Joy&Anger

Joy & Anger

Jennifer Blake

Fawcett Columbine · New York

A Fawcett Columbine Book
Published by Ballantine Books
Copyright © 1991 by Patricia Maxwell

Library of Congress Cataloging-in-Publication Data
Blake, Jennifer, 1942–
Joy and anger: a novel/Jennifer Blake.—1st ed.
p. cm.
ISBN 0-449-90621-3
I. Title.
PS3563.A923J68   1991
813'.54—dc20   90-85130
CIP

Design by Holly Johnson

Manufactured in the United States of America

First Edition: July 1991
10 9 8 7 6 5 4 3 2 1

Acknowledgments

I am deeply indebted to Shirley and Nelson Faucheux of Grand Point, Louisiana, for their bountiful hospitality—including some of the best jambalaya and crawfish bisque in the state—during the time I spent researching this book, and for endless lessons in the manners, mores, and joyous way of life of the Cajuns of the Acadian Coast above New Orleans. To Nelson, also, a special thanks for acting as guide for the winding back ways of the Blind River, for sharing his knowledge of river and swamp lore, and for the tale of the overturned pirogue that came from his childhood.

I would also like to express my appreciation to Tony Bacala of the Ascension Parish Sheriff's Office for his insight into the problem of drug trafficking within the state, and to Julie Champagne of the St. James Parish Library, Lutcher, Louisiana, for her aid in researching minor points and solving major problems.

Per son joy pot malautz sanar,
E per a ira sa morir.

Through its joy love can cure evils,
just as through its anger love can kill.

—Guilhem IX, Duke of Aquitane

Joy&Anger

Chapter 1

The swamp was not a friendly place, especially as evening faded into night. There was a primeval quality in the dank darkness under the towering old cypress trees surrounded by their humped roots known as cypress knees, in the rotting logs, dark green palmetto palms, and mangrove trees that crowded the water's edge. The rampant growth of vines and mats of fern that entwined the tree limbs, the singing, stinging insects, and night creatures that watched with eyes glowing red in the lantern light made it seem impossibly wild, incredibly far from civilization. The silent gliding of the pirogue through the mist rising from the river was like a journey into another time.

Great. It was going to be great.

Julie Bullard grinned a little to herself. Imagination was not a bad thing in a movie director; she was already picturing the images she wanted to put on film. The locations for the scenes she needed, most in daylight but also one at night, were just around the next bend, she knew it. This trip in the old-fashioned wooden boat was going to be a worthwhile excursion, a most profitable evening.

The narrow pirogue rocked, swinging to the right as it surged forward to skirt a loglike shape in the water near the bank. Julie tightened her grip on the plank seat as she looked back at her guide. He was standing in the rear of the boat, lifting his long pole with a muddy swirl as he used it to propel the shallow craft along the winding river's course. The bowlegged Cajun, his face a network of wrinkles as intricate as the waterways through the Louisiana swampland, his eyes gleaming in the faint light of the camper's lantern in the prow, nodded toward the long shape in the water. "That old 'gator, he comin' to see what we want, that's all."

Julie glanced at the alligator in mock nervousness. "You're absolutely certain alligators don't eat people?"

He gave her a toothless smile. "I guarantee! Not live people, any rate. Might turn the boat over, just curious like. Best go 'round him."

"Right," Julie said, her tone dry as she faced forward again.

Her guide chuckled.

Julie wasn't really afraid of the night or anything in it. She believed the old Cajun when he said alligators seldom killed anything larger than the stray raccoon or opossum, and that the poisonous water snakes with picturesque names like cottonmouth and copperhead moccasin that made arrow-shaped wakes in the water were more afraid of her than she was of them. Though she hid it well, she was thrilled to sense the swamp around her, moved by its primitive magic. If she could feel these things, surely she could make moviegoers feel them, too.

She had also been right to take her film on location instead of trying to do it on a bunch of sets made out of plastic and papier-mâché. Keeping the cost down was important; she knew that without having darling Allen striding up and down in his silk pajamas making noises like a producer. She was well aware, too, that she had to bring this movie in on time in order to prove herself as one of the few women directors of note in L.A. Still, there was something else just as important, and that was the integrity of the movie she was making.

It was she who had developed this property, writing the screenplay herself after putting up her own money to option the book by a new young Louisiana author. *Swamp Kingdom* was a tale of a young girl's coming-of-age, one celebrating the triumph of cultural background and tradition over wealth and its privileges. There was drama in it, provided by the custody battle between a Cajun man and his New Orleans socialite wife over their adolescent daughter, and plenty of action as the Cajun kidnaps his daughter from his wife's new townhouse apartment and takes her into the swamps, then has to fight the goons sent by his wife to bring the girl back. It had humor, sex, pathos—everything, in fact, including a good if not spectacular cast. There were no huge stars; Julie couldn't afford them. Regardless, she didn't see how it could fail to do well at the box office so long as she could transfer the story to the screen as she saw it in her mind.

Her father had told her she was foolish to try. The great William Bullard, winner of two Academy Awards for Best Director on the strength of his innovative approach to film, had advised her not to take chances. She should, he said, stick to the low-budget surfing movies and women's pictures with which she had made her mark.

That had hurt, her father's lack of faith. It had hurt that he couldn't see how much she had absorbed from watching him all these years, that he failed to recognize that she was capable of putting broader stories, larger themes, on film. It wasn't experience she was lacking; she had made her first grainy 16mm short feature more than fifteen years ago, when she was still at UCLA. She had been a surfing freak then, one of those tall, tan, blond California girls who haunt the beaches and talk the jargon of tunnels and rips like some second language. That first film had been made out of love of the ocean and fascination with the young men and women who challenged the waves. It had been crowned with the luck that comes to those who approach their subject with respect and confidence; she had caught something essential about the sport of surfing and the nomads it spawned. The film, blown up to 35mm, had been selected for showing in the Directors' Fortnight at Cannes, and she had not stopped making movies since.

There could be only one reason her father doubted her ability, and that was because she was a woman. She shouldn't have been surprised; he had always made it plain he expected his daughter to be ornamental and suitably adoring until she married and transferred her affections to her husband. He was an unrepentant chauvinist who thought a woman's place was in the kitchen and in bed, in alternating sequence. The strange thing was that Julie's mother had more or less conformed to that image, and he still had not been satisfied. He needed the excitement of other women, or of being out with the boys, sailing, fishing, hunting, bullfighting, stock-car racing—anything that risked life and limb and kept him away from home. He needed freedom, or its illusion. After a while, Julie's mother had given him all the freedom he wanted. Bull, as her father was known to his friends and even to Julie herself, had not been happy with that, either.

Following the divorce, Julie's mother had retreated to her home-
town in the central portion of Louisiana, taking Julie with her, refusing
to have anything more to do with the ersatz glamour of L.A.

Fake places had little appeal for Julie, either. That was why it was
so important that she have the real thing to film, real New Orleans
streets, real jazz, real swampland. She was glad to be shooting in her
mother's part of the country since it gave her the opportunity to spend
time where she had lived until she was a teenager, until her mother
died, but that consideration was secondary.

Julie had been filming in New Orleans for the best part of a month.
Now she had at least another four weeks of work here in the swampland northwest of the city before she could wrap up *Swamp Kingdom*.
She thought she was going to make it on time and under budget, in
spite of a rash of minor accidents on the set and petty problems with
absenteeism and the theft of supplies. She would be both glad and sorry
when it was done, glad because of the unexpected strain of trying to
fulfill the promise of the story and portray the Cajun life-style and the
beauty of the swamp exactly right, and sorry because she would be
ending a project that gave her an unusual sense of achievement.

She was creating a solid piece of work here with her crew. She
had to keep telling herself that, regardless of what anyone else thought
or said. Sometimes, she actually believed it for whole hours at a time.

The pirogue glided along near the bank of the river, the Blind
River, it was called. The waterway, in ancient times a channel of the
Mississippi before the great river had made one of its many changes
of course, was looping but well defined. So old it was no longer
connected in any way to the Mississippi, it had no discernible current,
though it meandered in a general southeasterly direction. It had once
been called Bayou Acadian, Julie had learned. That was until the
thirties when English-speaking logging crews came into the swamps
to clear the virgin cypress. It had gained its new name then because
the loggers found the old one hard to say, and because the dark color
of the water caused by the acid from constantly dripping tree sap made
the water so opaque little could be seen below the surface.

There was no moon tonight in the dense blue-black arch of the
sky overhead. The pale stars in the Milky Way seemed to be tangled

in a great gauze veil that reached down on each side to near treetop level. A mellow fall breeze, damp and smelling of fish yet fresh with a hint of salt from the distant Gulf, stirred Julie's hair against the tops of her shoulders. A leaf, one of the few beginning to turn though it was already October, drifted down to swirl in the wake of the pirogue's passing. The only sounds were the dipping of the guide's pole and the chorus of the peeper frogs, with the occasional whine of a mosquito, the call of a hunting owl, or bellow of an alligator.

Julie breathed deep, and let the air escape from her lungs on a slow sigh. It was so peaceful, floating through the night in the dim glow of the lantern. Her guide, Joseph, had wanted to take her out in his skiff with the outboard motor attached, and she had let him make the first ten miles or so of the river in it for the sake of speed. Then she had insisted on transferring to the pirogue they had towed behind them. One reason was that she wanted to see how one of the shallow-draft boats handled, but she also craved the slower ride and the quiet so she could think.

It had been a good choice. Once past the big canals, the fishing and hunting camps, the drinking places, and the small wooden chapel on the upper reaches, she had had time to really see the river. She had had time to notice the different trees and plants and animals, time to see the various canals, bayous, sloughs, and narrow, almost hidden runs leading into the river as the guide pointed them out before the light began to fail. There was definitely something to be said for doing things the old way, for slowing down, taking it easy. She had been too involved with the problems of her movie lately, too anxious about it.

She should try to take everything at a less hectic pace, and she would, too, as soon as *Swamp Kingdom* was in the can. If Allen wasn't too busy, maybe she could talk him into flying down to the islands or to Belize, maybe renting a beach cottage and playing castaways for a few weeks. It was unlikely, but she could try.

Ahead of the boat, the river channel widened. A stretch of water appeared that opened out into an area the size of two football fields. It was edged by patches of cattails and the tall water weeds known as cut grass, and had several stands of cypress trees spotted here and there,

lifting branches festooned with lacelike leaves and draperies of gray
Spanish moss toward the night sky. Julie leaned forward to see better,
at the same time catching the full skirt of her white cotton dress and
wrapping it around her knees to keep it out of the dampness in the
bottom of the pirogue. This could be the first of the two sites she was
looking for, a spot wide enough for boats to maneuver. There were
no houses in sight, no camps, no moored houseboats, no distracting
power lines or boat ramps, only a natural and private lagoonlike stretch
in the river. It was wonderful, almost too good to be true.

A low humming sound, almost like a giant insect, caught Julie's
attention. It throbbed in the night, rising and falling, growing ever
louder. Just in front of the pirogue there was a splash, as if some animal
disturbed by either the low-pitched roaring noise or the pirogue's
approach had launched itself from the riverbank into the water.

"What's that?" Julie asked. At the same instant, she caught the
ripple of a small wave at the edge of the lantern's glow, saw the head
and upper body of a fur-bearing creature she thought she recognized
as a nutria.

Joseph gave a chuckle. "Why, I think, me, that's the Swamp Rat!"

Julie turned to look back over her shoulder at him. "You mean
that thing's a big rat?"

"*Mais non, chère,*" the old man replied, dismissing the swimming
nutria with a shrug as he listened with his eyes half-closed and his head
tipped to one side. "I speak of the man in the air boat."

Either her guide wasn't understanding her, or she wasn't understanding him, Julie thought. Before she could decide which, a double
shaft of light striking through the trees on the far side of the open
water turned her attention in that direction. The yellow beams swept
this way and that, bobbling, turning, splintering through the branches
and hanging vines, gilding the tatters of swaying moss. At the same
time, the droning roar, accompanied by a hissing rush, grew louder.

Abruptly Julie understood. An air boat. She had seen pictures of
one, a craft propelled by an engine sitting up high in the back with
blades like a fan, one that maneuvered at high speed on a cushion of
air. Developed for the kind of watery terrain that could go from forty
feet deep to only four inches in seconds, it could travel over little more

than a heavy dew. This one was certainly moving fast, taking the curves of the winding river channel that lay on the far side of the open area at a breakneck pace.

It was odd, but there seemed to be an echo of the air boat engine's muted roar. An instant later, Julie realized that echo was coming from overhead. There was a plane approaching, a seaplane, awkward looking with its big pontoons. It was descending as it drew nearer, as if the pilot meant to land, though Julie knew from the location scouting reports that there was no airport nearer than New Orleans International more than forty miles away.

She wondered if the plane was in trouble, though there was no sign of it. As she watched, the plane's headlights came on, stabbing into the treetops. Its motor slowed to just above stalling, almost as if it were going into a glide.

Behind her, the old guide muttered something in Cajun French patois. He stood frowning with his pole held out of the water, dripping, while the pirogue drifted from the narrow, tree-lined river channel out onto the open area of water under its own momentum.

The air boat rounded a curve in the far reaches of the river, broke into a tree-lined straightaway much like the one Julie and her guide had just left, and came speeding toward them, trailing a comet's tail of boiling spume. It hurtled from among the trees and out onto the open water. The man at the controls was a shadowy figure behind the glare of the air boat's headlights. His shoulders were broad, his grasp on the controls steady. The wind ruffled his hair into close waves against his scalp. He was watching the plane with his head tilted back in a way that was taut and intent. He did not slacken his speed.

The plane came on, dropping lower, skimming the tops of the trees. It swept out over the open space, setting the tree branches to waving. Its lights made a moving white glare on the water, mingling with the yellow beams from the air boat. The paths of the plane and the air boat came nearer, converging.

They crossed in a rushing roar. An instant later, they divided again as the plane swooped on past.

The man in the air boat swung his head to follow the flight of the plane. He held his craft steady.

The muttering of Julie's guide grew louder. He shouted a warning as he lifted his pole and swung it above Julie's head.

The air boat was coming straight at the pirogue on a direct course with the tunnellike river channel with its archway of trees that the wooden boat had just left. The air boat's driver had not seen the other craft, hadn't even looked. In seconds, the air boat would be upon them. There was no way to stop it, no way to avoid a collision. Julie gripped the side of the pirogue, ready to jump.

Then the air boat's driver turned his head, saw them. He swung his control bars hard, flinging his weight to the same side. The engine whined as the craft skimmed past on one pontoon in a hurricane sweep of wind and water.

Julie lurched away from the bright glare of lights, the roar, the hurtling shape. The unstable wooden boat pitched violently as the air boat's wind blast and shallow wake caught it. She heard the guide yell, saw him fling himself to the opposite side to counteract the roll. It was too late. Julie was thrown over the gunwale, tumbling in space.

The murky water rose up to take her, closing over her head, drawing her down. It was black and cold and thick, pressing in upon her. Her breath burned in her chest. She turned in slow motion with the skirt of her dress wrapping around her upper body, confining her arms. Something touched her leg, scratchy yet slimy, a sinker as it was called, or old submerged cypress log. Revulsion sent energy surging along her veins, and she thrust upward with a hard kick that tore the sandals from her feet. She bated her skirt away from her chest, pulling for the surface with reaching arms. She broke the top of the water with a gasp that hurt her throat.

There was the rumbling purr of an idling engine just behind her, almost on top of her. A deep voice spoke from above her head, the words short. "Here, take my hand. I was beginning to think I was going to have to come in after you."

Julie thrashed around in the water to see the air boat with its driver kneeling, leaning over the rubberized pontoons as he reached down to her. There was a frown between his dark brows, and his firmly molded lips were set in lines of irritation.

Julie felt the warm rise of her own anger. Treading water, she glanced around her for her guide and the pirogue. She saw the smaller boat several feet away, with the Cajun guide swimming strongly toward it. She looked back at the air boat driver.

"Thank you," she said, her tone sharp, "but I wouldn't want to put you to any trouble."

The man settled back, resting his arm on his bent knee. His expression eased into something approaching amusement. "Meaning that I've already caused you a great deal?"

"Meaning you ran us down because you weren't looking where you were going!"

"I had other things on my mind. Besides, old Joseph has been told a thousand times to keep his lantern clean and in plain sight instead of half-hidden on his forward seat."

"And on top of that, he was poling his pirogue much too fast," she agreed with scathing promptness. "In fact, Joseph is entirely to blame. None of it was your fault!"

The driver's face creased into a slow smile that rose to gleam in his eyes. "I didn't say that. If I admit I wasn't watching where I was going, will you get in the boat?"

Julie made no answer, turning instead to look toward her guide once more. Joseph had flipped the pirogue right side up and was hoisting himself aboard. She plunged away from the other man, swimming toward the pirogue with a fast and strong crawl learned in Pacific breakers.

The air boat motor grumbled, then took on a slightly faster tempo. A moment later, the craft glided between Julie and her objective.

She changed directions.

The boat kept pace, idling close alongside. She changed again, throwing the driver a glare over her shoulder. The boat motor was gunned, then dropped to an even lower idle. Julie turned her head on a hard stroke to see the driver leaning over the side once more, just above her.

She dodged, but a strong hand fastened on her arm, dragging her to a swirling halt. Before she could react, before she could accept what was happening, her waist was clamped by an arm like a vise and she was hoisted aboard the air boat. She tumbled over the rubber and fiberglass side, landing in the bottom. The driver shouted something she didn't catch at her guide, a confident spate of Cajun French that was answered by a laugh and a wave. At the same time, her abductor threw himself into the left-hand side of a pair of seats in the front of the boat. The air boat rumbled into a dull roar, then lifted and zoomed away.

Disbelief and the effort to gain and keep her balance held Julie where she was for an instant, then she dragged herself toward the front of the boat. Dripping water, with her dress sticking clammily to her skin, she staggered to her feet and lurched into the seat beside the driver. There was fear and rage boiling inside her as she leaned to grab a handful of his shirt in her fist. She jerked at him, once, twice. With the wind of their passage whipping the words from her mouth and the engine's growl half drowning them, she yelled, "Where are you taking me?"

He was broad and hard-muscled and completely immovable in her grasp. He turned his head to look at her with laughter crowding into his eyes. "Home," he said.

The answer along with the provocative expression on his face took her breath almost as much as the cool rush of the wind. "That," she said, her gaze steady, "is what you think!"

She swung to look over the side, half rising in her seat. He reached out to clamp an arm on her wrist, dragging her down again.

He removed his glance from the dark, tree-crowded river channel they had entered once more to look at her. "Let me clarify that. I didn't mean to *my* home. The movie location is where I had in mind—unless you would prefer otherwise."

"Not likely," she said through her teeth.

He lifted a shoulder with a faint grin. "I was afraid of that."

She subsided back into the other seat, uncertain whether to believe him or not. His grasp was warm and firm, but not hurtful. There was a strand of wet hair fluttering between her eyes. Lifting her free hand in distraction, she pushed it back, then ran her fingers through the sopping, tangled curls, loosening them where they were plastered to her head. Finally, she raised her voice to ask, "You know who I am?"

"It wasn't hard to guess." He released her as he answered. "You're not local or I would either know you or have heard of you long ago. You have both the charm and the cash to persuade old Joseph to come out on the bayou at night, no easy thing to do. The flimsy white dress you have on practically shouts California—besides which, even the tourists usually go for jeans or pants in a boat on the river. It follows that you must be with the movie company. You're too young for the part of the wife in the film, and too old for the daughter. My guess is you're the lady director."

"Brilliant," she said in acid tones.

He gave her a smiling look, but made no answer.

"Do you treat everyone like this, or did I say something to make you think I wanted to be abducted?"

He slackened speed a fraction, and the noise of the engine lowered. "The season here is fall, in case you haven't noticed. This may be south Louisiana and it may not seem cold, but it's still possible to catch a chill."

"To what?"

Annoyance crossed his face, then was gone. "If I sound quaint, it's a hazard around here. Cajuns also catch a heart attack or catch cancer, not to mention *la grippe*—that's the flu to you."

"I wasn't making fun of you."

"So I'm being too sensitive, in your view, of course. That's another hazard. But you're in my swamp now; you'll have to get used to it."

"Your swamp?" Julie did her best to keep anything other than neutral curiosity from her voice.

He looked at her in the glow of the dash light, narrowing his lashes against the wind in their faces. His voice quietly implacable, he repeated, "Mine."

"Why do you say that?"

"Because I know it, the backwater where the fish spawn and the alligators mate, the marshlands where the geese and ducks come winging in clouds in the winter, the *chenières*— oak-covered hills of seashells left by ancient Indians down below New Orleans—the logging and highway canals, the winding rivulets and bayous that lead in their own good time to Lake Maurepas and through Pass Manchac to Lake Pontchartrain and into the Gulf. I've known it since I was ten, when

I got lost in it my first and last time. It's mine because I made it mine."

"The Swamp Rat," she murmured, suddenly recalling the words the old Cajun guide had said.

"Some call me that. I don't claim it."

He was a good-looking man in a dark and rough-hewn fashion, of her own age at least and possibly four or five years older. His brows were thick, his nose high-bridged and straight between prominent cheekbones. His deep-set eyes, bracketed by radiating lines of laughter and framed in lashes long enough to tangle, appeared to be coffee brown. His hands on the controls of the boat were strong and well made, with more than one scar showing white against the deep tan. His shoulders were padded with muscles under his worn khaki shirt, and he sat with the relaxed ease of fine physical condition. Like the swamp he claimed, he was not quite tame, more than a little alien.

There were damp patches on the front of his shirt and down the legs of his jeans where he had held her against him. Remembering the moment when this man had caught her in his arms and dragged her aboard, Julie felt a tightening in the muscles of her abdomen and a faint shivery sensation across the back of her neck. She didn't like it, she didn't like it one bit.

"What do you do?" she asked. It was an innocuous gambit, a cocktail-party question useful in establishing a polite basis for conversation. At the same time, Julie wanted an answer for the sake of an idea that was slowly gathering in the back of her mind.

"Do? Nothing much."

The reply was not helpful. She had the feeling it was not meant to be. She persisted. "Do you work at one of the chemical plants around here, or a sugar refinery? Do you work offshore on the oil rigs? Fish commercially? What?"

"Nothing like that. You might say I'm retired."

"How nice for you—but aren't you a little young?"

His gaze on the river ahead, he said, "No."

It was possible that the man was right about the fall weather, especially when combined with a wet dress and a windy ride. There was gooseflesh rising along Julie's arms and legs, and her jaw had a tendency to quiver. She clasped her hands upon her arms, rubbing the chilled skin.

"Could—could you go just a little slower? I'm freezing."

"Faster is what you need," he said, and the air boat engine whined as the boat shot forward once more, planing over the water.

Julie set her teeth while shudders shook her that seemed to time themselves with the vibrations of the boat. The wind tore at her hair, drying it, while tears gathered in her eyes and streamed back across her temples. She ducked her head, enduring.

"We're almost there," her driver shouted.

It was true. She could see the pinkish glow of the extra mercury lamps on poles that the utility company had set to light up the location at night. Just visible through the trees was the metallic sheen of the trailer offices and motor homes in their staggered line, and also the bulk of the metal building that housed the St. James Parish Boat Club, which was allowing Excel Films to use its parking area and river access. In a moment she would have dry clothes and something hot to drink. And she would, she supposed, have to thank the Swamp Rat for bringing her home.

"I've just realized," she said as he cut the engine, letting the boat glide toward the boat pier built out into the water, "that I don't know your name."

A corner of his mouth lifted. "I thought you had one for me."

"It isn't very useful. For instance, I'm hardly likely to find it in the telephone book."

"Rey," he answered, "Rey Tabary."

"Cajun, I suppose?"

"French-Spanish Creole mixed with Cajun, if you know what that means."

"Of French and Spanish blood but born on foreign soil, in this case American, and mixed with the blood lines of a French family ousted from Nova Scotia by the British more than two hundred years ago."

His glance held surprise. "You've been studying state history."

"Actually, I was born here myself, though my ancestors are just plain English, Irish, and Welsh."

"Hardly plain," he said.

His smile as he spoke was so wry that it was difficult to tell if he meant to pay her a compliment. Not that she cared, one way or the other.

Tabary gunned the engine as they neared the bank so the boat skirted the wooden pier where the movie company's two cabin cruisers were tied up and angled toward the bank. There were a few people moving about, knocking together a wooden platform for the next day's shooting, talking in low voices, cooking something in a great aluminum pot over a gas burner. They looked toward the air boat with quick interest. It was unlikely that she would be able to get to her motor home without having to answer questions.

The air boat pushed through a stand of cut grass to ground itself on the muddy shoreline. With determined hospitality, Julie said, "I can offer you a drink, if you would care to stay and meet everyone."

"Another time, thanks. I have to be going." He didn't turn off the boat's motor as he stepped out. Wrapping a bowline around his palm to hold the boat steady, he gave Julie his other hand to help her over the side.

She jumped down, spraying his boots with the water dripping from her skirt. The words of appreciation she spoke were brief and to the point. She would have stepped away from him then, except that he did not release her hand.

She glanced back at him, pausing in her uncertainty. He was watching her, an arrested look in his eyes as he studied her in the light from the mercury vapor lamps on their poles. His clasp was light and warm, yet firm.

"Yes?" she said, with the slight lift of a brow.

He made no answer. Deliberately, he dropped the boat line he held, then reached to take her other hand, spreading her arms wide. He glanced over their slender lengths exposed by her short sleeves, first the fronts and then the backs. As she tried to pull away he smoothed his hands quickly upward to her shoulders, then pushed his fingers under her hair, brushing over the smooth skin of her neck.

"What are you doing?" she asked, her voice tight in the return of annoyance caused in no small part by the faint quiver in her voice.

He lowered his hands, trailing them down her arms again, where he retained possession of her wrists. He said softly, "Lift your skirts."

"You must be crazy."

"Not exactly," he answered, a glint of something very near mischief in his eyes. "But the only design I have on you is to inspect you for leeches."

"Leeches!"

"A definite possibility."

"You don't mean it."

"Of course, if you would rather let them suck your blood than show me your legs, that's your choice. But I warn you, they won't drop off until they're ten times their size, and the marks they leave can become scars."

"Let me go, and I'll look," she snapped.

"You can't see everything that needs to be seen."

His choice of words were suspect, but her skin was crawling with something more than wet and cold. Somehow, he had managed to step between her and the audience of crew and boat-club members, screening her from their view. The look in his eyes seemed watchful and tinged with audacity, so it was difficult to predict what he might do if she refused. Though his hold was light, she thought it might easily become unbreakable.

"Oh, for God's sake," she cried in exasperation. She jerked free, then picked up her dripping skirts, bunching them in her hands as she held them at midthigh.

He glanced down, then spun her around, his touch brief, impersonal. The moment of appraisal in that position seemed endless before he spoke again. "It's all right. You're clean."

"Thank you very much," she said in tight tones. She whirled back to face him.

"My pleasure." He hesitated, looking down at her with the amusement fading from his face. Then he gave a slow nod and stepped back. "And my apologies."

His apologies for what? For dumping her in the river, or for taking his time over the leeches. There was no chance to ask him.

He swung back to his air boat, leaping lightly over the side. The motor thundered as he backed it. He was gone, then, returning the way he had come in a rumbling rush and a head-high rooster tail of blown spray.

Julie stared after the boat until it swept around a bend, then looked down at herself, at her stained and bedraggled dress, at the mud oozing between her toes. Her hair was a mess, and her makeup, if she still had any, was probably running. More than that, she had spoken to the man who had pulled her out of the bayou like some kind of witch, or else like a bashful virgin. How she had come to behave with so little composure, so little sophistication, she didn't know.

A moment later, she shook her head with a tight laugh. What did she care what she looked like or what a man with a name like Swamp Rat thought about it?

Rey Tabary was, in fact, exactly the kind of man she liked least and mistrusted most, a take-charge macho male who seemed to think that strength was the proper response to any disagreement, the kind who thought women were amusing playthings and had a smart answer for everything. The exact opposite in every way possible of Allen Gravesend, Rey Tabary could never equal the man who was her fiancé as well as the producer of her movie.

More than that, Julie would swear there was something secretive about the Cajun. His answers to her questions had been deliberately evasive, and she knew he was shielding a portion of his thoughts behind those ridiculously long lashes.

Imagination again. The mystery, if there was one, was probably just that he was married. The man was nothing more than an arrogant know-it-all. Just like her father.

He was also the man she needed.

She needed him for her movie. For that, and nothing more. Nothing more at all.

The idea had come to her as the man talked about his swamp and his Cajun background. She wanted so much to show those things as they really were, to catch their spirit and their flavor without exploiting either. Both were so important to the true-to-life values of her movie, to the mechanics of it and also its heart. She had been worried from the beginning about this section that took place in the swamp, worried about the accents of the Cajun characters, about their customs and the outlook of the male lead, about the scenes showing fishing and high-speed boating on the winding waterways. She needed desperately to get the details right.

Rey Tabary was the man who could help her do that. All she had to do was convince him of it.

Chapter 2

Becoming involved with making a movie was the last thing Rey
Tabary wanted. He had no intention of being persuaded, and he made
that plain from the moment he began to understand what it was Julie
wanted of him. He said no, and kept on saying no while she explained
about the way she wanted to present the swamp, his swamp, and his
Cajun people. He refused while she tried to offer him the title of
technical director and a salary equal to half a year's pay for the average
man, with a bonus if the movie was completed ahead of schedule. He
declined with thanks as she told him the movie wouldn't be the same
without him.

It wasn't hard to remember what his answer should be. The hard
part was to keep giving it knowing that when she finally accepted it,
she would probably go away and never speak to him again.

Rey had wondered the night before exactly what color her eyes
were. Now he knew. They were green, the soft, pure green of winter
grass in these latitudes. They were also clear and earnest, intelligent and
without a sign of flirtation. He wasn't sure whether that restraint, that
lack of recourse to traditional methods of female persuasion, made it
easier or harder.

She didn't give up easily, which didn't help matters. There had
been a time when someone like her, a long-legged female with sunlight
caught in her hair and strong ideas, could have had anything she
wanted from him. Even now, he caught himself watching the tender
surfaces of her lips, following the way the light glinted on her gold-
tipped lashes and glanced across her cheekbones leaving the hollows
underneath in shadow. The top of her head was even with his chin,

and the dress she was wearing, made of cotton in an odd dusty green, had a wide belt of sand-colored suede that cinched her waist to such a small span that it made him want to spread his fingers around it.

There was nothing obvious or superficial about Julie Bullard. She was straightforward and businesslike. And yet there was something vulnerable, something too sensitive, too solemn about her. He wondered if anyone ever teased her, made her laugh, encouraged her to lose her composure and do and say whatever ridiculous, quirky thing came to mind. He doubted it.

She was waiting for him to say something again.

"There are other people who can help you, Miss Bullard," he said obligingly. "Old Joseph, for instance. Try him."

"I talked to him, and he said you were the best. Besides, half the time I'm not sure what Joseph is saying and the other half I don't think he understands me."

"He understands what he wants to understand," Rey answered, his tone dry.

Julie stared at Rey Tabary with a perplexed frown between her eyes. The man's easy attitude, his total lack of interest in what she was offering, were exasperating. He might at least have heard her out before turning her down. Instead, he refused to listen, just leaned against the support column of the old house of weathered wood, watching her as he waited for her to wind down and take her leave. Julie looked away, searching her mind for something more to say to convince him.

The house was on the Great River Road, the winding highway that followed the turns and bends of the Mississippi River. Shaded by ancient live oaks whose thick branches trailed on the ground, it was built of cypress that was silver gray with age and lack of paint. It was of no great size, six rooms plus an attic sleeping loft. It did not seem small, however, since the rooms were commodious and the house was raised on brick piers seven or eight feet tall for air circulation and protection from flood damage. The spaces between the piers had been filled in with bricks sometime in the last thirty or forty years to form an aboveground basement used for storage and as a garage. There were long porches, or galleries as they were known in this part of the country, on both the front and back. These were edged with a railing with plain balusters that was attached to square columns, which, in turn, supported the roof of rusted tin.

At the rear of the house where Rey and Julie stood on the gallery, the high steps led down to a patio of bricks laid by hand. At one corner of the patio was a stand of banana trees, one of which had a curving stalk of small green bananas tipped with a large lavender bloom. A cape jasmine shrub ten feet tall and six feet wide grew at the opposite house corner, while crepe myrtles with trunks twisted and silvered with age stood here and there on the lawn. Some distance away was a fall garden rowed with squash and stringbeans, new onions, turnip greens and collards, and lined with beds of herbs. Behind it was a chicken yard where a cluster of white leghorns scratched at the bare earth inside the fence. Strolling about the lawn, in lordly possession of it, was a peacock whose feathers shimmered blue and green in the sunlight and also a flock of four or five peahens.

"Why?" Julie said finally. "Why won't you at least think about what I'm asking? You said yourself that you had no regular job, nothing else pressing to be done."

"I said I was retired, not quite the same thing."

"Well, what's taking up your time that's so important you can't work with me for a few weeks? I would think that whatever it is could be set aside long enough to add to your income, maybe allow you to buy something you want or make a few improvements to your home."

"You think this place needs improving?" He glanced around at the house.

"I didn't say that," Julie said hastily as she heard the irony in his voice. "It's only what many people do with a windfall."

"This house belongs to my aunt, and it happens that she prefers the natural look. Cypress is practically indestructible, whether it's painted or not. Paint mildews in the damp, so once you start painting, you have to keep doing it. Money doesn't always enter into it—or neglect."

She stared at him a moment before giving him a stiff smile. "Point taken. Things are not always what they seem."

"Including me."

"Meaning?"

"What makes you so sure I'm the man for what you're offering? You know nothing about me."

"I know what I want."

"Well," he drawled, "it's nice to meet a woman so sure of her own mind, but how can you tell until you've had me."

A flush rose to burn across her cheekbones. Her voice stiff, she said, "I was speaking in a business sense."

"I know." His slow smile held equal parts of amusement and contrition. "But you left yourself so wide open it was irresistible. Sorry."

"Anyway, you have excellent qualifications," she went on quickly in an attempt to ignore the effect of both his comment and his apology. "You were raised in the swamp, and your grandfather and your father were famous for their knowledge of it, which they passed on to you. More than that, you have a degree from Southwestern in Louisiana history—not to mention one from Louisiana Tech in business administration."

"Joseph has been talking."

"I asked questions. I'm not going into this blind, you know; I wouldn't be here if I didn't think you have a great deal to contribute to *Swamp Kingdom.*"

He met her gaze a long moment, his own bleak. "Do you know that I was once a special agent with the DEA?"

"Joseph mentioned something about the drug agency."

"I left it," he said evenly, "under what you might call a cloud, a matter of drugs missing from a bust."

"Were you guilty?" Her green gaze was steady as she spoke.

A short laugh shook his chest. He said, "What kind of question is that? I'm not likely to admit it if I was, and if I deny it, who's going to believe me?"

"I might."

A suspended expression came and went across his face, as if the words she had spoken had triggered thoughts and emotions she could not follow, as if she had finally pierced the armor of his self-containment.

At the same time, she was struck by his relaxed stillness. He made no attempt to explain or defend himself, had not once touched his hair or his clothes, had not changed his stance or altered the set of his shoulders. Unlike most vitally attractive men she had known, the majority of them actors, he seemed unaware of how he looked. He was also unconcerned about how he appeared to her.

"On the other hand," he said with quiet deliberation, "you might say anything to get what you want."

She glanced away, past his shoulder. When she looked back again, there was rueful amusement curving her lips. She said evenly, "I might at that."

"In that case," he said, "I'll tell you I'm entirely guiltless. Do you believe it?"

"Why not?"

"Why not, indeed? But I still can't be technical director for your movie."

Julie could see that he meant what he said, that there was nothing she could say that was going to change his mind. It might be irrational to resent it, but she did. "You mean you don't want to be."

"I wouldn't say that."

"Only out of politeness, I'm sure," she returned.

They were interrupted by the hollow tread of footsteps. A diminutive woman who had been introduced on Julie's arrival as Aunt Tine bustled from the house out onto the gallery. She was carrying a tray laden with moisture-frosted glasses of iced tea and slices of rich yellow pound cake on a footed cake stand. Julie blinked as she realized that the glasses and stand were of fine crystal remarkably like Baccarat and the napkins, stiff with starch and edged with handmade lace, were of real linen.

"What you two found to argue 'bout already?" the older woman asked in lilting accented English that underlined her acerbity as she eyed her nephew. "When I was a girl, *mon cher,* I tell you, a nice-looking man and woman could find better things to do than get in a tiff."

"I'll bet they could," her nephew said with a slow grin as he moved to take the heavy tray from his aunt.

"None of that, no! We talk, we find out about each other's families and friends, whether the other liked to dance, important things like that."

"Miss Bullard wants me to work for her, on her movie." Rey moved toward the opposite end of the gallery where a table was set between two rocking chairs, next to a swing piled with faded chintz cushions. Aunt Tine whisked after him to set out the refreshments.

It seemed to Julie that a lightning glance was exchanged between the other two. Before she could consider the meaning of that silent communication, the older woman was speaking to her nephew. "So, you would be working with Paul, what's wrong with that?"

"Paul?" Julie asked.

"A friend," Rey answered. "He was hired as a stuntman by a woman with your outfit. I think Paul said she was your assistant."

"That would be Ofelia. She did tell me that she had rounded up most of the people we'll be needing, stunt people as well as extras. Since I only drove up from New Orleans yesterday morning, I haven't met everyone."

Julie's assistant, Ofelia Selby, was super efficient. She needed to be since she was doing double duty as both unit production manager and assistant director because of the tight budget. Ofelia had been at the swamp location doing advance work, getting ready for this important last half of the movie, for the best part of two weeks. Julie herself had been going over the film shot in New Orleans with the film editor, plus taking care of all the bureaucratic tangle of licenses and permits necessary in order to film in the swamp. She had come as soon as she could. The actors were scheduled to show up this afternoon and tomorrow.

"Donna—that's Paul's wife—is so excited she can't stand herself," Aunt Tine was saying. "Paul has promised to buy her a diamond ring and an aboveground swimming pool for their two boys with part of the fortune he's going to make. He means to use the rest to buy himself a shrimp boat. He's always had this dream to quit work and go shrimping for his living."

Julie took the food and drink handed to her as she settled into a rocker beside Rey. To the older woman, she said, "I've been trying to tell your nephew that the position as technical director will pay well, too, at least as much as doing stunts. And a stuntman, you know, can net as much as ten thousand dollars for a gag with even minor danger."

"That is so? But Rey cares nothing for the money. Why should he?"

Julie blinked at the question. At the same time she had the uncomfortable feeling that she had been a little crass. The smile that flitted across Rey Tabary's face as he saw her discomfiture confirmed it.

Her tone was defensive as she said, "There are few of us who couldn't use a little extra now and then."

"I was about to tell Miss Bullard," Rey said, using Julie's ploy of talking through his aunt, "that I want nothing to do with another movie showing Louisianians as backward, immoral, and with webs between our toes. Or one where the swamp is shown as a sewer filled with human and animal monsters."

"I wouldn't do that!" Julie protested.

"You might not set out to do it."

"But you think it would turn out that way because I know no better?"

"That's what usually happens."

"You exaggerate. There have been some fine movies made in the state, award-winning movies."

"If you mean with all-star casts and impressive story lines, yes. But one of those managed to show a wedding reception with a couple from the northern part of the state in formal clothes doing a wild clog dance to Cajun-style music at what was basically a redneck Episcopalian wedding reception. Everything about it was wrong. More than that, in the funeral scene the mother was left alone at her daughter's grave after the service. It never would have happened; she would have been supported on all sides by relatives, male and female."

"Yes," Aunt Tine put in, "and they had azaleas and crepe myrtle blooming at the same time, which is a thing I've never seen in my life. And you won't believe it, but the flowers in the grass at Easter were silk. Fake. For why, I ask you? As for the decorations for the wedding, for Christmas and Halloween? La! Do these Hollywood people have no taste. Or do they just think we have none?"

"I know which movie you mean," Julie said with a wry smile. "I expect they thought no one would notice the flowers—they didn't realize most southern women are gardeners. As for the excess decoration, the purpose was probably humor."

Aunt Tine shook her head. "It was a bad joke."

"The point," Rey said, "is that this was one of the better productions."

"You could prevent such things, you know. That's what a technical director is for." Julie's gaze was challenging.

"Seeing things that are wrong without having the power to change them sounds to me like a job guaranteed to cause ulcers."

He had a point. "Suppose," she returned after a moment, "that I promise you the final word on how the swamp and your people are portrayed? Suppose I offer you the opportunity to help plan scenes that would show both in their best light? What then?"

Rey shook his head. "I don't think it would work. Besides, I really have other fish to fry."

The quiet of the day was broken by the distant ringing of a telephone. Rey excused himself and went inside to get it. Something about the quickness of his departure made Julie think he was just as happy to have a reason to cut short their conversation.

"That clog dance, now, it was so without dignity," Aunt Tine said, reverting to the previous topic. "The Cajun waltz is a dance that's beautiful to see when done right, one of grace, with the hand held just so on the hip or behind the back and the skirts of the lady whirling. Why did they not do that? I like the picture shows; I even learned English when I was a girl by watching them, trying to understand the words. But these things they do, they make me crazy!"

"Me too," Julie said frankly, "which is why I'm so anxious to have your nephew work with me. I don't suppose you could persuade him to change his mind?"

The older woman shook her head. "Rey does not do that easily. I wish I could help, but no."

"If I could just get him to come to the set, to watch for a while, maybe see what I'm trying to do, it might be enough."

Rey's aunt looked pensive. She said slowly, "Now, that might be arranged. I think—yes, I think Rey must take me to see how a movie is made, to see the actors act."

Hope brought a flush to Julie's cheeks. She leaned toward the older woman. "He would really take you to the location?"

Aunt Tine nodded with mischief in her face. "I think, me, that I must have the autograph of the stars, this Vance Stuart and Madelyn de Wells that I have been reading about in all the papers. I am long a fan of Vance Stuart; I watch him every afternoon for many years on the soap stories. This can be done? Tomorrow, maybe?"

"By all means," Julie agreed promptly.

"There is another thing."

Julie looked at Aunt Tine with a certain wariness for the shrewd expression she saw in her fine old eyes. "Yes?"

"I have read about people being paid much money to have their houses used for the picture shows, to have the actors come in and pretend they live there. My house here is not fine, but it is old, nearly one hundred and fifty years, and a true Cajun home. I could use money to fix my roof that leaks in the extra bedroom; it's been an age since it was done, since before my man Etienne passed on. Tin roofs are so expensive now that so many put them on their fancy houses. You have a use for my house, yes?"

"I'm afraid I don't, not really," Julie said with regret. "Besides, you should know that so much money is paid because of the possibility of damage, because walls sometimes have to be torn out so the cameras can get the right angle, or floors can be ruined by dragging heavy equipment over them. You wouldn't want that if your house has any kind of historical value."

Aunt Tine's face settled into lines of disappointment; still, she smiled with a flicker of pride. "It's on the list of houses, yes, this national register."

"It's a lovely old place," Julie said, glancing around at the sun falling across the east end of the gallery, at the fig tree on that side, which still retained its velvet green leaves even at this season, still bore large yellow-tinted figs. The cackling of a chicken announcing the production of an egg only emphasized the drowsy peace. An idea gathered in her mind. It seemed so right that she spoke at once, without taking time to think about it.

"You know, Aunt Tine, people also get paid for giving house room to actors and other members of the crew. I expect the rent would come to enough to cover repairs for your roof."

"You will be here so long?"

"Not really, but we would expect to pay a premium because of the inconvenience to you."

"But—you would want the whole house, yes? I would have to move?"

"The coming and going at all hours would be less disturbing to you that way. Of course, you would have had to move if the house had been rented as a set, too."

The old woman shook her head. "It may be that it's just as well that it cannot be used. I spoke too quick, because you were here in front of me and it seemed a sign that you came, as if it was meant to be. Rey would not like to move while he is staying with me; the time is all wrong. Never mind. But suppose I only wanted to rent a single room, my extra bedroom. The leak, I swear on my rosary blessed by the pope, is only a very little one."

Julie stared at the older woman for a long moment, at her strong features that were so classically, indefinably French, the fine-textured skin that was crepelike with age and puckered around the eyes with her anxiety. In abrupt decision, she said, "If you really want to do that, then there's no problem. I'll take the room myself."

Julie left a short time later, before Rey returned to the gallery, before he had a chance to prevent his aunt from renting out her spare room. Julie had no idea he would try such a thing, but it seemed best not to take chances. She had made arrangements with Aunt Tine to have her things delivered on the following afternoon. She would move in when she could, depending on how preparations for shooting went today. The movie crew was in the process of setting up for an action scene at the open section of the river she had scouted the night before, one involving Rey's friend as stuntman, which would be shot tomorrow or the next day. It was a complicated process that might take time before it was done right.

She had more than one reason for taking the room. In the first place, it couldn't hurt to be in the same house with Rey Tabary. The more time she spent with him, the more likely it was that she could induce him to reconsider her offer. If he remained stubborn, well then, she would be on hand to pick his brain, acquiring his expertise for free. In addition, there was a lot she could learn from Aunt Tine in the way of Cajun customs and attitudes. She would see to it that the older woman was compensated for her help, of course; Aunt Tine had not refused to be a part of her team.

The last reason had to do with her assistant. Julie and Ofelia had often shared a motel room in the early days in order to save money. It was an arrangement with advantages, since it allowed them to work closely together, often into the small hours of the morning. However, those other films had been independent productions. *Swamp Kingdom* was Julie's first studio film. The budget was tight at twelve million, but not nearly as tight as the few hundred thousand they were accustomed to handling. They could afford separate accommodations.

Julie and Ofelia had been friends for years, since college in fact. Ofelia was a whiz at paperwork, at the organization of the cattle calls for extras, at the logistics of feeding a crew, supplying the set, and removing the worry from Julie of some of the thousands of details that went into making a movie. She was tall, hefty, and had a bawdy sense of humor. When they were both younger, Julie had been able to tolerate Ofelia's six-inch-long cigarettes, her refusal to fill her side of the refrigerator with anything more healthy than beer and chips, her free and easy attitude toward men, her late nights and habit of sleeping in until the last possible second. Julie couldn't take it anymore. She had found that out during the shooting time in New Orleans.

Julie knew, however, that behind Ofelia's bravado and brassy manner was a hypersensitive woman who agonized over her large size, moon face, and manless state. She had been dreading the ordeal of telling her assistant she would be lodging elsewhere. It was good to have an excuse that Ofelia could understand. She would let Ofelia have the suite at the motel in Gonzales twenty-odd miles away. The two of them would still be working at close quarters since they would be sharing the director's motor home. She and Ofelia always accomplished a great deal during breaks in their getaway place on wheels.

Julie wanted to find the right time to break the news. An opportunity came sooner than she expected.

She had gone to the motor home for a snack late that afternoon, after work was done for the day. While she waited for the water to boil for a cup of soup, she looked at the sketches for her male star's wardrobe that she had spread out on the dining table. She glanced up as Ofelia came banging inside, heading for the small bathroom. Ofelia's greeting was breezy. She was on her way out, she said; she just needed to make a few repairs before going for a beer with the cinematographer and a couple of the cameramen.

Julie got up, following the big woman, leaning on the frame of the bathroom door as she talked to her. She gave the other girl the news straight, adding her reasons.

"Hey, listen, don't worry about it," Ofelia said as she bent from the waist to brush out her long brown hair, then swung herself upright again with care in the tiny space. "Anything you can do to make this a better movie is all right by me, up to and including offering your own sweet self on the altar of excellence. I mean, you could always vamp this Cajun honey bun. I've seen him around, and I have to tell you I wouldn't mind sacrificing myself for the cause."

"I'm sure that won't be necessary," Julie said dryly.

"Too bad."

Ofelia gave her a lascivious grin as she twisted her thick, shining hair, her one vanity, into a Psyche knot and skewered it with one of what she called her Tokyo Rose chopsticks. The wooden ornaments were painted a blood red that clashed violently with the lime-green shirt she wore over a pair of well-packed jeans.

"You're sure you don't mind?" Julie turned to lean with her back against the door facing. "I don't want you to think I'm deserting you."

Ofelia swiped across her wide lips with cerise-colored lip gloss on her ring finger. "Don't be silly. I'm been sleeping by myself for years—when all else fails. Besides, I've discovered the joys of *bourée*, next to which all other forms of entertainment come up lacking."

"I'm almost afraid to ask what that is."

"What a filthy mind you have! My influence, I hope? Actually, it's a card game, one that makes blackjack in Vegas look like kid stuff. I came across a game at a local joint. These Cajuns have been playing it since God was in diapers, and they're sharp. The stakes ain't chicken feed, either. Since I've allowed myself to be fleeced so far, the guys have been letting me play. Tonight I mean to have my revenge."

"What kind of joint?" Julie asked doubtfully.

"Well, it's not your local Knights of Columbus hall, sweet thing. I think I heard somebody call it a honky-tonk, which struck me as totally charming. It's a roadhouse, if you must be elegant. But don't go all motherly on me. You ought to know it would take five men and a Mack truck to get me down, and even then they better watch themselves."

"That may be, but you'll remember that you're in the Bible Belt, where men are men and women are women, and anything suggestive could be seen as an invitation?"

"Oh, my! I'll have to practice fluttering my little old eyelashes, won't I?" Ofelia swung toward Julie, spreading her arms wide. "But just take a look here. What you see is not your regulation peek-a-boo lace skirt worn sans panties, and I'm not the bimbo type. I'm as safe as the Sears Tower. Worse luck."

"You look like some truck driver's idea of a nice armful," Julie said frankly.

"A companion for the road," Ofelia mocked, her face turning a mottled pink. "A real brick house to share the driving and change the flat tires? Now I'm terrified. Fortunately, my joint caters to fishermen and hunters instead of truck drivers. My greatest danger is being deep-sixed in the swamp after I'm rolled for my winnings."

"In that case, I hope you lose." Julie's voice held equal parts of affection and irritation.

"Screw you," Ofelia retorted amiably.

Julie let that comment pass as another question surfaced in her mind. "Since you've been on the spot here a few days, hobnobbing with the locals, have you heard anything about a private airstrip nearby?"

"Nope, though it would come in handy for bringing in supplies. What gives?"

Julie told her about the plane she had seen the night before and its odd actions.

Ofelia grinned at her in the mirror as she applied virulent blue eye shadow. "You did have an exciting evening, didn't you? Rescued by a Galahad of the swamps and nearly brained by a drug drop to boot."

"Nothing dropped. What are you talking about?"

"Must have been something somewhere. It's a favorite game, or so I'm told. The plane comes in from South or Central America at night, flying low, sometimes even cutting the engines. A fishing boat is waiting. The boat flashes its lights as a signal and the drop is made with the stuff in waterproof packaging and enough Styrofoam to float an aircraft carrier. The men in the boat fish the stuff out of the water, then take off to some place where the river or canal they're traveling on crosses a highway. They are met by a truck, the stuff is turned over to the folks in the vehicle. Voilà, it's gone. Cute, huh?"

"Modern pirates," Julie agreed, a frown between her eyes. She thought of Rey, so intent on the plane the night before. She thought, too, of his annoyance at the delay caused by the accident and his refusal to be detained overlong afterward. If he had been waiting for a drop, however, he had failed to signal the plane and had certainly missed it. He might have been racing to overtake the plane elsewhere on the winding river, but if so, he surely would not have troubled to snatch her out of the water and see her back to the location. Of course, there was still his dismissal from the DEA.

"Don't let it bother you," Ofelia said. "I also hear tell this area is the dumping ground for the bodies that get mysteriously dead down in New Orleans. It's only an hour's drive or less from downtown, and seems like the back of beyond with all the nice convenient swamp to hide the evidence. But what's it to us? We'll be around for a few weeks, then we're out of here. It's not our problem."

"I suppose you're right."

"Bet your sweet life I am," Ofelia said with a wink. A moment later, she was gone out the door, flipping the keys to an Excel Films truck in her hand as she went.

Julie left the motor home a short time later as twilight settled behind the trees, spreading its soft colors over the river. She enjoyed this time of day on location, the time when the noise and activity had ceased, when most of the crew had headed for their accommodations at the nearest motels or for the closest bars and restaurants.

She had some of her best ideas while roaming about the sets, looking at things from different angles, placing the actors in her mind's eye in different spots, in different character combinations. Though the movie's scenes had been blocked out in preproduction, it still remained fluid in her mind, always subject to small changes that would illuminate another layer of emotion or motivation. She never really stopped thinking about it on some level from the time production got under way until the last millimeter of film had been shot.

It was important that she know precisely what effect, what image she wanted, because that was the only way that she could maintain control. Control was important. Like a conductor who guides and directs an orchestra to elicit harmony and resonance from the musicians, it was her job to see that everyone on her movie worked together to create a unified product.

It was also her job to see that they enjoyed doing it. Some directors felt that dire conflict, the clashing of tempers, and the inflicting of psychic pain was the way to wring great performances from actors. She had never subscribed to that notion. To her it seemed that actors, like other professionals, should be able to do their best work in an atmosphere of relaxed understanding. Artistic pretensions did not concern her. She was in the business of entertaining, though she wanted to do the best work of which she was capable.

The thing she wanted most of all, however, was to be satisfied with what she was doing. A movie, even at best, represented a year out of her life by the time it went from preproduction and production through postproduction and the vagaries of eventual release. If she couldn't take satisfaction from what she was doing during that span of time, then she was in the wrong business.

Julie wandered down toward the water. The mercury lamps had come on, reflecting in the river's dark surface like sunspots in a murky steel mirror. Rose-red glints from the fading sunset shifted across its width, while the shadow of the great cypress tree that stood on the bank beside Julie was thrown to the opposite shore. To her right was a low bridge with stout pilings where the highway crossed the river and gave access to the boat club and the location. Paralleling the highway was a canal that had been dug decades before by the logging company as a means of getting the felled trees out of the swamp, but had since become a part of the area's system of waterways. Blind River merged with the canal just in front of the bridge. The two waterways formed a kind of triangular moat around the location, with the swamp coming up to the back of the boat club on the third side. It made the site easy to secure against unwanted visitors and petty pilfering with a single guard station set up at the place where the bridge over the canal reached the driveway into the parking lot.

Nearer at hand, almost under the big cypress, was the wooden pier where the two cabin cruisers were docked. Another boat had been added beside them, a sleek silver speedboat delivered that morning. Julie liked the looks of it, fast and high-tech in contrast to the dingy, round-bottomed aluminum skiff with its outboard motor, little more than a modernized pirogue, that was pulled up on the bank nearby. The skiff had also been brought in during the day. The two lighter boats, along with one of the cabin cruisers, would be used in the action scene to be shot tomorrow afternoon. The stuntman, substituting for Vance Stuart, would be in the skiff, the actors playing the goons hired by the disgruntled wife of the story would take the speedboat, while a tracking camera would be in the bigger boat.

The morning would be spent doing the preliminary shots with Vance. The actor had wanted to do his own stunts, but Julie couldn't allow that, even if the movie's bonding company would. There was no time to wait for any scrapes and bruises he might get to heal or, God forbid, for him to get out of the hospital if anything more serious happened. Unlike more static scenes, stunts were an unknown quantity.

"Getting ready to change the whole thing, Julie?"

She turned as Stan McNeilly, the stunt coordinator who was also in charge of special effects, came up behind her. He walked with a halting gait, a souvenir of his stuntman days, one he had picked up during the filming of some western back in the late fifties. The accident had ended one career for him, but started another as a director of stunts. He was good at it, conscientious with equipment, painstaking in his preparations, and extremely careful.

Julie smiled as she shook her head in answer to his question. "Only looking things over, thinking about tomorrow. Did I see you going through the stunt with the new man out on the water this afternoon?"

Stan nodded, the light behind him glittering in his thinning, sandy-gray hair, leaving his face in shadow. "Paul Lislet's his name. Seems he'll do all right, been around boats all his life."

"It bothers me that he's never done stunts before. You don't think we should have flown in a professional? This first one, especially, isn't exactly easy."

"The guy joined Screen Actors Guild, didn't he? A SAG card makes him a professional. Anyway, the gag's not that hard, just a chase scene, really. Lislet caught on quick. Besides, it'll take somebody who knows the river, knows where the stumps and sinkers are located, which way the channel goes, and so on. He'll actually be leading the other boats through the hazards."

They discussed the scene a few moments, going over the movements of the boats, the angles and frames and various special shots of wakes and skyline that Julie wanted and that the cinematographer, gangling, red-haired Andy Russell, had recommended. Finally, they fell silent.

Stan lit a cigarette in a flare of his lighter that showed clearly the splotches of freckles on his face from the sun exposure of too many locations. Dropping his hand holding the cigarette back behind him to keep the smoke away from Julie, he changed the subject.

"Ofelia said you weren't able to talk this Cajun you came in with last night into working for you."

"Not yet. He's supposed to show up tomorrow to look around. We'll see, then."

"Makes no difference either way. You've read enough, talked to enough people to be an expert yourself. What we aren't sure of, we can fake."

"I don't like faking it."

"I know that, but it's done all the time. The important thing is the overall impression, the illusion. That's what the people in the audience are going to remember, not the details."

"It's like the silk flowers in the grass in *Steel Magnolias,* Stan. There are people who will notice."

"Not enough to matter."

She shook her head. "It will matter to me. It bothers me not to get it right and know it's right."

"You sound like your old man."

"He has one or two good points."

"Yeah."

Stan took a drag on his cigarette, letting the smoke drift from his nostrils. The bitter edge to his voice was a reminder that Stan had little use for Bull Bullard. Julie's father, then just starting out in his career at the time, had directed the movie on which Stan had been crippled. Julie had never been quite sure what had happened, but she knew Stan blamed Bull for his injury.

Julie had known Stan since she was a child; before the accident Stan had been a regular at her parents' home. Afterward, and after the divorce, Stan had kept in touch for a while with cards and visits to Julie and her mother when he was passing through Louisiana. Julie could remember him taking them all out for picnics, talking to her mother in his soft voice, could recall him buying her an ice-cream cone on a hot summer day and taking her for a ride in his Chevrolet convertible. After a time, his visits had grown further apart, then ceased altogether.

Julie had looked up Stan after she moved to L.A. herself. They met from time to time, ran into each other at parties or on studio back lots. Stan had done some memorable pictures, but had not worked a great deal in the past couple of years. Julie had given him a call as a matter of course when she knew she would be needing a stunt coordinator for *Swamp Kingdom.* She had since decided that she had been lucky to get him.

They were quiet for long moments while Stan smoked and Julie hugged her arms around her against the evening coolness. The night drew in, the shadows thickening to darkness under the big old tree. Finally, Stan dropped his glowing cigarette butt on the ground and pressed the toe of his sneaker on it.

"Look, kid," he said, his voice a low growl, "don't sweat it. It's just a movie. There've been thousands made, some great, some lousy, most neither one nor the other. You do the best you can, then you forget it. That's all."

Julie turned her head to give him a warm smile. "I hate to be the one to break this to you, Stan, but Bogey you're not."

"The advice still goes. 'Night." He flicked his fingers at an imaginary hat brim, then limped away.

It was probably good advice he had given her. Julie wished she could take it. She really did.

Chapter 3

•

Would Rey Tabary show up?

The question nagged at Julie from the moment she got out of bed in the small hours of the next morning. It came and went in her mind, interfering with the thousand and one details that needed her attention. It was annoying that it wouldn't go away.

She worked for a while in her office, the metal building on a flatbed trailer with concrete steps set at the door, which served that purpose. Ofelia was on hand to help, though she spent the first hour moaning about her losses of the night before and clutching her head that ached from too many beers mixed with strawberry daiquiris.

Julie had had an early breakfast with Andy Russell and Stan McNeilly, the cinematographer and stunt coordinator. They had eaten it around her desk instead of inside the boat club where catering had set up shop by special permission. They had managed to work out a few problems. Afterward, the two men had gone off to set up the day's shooting. Julie looked through the pictures of extras suitable as fishermen and trappers for an upcoming scene, choosing the ones who looked promising so Ofelia could make appointments for her to see them in person. In another half hour, the sun would be up, and then they could all really get to work.

Julie's secretary arrived, a local girl who had been hired for the duration. The girl was competent at her job, but more than a little star-struck. Julie heard her catch her breath, then breathe a soft sigh along with a murmured good morning as the trailer's outer door opened. It was the mellow voice of Vance Stuart that answered her as his footsteps crossed the outer office. He tapped on Julie's door and walked in without waiting for an invitation. Crossing to her desk, he dropped into the chair sitting in front of it.

Julie continued marking the stack of photographs in front of her until she finished them. Pushing them to one side, she leaned back in her chair. The man before her was of medium height, with precisely cut brown hair and eyes of a meltingly soft blue enhanced by contact lenses he didn't need. Saved from a bland handsomeness by a lopsided grin, he had a tense air that was not helped at all by the casual way he draped himself over his chair or the comfortable movie-set chic of his tan cotton shirt and chinos.

"The makeup is fine," Julie said after a second's consideration, "but if you've been to wardrobe, I don't think much of the results."

"That's what I want to talk to you about," the actor said in disgruntled tones. "They tried to hand me a pair of worn-out jeans and a T-shirt that said 'Go Tigers!' for Christ's sake!"

"So?"

"I thought this Jean-Pierre character I'm playing's supposed to be a Cajun come back to his roots and all that."

"You think he would wear something different?"

Vance brushed a hand back over his temple, smoothing his hair. He looked at her from under his lashes. "What I had in mind was one of those pirate-looking shirts with sleeves gathered on the shoulders and an open neckline."

"To show off your manly chest?" Julie made no effort to hide her amusement.

"Yes—no, I mean—ah, Julie!"

"It pains me to be the one to break this to you, Vance, but Cajun costumes like that went out when they stopped making their own clothes, before the turn of the century. They wear jeans and T-shirts now just like everybody else."

"Well, dammit, Julie, can't we stretch it a little? It would be so cool, so Errol Flynnish, if you know what I mean. It might start a whole new fashion trend."

"Not a chance, not if it's all wrong. And it is. Back to wardrobe, my friend."

"You take the fun out of everything."

She gave him a bright smile. "It's a tough job, but—"

"—but somebody has to do it," he finished for her in exaggerated disgust.

"Right. As long as you're here, there's a favor I'd like to ask you to do for me."

Julie went on to tell him of Aunt Tine's proposed visit to the set with Rey Tabary and the older woman's request for Vance's autograph.

"You want me to make nice with this sweet old lady so you can snag yourself a technical director?" Vance's expression was pained.

"Not exactly. I just want you to be your usual gracious self so Aunt Tine isn't disappointed."

"And so this Tabary guy will think we're great folks to work with."

"It can't hurt." Her tone was defensive.

"I'm supposed to be on my best behavior for a backwoods swamp hick?"

"No, Vance," Julie said, a steely timbre under the softness of her voice as she stared at him, "you're supposed to do it for me."

He met her gaze for long moments, then abruptly he grinned. "Ah, well, since you put it that way."

He grumbled a few minutes more, though without heat. He also gave no sign of leaving. "You should have been with me and Madelyn last night in New Orleans," he said, sitting forward as he changed the subject. "We met this guy in a cocktail lounge. We got to talking and he took us home with him for dinner. You know, the hospitality of these people is really something else."

"Where is Madelyn this morning?"

"Still in the city, as far as I know. She said something about shopping, her and Summer and her mother. They'll be along after a while. But I was telling you about this meal we had. There was gumbo full of chicken and smoked turkey and the most fantastic andouille sausage, and the flavor—smoky and indescribable. The guy's wife served it over rice, no instant stuff, either. There was this great French bread and I brought a decent Chardonnay. Made a pig out of myself, is what I did. Thought I had a zit from it this morning, but it turned out to be a mosquito bite."

Food was a major source of conversation for Vance, as for most of the movie world. Julie sometimes wondered if it was because an appreciation of good food was supposed to show their sophistication, or if it was only that it preyed on their minds because nearly everyone limited their eating to some extent.

"I'm sorry I missed it," she said in controlled patience. "The gumbo, not the zit."

He flashed her his famous crooked grin. "Go ahead, laugh, but this face is my fortune."

Julie got to her feet and walked around her desk. Sunrises, like the sunsets, were subtle affairs in this latitude where the dawn was filtered through the swamp haze and tangled tree branches. The light had been increasing by increments, slowly illuminating the parking lot. For a long time, the scene beyond the glass at Julie's office window had been gray and dim, now all at once she could see people moving, see the glint of sunlight on car windshields and in dew-wet grass. Heading toward the door and the movie that waited, she said, "There speaks the man who wanted to risk his profile in a boat chase."

"Dumb, I'll admit. But I'd still do it, if you'd give me half a chance. It makes me feel helpless, sitting around while somebody else takes the risks. Besides, think of the attention from the tabloids if you come in tight so they can see it's me." He jumped to his feet, striding after her.

"Sorry, that's the system."

He caught up with her at the foot of the concrete steps outside, matching his pace to hers. "Listen, Julie, I meant what I said about you coming out with me, with or without Madelyn. I'd really like to get to know you before this movie is over."

Julie sent the actor a quick look. Vance Stuart was fair at his craft, reasonable, always on time, always searching for clues to the characters he played. He had ambition and drive, even if he did tend to be a bit flamboyant and egotistical at times. He had paid his dues in off-Broadway productions and summer stock before gaining fame as a hard-drinking playboy on one of the better afternoon soaps. The soap had given him a devoted following of fans who had made his name a box-office draw with feature films in the last three years. There was often a lovely young thing on his arm; women were easy for him, and he enjoyed them. The L.A. party scene was also to his taste, and he skated along with the crowd that bought its champagne in jumbo Nebuchadnezzar jars that held twenty bottles each and provided cocaine in coin-silver urns with razor blades on the side. It was on the party circuit that Allen had met him and decided he would be a good choice for Jean-Pierre.

Julie had, over the years, developed a sixth sense for men who were womanizers, men who tried to sweep her off her feet with their looks and personality. Some did it for the challenge of it, some for the ego boost, and others for what she could do for them. There had been no indication that Vance was one of those men, but she was wary.

"We work together every day," she said lightly.

"Work isn't what I had in mind."

"Well, it's what's on mine right now. And I believe I hear the wardrobe mistress calling your name."

He glanced over his shoulder at the wardrobe trailer, where a rotund woman with graying hair and her usual uniform of baggy double-knit pants and shirt stood staring after them. Accepting his dismissal with a grimace, he said, "We'll talk about it later."

"Maybe," Julie said, and left him with a wave.

The subject probably would come up again, Julie thought, though she wasn't looking forward to it. She had enough to worry about without having to consider how to turn aside the moves Vance might put on her without making it difficult to work with him. Of course, if the situation became too fraught, she could always bring up Allen's name. There weren't many actors who wanted to risk offending the producer.

The day turned warm and clear, the sun muted with the delicate haze of fall that made for fine shooting light without harsh shadows. The filming got off to a good start and took on a nice even rhythm, with blessedly few snags.

Julie took time out at midmorning to talk to an entertainment

editor from one of the big dailies. It was a major break in her routine
for a minor detail, but such print coverage was always important to
enlist the interest and cooperation of the community. Besides, when
it came to her movies, she was a firm believer in the old Hollywood
adage that any publicity was good publicity.

By early afternoon, they had miles of film of boats chasing each
other, including the close-ups with Vance in the speeding skiff. They
were ready for the final action sequence, the stunt with its tricky boat
maneuver.

Julie had kept a watch out most of the day for Rey and Aunt Tine.
She expected them to come by water, however, perhaps because that
was how Rey had left the other night, so she paid no attention to the
cars and trucks that came and went in a constant stream. It was jolting
to look up from a discussion with the cinematographer and see the tall
Cajun and his elderly aunt climbing out of a Jeep Cherokee.

They were not alone. With them was a brunette with the piquant
features, slim shape, and calm manner of a Degas ballerina. Julie
finished what she was saying to Andy Russell, then moved to intercept
the trio.

Aunt Tine introduced the woman with them as Donna Lislet, the
wife of the stuntman who was out on the canal getting ready for the
scene coming up. "I hope you don't mind that I asked her to come
with us. She's dying to see her husband in action. When she heard I
wanted to come, too, she practically forced Rey to bring us both."

"That's great," Julie said, exchanging a quick, smiling glance with
the older woman before turning to Donna. "You're certainly welcome, but I hope you won't be disappointed. There's not much excitement to shooting a movie most of the time, just a lot of
hurry-up-and-wait."

"I'm sure it's fascinating, anyway." The young wife's voice was
pleasant enough but cool, as if she were determined not to appear too
impressed by her surroundings. Still, her eyes, brown and shining,
behind her huge sunshades with purple lenses, missed little.

Aunt Tine wanted to know about everything. Julie tried to oblige
her with answers while at the same time keeping up with what was
going forward with the crew. Stan and Ofelia and a half-dozen others

were getting the boats ready. The scene as written called for a high-speed chase with, supposedly, the Cajun Jean-Pierre in his beat-up, round-bottomed aluminum skiff equipped with a 150-horsepower outboard motor outmaneuvering the goons hired by his wife who would be in the speedboat.

Most of the long scene had been filmed, with the boats racing along the canals below the boat club or else streaking downriver at breakneck speed with close sweeps around the hairpin curves. They would pick up now at the place where the river widened, where Julie's pirogue had nearly come to grief two nights before. The aluminum skiff and the speedboat would play an elaborate game of tag among the cypress trees and dead logs. At the end of the game, Paul Lislet, taking Vance's place as Jean-Pierre in the skiff, was supposed to use a huge dead cypress tree at the edge of the river's channel, one that had fallen into the water but was still attached to its stump, so that it formed a makeshift boat ramp. The scene called for the skiff to hit this ramp and become airborne, jumping a nest of cypress knees that would then trap the speedboat while the skiff made its getaway down the river.

A hastily constructed floating platform had been towed downriver and set in place as a camera point for the scene. Julie and the others would be leaving for that platform in just a few minutes.

Vance Stuart, as agreed, emerged from his motor home and sauntered up with a casual air to join the group. His attitude toward Aunt Tine was slightly deferential, and he was appreciative of her compliments to his talent. He even produced a copy of the script that he autographed for her, then, moved perhaps by the older woman's pink-cheeked pleasure, walked away a short distance with her while he pointed out what he had been doing that day with the boats.

Rey Tabary stood to one side, his manner casual. If he was there under duress, he didn't make a point of it. Still, the look in his eyes as they rested on Julie, then moved to his aunt and the actor, held a certain ironic humor. Julie, catching that look, thought it likely that he suspected her plot with his aunt. She didn't mind, since it had succeeded. It was now up to her to take advantage of this opportunity to talk to him further.

A car horn blew a shrill blast. A black Lincoln Town Car with a uniformed driver behind the wheel came barreling over the highway bridge and turned into the boat-club parking lot.

As the car drew up in a swirl of dust Madelyn de Wells, the actress, emerged from it, tucking a Fendi leather purse under her arm. She sauntered toward Julie and the others, her head with its carefully curled dark hair held high so her heart-shaped face caught the light at a flattering angle. The smile on her red lips was one that a movie columnist had called, not without reason, rapacious. Her closely fitted black and acid-yellow YSL suit seemed out of place on the rough location, though it suited the character she was to portray.

Behind Madelyn came Summer Davett, who had the role of the adolescent daughter Alicia in the movie, and also Summer's mother, Annette Davett. The two of them trailed the sophisticated actress as if they were not quite sure where they were supposed to be.

"Don't look so amazed," Madelyn told Julie with the tinkling laugh perfected in a long succession of roles as the heartless other woman. "I know I had no call for today, but a hum on the grapevine said there would be interesting things happening this afternoon. We girls came straight here instead of going to the motel, just in case."

She was talking, at least in part, about the stunt, Julie thought. Madelyn enjoyed watching dangerous scenes and seldom missed one. She wasn't alone, of course; spectators on a location increased in direct proportion to the difficulty of the stunts being filmed. It disturbed Julie to know that the grapevine listed the one scheduled for today as being of above-average interest.

That Madelyn and the others had heard the rumor in New Orleans wasn't particularly surprising. The gossip machine on a location was formidable; a whispered tale could go from one end to the other and out to the tabloids in less time than it took to sneeze. It was caused in part by the nature of the operation, its often isolated position within an area or a community coupled with an intense concentration on the project at hand. There was also the perceived correlation between notoriety and success and the uncertainty of film life, where any bit of information could mean the difference between working or not working, success or failure.

Introductions were made. Madelyn, who had hardly taken her eyes from Rey from the moment she left the car, moved to his side. She attached herself to him, twining an arm around his as naturally as a wisteria vine around a trellis.

"You're the Swamp Rat, then? I heard about you, too. Will you really be joining us?"

Julie had mentioned Rey to Ofelia and Stan but to no one else. The efficiency of the grapevine could sometimes be annoying. She spoke quickly: "That hasn't been decided yet. Maybe you could help persuade him."

Madelyn barely glanced in Julie's direction. Her gaze openly caressing as she smiled up at Rey, she said, "I would dearly love to try. Why not come and have a drink with me in my motor home and tell me about it?"

Donna Lislet made a slight sound that had the timbre of distaste. Julie glanced at the stuntman's wife to find her watching the actress with narrow eyes. Madelyn, with her total disregard for any thoughts or feelings except her own, often affected other women with instant antipathy. It never bothered her.

Hypocrisy was not one of the actress's faults, though she had others. Madelyn was supremely self-centered. She had a well-developed appreciation for money, or at least for the jewelry and clothes, cars, and other fine things it could bring. Most of all, however, she adored men. An unusual new specimen was to her like a gourmet meal to a peckish gourmand. It was to be hoped that Madelyn's presence might encourage Rey Tabary to agree to what Julie wanted, for detaching her from him might be difficult.

Rey, however, held his own ground without need of help. "I appreciate the invitation," he said to the actress with a brief smile, "but I had better look after my aunt before she starts chasing the leading man."

"Before I what?" Aunt Tine asked in scandalized tones as she moved with Vance to rejoin the others.

Her nephew gave her a quick grin. At the same time, he detached his arm from Madelyn's hold with firm movements, turning to the child actress and her mother for a delayed greeting.

The young girl, more than precocious due to a life spent on various movie sets, had been watching the byplay between the Cajun and the actress. As Rey shook hands with her the girl gave him a knowing smile. Rey returned the look with polite imperturbability. The girl's grin faded, and she retreated into her usual petulance.

A twelve-year-old small for her age with straight, sandy-blonde hair and irregular features, Summer had one of those mobile faces that the camera translates as fascinating. She could play an age span from around seven to over fourteen and any personality from a whining brat to a pragmatic angel. In *Swamp Kingdom,* she was supposed to turn from a priggish little rich girl in frilly dresses, her mother's expensively dressed toy who has been taught to fear everything, into a self-sufficient tomboy who fears nothing. She had been outstanding as an actress so far, though somewhat difficult to handle on the set and prone to tantrums both on and off.

"I hope you find your visit with us enjoyable," Annette Davett said to Rey and his aunt in her reedy, breathless voice, "but I'm sure you will. Though we actors have our peculiar ways, we're really quite harmless once you get to know us."

Summer's mother paused expectantly. As her audience made no more than a polite response, disappointment settled over her features. Annette had once been a child star herself, and never stopped expecting people to recognize her. Unlike her daughter, she had been a petite blonde of uncommon prettiness with bouncing corkscrew curls and dimples. However, her career had lasted no more than five or six years since she had never been able to make the transition to adult features. She had grown into a faded woman with a whining manner and an endless supply of stories about her glory days. She was rather pathetic in her determination to relive those days through her daughter, and in her insistence that Summer was going to be a great star. She seemed to have taken on the persona of the traditional stage mother, using an encroaching manner and conniving ways to gain more lines, better camera angles, greater publicity for her child. The result was that Annette was shunned by the crew and patronized by the actors. Julie felt rather sorry for her, but dealt with her as seldom and as briefly as possible.

Donna Lislet had moved away from the others to look out over the water with one hand protecting her eyes from the bright sunlight. She began to wave. A slim figure in the aluminum skiff floating out on the canal, obviously her husband, stood up. His smile flashed in the tan of his face as he gave her a jaunty wave. Seeing Rey, he sent him a thumbs-up signal.

The stuntman was being coached by Stan McNeilly, who was shouting across the water from the cabin cruiser idling nearby. The stunt coordinator turned from Paul Lislet and spoke to the man at the wheel of the cabin cruiser. The boat made a tight turn and headed toward the pier.

"It's time to start downriver," Julie said to Rey and the others. "Shall we?"

Summer was biting her bottom lip as she watched the boats. She glanced at Rey Tabary in speculation that sat oddly on her piquant features, then looked toward Julie. Her brown eyes earnest, she said, "I'd like to watch, too. Could Mother and I go?"

Before Julie could answer, Annette Davett said, "Don't be a silly, Summer; you know you'd just be in the way. Besides, you have work to do, studying your fishing scene for tomorrow."

"Oh, Mother!" the girl cried.

"Your work is more important. You know it is."

Annette Davett's high scolding tone made Julie want to contradict her and take the girl with her. However, she only smiled and clasped Summer's shoulder in a brief gesture before turning away toward the cabin cruiser.

They piled aboard the powerful craft that sat with its motor idling. It pulled away from the pier, then picked up speed, surging away down the curving river, cleaving the water in a deep wake that spread out to lap the banks on both sides behind them. The sun on the water was dazzling. A great white crane, lifting into flight at the cruiser's approach, flapped in graceful slow motion in silhouette against the faceted diamond glitter. The trees lining the shore made an edging of shadow that was cool and dim in contrast.

Julie faced into the wind of their passage, enjoying the gentle buffeting. It reminded her of the ride with Rey Tabary two nights before, and she turned her head to look at him. He was watching her, his own gaze serious, faintly distracted, though his mouth curved in a brief smile as he met her gaze.

"It was good of you to bring your aunt today," she said.

"Is that what happened?" he asked quietly. "I thought she brought me."

"Whichever, I trust you won't regret it."

His gaze flickered over her, coming to rest on her face once more where the sun turned the tan of her skin across her cheekbones to a peach-tinted golden translucence. "I probably will, but what's a few regrets?"

Something in his words brought an image of Allen to Julie's mind. She tried to picture the man she lived with expressing anything similar, but it was no use. Regrets were something that Allen tried to prevent at all costs. He considered anything else unintelligent, lacking in foresight. It was a good trait, a safe trait, in a producer.

The shooting platform, sitting on heavy-duty pontoons at the water's edge, was somewhat crowded with the extra people in addition to the equipment, but there was nothing particularly unusual in that. Julie left Rey, Aunt Tine, and the others standing to one side while she consulted with the cinematographer, then put on earphones to listen to the final instructions that Stan, still in the cabin cruiser, was giving to Paul Lislet and the actors playing the villainous goons. The skiff and speedboat circled in apparent aimlessness or else wallowed in each other's wakes while the master camera on its Chapman crane, as well as the other cameras and sound equipment on the platform and in the cabin cruiser were checked. As the waiting stretched, Ofelia broke out cold drinks for everyone.

Finally, everything was in place for the take. Julie gave the order for action that was echoed by Ofelia near the master camera and Stan in the cabin cruiser.

Julie was always tense during action scenes. They seldom went exactly as planned, and the surprises were not always pleasant or cheap to fix. Effects that seemed great on paper could be impossible to capture in a realistic way on film, or else looked downright ridiculous. Crew members who would follow her orders to the letter for a dramatic or romantic scene suddenly developed all sorts of wild-haired ideas when action sequences were in progress. The tenuous feel of her control, then, was disturbing, especially since she was still responsible.

Everything seemed to be going fine. The skiff broke from the tree tunnel of the river channel in planing flight, leading a foaming wake that divided behind it like a giant zipper. It zigzagged across the open, avoiding stumps and half-submerged logs while Paul Lislet crouched at the rear controls, looking back over his shoulder at the speedboat that came winging after him. One of the two men in dark suits in the speedboat leaned out with an AK-47 submachine gun, triggering off a burst of fire. The shots exploded with an echoing whine, pocking the water in a series. The skiff fishtailed, swinging wide to dance back over the speedboat's wake, then curved away to flash through the close-growing stand of cypress trees near the opposite shore from the platform. In a bravura display of boatmanship and steady nerves, the stuntman sent the skiff hurtling through them, playing hide-and-seek with the sunlight and dense shadow in a lightning series of now-you-see-it, now-you-don't images that would be spectacular on film.

Behind the two racing boats, the cabin cruiser burst from the river channel, following the wake of the speedboat. Stan could be seen beside the tracking camera, still shouting instructions into a walkie-talkie, leaning to yell something, too, at the cameraman. Whether any of the other men could hear him was hard to say with the roaring of the engines that rolled over the water and bounced back from the encircling tree line.

From the corner of her eyes, Julie saw Rey move to the edge of the shooting platform, grasping an upright with one hand as he followed the action with narrowed eyes. She knew an instant of satisfaction that what was taking place out on the water, the scene she and her crew had concocted, was exciting enough to hold his interest.

Now the skiff was circling once more in a wide, sideslipping glide at full throttle, flirting with the speedboat even as more shots rang out. The lighter boat came on around, running in behind the cabin cruiser so the camera could swing around and get a head-on shot. Then Paul Lislet veered away from the other boats to push the skiff into another wide turn, enticing, leading the speedboat toward the thick, bafflelike growth of cypress trees once more, and the makeshift launch ramp and cluster of blackish-brown stubs that were the cypress knees.

Rey suddenly pushed away from the upright, putting his hands on his hips as he watched the boats. He whipped his head around, looking for Julie, finding her. "Stop it," he called out. "Stop it, now!"

She took off her earphones as she turned toward him, uncertain with the noise and her concentration on the action out on the water that he had said what she thought. "What is it?"

"There's something wrong, the skiff isn't steering right," he said in hard tones. "Look at it!"

She could see nothing. The smaller boat had not slackened speed. It seemed to be answering the movements of the man at the controls. Or was it? Was there a lag between the motions of the stuntman and the answering turn of the boat? Was there a wobble in the boat's wake as it headed at breakneck speed toward the dark cypress trees.

"Cut!" she shouted. "Cut! Cut!"

Julie heard the call echo over the water, heard it picked up by Ofelia and Stan and repeated in staticky miniature in her headphones. Men cursed and cameras ground to a stop.

But it was too late. The skiff hurtled among the cypress tree with the speedboat close behind. They were both swallowed in dimness, then came a cracking snap. The skiff spun broadside in a spray of water. It slammed against a tall cypress tree with a booming, hollow thud and the high-pitched shriek of ripping metal before bouncing off again into the path of the other boat. The speedboat, unable to stop, struck the skiff nose-high. Fiberglass flew, crunching, crackling, as the second boat tumbled over the first in a spinning arc and the sudden revving roar of the engine. The speedboat came down, slapping the water in a cracking report as the engine coughed and died.

Donna Lislet screamed, a sound that seemed to tear from her throat. Rey Tabary was at her side in three strides, holding her, hiding her face against his broad shoulder. He held her tight, blocking her view with his body of the spreading red stain in the dark brown swamp water.

Chapter 4

"If you can't do the job, Miss Bullard, if you can't turn out some kind of movie here without costing us two arms and a leg, then we'll have to take over the production."

"Take over," Julie repeated, her voice stifled as she faced the man who had commandeered her office and was sitting in her chair.

"We would bring in another director for starters, somebody who will pay more attention to where the money's being spent."

"You can't do that!" Julie said, leaning across her desk with her palms flat on its surface.

"I can, and you know it," the man said, his smile tight. "I make the recommendation, and that's it."

Julie had not expected this meeting with the accountant from the movie's insurers to be pleasant, but she hadn't expected it to be enraging. A part of the short fuse on her temper came from having her movie location shut down for the best part of four days while the St. James Parish Sheriff's Office conducted its investigation into the accident. Answering the questions of the officers and other governmental officials, plus fielding the queries made in varying degrees of politeness by the news media, had not improved it. Regardless, the main cause was the bonding-company accountant, Davies. That he had spent the past few days rummaging through her papers, using her supplies, and sweating all over her desk chair, her blotting pad, and her phone was nearly more than she could bear. She disliked intensely to have anyone invading her work space, shuffling through her papers, looking at her mail. Worst of all was his patronizing attitude. He was an overweight man with receding hair, bad skin, and body odor, who made up for the deficiencies of nature by flaunting whatever authority he could claim, and enjoying it.

"Face it," Davies went on. "This boat accident has made a shambles of your budget. Replacing the damaged equipment and picking up the funeral expenses for Lislet and the hospital bills for the other two stuntmen—plus the tab while the crew is idle, eating their heads off and taking up motel space—will cost a mint. I doubt it will be two weeks before the money will run out and my company will have to kick in to make up the loss. We would be within our rights to bring in a team of accountants tomorrow to take a hard look at the story you're doing, cut to the bone, get rid of all the ruffles and bows—er, flourishes."

Julie gave him a hard stare. "There are no ruffles and bows, as you call them, on this production. Every scene, every line of dialogue, and every shot has purpose and meaning."

"Don't get all hot under the collar; I'm not saying things are slack around here because you are a woman director."

"Aren't you." It was not a question.

"The job's one that requires tough decisions and the ba—er, the willpower to see them through."

"You're partly right."

"Yes, well, and there's no point in trotting out that song and dance about integrity and story continuity, either; I've heard it all before. None of it matters a damn, not with the kind of money it takes to make a movie these days. What we need is for somebody to get the job done and over with; it's as simple as that. Either you do it, or somebody else will."

"Accountants." Her voice was flat with revulsion.

"If that's what it takes. I'm sure we understand each other, though I will, of course, be speaking to Gravesend."

"I doubt there is much you can tell my fiancé about the situation that he doesn't already know." It wasn't often that Julie paraded her relationship with Allen, but there was a snide sound in the man's voice she couldn't stomach.

"Nonetheless, I'll be getting in touch."

"Do that, if it makes you feel better," Julie said tightly.

"And we'll be keeping a close eye on things here. You'll be subject to an audit without notice."

"I do understand. In the meantime, I have work to do. I regret having to throw you out of my office, but it's the place where I do my job. I know you'd like to see that get under way again."

A flush spread over the man's pallid face, but he began to gather his papers together.

As much satisfaction as it gave her to shut the door behind the bonding-company man, Julie still couldn't bring her mind to bear on her work when he was gone. In the first place, no amount of room spray could rid her office of Davies's stench; in the second, her mind was too unsettled.

She was responsible for the death of Paul Lislet. Oh, she had nothing to do with the steering cable that had been found eaten away by battery acid, but hers had been the final okay on the stunt that had taken his life. She should have been less reckless in approving the suggestions made by Stan and even Paul Lislet himself, should have opted for a more prudent sort of chase scene. She should have checked to see that the skiff had been thoroughly inspected by her own people instead of accepting the word of the boat company which delivered it that it was in perfect condition.

None of these things might have done any good, it was true. There was nothing unusual about a stuntman getting caught wrong in a stunt; even the best of them had had most of the bones in their bodies broken at least once. It was the nature of the game. Things that looked dangerous on film often appeared that way precisely because they were dangerous. That was the reason why the job paid so well, because of the hazards involved. Even deaths weren't uncommon.

But it had never happened on one of her pictures.

She couldn't get the image of the moment when the two boats collided out of her head. She saw it over and over like replaying a film clip, heard Rey's soft curse and Aunt Tine's gasp of horror that she hadn't even been aware of at the time, lived with the reverberation of Donna Lislet's screams sounding in her ears.

Once or twice, she thought that she would like to forget *Swamp Kingdom* altogether, thought she didn't have the heart to finish it. The idea of leaving Louisiana and heading back to Los Angeles, of lying on the beach and soaking up the sun and wind, forgetting until another story idea came along, had such intense appeal that it was all she could do not to start packing her bags.

It was impossible. There were too many people depending on her, too much money riding on this picture for her to abandon it. Besides, she still had to prove that she could do it. More than ever, she needed to prove that.

Paul Lislet's funeral was that afternoon; it had been delayed because of the autopsy required in cases of unnatural death. Julie had sent flowers, both in her name and in that of Excel Films. She tried to tell herself that was enough, that nothing more would be expected. It wasn't true, and she knew it. Still, the idea of putting in an appearance, facing the friends and family of the dead man, was demoralizing. She disliked attending funerals at the best of times; she wasn't sure she had the nerve to show up at this one.

Worrying over the whole thing, she decided finally, was more painful than doing something about it. As lunchtime came and she still had accomplished nothing she slammed down her pen and left the office, heading for her motel.

The nearest thing Julie had to a dress suitable for a funeral was one of navy voile with a matching broad-brimmed hat. She felt over-dressed as she stood at the back of the church for the Mass, much too smartly turned out for the simple, moving service in the old Victorian chapel. At least she had not had to enter alone. Stan had come with her, offering his escort at the last moment. She was grateful.

At the cemetery, she and the stunt coordinator stood well back from the green canopy with its rows of chairs and smell of carnations and chrysanthemums wilting in the heat. Stan wanted to leave when the last prayer was said and the mourners finally began to stir and disperse, but Julie, since she was there, intended to do the thing right. She waited until the crowd around Donna Lislet had thinned, then stepped to intercept the stuntman's widow.

"I wanted to say how sorry I am," Julie said, touching the woman's arm in a brief gesture of sympathy before drawing back. She barely glanced at the man who supported Donna with an arm around her waist, though she had known all along that Rey Tabary was there. And she did her best not to look at the two sandy-haired boys, one young enough to be carried in Rey's arms, the other leaning against his mother. "I'm sure it doesn't help, but I could not be more sincere."

"No," Donna Lislet said in choked tones, her face twisting with the tears that smeared her makeup, "it doesn't help."

Rey's features were bleak as he met Julie's gaze, the skin taut around his eyes. Still he spoke softly. "Miss Bullard isn't to blame. Paul knew the dangers, and accepted them."

Donna glanced up at him in accusation, her dark eyes drowning in tears. Their glances caught and held. After a moment, the widow sighed, then turned back to Julie. "Yes, I suppose so. I—thank you, Miss Bullard."

Julie moved back to let them pass. There was a heavy sensation in her chest that had grown familiar in the past two days, one it almost seemed would be relieved if she could shed a tear or two herself. She watched the couple move with the children toward Rey's Jeep Cherokee, and was caught by the way they walked so close together, the way the widow leaned against the strength of her husband's friend, the intimacy of their bond of shared grief.

To stare at them seemed, suddenly, a form of voyeurism. Julie looked away across the cemetery with its aboveground tombs of marble and granite unique to this lower portion of Louisiana, at the stone crosses and vases and the lichen-splotched inscriptions that hinted at old tragedies, old griefs. Time had made them benign, bearable. No doubt it would do the same for Paul Lislet's death. Someday.

"Here, now, *chère,*" Aunt Tine spoke from behind her. "Where you been keeping yourself, I ask? I've been expecting to have you move in any day now."

Julie turned, smiling with an effort. "Were you? I wasn't sure our agreement still held after what happened, wasn't sure your nephew especially would want me anywhere around."

"Rey? What has he to say to anything, I ask you? But of course he will not mind. You will come this evening, then? I aired out your room four days ago, and put on fresh sheets scented with vetiver just like my *grand-mère* used to do. Rey checked the window air conditioner and said all is well. I will expect you by dinner, no later; my neighbor brought me some fine shrimps this morning and I'm making a big *étouffée,* enough to take some to Donna, too."

Julie agreed; there seemed nothing else to do in the face of such determined hospitality. And she was grateful. Aunt Tine's calm acceptance of the accident, her invitation, which showed that life continued for her with the attending to human comfort, human hunger, was soothing. She wondered if it was meant that way, if Aunt Tine could see her need, or if it was just a part of the older woman's nature or her heritage to be practical and kind.

Rey was not at the house when Julie arrived with her belongings just after sundown. Aunt Tine helped her bring in her suitcases and laptop computer, the boxes that contained her portable office, and the few other odds and ends that she carried with her to make location accommodations seem more welcoming. Promising a glass of wine on the gallery when she was ready, the older woman left her to settle into her new quarters.

The room was large and airy, with narrow French doors that opened out onto the back gallery. There was also a pair of windows and an inside door that led into the dining room. The house, in typical French country style, had no hallways, unless the front and back galleries could be counted as such since all rooms had access to one or the other. All the rooms, three on the front and three on the back, opened into each other for a feeling that was cozy and intimate, if somewhat low on privacy. Julie's bedroom was on the back, along with the dining room and another room that had once been a bedchamber but had been made into a modern kitchen. Aunt Tine's bedroom was on the front right corner, so that she and Julie shared one of the pair of small baths built between the rooms. There was a formal parlor in the center front, then the bedroom used by Rey on the other front corner. The narrow staircase that mounted to the attic sleeping loft rose from one end of the front gallery.

The furnishings in Julie's bedroom were simple. The four-poster bed was of plain rosewood, though with a soft patina of age and polish. The rosewood armoire had a beveled mirror on the door. The bedspread, bolster cover, and pillow shams were made of stiffly starched drawn work in white cotton, obviously done by hand. There was an ivory crucifix above the bed and a pair of cupid prints in oval frames on either side of the French doors. The floor of random-width cypress planking was scattered with rag rugs in blue and rose and green that had faded with age and washing to gently blended softness.

The bathroom was just as old-fashioned in its way. The tub had claw feet, the commode had a wooden lid, and the basin was set into the top of an old washstand with ceramic pulls on the drawers and a mirror that tilted. The towels were thick, however, and the hot water plentiful. It wasn't long before Julie had taken a bath and changed into a pair of jeans and knit shirt. She put everything away, even laying out her portable office on one of the extra tables that filled in the corners of the bedroom. Left to herself, she would have stayed in her room, working a little, avoiding everyone. She could not ignore Aunt Tine's invitation, however. She went in search of her hostess.

"You see what I mean about Rey, that he will not interfere with what I do, or you?" Aunt Tine said as she and Julie sipped their wine while rocking slowly on the back porch in the gathering dusk. "When I told him that you were coming this evening, he only said that it was good."

"I'm glad to know that he isn't gone because of me—I had noticed that his Cherokee isn't here."

"He's still at the Lislet place, I think. He feels so for them, not only Donna and the two boys, but Paul's mother and father and his brothers and sisters. He will stay as long as he's needed."

"Just so as I'm not hampering either of you. I hope you'll tell me if I'm ever in the way."

"I will be glad for your company, especially tonight. I don't feel like eating alone." The older woman made a rueful grimace.

"You don't expect Rey for dinner?"

"Not really, but then I never do. He comes and goes as he pleases, at all kinds of odd hours. If there's food in the icebox he eats, if not, he cooks for himself. He helps me about the place when he can, and

I don't ask for more. When he comes, I'm glad; when he goes away again I am not sad, because I know he will return."

Julie gazed at Aunt Tine with increased interest. "Are you saying your nephew doesn't always live with you?"

"Why no, *chère;* why should you think so? He stays most of the time in New Orleans."

"I suppose I must have taken it for granted from the way he talked about himself and the swamp. He might have told me."

"He does enjoy a joke," Rey's aunt said with an indulgent smile.

"If he wanted to make me feel stupid, he certainly succeeded."

"No, no, it was all in fun. He likes to pretend sometimes, as he said to you earlier, that he has webs between his toes, likes to see how long people will believe it."

"Isn't that a little juvenile?"

"It may be, but so much of what he does is so serious that—but never mind. He was certainly raised on the river, the bayous, and canals. He grew up just down the road, he and Paul. They used to bring me something to cook every day, crawfish, an alligator tail, blackbirds, a mess of *sacque-au-lait*—that's the fish you know as white perch or crappie."

"They . . . must have been a pair," Julie said. She was not sure she wanted to hear about Paul, but it might be helpful to know more of the life of a man like Rey. For her movie, naturally.

"Oh, but they were. One summer, when they were maybe thirteen, fourteen, they found an old pirogue after a flood. They took it out on the Mississippi often to fish and to swim. Sometimes when they saw a rich man's yacht coming, they would overturn the pirogue—not a hard thing to do, as you discovered—pretending they had been swamped by the larger boat. They would swim beneath the pirogue and hide, breathing in the air pocket that is always trapped on the underside. The people in the yacht would stop and spend ages searching. The boys would then allow themselves to be found and rescued and made much over, sometimes even given money for their terrible ordeal. Ah, but then one day a friend of Rey's papa who was fishing on the river saw this trick. Ten minutes after Rey and Paul got home, their pirogue was a bonfire!"

Julie joined in Aunt Tine's quiet laughter before taking a sip of her wine. "You started to say, about his doing serious things . . . ?"

"Pay no attention to an old lady with a poor memory and a wandering tongue," Aunt Tine said, fluttering one hand in a careless gesture. "I was forgetting that Rey is no longer with the drug agency. How the years do get away."

To pursue the question could only embarrass Aunt Tine. Julie fell silent. Beyond the gallery, the air was sultry. A chicken or peahen clucked as it went to roost in the pen below the garden. Crickets and peeper frogs called in a monotonous yet peaceful dirge, with now and then the chirp of a tree frog, a sound that Julie had learned as a child to connect with rain. There was no sign of wet weather for the moment; still, she sat listening and watching as the night drew in.

After a while, she said, "What of Rey's parents? Do they still live nearby?"

"My brother and his wife were killed in a highway accident when Rey was away at college."

"Oh, I'm sorry," she said softly. "Did he have brothers and sisters?"

"He has a younger sister, married with three children, who lives in Atlanta. And there is a grandmother, his mother's mother, in New Orleans. That is all, except for me, now that Paul is gone. Rey and Paul were as near to being brothers as they could be without a blood tie between them."

"I hadn't realized they were quite so close."

"Ah, yes." Aunt Tine gave a slow nod. "They ran in the swamp together, had mumps and measles together, played football together; they shared everything. For a short time in high school, they were both in love with Donna, then that passed. Rey is taking Paul's death hard. I think he feels he should have seen what was coming sooner the other day, should have done something, somehow, to stop it."

"There was nothing anyone could have done." Julie's voice was flat as she spoke. At least that much of what Rey felt she could understand.

Aunt Tine sighed. "I know, but there it is."

They talked of other things, among them the closing of the investigation by the parish sheriff and also about the relief of finally having a verdict of accidental death. In the process, Julie learned that the sheriff was related to Aunt Tine. She was, by that time, unsurprised, since she had begun to realize the close-knit character of the community. She and the older woman did not linger long after the last of the wine was gone, however, but went inside to dinner.

The *étouffée* was wonderful, as good as any Julie had sampled in a New Orleans restaurant during her recent sojourn in the city. The tender fall snap beans and squash fresh from Aunt Tine's garden were perfect with it, as was the bread pudding served with a raisin-and-pineapple sauce. Julie, when Aunt Tine spurned her extravagant compliments, did her best to describe for the older woman the cardboard-and-plastic food from the catering unit that would have been her alternative if she had stayed at the location. Aunt Tine could not be brought to believe the difference. It was with great amicability that they cleared the table and dealt with the dishes together. When they were done, Aunt Tine offered to share her bedroom TV set, but Julie declined with thanks. Pleading the necessity for working out a new shooting schedule, she retreated to her room.

She could hear the low mutter of the television in the adjoining room beyond the connecting bathroom for an hour or so. By the time it ceased, she had mapped out a storyboard using Summer and Vance, carefully avoiding any further filming of the action scene on the river. She would get to that again later since it would have to be done, but she couldn't face it just now.

It was the lightning flashes beyond the curtains at the windows that distracted her. She got up and moved to open the French doors. The wind swept inside, cool and refreshing, carrying the smell of rain. That freshness made the air in the room seem stale and overrefrigerated, and she went to switch off the window unit.

Back at the French doors, she stepped outside as she heard the low rumble of thunder. The storm was no more than halfhearted; the lightning flickers were an intermittent pale glimmer high overhead that barely penetrated the night darkness, the thunder like a murmurous afterthought. The rain, when it came, pattered lightly across the yard beyond the gallery and scattered drops unevenly over the tin roof overhead.

Louisiana rain. It had always seemed to Julie that it was wetter than rain elsewhere, more pervasive, more natural. In California, moisture falling from a clouded sky seemed an affront to the endless progression of sunlit days. In other places, the islands and the mountains, it had a definite season and seldom fell otherwise. But in Louisiana, it was always a possibility, often a probability. The falling water was cursed and blessed, but seldom ignored, for it could too easily become a gully-washer or frog-strangler, as the country people described it; it could rise into a flash flood, or else blow up into a tornado or hurricane.

Beyond the gallery railing, the rain grew heavier, took on a steady, relentless sound. It clattered musically on the tin roof, good sleeping rain. Weariness crept over Julie, dragging at her shoulders. It was time to call it a night.

She emerged from the bathroom a short time later with a short robe of white silk wrapped around her and a hairbrush in her hand. She was holding her head to one side, brushing the tangles from the back of her hair, when she came to an abrupt halt.

She was not alone. The long form of a man was stretched out across the foot of her bed. Rey Tabary lay watching her with his head propped on his hand and a frown between his eyes.

"You left your door wide open," he said, "not a good policy."

"I was enjoying the coolness. Besides, I thought—"

"You thought you were out in the country where there was no danger from—intruders."

"Something like that." She lifted her chin as she continued brushing her hair.

"See how wrong you were?"

"I do get the picture," she said in clipped tones as she abandoned her pretense of unconcern. "Now, if you'll please leave, I'd like to go to bed."

He looked at her a long moment before he shook his head. "You left yourself wide open again, didn't you? Are you that careless, or do you really want to hear what I'll say?"

"I don't play games," she answered, trying to ignore the acceleration of her pulse. "I was telling you in plain English what I would like you to do."

"And is there nothing else you would like me to—no, forget I said that. You don't like games. I'll do my best to remember, since we're going to be working together."

It was done with such offhand ease that she might have missed it if it hadn't been for the expectant look in his coffee-brown eyes. She pushed her hairbrush into her deep robe pocket and shook back her hair. "Are we going to be working together?"

"We are," he said, "if we can clear up a detail or two." He raised himself upright with the ease of well-oiled muscles, sitting on the edge of the bed with one knee doubled under him and a long leg stretching to the floor.

"Such as?"

"To begin with, I want to do the stunts Paul was going to be doing, including the one he didn't finish."

She stared at the firm molding of his features, meeting his steady gaze, but he gave nothing away. "Why?"

"The money, of course."

"Somehow," she said slowly, "I don't think that's it."

"A whim, then? A salute? A reparation? To prove the job can be done by a Cajun. Take your pick."

A spasm of doubt and pain crossed her face, but she left the challenge alone. "Agreed, then, if you're sure. Is that all?"

"I want the final control for local customs and swamp lore that you offered when we talked before."

"I have no quarrel with that. And?"

"What makes you think there's more?" he asked, amusement rising into his eyes.

"Experience and intuition. Well?"

He hesitated an instant, then nodded. "I would like you to give Donna a job, just a small part, something to let her earn a few dollars and take her mind off the accident."

"I don't see how working on the location where her husband was killed is going to take her mind off it," Julie said frankly.

"I don't say she's thinking straight just now, but it's what she wants. Donna is a teacher, though she hasn't worked for several years. She intends to go back to it after midterm, when she has a promise of a position. Anyway, she thinks this will help, so I said I would ask."

Donna probably had visions of herself as an actress, Julie thought. She had seen it a thousand times, young women with some pretension to beauty who expected to change their lives by their brief contact with a movie company. It could be that, or else Donna Lislet wanted to join the company to be close to Rey, since that was where he would be spending his time. A moment later, as Julie caught the sardonic expression rising in his eyes, she was assailed by embarrassment for her cynicism.

She gave a brief nod. "We'll be shooting a few street scenes, maybe a store interior or two, in one of the towns nearby, Lutcher or Gramercy, in the next couple of weeks. We can use Donna as an extra for those, if she'll go see Ofelia and fill out a card for her and have a Polaroid shot made. Will that be all right?"

"I'm sure she'll be happy with it."

"Good," Julie said, lifting a hand in a casual gesture to make sure the top of her bathrobe was closed. "Then if that's all?"

He disregarded the hint as if she had not spoken. "Do I make you nervous?"

She gave him a level look, one he returned with patience and lambent curiosity. It seemed he really had stopped playing games. "To be honest," she said slowly, "I don't like being at a disadvantage. And I don't like people invading my territory without permission."

"Your territory."

"My room, my office, the area I move around in," she said, making an encompassing gesture with her hand.

"I seem to have heard of that phobia," he said laconically. "Are you sure you aren't disturbed because, in spite of being a liberated California type, you don't like it because I'm dressed and you are wearing nothing except a housecoat?"

She flushed, and that made her angry, for she had always prided herself on a lack of prudishness about her body. Since she was a teenager, she had walked the beach wearing bikinis too small to make a decent ladies' handkerchief and had slept in the altogether for years.

Nervousness over mere nudity, she would have said, was the last thing on her mind. And yet, he wasn't too far from wrong.

"My nakedness, if that's the phrase you're looking for, has nothing to do with it," she said. "You're a stranger here in my room in the middle of the night. What do you expect?"

"I think it's more to the point to ask what you expect."

"Nothing! Exactly—nothing."

"Good, because that's exactly what's going to take place here. I promise. So why not sit down and talk about the scenes you intend to put on film come Monday morning, tell me how I can help you with them?"

"Now?"

"What better time? There's nobody to interrupt, no technical problems needing your attention, no lights or cameras or crew, just the two of us and a lot of empty hours."

There was a rough timbre to his last words and darkness in the depths of his eyes. She wondered, suddenly, if he needed someone, some occupation to distract him from thoughts of Paul. Her sleepiness had fled, and it was now possible that she could also use some distraction. Lowering her lashes, she said abruptly, "All right, since you put it that way."

Walking to the head of the bed, she turned back the covers and piled the pillows against the headboard, then settled herself against them. There was a straight chair at the table where she had been working earlier that she could have drawn up and used, but she refused to give the man at the end of her bed the chance for some further insinuating comment.

The shadow of a smile flitted over Rey Tabary's mouth as he watched her, his gaze lingering on the soft dampness of her hair, the clarity of her skin without a trace of makeup. Still, he only made himself comfortable facing her, with his back resting against the post behind him.

It was difficult for Julie to focus on the business at hand, until she began to ask some of the questions that had been plaguing her. Once she got into them, once she began to concentrate on her story, she forgot everything else.

Rey was surprisingly quick at grasping the ideas behind a scene and at understanding her vision of it. His opinions were clear and definite, and he was prepared to give reasons and cite facts and figures to support them. There was nothing dogmatic about him, however; he accepted a certain amount of adjustment for the sake of economics or artistic value. The fact that his temper remained even impressed Julie. In her experience, there were few men who could negotiate at length with a woman without some fraying of their egos, especially on such nebulous matters as customs and habits.

Julie dragged out a copy of the script for him, flipping through it to show him bits and pieces that needed his attention. She also showed him the storyboard she was working on. He gave her several important tips, laying them out as if they were nothing.

"Look here at this scene where Jean-Pierre is stalking his wife's hired men through this section of swamp," he said, pointing to the scene in the script that would be coming up in another week or so. "He's supposed to be chasing after them in a footrace, using the cover to circle around them and head them off. It won't work."

"What do you mean, it won't work?"

Julie pushed away from the headboard, moving to lie across the mattress on her stomach to look at the lines he indicated. He leaned toward her to show her, flipping the bound pages around so they both could see them.

"The swamp is full of palmetto, the low-growing palms you've seen. They rattle when you move through them. Your Jean-Pierre will have to get down low, almost crawl. If he runs flat out the way this says, he'll sound like a herd of elephants crashing around. The noise will carry for miles."

She smiled. "Vance won't like the idea of crawling in the mud."

"Can't be helped. And this action scene where Jean-Pierre runs circles around the guys in the speedboat, then heads downriver and branches off up a bayou. He can't just run into a bayou like that and hope to get away with it unless he has a lot of time. The river isn't a highway. The foam from his boat's wake would leave a trail that could take fifteen, twenty minutes to break up. What he could do instead would be to run into some rivulet as a decoy, maybe one with a dead end that will confuse the other guys. He cuts his motor and paddles back out into the river again. Then he paddles along to the bayou he really wants, turns into it. After a few hundred feet, he could use his trolling motor—I think I saw one on the skiff—and there you are. No wake, no foam, a quiet getaway."

He was talking about the end to the scene Paul had been working on. "Yes, I see what you mean," Julie said, her voice stiff, "but it will be a while before we have to worry about that one."

"Why? It has to be done."

"I'd just—rather not think about it."

"That won't make it go away. You may as well do it and get it over with."

There was in his words an echo of all the male adventure films she had ever seen: Bite the bullet. Take the plunge. Get back on the horse after a fall. It was the kind of thing Bull Bullard, her father, was fond of saying.

Her tone cool, she said, "I'll decide when it gets done."

He turned his head to look at her as stiffness moved over his features. The words soft, he said, "Right—boss lady."

He was so close there on the mattress that his shoulder brushed hers. She could smell the faint spice of his after-shave lotion, see the dark, fathomless depths of his eyes and the way his lashes grew, crossing over each other, curving down to touch the crinkled skin under his eyes. She sensed the force inside him, was aware of the width of his shoulders under his T-shirt, the musculature of his thighs where his jeans were pulled taut over them.

Outside, the rain beat down, vibrating on the tin roof, catching silver glints as it fell past the windows. The air was heavy, moist with the rain's breath coming through the open doors. It seemed to wrap around them, enclosing them in unwanted intimacy. Somewhere deep inside Julie there was a slow, drawing ache that rose to cut off her breath.

"I—didn't mean to throw my weight around," she said, her lashes shielding her eyes as she eased away from him. "It's just been a long day and—I'm not comfortable talking about that scene. Could we leave it for now, call it a night?"

He watched her for a long moment before he straightened abruptly, getting to his feet. He picked up the script, rolling it in his hands as he turned toward the French doors. "It might be just as well," he said.

With the distance between them, Julie felt the strain recede. Concern that she may have been too harsh, too obviously affected by his nearness, assailed her. She moistened her lips. "I'd like you to know that I appreciate your decision to work with us on *Swamp Kingdom*. I feel sure it will be a better movie because of it, especially after tonight."

"We'll see, won't we?" he answered. "You had better come and lock the door behind me."

She slid off the bed, but made no move to walk closer to him. "I'll do that."

His regard was measuring, thoughtful. "Incidentally," he said, "there's a bucket out here on the gallery. Aunt Tine sent it, in case the roof starts leaking."

"That was thoughtful of her." So that was the reason he had come. Or was it? It was impossible to tell.

"I could show you where it should be set to catch the water."

She spoke hastily: "That's all right, I can manage."

The corner of his mouth tugged in the intimation of a smile. "I figured you might." He watched her a few seconds longer, then, with a slight shake of his head, stepped out the door and closed it quietly behind him.

"And a good-night to you, too," Julie muttered to herself, but she waited until his footsteps faded from hearing along the gallery before she moved from where she stood.

Chapter 5

Ofelia sauntered over to Julie's table in the boat club with a half-dozen doughnuts in one hand and a giant-size cup of coffee in the other. She dropped into a chair and spread out her breakfast. Tearing open three packages of artificial sweetener with a single rip, she poured them into her coffee. "So okay, tell me," she said, "what did you have to do to get Alligator Tabary to agree?"

"Alligator who?"

"The Galahad of the swamp, remember him? He can't be a Crocodile Dundee, as there are no crocs in this part of the world, but if you tell me the man doesn't wrestle alligators, you'll spoil my girlish dreams."

"Sorry."

"Ah, damn, I asked you not to tell me! But I want all the other juicy details."

"Sorry again," Julie said with the flash of a smile.

"Spoilsport."

"Actually, he decided all by himself; I had nothing to do with it."

"Sure, whatever you say. Anyway, he's made himself at home, I'll give him that."

Julie had left Aunt Tine's house for the location in the early dawn, being as quiet as she could so as not to wake the house. It had not occurred to her to notice if Rey's Cherokee was gone. She swallowed the bite of her bacon-and-egg biscuit she had just taken before she asked, "He's here already?"

"Been here for hours, looking things over, asking questions. Even as we speak, he's being invited to have gourmet coffee and an omelet in Madelyn's motor home, both whipped up with her own lily-pale hands. Will he accept? Stay tuned."

"Good grief."

"Exactly. But don't think Madelyn has gone all domestic for nothing. She has visions of herself retiring from her illustrious career and taking up the part of glamorous wife of a New Orleans aristocrat."

"So?"

"So what?" Ofelia said, downing a doughnut in two bites.

"So what has that to do with Rey Tabary?"

Ofelia widened her eyes in mock surprise. "You didn't know? How about that? Madelyn's private sources tell her that our swamp man is the playboy of N'awlins, no less. Very high-toned, old money, Pickwick Club and Krewe of Comus, apartment at One River Place, Maserati and private plane—the works."

"Oh, come on," Julie said with a wide smile as she waited for the punch line of Ofelia's joke.

The other woman washed down another doughnut with a gulp of coffee. "I wouldn't kid you. Madelyn swears it's the facts. And she's putting her wiles where her mouth is."

"It's ridiculous," Julie said with finality. "The man used to work with the DEA."

"He resigned a few years back, when his rich Creole grandmother had a heart attack and couldn't look after the family enterprises anymore."

Julie frowned. That part was just plausible enough to be true, just unreal enough to suit Rey's offbeat sense of humor. "Why isn't he looking after these enterprises himself instead of puttering around in the swamp—or on this location for that matter?"

"Who knows," Ofelia said, stuffing her last doughnut into her mouth and licking her fingers. "I guess you'll have to ask him."

"You ask. I have better things to worry about," Julie said firmly. "So long as he keeps this movie straight on swamp and Cajun lore, I don't care what else he does."

"Oh, right, me either," Ofelia said with droll sarcasm as she reached for her cigarettes and cheap plastic lighter.

Julie, ignoring the comment, pushed back her chair and strode away, back to work.

Julie really meant what she said. She had spent more than enough time thinking about Rey Tabary. She needed to concentrate on the job at hand, get the film back on track and in the can. Speculation about Rey's background would do nothing to further that cause.

Nevertheless, she saw no reason to let an opportunity pass to double-check Ofelia's story. As she passed Madelyn's motor home the actress was standing in the doorway, leaning on the frame. She was in elegant loungewear straight from the thirties, a pair of wide-legged white satin pajamas that draped with perfect fidelity over her voluptuous curves, with a white turban over her hair and vivid red makeup. Her expression was less than satisfied as she watched Rey down by the river. The new technical director was on the boat pier, where he appeared to be busy showing Vance and Summer the finer points of fishing. Apparently he had declined the gourmet breakfast.

"Ofelia is either a very silly woman or else a troublemaker," Madelyn said with a twist of her lips when Julie had repeated what her assistant had said. "Why would she go running to you with my news about our new man, unless, of course, she wanted to make you feel foolish? That's possible, I suppose. Dear Ofelia has always been jealous of you."

"Jealous? Ofelia?" Julie said with a lifted brow and a quick smile. "I can't think of anything less likely."

"Come on. You have everything she wants most, looks, brains, a waistline—not to mention Allen's backing as a director and a crack at the big time. Why shouldn't she be jealous?"

"She enjoys her job and her own kind of fun too much for that kind of yearning."

"Think what you like, but she still had to crow about Rey to you, didn't she?"

There was a bitter edge to much of what Madelyn had to say about most people, particularly women. After so many years of fighting for plum roles, fighting to stay close to the top, she seemed to view them as natural adversaries. Julie knew better than to accept what she said without making allowances.

Honing in on the other's woman last words, Julie said, "It's true about him, then?"

Madelyn smoothed a stray wisp of hair under her turban at the temple. "Naturally it's true, dear; I never make mistakes about men. I knew who he was the instant I saw him here; he was pointed out to me in New Orleans weeks ago. He was escorting his grande dame of a grandmother at the time, at a marvelous restaurant called the Versailles."

"You never mentioned it."

"How could I know you would be interested? After all, you have Allen."

The words were softly suggestive. Julie merely smiled. "It just seems curious, this double identity."

"Oh, I don't think you can call it that. He actually doesn't like to talk about himself. Can you imagine? I adore it after years of being around actors who think everyone is fascinated by the minute details of their lives. Don't you?"

"I'm not too sure," Julie said. "I don't much care for secrets."

Madelyn opened her mouth to answer, but the words were drowned by a scream. It was Summer, down by the water. The sound was shrill and loud, but had the ring of near-hysterical anger instead of pain. Julie turned in time to see the young girl throw her fishing rod down on the ground and begin to jump up and down, pulling at her hair with her hands.

Vance backed away with an imprecation and a shake of his head. Rey seemed stunned into immobility as he stood looking down at Summer. When he made no move, the girl screamed louder, then took a running step forward and began to stamp with both feet on the rod she had dropped.

Rey reached out in swift reaction, catching Summer by both shoulders and holding her immobile as he spoke in terse phrases. What he said could not be heard, but Summer stopped screaming abruptly.

She snatched her upper arms from Rey's grasp. Whirling, she ran toward the motor home that she shared with her mother.

Julie moved quickly to intercept the girl, catching her arm so that Summer was whirled to a halt. "What is it?" Julie asked in concern. "What's wrong?"

Summer glared up at her with her young face contorted with rage and the pain of injured pride. "He called me a child, a spoiled brat! I'm not a child and I'm not spoiled, and I'll show him. I don't care if I never learn how to fish. I don't care if I never do any old fishing scene. I won't do it! Not ever. So there!"

The girl twisted free and raced, arms and legs churning, toward her motor home, which sat beyond the one used by Madelyn. She shot inside and slammed the door. Julie shook her head, waiting with certainty for what would happen next. It was not a long wait.

Annette Davett emerged from the motor home with her bleached hair flying around her head like cotton fluff and her mouth set in a grim line. Marching up to Julie, she demanded, "What has that man done to my child? How dare he lay hands on her! I have never seen her so terrified in my life. I demand that he apologize or I will file a complaint with the police!"

"I don't think that will be necessary," Julie said in soothing tones. "I'm sure the whole thing was just a misunderstanding."

"A misunderstanding! It was child molestation, that's what it was!"

"Hardly that," Julie began in firm tones.

"Not at all," Rey said as he walked up behind her, "especially compared with my first impulse. Your daughter, Mrs. Davett, is a destructive menace. She just demolished a rod and reel worth several hundred dollars simply because she couldn't throw it right the first time or two she tried, and because I pointed out she was holding it wrong."

"My daughter is a highly strung artiste who lives on emotion," Annette said, drawing herself up with hauteur. "She isn't to be judged as other children. But no matter what she did, you had no right to touch her!"

"Touch her? She's lucky I didn't paddle her backside for her. The rod and reel she mangled belonged to me."

Annette Davett's gaze flickered. "Oh. You will, of course, be compensated, but it makes no difference. I insist that you apologize to Summer."

"I'll apologize to Summer when she apologizes to me, and not before. In the meantime, she can look like a fool when she plays her fishing scene, if that's the way she wants it. I have no time to waste teaching a girl too 'highly strung' to control her own temper."

Annette gave him a grim smile. "Summer says she isn't going to play that scene."

"It makes no difference to me."

"It does to me," Julie broke in, her voice firm. After hearing the whole story, she had lost any inclination she might have had to placate either Summer or her mother. "I believe, Annette, that I would look at your daughter's contract before supporting her in any statement she may have made in the heat of anger. The fishing scene will be done, one way or another. And it will be done today."

Summer's mother looked from Julie to Rey with her lips pursed. "We'll see about that," she began.

"Wait. Wait, Mother."

It was Summer, speaking from the door of the motor home. Annette Davett turned with angry amazement widening her eyes. The girl, her footsteps dragging, walked down the motor-home steps and came to where the three of them stood. She halted, looking up at Rey. "I didn't know the rod and reel were yours; I thought they were props," she said. "I'll buy you another set."

Rey's expression did not relent. "I prefer to buy my own."

"I want to do it. Really." The girl took a deep breath, her pale face slowly suffusing with color. "Then—then I want you to teach me to use it, just like you were doing."

"Is there any reason I should?" Rey asked.

"Can't you see she's trying to say she's sorry," Annette Davett said, clasping her hands together in an agony of sympathy.

"Is she?" Rey said quietly. "I didn't hear it."

A thousand emotions chased themselves across Summer's expressive face, from rebellion and pride to guilt and embarrassment. Finally, she cleared her throat and spoke. "I'm sorry. Honest."

A slow smile, amazing in its warmth and approval, creased Rey's face. "And I'm sorry if I hurt you."

"You didn't. I was just—mad."

"There's nothing wrong with being mad; it's what you do about it that counts."

"Will you teach me to fish? I—think the fishing scene will be good, but I don't want to look silly, or do it all wrong."

Rey gave a considering nod, his gaze serious as he met that of the younger girl. "I can salvage the reel, but the rod is shot. What do you say we go pick up another one at my aunt's house—a cheap one?"

"Now?" Summer asked, a smile dawning on her face. She reached to grab his hand. "Let's go!"

Rey didn't move. "I think you forgot something."

"What?" Summer's smile turned to an instant scowl.

"I didn't hear you ask your mother if you could go off with a child molester."

The girl looked over her shoulder at Annette. "We'll be back in a little while, Mother."

Rey still didn't stir, nor did he speak. Summer tugged at him, her frown deepening. She said, "I told her. What more do you want?"

"Permission."

The girl swung his hand in both of hers. "You're an irritating man."

"Too bad."

"Oh, all right then! Mother, may I go?"

Annette Davett appeared more annoyed than pleased by her daughter's show of compliance. Her voice snappish, she said, "See that you aren't gone long."

Rey turned to look at Julie. "I should have asked you if this is going to interfere with your shooting schedule."

"We'll shoot around Summer, if it really won't be long before she's ready."

He nodded and led the girl away. Annette Davett swung around and walked with stiff steps back to her motor home. The door slammed behind her.

"My, my," Madelyn said as she strolled down the steps of her motor home to join Julie.

"Right," Julie said in dry agreement.

"What do you think got into our Summer, as if I couldn't guess."

"Just adolescence, I suppose."

"Poor little thing. It appears she's fast developing a crush on our technical director. Smitten by the first strong man to cross her path. How sad."

Julie could not quite bring herself to agree, though she frowned after the pair. "Annette is right in a way: Summer is high-strung. It can't be good for her to form too close an attachment to someone who may not be here next week, even if she does need a father."

"Oh, I doubt she'll come to any harm. Anyway, so long as she cooperates, the reasons aren't important." When Julie did not answer, the actress went on. "The Cajun is quite something. Summer can hardly be blamed for succumbing."

"Really, Madelyn," Julie protested.

"Oh, come on. Don't tell me you don't find that masterful air compelling?"

"I'm not twelve," Julie said. "I prefer a little more subtlety."

"I'm sure Tabary can oblige."

"That may be. However, as you pointed out, I have Allen."

"A subtle man if there ever was one." Madelyn's smile held an edge of derision.

"Exactly so," Julie answered, her voice even. Turning, she walked away.

Julie wasn't too surprised to hear from Allen later in the morning. In the first place, he had a knack for sensing when he was on her mind, and in the second, she had been waiting for him to get in touch with her ever since Paul Lislet's death. She had spoken to his secretary, leaving a series of urgent messages. The woman had been apologetic, but could only tell her that Allen had flown to Europe on business. His itinerary had been uncertain when he left, and the woman had no idea when he would return.

Julie might have been annoyed, except that she realized she had been so wrapped up in *Swamp Kingdom* that she had not asked what Allen's plans were for the final weeks of shooting. She had assumed he would be in L.A. making postproduction arrangements.

He had been in Paris and Switzerland instead, it seemed, returning only the evening before. The purpose of the trip had been a series of delicate negotiations putting together a picture with a budget reaching toward fifty million, one that would be financed by a group made up mostly of Arab and South American businessmen. Though Allen was too diplomatic to say so over the phone, Julie knew the picture was not one that she would be directing. She resented his failure to mention it to her, however, and showed it by glossing over his explanation and turning the conversation to her problems.

"Poor darling," Allen said, his voice coming quiet and caring over the line. "The roof did rather fall in on you, didn't it? I'll fly down there at once."

Julie could almost see Allen ensconced in his office, probably leaning back in his black leather chair with his Top-Siders propped on his desk and a tray of Earl Grey tea, brioches, and fruit at his elbow. Relaxed, urbane, slender, with fine brown hair, eyes the color of a winter sky, and a trace of northeastern prep school in his voice, he was the perfect amalgamation of California and Massachusetts.

She smiled. "There's no need for you to come, especially while you're involved in this other deal. Really, I think everything is under control. The only thing is this claim representative. I could do without his harassment."

"The insurance company does have a legitimate interest."

"I realize that," Julie answered, infusing her voice with quiet reason, "but this guy didn't have to be so obnoxious about it."

"I'll have a talk with him. How about that?"

"Thank you."

"How are you keeping yourself?" he went on, his voice dropping a note. "Do you miss me?"

"Of course, now and then when I have time to think about it. I've moved into the hinterland, you know."

"I heard about that, and about your new technical director. Tell me about him."

"You heard? From whom?"

"I don't remember exactly. I think something was in one of the ten thousand messages on my desk when I got back. So how is the guy working out?"

Julie explained about Rey in some detail, though without mentioning Madelyn's more recent revelations. They had no real bearing on his usefulness to the picture and could be of no particular interest to Allen.

"It sounds as if you're getting your money's worth if Tabary is going to do the stunts, too."

"I hadn't thought of it that way, but I suppose so."

"Yes, well, you do need to watch these things. Your bonding-company man was right about the budget; we're cutting it pretty fine. Tell you what. I'll be winding up this new deal in a few days. I'll fly down then and look things over. Maybe we can find a few hours here and there to spend together; it seems forever since we had time to just talk."

"I'll look forward to it," Julie said.

They spoke for a few minutes more before hanging up. Julie sat for long moments afterward with her hand still on the receiver in its cradle. It would be nice to see Allen, to have him on the set to back her up and take an interest in what she was doing. At the same time, she was disturbed by a vague feeling that he might be coming to check up on her. He had always expressed support for her talent, maintaining that it was inherited straight from Bull, a director he admired beyond most. He had never interfered in any of the films she had done under his auspices, with the possible exception of an aesthetic suggestion here and there and an incisive critique of the final editing. Still, this time it was different. The budget for *Swamp Kingdom* wasn't fifty million, but it was still generous by most standards. That kind of money made a difference. That kind of money made people nervous, even Allen.

There was also this new project of Allen's to be considered. If he was in the midst of putting together a deal of such magnitude, then he wouldn't want any hint of money problems with his current production to start floating around. That possibility alone might be cause enough for him to decide to take a closer look at what she was doing.

Julie didn't like having to think that way. She and Allen had been together so long, nearly seven years. They were comfortable with each other, living together when their jobs permitted with ease and affection. He was her mentor, her confidant, the man who had taught her to trust herself and her talent. He had never tried to stop her from doing anything she wanted to do. If there was no great passion in their reunions after absences, there were also no recriminations over the time spent apart. He had helped form her tastes in art and music, food and wine without seeking to impose his own. He had provided a sense of security for her, of gentle acceptance, and of family. She had been his protégée and his pride.

Allen had changed, though, since she had started this movie. Julie wasn't sure why, whether it really had to do with the amount of money at stake or was perhaps the result of the increase in her own ambition. He had become more distant, more concerned yet less involved with what she was doing. He had visited once or twice while they were shooting in New Orleans, but returned to L.A. after only a day or two. He had listened to her ideas and encouraged her in a vague manner, but asked few questions. She had thought maybe his lack of interest in discussing it meant that he felt she had reached a point where she needed no help. Now she was not so sure.

Filming for the day went off without incident and with a minimum of mistakes. The fishing scene, a prickly tender incident between Jean-Pierre and his daughter as they grow to know each other and Alicia begins to appreciate the freedom of the swamp, turned out to be one of the best shoots they had done. Rey contributed much to it with his guidance on fishing technique and bits about the swamp that were incorporated into the dialogue. Julie, watching Vance as the cameras rolled, thought that the actor had also taken on a shading of Rey's accent and way of moving, and even his firm yet responsive manner toward Summer. Julie was satisfied, even more than satisfied.

The storyboard for the next shoot was the long chase scene on foot through the swamp with Jean-Pierre and the two men sent by his wife exchanging the roles of the hunter and the hunted back and forth. Julie had blocked out a possible two days for it. Afterward they would try the scene where the wife, Dorothea, played by Madelyn, tracks her husband down and threatens him with a gun, then is tricked into a long trek through the swamp to his fishing camp that leaves her dirty, disheveled, and much chastened. Julie had in mind, also, a few more scenes with Summer and Jean-Pierre in the swamp, developing their relationship and showing the girl's wonder and growing appreciation of her father's world. That would take them to the coming weekend, if not beyond.

On the following Monday, they would pick up with a number of scenes inside the fishing camp—a cabin Ofelia had already scouted out for their use—especially one where Madelyn as Dorothea makes an effort to entice Jean-Pierre back to New Orleans and comes close to succumbing herself to the lure of old love and the swamp in the moonlight. That last scene would be pivotal, as both characters acknowledged the desire that had brought them together in the first place but are forced to face their insurmountable differences. Altogether, Julie thought, she was looking at two more weeks of shooting on those scenes. The action sequences were all that would be left then, those Rey was supposed to do as stuntman in place of his friend Paul. One was of particular importance since it involved Summer and an explosion that marked the climax of the story. Two days, possibly three, should suffice there, then Julie would move her cameras and crew out of the swamp and into the small town chosen by Ofelia for street and store interior scenes. Those would not take long at all, unless Julie came up with something else. She would really like to show, somehow, a little more of the flavor of the Cajun way of life.

She was concentrating on laying out the days of shooting late that evening when a tap came on her office door. Rey put his head inside.

"Ready?" he asked. "Aunt Tine will have dinner cooked."

"In a moment. You go on ahead." She barely glanced up before returning her frowning attention to the storyboard.

"Got a problem?"

"Nothing special."

"Technical?"

"Not exactly," she answered, then looked up as she realized he might be offering his help. "Well, maybe."

He came forward, moving to sit on the corner of her desk. "Yes?"

"There was supposed to be a moonlight swim in the river, a sort of dreamy sequence between Jean-Pierre and Dorothea—Vance and Madelyn—showing the strength of their past attraction and the under-lying sexual tension that still drives them in their feud over their daughter. As it evolves, the attraction breaks down, showing the futility of any hope that they might get back together. I intended it to have this earthy romanticism to it, misty yet sexy. That was before I had my own midnight dunking. Now I don't know what to do as a substitute that will give the same feeling."

He lifted a brow. "I don't see what's wrong with the original idea."

"Come on," she said with a laugh. "That water is cold, and what about the leeches?"

"It isn't that cold if you're swimming. As for the leeches, I didn't find any, did I?"

"No, but you could have." A suspicion struck her as she added ominously, "Couldn't you?"

"There was a slight chance," he told her, his grin unrepentant.

She dropped her head into her cupped hands. "I don't believe it. Had again."

"Not exactly," he said in pensive tones, then added hastily as her head came up. "There are just more leeches in the summer, when the water's warmer."

"I'm sure," was Julie's dour comment as she relaxed again. "Any-way, it's too dark out there in the water, and it's too full of logs and cypress knees and bits of floating junk, and that's without the snakes and alligators. Forget it. I'll have to think of some other scene."

"I thought that's what scriptwriters were for."

"I'm the writer in this case. So far, nothing fits."

Rey got to his feet, leaning over her. "Beating your brains out isn't going to help. Come on and eat. Who knows, you may have a brainstorm over the jambalaya."

She didn't, but then she didn't expect to. Rey's arrival had sent her concentration to the four winds. She found herself trying to picture him as a man about town, squiring his aristocratic grandmother. It wasn't easy. The problem was not his manners or even his casual dress, rather it was the natural way he fitted into the swamp, his rough vehicle, the rural countryside, the faintly run-down look of his aunt's house. He was at home. There was no pretense about it, he belonged. How was it possible, then, that he could also belong elsewhere, with the Pickwick Club and at One River Place, for instance?

She had told herself it made no difference, and it didn't, not really. Yet she could not seem to stop making comparisons in her head, could not help wondering.

Aunt Tine had made a pot of soup rich with meat stock and garden-fresh vegetables. She was not there, however, but had left a note saying she was going to a bingo game in LaPlace. Julie and Rey ate and cleaned up after themselves, all the while arguing back and forth about the swimming scene.

Finally, Rey said, "All right, get your bathing suit and come on."

"You mean—no thanks! I've already had the privilege of paddling around in Blind River, and I don't think I want to repeat it."

"It isn't the same. Besides, where's your dedication to your job? What happened to your urge for authenticity? What became of your need to be true to the story you're putting on film?"

"Jettisoned," she said with finality, "for safety and sanity."

"Coward. Well enough, so you won't go swimming. At least come out in the boat with me, let me show you this place I know that would be great for what you have in mind."

She was going to regret it; there was not a doubt of that in her mind. Still, she went. The place he wanted to show her must be special to make him so insistent. Besides, he had proven himself so resourceful thus far that she was afraid she might miss something special for her movie if she refused.

It was special. It was off the river and down a bayou that looked barely wide enough to take the air boat Rey had launched for their use. The narrow run snaked for what seemed like miles, then slowly widened into a cul-de-sac, a complete circular dead end. The secluded pool was ringed with black and towering cypresses, feather-edged with cut grass and rafts of lily pads showing ghostly white blossoms. It steamed in the moonlight, with a gentle mist glowing across its still, dark surface, giving it the luminescence of a moonstone. It was a watery Eden, one so private and insubstantial that it seemed it might well vanish with the dawn.

Rey cut the engine and they drifted with their own momentum to the pool's center. Julie, staring around her, was silent. She could smell the perfume of the water lilies, sweet and haunting with a hint of musk. Night insects sang a soft obbligato. The streamers of moss on the trees swayed as if to unheard music, their coating of mist gleaming silver as it caught the moon's pale light.

She didn't hear Rey leave the boat. One moment he was there, the next he had slipped over the side, leaving his clothing in a heap on the seat. He surfaced long yards in front of her, his head breaking the top of the water with hardly a sound, the moonshine catching in his hair, glittering in the droplet he flung from it in a spray with an eerie blue sheen. He surged through the water with powerful reaches of his arms, his wet shoulders cleaving the surface, leaving dancing bubbles of foam like champagne in his wake.

He was a creature of the night and the swamp, splendid, untamed, in his element. The mist made a nimbus around him, shimmering over his long length, now concealing, now revealing him. The luster of the brightening moon touched the shape of his head, the turn of an arm, the curve of a thigh, painting them with silver. It rippled over the place where he dived, making iridescent swirls in the water.

He was gone. Julie swung this way and that in her seat, waiting for him to surface again. She thought of alligators that clamped down on their prey and held them underwater to drown. She suspected a hoax that would be followed by an attempt to tip her into the river, and scanned the top of the water nearest the air boat. There was nothing.

She called out, but there was no answer. Caught between fear and irritation, exasperation and a species of panic, she could think of only one thing to do. Skimming out of the skirt and shirt she had worn to work that day, kicking off her espadrilles, she dived into the water.

She surfaced into Rey's arms. Swirling around to face him, she glared at him in anger.

"Are you cold?" he asked, his voice quiet, persuasive.

"Not in the least," she snapped.

"Have you seen a snake, or an alligator?"

"Only a snake of the human species."

"Well, then," he said, and pulled away, gliding backward in unmistakable invitation.

What did she have to lose? Joining Rey in his water play, she matched him stroke for stroke, rolling, diving, cavorting with him in the moonlight. They were well paired, both able swimmers, both used to watery diversions. A rapport seemed to build between them, so they formed figures of strength and grace, rolling together, turning, reversing as if on cue. And they both surfaced near the air boat at the same time, and reached for it, clinging, while their bodies slowly drifted to entwine, and their breathing, coming fast and hard from effort, deepened still further.

Julie met his dark gaze, holding it, unable to look away, though she knew it was folly. Her skin felt heated from exertion and something more that came from inside. Her heart beat with heavy thuds in her chest. There was an intolerable tightness in her throat and her arms and legs felt weighted, unresponsive. His touch, gently gliding to hold her, was warm, without constraint. The look on his face was suspended, with an edge of pain. His lowered his gaze to her parted lips, then slowly bent his head to touch his mouth to hers.

She could have stopped him with a word, a gesture, a single movement. She did not. His kiss seemed inevitable, necessary. She wanted it, could not have borne, at that moment, to be denied it.

It was the night and the water and the isolation, along with some primitive, mindless bonding caused by the moon. It was curiosity and chemistry and the residue of fear and anger. It was a discovered affinity of mind and body. It was purest aching need.

His mouth was warm and sweet, melding to hers in a tender onslaught that made the sensitive surfaces of her lips tingle. His tongue soothed them, incited them, found their moist corners, then gently invaded. She met it with her own, testing the grainy smoothness, accepting, inviting. They eased closer in delicate mutual exploration, while inside Julie there was rising wonder and the first soft ringing notes of dread.

They drew back as slowly as they had come together, and as carefully. Face-to-face in the water, their arms entwined, their legs gently gliding, riding together, they looked at each other. And they waited to see who would make the next move.

Chapter 6

"Am I encroaching on your territory?" Rey asked, the words soft, his breath brushing her cheek.

"Yes." Her answer was just as quiet as she lowered her gaze to the firm formation of his collarbone and the hollow of his throat that was shadowed with dark, curling hair. "Is it deliberate?"

"You might say so. What are you going to do about it?"

"Pretend."

"Pretend?"

"That you're keeping me warm."

He tilted his head there in the moon's glow. "I like that idea. Suppose we pretend, too, that there's no such person as Allen."

"But there is," she said. She met his gaze, her own troubled, and even regretful, though she did not know it.

"Where does that leave us?"

Her chest rose and fell in a sigh that made the lace of the scrap of a bra she wore glimmer just under the water. "With a midnight swim scene to plan?"

It was a long moment before he spoke. "You agree that I was right about it?"

"Your argument is very—effective."

"But not quite effective enough." The curve of his mouth was wry. His hand at her waist tightened in a last caress, then he disengaged himself from her with slow care. Reaching higher on the frame of the air boat, he vaulted up and over the side, then turned to pull Julie on board. He handed her a towel from behind the seats and, while she dried herself, skimmed into his clothing. He also produced a stadium blanket in red and blue plaid, which he draped across her lap. She glanced at him with irony for his obvious preparedness. He returned it with an unabashed grin before he started the air boat and sent it flying back the way they had come.

They reached the house before Julie's hair had time to dry completely. Neither had spoken on the swift journey, nor did they speak as they entered the house. Rey held the back door for her, then followed her as she turned right into the kitchen. Julie filled Aunt Tine's brass kettle with water while Rey took down the coffee and began to spoon it into the drip pot. It was only as Julie got down the cups and turned to find Rey setting out the cream and sugar that the strangeness of their cooperation, their certainty of what both intended, struck her.

It was a small thing, yet added to the events of the night, it was troubling.

The smell of coffee was heavy in the room, and so was the silence. The soft popping of the gas under the heating kettle seemed loud. When the voice sounded, crackling with static, Julie flinched and looked toward the radio that sat on top of the refrigerator.

"That's Aunt Tine's private vice," Rey said. "A police scanner. They change the frequency now and then to foil the crooks and old ladies with a nose for sensationalism, but her third cousin keeps her up-to-date."

"The sheriff."

"You've got it."

"I'm shocked," Julie said. "First gambling at bingo, and now police-car chasing."

"Aunt Tine says it keeps her off the streets. I've never quite dared ask in what sense."

"I wouldn't, if I were you." The brief moment of banter had eased the tension between them. Julie wondered if that had been it's purpose. She said, "If we're really going to map out the swimming scene, we'll need something to work with. I'll get a pad and pen."

"Everything we need is here." Rey opened a drawer, taking out writing materials. He laid them out on the kitchen table, a worktable covered with a plastic cloth scarred with much use and with a pair of plain wooden chairs set at each end.

Julie picked up the cups she had taken from the cabinet, turning toward the table also. In an effort to keep some kind of conversation going, she said, "At least I won't have to tell Madelyn that her favorite part had been cut. She'd have pitched a fit if she thought she wasn't going to get to do her nude scene."

"I saw that in the script," Rey said as he moved to pour the coffee water, then put the dripping pot on the table. "Will she really do it?"

"She can't wait. It's the fashion these days. You are nothing as an actress if you haven't shown your boobs, or as an actor if your buns haven't flashed across the screen. Only Vance isn't happy with the idea. He doesn't want to show his. Actually, I don't see the purpose myself—I mean one set of either is like any other, isn't it? But it seems natural enough for the swimming scene. Frontal nudity below the waist is out, though. I draw the line there."

"Why?" he asked as he pulled out a chair for her.

She looked at him before she sat down. He was not being facetious, she thought, nor was he, like many men, attempting to disconcert her by sexual innuendo or prolonging the discussion of a subject with lascivious undertones. It seemed he was interested in her motives as a director.

"First, because it would call for an X rating, and the top movie houses don't show X-rated movies. But also because it detracts from the story and the mood of the scene, and adds nothing to the character the actor or actress may be playing."

He leaned back in the chair he had taken across from her, resting his wrist on the table edge. "And the appeal to so-called prurient interest?"

"A group of words which mean, basically, that the sight of naked bodies on the screen produce the desire in the audience to make it with the actor or actress—or their available partners—instead of paying attention to the movie. To me that means detracting from the story."

He laughed, a low sound rich with humor and a shading of appreciation, as he shook his head.

"What?" She glanced at him from under her lashes as she picked up the coffeepot to see if it had finished dripping. It hadn't. She set it back down.

"I don't understand why your producer friend never married you. He must be blind and deaf, and a first-class idiot on top of it."

She touched the tip of her forefinger to the wet ring left where the coffeepot had been sitting, stirring it a little. "Oh, we've talked about it, off and on. Somehow our schedules never quite meshed. When I was interested, he thought I was too young, didn't know my own mind, or should wait until I had had a chance to establish myself in a career. When he was ready, I was usually packing to go off on location somewhere."

"Sounds like a lukewarm arrangement."

She frowned. "Allen is almost fourteen years older than I am and a wise man who doesn't rush into things, or try to rush me. He taught me most of what I know about the business side of films, as opposed to the creative end, which I learned from watching my father. He introduced me to people, gave me stability, taught me to value myself as a person, as someone else beside Bull Bullard's daughter."

"Lukewarm."

"I suppose it may look that way to someone on the outside, but Allen has always been more than some shrink's idea of a father figure, if that's what you're getting at. He understands me, and he allows me to be me."

"He doesn't invade your territory," Rey said, his gaze steady on her face.

"Only on invitation," she said shortly, then counterattacked. "But what about you? How is it you haven't married?"

"I did. She died, along with our child. She went into early labor one night, at just under seven months. I should have been there, but I wasn't."

It seemed that an expression of sympathy was in order, but the closed-in expression on his face did not encourage it. She picked up the coffeepot that had completed dripping. As she poured out the rich brew she asked, "Where were you?"

"I had been with the DEA a couple of years and was a fanatic about it; I was going to save the world. I took assignments I should have let pass. Afterward, I could take as many as came my way, but they didn't seem as important anymore."

He stopped speaking suddenly, as if he had said more than he intended.

"I used to enjoy making movies more than I do now," Julie said, as much for something to fill the silence as for anything else. "I felt I was creating dreamworlds, superior fantasies that would make every-day life easier for people to bear and show them something about themselves at the same time. I'm not that arrogant any longer. I just try to tell stories and hope they turn out to have something of value in them."

The tense lines beside his eyes had eased as he listened to her. Now he said, "Would you like to quit?"

"I don't think so, at least I don't most of the time. There are days when it crosses my mind, days when the actors are more interested in playing petty tricks on each other than in understanding what I'm trying to say, days when everything goes wrong. But there are also days when some scene that's just a vision in my mind comes out on the screen with more beauty and rightness than I ever dreamed. Then I can't imagine doing anything else."

"What does your dad think about you following in his footsteps?"

"Proud, I suppose, with a hint of disbelief. He always tells every-body about my movies and twists their arms to make them go see them. But he didn't want me making this one, afraid I had bitten off more than I could chew."

"And have you?" The words were quiet, but had as much challenge as curiosity in them.

She made a brief gesture of futility. "Who knows? All I can do is work at it. Speaking of which, there is this swimming scene—"

The level of coffee in the pot dropped as they talked it over, throwing out ideas, sketching images and camera angles, questioning motivation and therefore attitudes. Julie jotted down every idea either of them produced, though she scratched out half of them as overdone or unworkable.

"The way I see it from the script," Rey said at one point, "Jean-

Pierre has a hard time at first believing that his life is in danger. He embarks on this chase through the swamp and up and down waterways as a fun caper, almost a game to bamboozle the city dudes who come into his part of the world without knowing what's facing them. It seems to me that the swimming scene adds to this. It shows something of the closeness, the sexual attraction based on tenderness that was between him and his wife in the beginning and which makes it so hard for him to realize she would actually try to kill him."

"You have a point. I had been thinking of it as a metaphor for the pain of the recognition that the love between them is finally gone. It can still be that, but what you are saying adds another dimension. For what I wanted, the cameras could stop rolling after, say, a few kisses and heavy breathing with the removal of a piece or two of clothing. But maybe it needs to go further."

"I thought you meant to show a full love scene all the time, something with body positions and exertion."

She shrugged. "A love scene can mean anything from a single glance with violins to the point where bodies get tangled up under the sheets and the camera pans to crashing waves and thrashing palm trees."

"I think you should go for tangled bodies," he said with laughter threading his voice, "though making love in water over your head isn't easy."

"No?" she asked with a lifted brow, ignoring the slow rise of heat under her skin.

"No. You'd better pan to something pretty quick."

She narrowed her eyes, propping her chin in the palm of her hand. "I keep thinking about the water lilies floating on the pool out there. Aren't they supposed to be symbols of fertility?"

"You may be thinking of lotus blossoms. Buddha was born in one, or something like that."

"They would still be beautiful in the moonlight, dipping and swaying, moving back and forth."

"An inspiration," he said, his voice catching a little in his throat.

She met his gaze and the brightness that shone deep in his dark eyes. She protested, "This is serious!"

"I know," he said as he rose to his feet and began to gather up the coffee things. "I wish I had thought of it."

"Yes, well. Speaking of scenes shot for beauty and serious purpose, I've been noticing the sunsets on the river. They are so vivid, have so much color in them."

"The direct result of the air pollution hanging in the atmosphere from the chemical plants along the river," he said.

"That may be, but I think I'd like to get some footage of them, maybe show old Joseph poling his pirogue at sundown for the title credits. The mood would be peaceful, nostalgic even, then Jean-Pierre could flash past Joseph in his skiff at breakneck speed, heading for New Orleans to bring back his daughter. Do you think old Joseph will go for it?"

"I don't know why not," Rey said over his shoulder as he turned on the water to rinse the coffee cups. "Probably set him up for weeks, the idea of being an actor. Though there's no telling what he might charge for the use of his pirogue if he finds out how much it means to you."

"I'll keep that in mind when I talk to him," she said dryly.

Julie tore off the pages of notes she had made and tucked them in the pocket of her skirt. She moved then to help Rey put away the things they had used. When the cabinets were clear, she did not linger, but said good night and made her way to her room.

She wasn't sleepy; she was used to drinking countless cups of coffee during any given day, but not as strong as Rey's and not at such a late hour. She sat going over the notes for the swimming scene, mapping it out a little more exactly. Satisfied there was nothing more to be added, she finally put them away. She thought of reading awhile, but her first and most pressing need was a shower. She had forgotten what she must look like with her hair dried close to her head, parting as it pleased. She refused to look in the mirror as she removed her shirt and skirt and underclothes and padded into the bathroom to start the water running.

The claw-foot tub was fitted with a shower head and an attached rectangular frame to hold the lightweight nylon curtain. It was a little like taking a shower in a tent. The soap Aunt Tine had provided was scented with English lavender and its lather was rich and thick and aromatic. It made an excellent shampoo that Julie worked through her hair with slow pleasure, then rinsed it with the water beating down over her head and face, chasing the gliding suds down the hollows and curves of her body, carrying with it river water and memories.

It was a moment before she heard the knock, and then she wasn't sure she had not imagined it. She turned off the water. Wiping at her eyes, reaching through the curtain for a towel, she called out, "Who is it?"

"The leech inspector," came the answer from the other side of the bathroom door.

Rey. His voice was threaded with humor and something more that sent a tremor along her spine. She grabbed the towel, drying her face as she held it in front of her. Wrapping it about her, she stepped out of the tub. "How did you get in my room? I know I locked the door this time!"

"There are advantages to living in the same house, especially an old house. All the locks, and keys, are the same."

"Wonderful." There was an breathless quality to her voice that she controlled only with an effort. "Thanks all the same, but I don't have any leeches."

The bathroom door swung open on slowly creaking hinges. Rey stood leaning with his forearm braced on the frame. Pushing away from it, he said, "Are you sure? They sometimes require a close search."

He wore only a pair of jeans and his hair was jet black from his shower, curling forward with the dampness to brush his forehead. He was tall and broad there in that small room, but his movements were easy and smooth, with no attempt at confinement, no threat in them. His gaze, dark and promising yet shadowed by doubt, held hers.

He reached to touch his hands to hers where they were clenched on the towel she held, curling his fingers around them, brushing the backs with his thumbs. The night-fresh smell of him, cleanly masculine and wholesome, crept in upon her senses. She felt in her veins the first sweet numbing rush of desire and the rise of exacting curiosity. Accepting these things, she flushed delicately rose red.

She wanted him and disdained to pretend otherwise. She wanted to know his strength and humor and caring, and also the part of him that was different, foreign. She wanted to be held, to be loved, to be caught in the surge of his passion. She wanted to forget, to allow herself to be carried away; she wanted to feel until feeling became too much to bear and she could lose herself in her own flowing joy. She wanted him.

Releasing her grasp on the towel, she let it fall. She touched his chest, spreading her fingers, trailing the tips through the soft mat of hair that grew there, pressing her palms to the heat and thudding life of him. Then she lifted her mouth to his.

"Is this an invitation?" he whispered, his breath warm and sweet against her lips.

"Yes, please," she answered, and let her lashes drift down, closing out the brightness of the light, taking it inside.

He bent to put an arm behind her knees and another at her back, swinging her up against him. He strode with her into the bedroom, where he placed her on the mattress of the four-poster bed. Removing his jeans, he joined her there. She drew him to her, pressing against his long length, taking pleasure in the hard resilience of his body against her softness.

The curves of his lips were firm, the inner surfaces of his mouth like warm silk. His caresses were sure and unerring. He sought the warm hollows of her delight, and allowed her free exploration. Tending the flame of each other's need, they stretched enchantment past enduring and, when the time came, surrendered to surcease with grace and a murmuring sigh.

The tumult of their joining was no surprise, but rather a glad shock. It caught them in a frenzy of panting effort, taking them deep, sounding their minds, scouring their souls. It was a revelation, unending, without recourse. And when it passed, they lay listening in dazed wonder to each other's heartbeats.

Rey stirred, brushing Julie's hair from her face, reaching to draw the sheet up over them. Propped on one elbow, he whispered in her ear, "Why is it, do you suppose, that I keep thinking of water lilies?"

"Who knows?" she answered without opening her eyes. Smiling, she slept in his arms.

He was gone when she awoke. His devotion to duty was more than a little excessive, she thought as she stretched with her arms above her head, pushing against the headboard while she flexed her muscles in mellow well-being.

She rolled on her side, reaching out to smooth her hand across the other pillow that was indented with the shape of his head. Slowly, her smile faded. Why had he left so early, creeping away without a word, as if from some one-night stand?

She had betrayed Allen. She had gone to bed with another man without a qualm or thought for the consequences. She had never done that before. How had it happened? How had she come to do that to Allen? She was amazed at herself. She had gone to bed with a man of the swamps, one who had another image entirely when he was in New Orleans. Who was he, what was he? The answer had not seemed important until this moment. Now it was urgent.

She turned to gaze at the ceiling, the walls, the windows, as if for clues.

Her thoughts, her misgivings, scattered. It wasn't just daylight outside. The sun was shining brightly.

She leaped from the bed, scrambled for underwear, snatched jeans and a cotton sweater from the armoire, and headed for the bathroom. Today they were supposed to be shooting the scene where Vance's Cajun character, Jean-Pierre, played hide-and-seek with his wife's hired killers on foot in the swamp. Everybody would be standing around, kicking their heels at full pay and wondering where she was and when they were going to get started.

The shoot was well under way when Julie arrived, though no camera was in gear. Ofelia and Stan had organized most of it from the detailed storyboard Julie had prepared the day before. They were using the swampland just behind the boat club, so equipment and comfort logistics were not a problem. The special effects, the small explosions keyed to the shots fired from automatic weapons by the hired goons, had been put in place the day before and were in the process of being charged. Rey had already walked through the scene with Vance, giving him pointers on how to avoid being slashed to pieces by the cut grass, how to move to make the least noise, particularly through the rattling palmetto, how to watch for swamp rattlers and even smell them, and a dozen other small things. In addition, he had cued the actors playing the goons to do the exact opposite of Vance, so that the contrast would make Vance's Jean-Pierre appear a master of the swamp.

The alligators arrived at the same time Julie did. Old and huge, sluggish from the early-morning cool and from gorging the night before on several pounds of raw chicken each, they lay in their cages viewing all and sundry with jaundiced eyes. They were supposed to add color, and also block the path of the killers at the crucial point, a trap set by Jean-Pierre.

Stan took charge of them, pointing out where they were to be placed. "Chain them down good," he called after the slouching, bearded alligator keeper and his two black helpers. "We don't want them running around loose, screwing up the shooting."

"These beasties ain't running nowhere," their keeper drawled over his shoulder. "They wouldn't run if you beat 'em with a stick!"

The cameras were set up and the actual shooting got under way. They had to make several takes of the first segment of the chase because Vance had a tendency to avoid the muddy ooze left from the recent rain. When running through the undergrowth, he raised his chin to hold his face tilted back to protect it from injury instead of keeping it tucked under as if to watch his feet and his back trail. He finally got the hang of it, however, and things went faster. Vance and the goons walked and ran through the area of explosives several times with the cameras off, then made that shot, with the swamp roaring with the blasts, in one take.

They broke for lunch. Afterward, in order to give Vance a breather, they took up the pursuit by the goons at the point where they lose Jean-Pierre and stumble around in growing terror, viciously blaming each other for their plight.

"All right, everybody stand clear!" Stan called. "How are the alligators doing? Fine. Remember we can only do this once, so make it look good. Okay, here we go."

The actors playing the goons had their various scratches and dirt streaks touched up, then moved over to the prop man to pick up their AK-47 weapons. They had to wait a moment while the blanks they had been using were removed and more ammo was shaken out of the box and loaded. The two men took the weapons in a gingerly way, then moved off toward their places.

"Wait a minute!" Rey said, stepping swiftly to stand in front of the two with his hands on his hips. "Hold it right there."

Julie, conferring with Andy Russell, the redheaded cinematographer, turned at the sound of Rey's voice. She had been aware of him all day, of his presence as he moved here and there in the background, his occasional humorous asides and trenchant comments as he pointed out problems and offered solutions. Now and then they had exchanged a smile. She had wanted to have her sandwich with him at lunch, but a problem had come up and she had eaten at her desk with the telephone glued to her ear instead of joining everyone else in the boat club.

She reached Rey's side at the same time that Stan limped over to join him. The stunt coordinator spoke first. "You got a problem, Tabary?"

"You might say so. Your prop man just loaded these weapons with live ammo."

"That's right."

"There are too many people around here to be shooting off submachine guns, not to mention how close we are here to a main highway. What's the idea?"

"The idea," Stan replied with heavy sarcasm, "is to make a couple of alligators dead. The firing will be short and sweet and aimed toward the ground. There'll be no danger. Now if you don't mind, we'd like to get on with it."

Rey didn't move. His face grim, he said, "I mind."

"What the hell are you talking about?"

"Wait, Stan," Julie said, placing her hand on the stunt coordinator's arm. "Hear him out."

"You're ready to kill two animals for nothing more than a few feet of film," Rey said, "just to have them bleed in Technicolor to provide a thrill for the audience."

"They're alligators for God's sake!" Stan yelled. "They're not an endangered species, not anymore! People shoot 'em, hunt 'em all the time."

"Not all the time; there's a hunting season and some even abide by it. But the people who hunt them around here don't take pictures of their death wallows."

Julie could see the veins in Stan's face throbbing, see his lips quivering with his anger. She was also aware of the silence that had fallen over the set as the crew stood following the argument. The quiet of the swamp hovered around them, broken only by the whine of a mosquito and the soft whisper of a breeze brushing through the palmetto.

Before the older man could frame an answer, she said, "The purpose of having the killers shoot the alligators is to show the terror of the men from the city at being in the swamp and at the mercy of Jean-Pierre. They lash out indiscriminately at anything that moves, since they can't strike at their real target."

Rey's gaze was hard as he turned it on Julie. "As motivation, it's great, but why can't you just have them fire blanks, then splatter their feet with a little artificial blood instead of sacrificing living alligators."

"It's such a small thing—" she began.

"It isn't small. Alligators enjoy the sun and rain and moonlight; they bellow their pleasure in mating and sing to their young. They don't give up life any more easily than you would."

Ofelia's voice cracked out from somewhere behind the cameras. "What'd I tell you? Alligator Tabary."

"Shit," Stan said. "Come on, Julie, let's get rolling."

Julie didn't move, nor did she look away from the bold sun-browned planes of Rey's face or the coffee-brown depths of his eyes. At last she spoke over her shoulder. "Unload the weapons."

"Julie—" Stan began.

She turned on the stunt coordinator then. "You heard me. Make it look good, the way you know you can. Do whatever it takes with special effects to get the point across, but I don't want so much as a scratch on the alligators."

The older man's lips tightened, though he gave a slow nod. "You're the boss."

"Thank you, Stan." She touched his arm again, then swung toward the crew. Her voice carrying, she called, "All right, let's take a half-hour break, then we'll do it."

That wasn't the end of it.

Stan wasn't far behind Julie when she left the set as the light faded later that evening. When he lifted a hand to beckon, she waited for him, with his halting gait, to catch up. They walked without speaking for several yards, threading their way along the path beaten down by their coming and going during the day, ducking under palmetto fronds, and stepping over rotting tree trunks barnacled with lichen and small green ferns. Voices wafted back to them with now and then a spurt of laughter from the members of the crew who had left before them, while more stragglers could be heard coming along behind. Julie wondered where Rey was. It had been at least an hour since she had seen him; he must have gone home before the last scene was done.

For the moment, she and Stan had the trail to themselves except for a blue crane that stood sentinel over a small patch of marsh off to one side, and a squirrel that crossed the path in front of them then scrambled up a tree and flattened himself on a limb, hiding. Stan watched the squirrel for a few seconds, then looked both ahead and behind them before bringing his gaze back to Julie.

"So all right," he said, "what's going on between you and Tabary?"

"Since when did you start checking on my love life?" Julie asked, keeping her voice light.

"I don't give a damn about your love life," he replied. "What I care about is the way this movie is going. Looks to me like you're losing your hold on it, like maybe you're letting Tabary run things."

"That isn't true, and you know it." Julie caught at a branch of wax myrtle as she passed, shredding the leaves so that the spicy, aromatic scent rose around them.

"No? You take every piece of advice that falls out of his mouth as if it was gospel. You do double back flips trying to make things the way he says they should be. You side with him every time any question comes up about the way things are shot."

"He was right about the alligators," Julie said, holding on to her temper by strong effort. "It's a wonder we didn't have the SPCA out there today monitoring us."

"Oh, come on! For a dog or a horse, maybe."

"You never can tell, and it's the kind of publicity we don't need."

A stubborn look came over the stunt coordinator's lined face. "You didn't have to side with Tabary like that. It wasn't right. A movie crew is like family. You don't show up family for the sake of some local yokel, even if there is something going on between you and him."

Julie broke the stem of the wax myrtle into small pieces and let them drop on the toes of her shoes as she walked. She didn't like to think that the attraction between Rey and herself was so obvious. Stan knew her fairly well, of course, but if he had noticed, it wouldn't be long before others did. As for the rest of what he had said, there was something to it. There was indeed a brand of kinship that sprang up between people on location, one made up of shared effort, shared hardships, and near-constant communication in a moviemaking jargon that made little sense to outsiders. She had violated it by her public support of Rey's argument. The fact that Stan had forced the confrontation made no difference. She should have taken both men to one side for a private discussion, a private decision that could have been given the appearance of joint agreement.

"You may be right," she said abruptly. "But you should remember that Rey Tabary was hired for a purpose. If we pay no attention to what he said, then it's money wasted."

"As far as I'm concerned, that's just what it is, wasted money. I don't think it would be any great loss if we got rid of him."

Julie gave Stan a sharp glance. "Rey is the authority on the swamp. He knows what's right, what works. We don't," she added pointedly, "not any of us."

"We could figure it out. I could've showed Vance how to run through the bushes, if Tabary hadn't got there first. C'mon, Julie. You know you need to cut costs, so cut Tabary—unless you got other reasons for keeping him around."

"What is it, Stan?" she asked, annoyance for his innuendo making her voice hard. "Exactly what do you have against Rey?"

The stuntman looked away toward where the trailers and motor homes of the location could just be seen through the trees. "He's too sure of himself. Besides that, I think he's interested in something more around here than being a technical director. He pokes his nose in things where it don't belong, shows up places he has no business. I just don't like it."

"I think you're exaggerating. He's only trying to do his job."

"Maybe, but I tell you again, I don't like it, and I don't like him."

They had reached the edge of the boat club parking lot. Stan did not wait for Julie's reply, but limped away from her, heading toward the clubhouse.

Julie stood for a moment, then turned toward her office trailer. Was he right? Was Rey prying into places he didn't belong? Why would he do that? What purpose could there be?

Still, even if Stan was right, why was he so upset? Most people were curious about the movie business and the ins and outs of how a story was put on film. There was nothing wrong with trying to learn about it so long as the process didn't interfere with production. Stan was getting all bent out of shape over nothing.

And yet, even Ofelia had said that Rey was everywhere, talking to everybody. It might just be possible that he was taking more than an average interest.

She could find out, Julie thought. If she did, and if what Stan said proved to be true, then one thing was certain. She wasn't going to like it either.

Chapter 7

There was someone in her office. Her secretary had left for the day at her usual time. The outer office was empty and still, its ashtrays emptied, its magazines stacked in neat piles. Julie's office door was supposed to be locked when her secretary left, but it stood half-open. From behind it could be heard the sound of papers rustling and the slow roll of a file drawer closing.

Julie marched to the door, pushing it open so that it banged against the wall. Rey looked up from where he stood beside the file drawer, thumbing through the folder in his hand. He met her gaze, his own suspended between surprise and wry acknowledgment of trouble.

"Is there something I can help you find?" Julie asked, her voice lilting with the spurious offer of assistance.

"Don't tell me," he answered. "I expect your office is a part of your territory, too."

Heat rose in her face at the memory of the night before and his use of those words, and also at the warmth in his eyes. She kept her voice even, however. "One thing this office isn't is a public facility. Would you like to explain what you're doing?"

His smile faded. "I'm not sure I would when you ask in that tone of voice."

"My tone suits the occasion." Even as she spoke she was forced to wonder if what she said was true. It was possible she had been influenced by Stan's suspicions and her own ambivalence over this man. Regardless, it went against the grain to have anyone, even Rey, touch her things without her knowledge or permission.

"Yes, well," Rey said after a pause. "I'm sorry, but I was waiting for you and suddenly thought about finding out what I needed to know. Next time, I'll ask. All right?"

The calm apology, the wry grimace that went with it, were so disarming that it wasn't easy to stay angry. "What was it you wanted?"

"I was interested in the name of the company that provided the boat for Paul's stunt. There's a question in Donna's mind, and mine, about liability for the accident."

Julie stared at him with a sinking sensation in her chest before she moved slowly to sit down in her desk chair. "You mean," she said in stifled tones, "that Donna Lislet is thinking of filing suit?"

"I didn't say that."

"The way things have been going, it's exactly what will happen. Excel Films, Inc., and the studio will naturally be named in it along with the boat company. The bonding company will come down on us like a ton of bricks. Davies will be ecstatic. It's all the excuse he'll need to take *Swamp Kingdom* away from me."

"What are you talking about?" Rey asked, a frown gathering between his eyes.

She told him in a few succinct phrases, adding as she finished, "I don't see why Donna wants to carry through with this. She will have the accidental-death benefits from the company insurance."

"That doesn't give her the peace of mind of knowing exactly what caused Paul's death, something that might show up in an investigation."

"It was an accident, pure and simple!" Julie exclaimed. "You saw it, we all did. The skiff's steering cable broke under stress after being damaged by battery acid."

Rey shook his head. "I can't believe Paul would have run that skiff at such high speeds without looking over it first. He would have noticed any acid corrosion. It must have been something else."

Julie threaded the fingers of one hand through her hair. "You can ask at the boat company, but I don't know what they can tell you. The skiff was four or five years old and had seen hard use, instead of being bought new like the cabin cruiser and the speedboat. It was supposed to look beat-up, as if it was something Jean-Pierre might have used for years."

"Who checked it out when it was brought in?"

"Ofelia signed the invoice, and Stan and one of the mechanics gave both it and the speedboat a quick once-over. The skiff was supposed to be recently reconditioned with a new one-fifty motor, so it seems nobody really went over it inch by inch. Most stuntmen, the professionals anyway, do like to check out their own equipment; they don't trust anybody else. People on the set usually figure there's no use duplicating the effort."

"It was just a misunderstanding then, the way you see it."

"I don't know what else to tell you." She paused, her gaze as she looked away from him clouded with painful introspection. "You know, I used to say I didn't see how John Landis, the director of *Twilight Zone: The Movie,* could have endangered the lives of Vic Morrow and those two children who were killed during the filming. It seemed so reckless, so unfeeling. I have a better understanding of it now. Somehow, you get used to the people around you taking chances; you get used to exposing people to small dangers. Little by little you make the dangers bigger. When you get by with it, when nothing major happens, somehow you think that it never will."

Rey tossed the folder on top of the file cabinet, then sat down on the desk corner beside Julie. "The scene you set up wasn't that dangerous. The accident shouldn't have happened, and wouldn't have, if something hadn't gone wrong in that boat. There's no reason to blame yourself."

"I'm the director. I call the shots, so I'm responsible for whatever happens on the set."

"If I remember right, even Landis was cleared of criminal charges."

"The civil settlements dragged out for years and came to millions."

"Donna hasn't said she'll sue. She just wants—needs—to learn the truth and put this incident behind her."

"It would be nice if I could do that myself."

Rey nodded his agreement. There was an expression disturbing in its intensity on his face for an instant. Then it was gone. His tone degrees lighter, he said, "What do you say to fried shrimp and catfish for dinner. Tonight Aunt Tine has a Catholic Daughter's baby shower, and we have to fend for ourselves."

"Sounds fine, but I'm not that great with a frying pan." Julie sat back in her chair.

"I don't intend to cook, either," he said. "What I had in mind was Middendorf's. They serve the best fried seafood around, and as a bonus you get to see Lake Maurepas and Pass Manchac, the channel between Lake Maurepas and Lake Pontchartrain."

Lake Maurepas, Julie remembered, was where the Blind River ended. "Will we be going by boat?"

"If that's what you want." His smile was guileless.

"No, no, by land will be just fine."

"What?" he asked as he reached to catch hold of the arms of her swivel chair and swing her to face him. "No moonlight swim?"

"Not—this evening." Her gaze was shadowed, and she clasped her hands together over her midsection, holding them close against her.

"Too bad," he said softly. "I'll have to think of something else."

He leaned to touch his mouth to her cool lips, warming them, teasing the moist line where they came together with his tongue until they seemed to pulse with the rapid beat of her heart. She unclasped her fingers and placed them on his shoulders, drawing him closer, increasing the pressure of her mouth on his.

"Well, well. How very interesting," came the drawl from the doorway.

Rey lifted his head, drawing back without haste. Julie discovered she had been holding her breath and inhaled slow and deep before she turned to look at Vance standing poised with one hand on the doorknob.

"Did you want something?" she asked.

The actor's eyes were dark with jealousy and injured conceit as he stared at Julie. "I'm sure I did, but I've forgotten what," he answered with brittle sarcasm. "I'll come back later, what do you say? Oh, and I'll close the door behind me. I don't know if Allen knows what's going on here, but in case he doesn't, I'm sure you wouldn't want the news to get around."

———

The drive to Middendorf's Restaurant was not lively. Rey held the Cherokee on the road with only a small portion of his mind on what he was doing. He took Airline, otherwise known as US 61, to the cut-across to Interstate 10, then branched off 10 to I-55 and headed north. Night fell quickly and there wasn't a great deal to see. He pointed out the canal dug along the interstate to carry the big barges used to set the pilings for the wide roadway through the swamp. He and Julie mentioned in passing the suicidal impulses of possums and raccoons on Louisiana roads at night, creating the pitiful bundles of fur that were dealt with by buzzards. It did nothing to lighten the mood.

Rey glanced at Julie from time to time. She was withdrawn, apparently lost in her own thoughts. He wondered what they were, but was afraid he knew.

He had rushed her, and he knew it. The trouble was, there was so little time—not that that was any excuse. He had lost it. That was the simple truth. He could no more have stopped himself from going to her room the night before than he could have stopped his own heartbeat. The power of his attraction to her was crazy, an aberration that set off alarm bells in the back of his head, but it was something that had to be faced. It had to be taken into account and allowances made for it.

He glanced at her in the green reflection from the dashboard. Her features were set in firm lines and there was a determined tilt to her chin. Her mouth was well defined, gently curving, its smoothness like an invitation. She was so self-possessed, so secure within herself, that he felt the stir of challenge. He wanted to disarm her defenses, to persuade her to allow him into her thoughts, her dreams. He wanted to know everything there was to know about her, from her favorite color to the way she meant to vote in the next election. The more he knew, the safer he would feel.

He had wanted to apply his fist to the face of Vance Stuart. Conceited horse's ass. What made the actor think he could get away with using that snide tone to Julie? What had there ever been between the two of them to allow it? Just how valuable was he to Excel Films, and to Julie?

Rey watched the road unwinding under his headlights with narrowed eyes. He had no right to ask such questions. Anyway, it was possible his own indiscretion may have been all the actor needed. He should have known better than to get too close to Julie while she was at the location. He would have kept his distance except that it had been important to do something to mend the breach caused by his bungling, to reestablish the closeness between them.

He glanced at the woman beside him again, caught by the movement as she glanced at him then turned her head once more to stare out at the passing swampland and the trees that crowded the highway right of way like a screen for the swamp beyond. Considering a few of the many things he wanted to know about her, he said, "If you went to school in Louisiana as you said, how did you wind up in L.A.?"

The look she turned on him was serious, but she answered readily enough. "Bull asked me to come and live with him after my mother died. I had been out to California once or twice during school vacations, enough to develop a taste for the sun and fun of Malibu, where Bull lived. I went."

"And it worked out, living with your dad?"

"At first," she answered, relaxing as if it was a relief to have something to talk about, leaning her head back on the headrest and turning toward him. "Bull was free-handed; gave me a car, opened charge accounts, passed out twenty-dollar bills as if there was an endless supply."

"Sounds like a teenager's dream."

"Yes, but he also wanted to choose my friends and tell me what to think. He had never been around while I was growing up, but suddenly he was the final authority, the ultimate paternalistic head of the house. I was supposed to account to him for every moment of my time. I thought then that he was making unreasonable rules and flexing his muscles to see that I followed them just for the ego trip. Now, I realize he was frightened of the responsibility of having a wild child on his hands."

The descriptive phrase seemed so unlikely he had to smile. "Were you a wild child?"

"I thought I was pretty bad," she admitted, "though probably I was normal for the time. Anyway, I moved out, lived for a while in a beach house with four other girls and a couple of brotherly-type boys."

"Dropped out of college?"

"For a year or so."

"And then?" he persisted.

"Then I got bored. I started fooling around with a sixteen-millimeter camera Bull had given me, shooting the surfers, the waves, the appeal of that way of life and it's dead-end nature. I ran into technical problems, questions, and who better to ask than Bull?"

Rey, passing an eighteen-wheeler with smooth precision, said almost at random, "Apparently he gave you the answers."

"It changed everything. We learned to talk to each other without shouting, listen to each other without just waiting to jump in and say our piece. I went back to school, but kept my own apartment, and when I wasn't watching Bull at work, I was filming everything that moved."

There was something subdued in her voice, reinforcing the undertone of depression that threaded it. He probed for the reason with caution. "You've been on your own a long time, then."

"You might say so. Except for Allen."

He had almost forgotten Allen. It was telling, he thought, that Julie had not.

It was she who broke the silence next. "The swamp out there seems so vast, as if it goes on forever."

"It's not as big as it used to be; too much logging, too many housing developments and industrial parks."

"Why is it that the Cajuns settled in it? There must have been better places to live in those days, at the end of the eighteenth century."

"They took the land the Spanish, who held Louisiana at the time, gave them, and were glad to get it. Actually, they didn't settle in the swamp itself, but along the rivers and bayous. But the swamp was always at their back door. They explored it, made themselves at home in it, I guess, for the same reason men climb mountains."

"Because it was there," she said in dry recognition. "What about your ancestors? Is that what they did?"

There was an odd, intent look in her eyes as she asked the question, but Rey could not decipher its meaning. He answered almost at random as he considered it. "More or less. It's been a family pastime, up until modern times. Most of my cousins are too busy making a living these days to learn it the way their fathers did."

"What did your father do—for a living, I mean?"

"Farmed for a while, then went to work at the chemical plant down the road. His brother, Aunt Tine's husband, worked for Colonial Sugar. I used to love to see him come home. He looked like a piece of marzipan, always covered with the sugar crystals that fogged in the air. Aunt Tine called him the sweetest man alive."

"She would," Julie said, a smile in her voice, though it did not quite banish the troubled look in her eyes.

They topped a rise, and Lake Maurepas lay before them. Rey pointed out the wide, dark body of water that lay off to the left, lined with yellow lights winking away into the distance. To the right flowed the more narrow pass that led to the inland sea of fresh and salt water named after the minister of the navy under Louis XIV, the Comte de Pontchartrain. They crossed the humped-back bridge over it that was high enough to allow barge traffic and larger fishing boats to pass to the other lake, then swung into the parking lot of Middendorf's.

The restaurant was unpretentious, a long low building with red-striped awnings and a giant red and yellow sign designed to attract the attention of Yankee tourists speeding toward Baton Rouge or New Orleans along the interstate. It had been in operation more than fifty years, serving up fresh seafood to lake fishermen and local residents, to New Orleanians looking for simple fare, and good old boys from north Louisiana and Mississippi going back and forth to football games at LSU and the Super Dome, in addition to the tourists in season.

Inside, it had a homey decor of wood paneling and checked tablecloths. It hummed with the low voices of diners and smelled of crab meat, corn meal, and warm peanut oil. Rey and Julie were met by a smiling hostess who guided them toward the corner table Rey requested. As they followed her toward it, Rey answered several greetings from friends. They also waved in passing at three different tables of movie crew members who had heard about the place.

The menu included steak and chicken and even hamburgers, but these were swamped by the offerings of oysters on the half shell and boiled crawfish, barbecued shrimp, broiled flounder with lemon butter, and every variety of fried seafood. Side dishes ran to green salad and coleslaw, fried potatoes and hush puppies. The food wasn't fancy, but it was plentiful and cooked to perfection.

Rey asked for a bottle of Pouilly-Fuissé of good but undistinguished vintage, then enjoyed the debate with Julie over whether the wine was still too good to go with fried food while they sipped it and studied the menu. He ordered the house specialty, thin fillets of pond-raised catfish fried light golden brown, while Julie opted for safety and a taste of several things by having a seafood platter combining shrimp, oysters, catfish, and stuffed crab.

When the waitress who took their orders gathered up their menus and went away, Rey refilled their wineglasses, then leaned back in his chair. He gathered his resolve, then said quietly, "Do you want to talk about it, or would you rather ignore it?"

"Excuse me?" She drank a little of her wine. The table candle in its hurricane globe made a pale gold fire in the bottom of her glass. The refraction of it flickered over her face, emphasizing her look of unnatural calm.

"Something is bothering you. I'd like to know what it is."

It seemed for an instant as if she meant to evade the question. Then she gave a short nod. "Actually, there is something. I hear you have a reputation as a man-about-town in certain echelons of New Orleans society. How is that possible for a back-country Cajun known as the Swamp Rat?"

Rey had braced himself for several things, but not that one. It was, he thought, a side issue. His voice dry and a little deeper than he had intended, he asked, "Madelyn?"

"The information came from her in a roundabout way."

"She exaggerates."

"But you do have an apartment in New Orleans?" It was an accusation.

"I do."

"A very nice apartment, I've heard. And you drive an Italian sports car, which costs enough to keep an average family for years?"

"Madelyn has been a busy girl."

"And fly your own plane?"

His sigh was a resigned affirmative. "Did she happen to go on record with my collection of old-master drawings and sixty-foot yacht on Lake Pontchartrain?"

"No, but there was some mention of the Krewe of Comus."

"I know you were no end of impressed by a Mardi Gras club affiliation."

"Being from Louisiana, I know its approximate social value—an indication of distinguished lineage. What is it with you? I gave you an opening back there in the car to tell me about your New Orleans family connections as well as your Cajun ones. Why didn't you mention them? What are you hiding? You can't be afraid people won't like you for your own *dolce* self?"

He studied her face, trying to judge whether the coolness of her tone came from disappointment, disgust, or possibly well-restrained curiosity. "Can't I? Then you have never been chased by Madelyn de Wells."

"I'm not joking."

"Neither am I," Rey said soberly. "I didn't tell you at first because I didn't think it mattered. I'm not in the habit of walking up to women and saying, 'Hey, I'm a rich man and marginally acceptable socially.'"

"No, of course not. And anyway it's so much more fun for you, playing people for idiots."

The flash in the absinthe green of her eyes was definitely anger. He tried to deflect it. "That's not quite right. You were so certain I could use money that it didn't seem polite to tell you otherwise. In any case, I never expected to work with you, much less live with you under the same roof."

"Surely there was a minute or two between the time you decided you might condescend to help me out and the instant you slid out of my bed at the crack of dawn when you could have said, 'Oh, by the way, I'm not what you think.' "

He sat watching her, admiring the rose flush of her face in the candlelight and the way the cotton sweater she wore lifted and fell over the soft curves of her breasts with the quick breathing of her anger. He gave himself a mental shake. That kind of bemusement wasn't helpful. He was in trouble. And he thought he was beginning to see a few of the reasons for it.

"I'm sorry," he said abruptly.

"Oh, please, not again," she said in scathing rejection of that quiet apology. "There is no condescension more complete than when a man accepts full blame."

He leaned toward her, keeping his voice quiet. "I accept blame for nothing except not waking you up this morning to say good-bye."

"Who said it was needed?" she shot back at him.

"Nobody, but I have a feeling I wouldn't be quite so deep in it if I had not let you sleep this morning, if I had made sure you knew I didn't leave early because I wanted to go. I left, you know, because of Aunt Tine."

She was quick. She only stared at him for the blink of an eye before she said, "Oh."

"Right. Aunt Tine well understands the way of the flesh, and gets as much enjoyment out of watching it on the soap operas and gossiping about it with her friends as any lady of mature years, but she would not be happy if she found out that I didn't sleep in my own bed last night. It's her house; it seemed best to abide by her ideas of right and wrong."

"I expect," Julie said almost inaudibly, "that she would be even less happy with me than with you."

Rey was saved from having to answer by the arrival of their food. When it had been placed before them, they ate in silence for long moments. The tension between them seemed to grow with a life of its own. Julie kept her eyes downcast, though a tiny frown came and went between the wings of her brows. Finally, she put down her fork. Rey, seeing the earnest look in her eyes, felt his stomach muscles clench as if in expectation of a blow.

"Look," she said, her tones husky and stumbling as she hurried to get the words out. "I think we—I made a mistake last night. Things got out of hand. I know I am as much to blame as you; I sent the wrong signals, failed to back off when I should. I won't try to explain it, because I'm not sure I can. But I'm not comfortable being with you while I'm still involved with Allen. I—feel so guilty."

Rey was suddenly not hungry anymore. He drank the last of his wine and sat holding the glass, then placed it carefully back on the table. The words flat, he said, "Is this in honor of Vance's remarks this evening?"

She shook her head. "It's been coming on since I woke up this morning. We've been together a long time, Allen and I, through good times and bad times. We respect each other, understand each other. He deserves better than this from me."

There were a great many things he could say, Rey knew, but he wasn't sure they would make any difference. What was required now was the gentlemanly gesture, no matter how much he disliked it. His voice even, he said, "There was no obligation attached to last night, of any kind."

"That's all right, then," she replied without looking at him.

"I think," he said, the words shaded with irony, "that this is the first time I've been rejected because I have money."

"That isn't it," she said in quick denial. "It's just that we're so different, our lives are so different. We started off with such misunderstanding, something you apparently enjoy, though I don't. Even if it wasn't for Allen, it's just—"

"Something isn't right."

"Yes," she said with a flicker of gratitude in her voice for his helpfulness. "We will just—forget it happened."

He clenched his teeth to stop the retort that sprang first to mind. Instead, he said, "And go on working on the movie, living under the same roof, for as long as you're here on location?"

"Preferably, if you think it's possible."

"It isn't impossible, if that's what you want."

"I—good, then. I would have hated to have to leave Aunt Tine's so soon, or try to explain to her why I was going."

He was able to give her some semblance of a smile. "Something to be avoided at all costs. She would have the truth out of you in no time flat."

"I don't doubt it." Julie's lips curved a fraction, though the look in her eyes remained troubled.

"After which, I might have to leave myself."

"Surely not."

"Oh, not for my sins, black as they might be painted. What she wouldn't forgive would be my chasing you away."

"She does have her heart set on a new roof."

That wasn't what Rey had meant, but he let it pass since he didn't quite trust himself to explain. Instead, he mentioned the possibility of dessert. When it was declined, he signaled for the check.

Rey half expected Julie to insist on putting the meal on Excel Films plastic, or at least paying for half of it. That she didn't might have been tact, but could also mean a concession to his sudden monied status. Either way, he was glad to be left alone to attend to payment while she went to wash her hands.

He extracted bills from his wallet for the tip and dropped them on the table. As he reached for the check to take it to the cashier he noticed the inch or so of wine left in the bottle. Pouring it into his glass, he picked it up. A grim smile tugged at his lips as his gaze rested on the wine. For a long moment he sat contemplating the rippling of the cool yellow liquid caused by the faint tremor of his hand. With an abrupt movement, he drank it down and returned the glass to its place. He left the table without looking back.

Chapter 8

Julie did not sleep well. The evening with Rey played itself over and over in her mind like a set of film rushes with a problem. It seemed that some of what had been said needed dubbing in again. The tone was off here, the inflection of his voice there, one or two pieces of dialogue didn't quite go with the accompanying facial expressions.

Rey's reaction to her decision to halt the intimacy between them had been generous. She could not have asked for a more obliging attitude or more help in getting through a difficult moment. She had expected something else, though she was not sure what. Disbelief maybe, or anger, even accusations. She was grateful for his detached acceptance, yet at the same time it didn't seem quite right.

The explanation, of course, could be that he didn't care enough one way or the other to make an issue of it, especially since she had chosen to bring it up in a crowded restaurant. That idea didn't sit well either, but it was difficult to tell whether the problem was in something he had said or done or only in her own injured *amour propre*.

She felt so foolish. How could she know her own mind so little that she could make love to Rey one night and want to run away from him the next? What was it about him, about the sweet beguilement of his touch, that so disturbed her that she was panicked by the thought of continuing with him yet pained by his acceptance of her dismissal? She had pleaded her attachment to Allen, and it was true that she was uncomfortable betraying the person who had been the stable center of her life for so long. But was that all?

Rey was a complicated man. She had at first thought that he was a regular macho male, with too much ego and not enough finesse. She had been wrong. There was more to him than that, though how much more was hard to say. He was so good at obscuring who and what he really was, hiding behind humor and a casual disregard for exact detail, that it seemed there could be anything. Or something not quite right. It made her afraid. Afraid not only of who and what he was, but of what he could do to her safe, well-regulated life.

It didn't matter, of course. She had solved the problem of Rey, and now she was free of the mental quandary he had caused, free to get back to making her movie. In a few days it would be in the can and she would be gone. Back to L.A. Back to Allen and the next movie. And the next.

Working fourteen hours a day and more over the next three days helped Julie to ignore all outside influences and concentrate on the job at hand. It also ate up film. Several scenes with Summer and Vance at the swamp fishing camp got themselves made, developing the warmth of the relationship between the two. There was also a scene that turned out well with the two of them out in the skiff as a storm came up. Braving the waves together in the unstable boat, Jean-Pierre and his daughter could be seen drawing closer together, while Summer as Alicia almost visibly drew courage from her father.

The scene where Madelyn, playing the wife, Dorothea, as a woman disgusted with the ineptness of her hirelings, who herself chases after Jean-Pierre into the swamp with a gun, turned out well. Madelyn gave a magnificent impression of a harridan losing her designer elegance under layers of mud while forced to come to terms with the impenetrability of the swamp or her husband's defenses. The nude swimming scene, shot at night, had a stark beauty and surrealistic impression of submerged emotion that surprised Julie and sent both Vance and Madelyn, when they saw the rushes, into transports of self-congratulation.

Rey was always there. Julie spoke to him often, brief, impersonal questions and answers with hardly a glance exchanged between them. He was everywhere she looked, laughing, talking, explaining, correcting everything from the pronunciation of a word to the kind of pots and pans on view in the kitchen of the fishing camp. He teased and cajoled Summer into flirtatious smiles and happy cooperation, soothed

Madelyn's sensibilities, and challenged Vance to more intense effort. Somehow, he had insinuated himself into the good graces of the camera crew, trading quips and shooting the bull with such likable ease that they often let him get behind the cameras. He even became Ofelia's buddy, sharing her beer and her jokes, which, from the husky richness of her laughter, were definitely ribald if not downright raunchy. In his off hours, he could often be seen drinking coffee with the parish police and the state game warden, who patrolled the highways and waterways of the swamp and used the boat club as an unofficial rest stop while making their rounds.

Vance strolled into Julie's office well after dark on the third evening, apparently for no other purpose than to broach the subject of the technical director. Flinging himself down in the chair across from her, he said without preamble, "What's with you and Tabary? You're so polite to each other it sets my teeth on edge, and I just saw him going into Ofelia's rolling bordello of a motor home with her. Willingly, too."

"Mind your own business, Vance," she said, her voice cool.

"Oh, it's that way, is it? I wasn't sure there was any other business to mind, but now I *am* curious. What happened? A lovers' quarrel? Or did you just decide it wasn't worth risking your good thing with Allen?"

She looked him square in the eyes. "What do you care?"

"Why wouldn't I?" he said indignantly. "Here you are, Lady Cool, the director with a rep for being untouchable, and what happens? You pass me by with a pat on the head and lose it for a swamp thing."

"I haven't lost it, as you so elegantly put it."

"Could have fooled me."

"No doubt. But what did you hope to gain? The distinction of going to bed with me? The thrill of seeing our names linked in the tabloids? Thank you so much. I have a flash for you, Vance. If you want to impress a woman, much less a director, you might try a little honest emotion."

He sat studying her, then reached into his shirt pocket and pulled out a brown twist of something that looked like dirty rope. He put it in his mouth, bit off a piece, and started to chew.

"Chewing tobacco? You?"

He made a sound of assent as he shifted his chew. "One of the local guys gave it to me. It's called Perique, a pure Indian tobacco that's grown no place else in the world except here by a couple of old families. Good stuff, but not dope."

"I did wonder."

"Yeah. The hard stuff's available, of course."

"Of course," Julie echoed without inflection.

He watched her a second before he said, "You know, Julie, you can be a real bitch."

"That isn't news," she answered, refusing to rise to the bait.

"It is to me. I had the idea you were basically a sweetheart, a pussycat, even if you were a bit too devoted to the grind. Annette tried to tell me it wasn't so, but I thought she was just running her mouth."

"A pussycat I certainly am not," Julie said, with anger rising in her eyes.

"Right. You can ruin a career without turning a hair, can't you? Maybe I should be worried."

"I don't know what you're talking about."

"Sure you do. You prevented Annette Davett's chance for the big time with just four little words. She told me all about it. She was auditioning for a major part in one of Bull's movies. You were hanging around, waiting for dear old Dad to take you somewhere. You wanted him to hurry, so when he asked you what you thought about Annette, you said, and I quote, 'Her voice sounds funny.'"

Julie searched her mind for some memory of the incident, but could come up with nothing. That meant little, she knew; Bull had often asked for her opinion over the years. He might have little respect for the basic intelligence of women, but he nourished a touching faith in their intuition.

Finally she said, "That must have been years ago."

"Oh, it was; you were still in your teens. But you don't remember, do you? That makes it worse."

"Because it's supposed to show that I didn't care enough to keep it in mind? I never intended to blight anybody's life. If it happened, I'm sorry, but there was nothing malicious about it. The fact is,

Annette's voice was, and still is, a problem. Why didn't she work on it, lower it, make it stronger?"

Vance moved his shoulders under his loose cotton shirt. "How should I know? Probably because it was easier to blame you."

"I also don't understand why Annette allowed her daughter to work on this movie if she dislikes me so much."

"Oh, I can tell you that. She figures you owe her one. If the payoff comes through Summer, that's fine, but it's still justice as far as Annette's concerned. What goes around, comes around."

"You'd think she would have too much pride."

"Actors don't have pride," he said, the contact-lens blue of his eyes dark with distasteful self-knowledge. "What they have instead is ego. Insecure, destructive ego that doesn't tolerate injury too well."

There came the sound of the trailer door opening and the firm tread of footsteps in the outer office. Julie could not see into the next room from the placement of her desk, but Vance, sitting in the chair opposite, could. She glanced toward the sound anyway, in partial recognition of that even stride. At the same time, Vance leaped to his feet and rounded the desk. Before she could avoid him, he bent over her, raised her chin with his cupped hand, and pressed his mouth to her lips.

The kiss was fleeting, dry, almost impersonal. An instant later, the actor straightened. His voice strained, he said, "I did warn you."

He backed away then. Turning toward the doorway, he gave the man standing there a triumphant smile. He stepped past him, then strolled across the outer office and left the trailer.

"I can come back later," Rey said in neutral tones, "if now isn't convenient."

Julie took a deep breath. She lifted a hand toward her mouth as if she would wipe it, then let it fall again. Her voice clipped, she said, "Now is fine. What you just saw was an act of petty revenge staged for your benefit and my embarrassment. The less attention given to it, the better."

"I'd like to give Stuart my attention." The words were grim.

"For what purpose? It would only let him know he got a rise out of you."

"The purpose would be to make certain it doesn't happen again."

"I think I can guarantee that."

"Can you? What are you going to do, threaten to fire him? You know, and he knows, that it would be too expensive to replace him at this stage."

"I can edit his scenes so this movie belongs to Summer. She's close to taking it away from him anyway, so it wouldn't be hard."

He stared down at her for long seconds, then a laugh left him. "A mean boss lady. Remind me not to tangle with you."

His comment, coming on top of Vance's accusation, caught Julie in the raw. Sitting up with her back locked straight, she said, "I'll do that. Now, was there something you needed?"

Amusement flickered in his eyes, and the atmosphere in the office slowly became charged with tension. Heat rose in Julie's face as she realized that she had left herself open for some suggestive remark once more. The fact that Rey refrained from making it only pointed up her slip, Freudian or otherwise.

Before she could retrieve the situation, he cleared his throat. "Actually," he said, "it's about something you need."

"Which is?" She kept her voice even with an effort.

"The completion of the boat-chase stunt that you've been putting off. I mentioned it to Ofelia and she says she thinks you've about worked your way down to it. I just wanted you to know that I'm ready to do it when you are."

She was never going to be ready; she knew that well enough. Regardless, it had to be done. "Good," she said, unclenching her jaw so she could speak. "What about tomorrow afternoon?"

"Fine," he answered.

"Fine," she echoed, but she refused to meet his eyes as she said it.

"Tell me something, Stan?"

Julie was standing on the floating shooting platform, waiting while the head cameraman got his equipment in order, waiting for the boats to be checked and maneuvered into position, waiting for the sun to get exactly right. They wouldn't be shooting the entire boat-chase scene again, but would use the footage shot with Paul in the canal and along the lower section of the Blind River before the boats reached the open stretch. That meant the weather, time of day, angle of the sun, and outward appearance of the boats had to be exactly the same. It all took time and effort.

The speedboat had been repaired and repainted to look like new, but the skiff had been gone over with particular care since it was not the same one as before; the other had been too badly damaged to salvage. Every effort had been made to find an exact replacement as to model and general condition, but the new one had to have a stripe repainted then bleached to the proper sun-faded color, have a dent or two put in the right spots, and its black plastic state registration letters replaced then peeled in the right places to mimic the crumbling originals.

At the sound of Julie's voice, the stunt coordinator turned from where he was conferring with the script supervisor, the young woman in charge of continuity whose responsibility it was to see that everything matched. He limped toward Julie. His expression harassed, his arms spread wide, he asked, "What?"

"Don't panic, I haven't found something else wrong," she said. "I was just wondering. Do you think I'm trying to do too much with this chase scene? Am I cutting it too close, trying to make it too realistic?"

"You got the jitters, huh?"

"You might say that."

"Don't worry about it. It'll be all right."

"That's what you said before."

He grunted. "Yeah, well, it should have been. But this time Tabary is out there. He may not look as spiffy as usual in his dun-colored wig, but if anybody can control the skiff, he can."

Julie grinned a little as she remembered Rey's look of disgust as he was handed the wig that matched Vance's hair coloring. The humor faded quickly. "I mean it, Stan. Am I asking too much?"

"Tell you what, girl; if you can still wonder about it, you ain't. It's when directors stop wondering and start thinking anything they want done ought to get done that they get dangerous."

She gave a slow nod. "Thanks, Stan."

"Don't mention it," he replied, and turned away to yell at an electrician's helper who was letting a cable dangle in the water.

It wasn't just the stunt that had Julie on edge. There were at least a dozen fishing boats buzzing slowly up and down the river and circling near the shoot that had nothing to do with the movie company. In them were local men and boys with an occasional girl, people who had heard about the stunt and turned out to see it. Excel Films could control who came and went at the location, could keep out unauthorized visitors and curiosity seekers and people who might tamper with props or machinery for the sake of a souvenir, but they couldn't control the river. At least there was an off-duty policeman in an air boat standing by to prevent the lookers from encroaching on the scene of the action. The sightseers were keeping clear for the most part, but were a distraction and could become a danger if one strayed into the path of the speeding boats once shooting started.

Another distraction was the presence of Paul Lislet's widow on the platform. Donna Lislet wore a gray dress with her hair pulled back in a plain metal clasp, her face pale. She was plainly nervous, yet just as plainly determined to stay where she was until the cameras stopped rolling.

Madelyn had also turned out for the event, presenting, as usual, a brilliant and attention-getting appearance, in acid-yellow designer slacks and shirt, three-inch high yellow sandals, and sunglasses with yellow frames. Summer was also on hand with her mother. Rey, it seemed, had his own cheering section. Julie hoped there was something to cheer about.

Aunt Tine was not there. She could not bear to watch, she said, not again. She would wait at the house until she heard all was well.

Aunt Tine had the right idea, Julie thought. She would have liked to stay away herself until it was over. Failing that, she wished she could clear the set, send everybody packing who didn't have a definite job to do.

She couldn't help thinking there was something ghoulish about the intense interest directed toward the skiff and the speedboat out on the water. Like the spectators at the bouts between gladiators in ancient

Rome, at modern car races and the futuristic takeoffs, and landings of
the space shuttle, there was some kind of primitive urge that drew
people to watch men risk injury and death. That she was pandering
to that urge by filming such scenes did nothing to help her feelings
at the moment.

If the truth were known, Julie would really have liked to call the
whole thing off. She could not. The arrangements had been made, the
crew and technicians assembled, the money spent. And the money was
continuing to be poured out at the rate of several thousand dollars per
hour. There was no way a sudden cancellation could be explained, not
without having words like *wishy-washy* and *female whim* tossed
around, not without destroying her chances to become a front-rank
director. Still, what did that matter compared with a human life?

Donna Lislet was standing alone, watching the preparation out on
the water with desolate eyes. Madelyn and the others were paying her
no attention, had not, so far as Julie was aware, spoken a word to her
since Rey had left her at the platform. The young widow's isolation
bothered Julie, that and the nagging sense of responsibility she still
carried about the death of her husband. Julie walked toward the other
young woman with slow steps.

"You're very brave to come here today," Julie said when the two
of them had exchanged greetings.

"It isn't bravery," Donna said. "It's more like an exorcism, I think.
I've had such nightmares that I thought—I don't know whether you
can understand, but it seems that if I can watch Rey do the stunt right,
it will give me another image to take the place of—"

As the widow fumbled for words Julie sought to help her. "I see
what you mean. I suppose all of us handle things in our own way."

"I've been wanting to thank you for the chance to work on the
set. I can't tell you how thrilled I am. I can't wait to begin."

Julie replied suitably, enlarging on the theme to describe a few of
the town scenes the other woman might participate in when they
started shooting them. Donna Lislet was a woman of even tempera-
ment and reasonable intelligence, judging by her comments. Her manner was stilted, however, as if she did not quite trust Julie enough to
be herself around her. Or perhaps it was simply that Donna blamed

Julie for her husband's death. At any rate, the widow's interest, except when the discussion was of movie scenes where she herself might play a part, was about evenly divided between what Julie was saying and what Rey was doing in the skiff out on the water. Julie was rescued from the awkward situation at last by the signal that all was ready. With a quick smile and a murmured word of reassurance, she moved away from the widow to take up her position.

The command was given for the cameras to roll. The skiff came racing down the river, breaking from the dark tunnel of the trees into the open stretch, with the speedboat close behind and the cabin cruiser with Stan and the cameraman now on board following. The wakes of the three crafts boiled and foamed, spreading backward behind them.

Just as before, the shots rang out from the speedboat as one of the two men in dark suits fired a submachine gun. The special-effects explosions made a series of fountain jets off to the left of the skiff, the timing right on target with the speed of the smaller boat. And just as before, the skiff swerved in a dizzy circle, dancing back over its own wake and that of the speedboat to streak between the other boat and the cabin cruiser. Then with Rey at the steering wheel it went hurtling toward the baffle of cypress trees in its first lightning pass through them.

There was no need for instructions, no need for shouted commands. The execution of the stunt was perfection, the timing flawless. Julie stood silent with her walkie-talkie forgotten in her hand, watching.

She had thought Paul Lislet drove a fast boat, but it seemed to her that Rey was sending the skiff flashing over the water at a pace almost too fast to follow with a camera. The craft was planing until more than three-quarters of it was out of the water, until it appeared that at any moment it might soar into flight. His turns were tighter, more controlled than his friend's had been, and as he zoomed through the cypress trees in that stunning pattern of flashing sun and shadow that had so captivated Julie before, she was sickeningly sure that he was cutting closer to the snags and stumps, and to the knobbed and shining cypress knees.

Behind her, she heard a moan as Donna Lislet whispered with tears choking her voice, "Dear God. Oh, my dear God." Madelyn was panting with excitement, her lips parted as she kept her rapt gaze on Rey. Annette Davett looked dazed, frightened out of her wits. She had her arms fastened around her daughter, who was standing biting her lips with her eyes suspiciously red in her pale face.

Julie could spare them little sympathy, little thought. Her throat seemed to have closed, so she could not draw breath. Her heart jarred against her ribs with every beat while the sound of it pulsed with soft thunder in her ears. Sickness shifted inside her, causing cool moisture to break out along her hairline. There rose in her mind the need to stop the torment, stop the boats, stop the scene unfolding and its horrifying finale. The word that would do that hovered, white-hot and ready, at the forefront of her mind. She could hear it ringing in her head, feel the sharp edges of its tones, taste its force and effect.

She could not say it. Fear held her mute, the fear that any sound she might make could cause the instant of inattention that would precipitate disaster. She was also silent out of respect for the professionalism and precision of the feat unfolding in front of her.

She had known that Rey was working with Stan on the stunt, mapping out the movements of the boats, but she had not known to what degree they had choreographed them, timed them, woven the boats and their wakes into an intricate pattern that was as beautiful to watch in its unfolding as it was exciting.

More shots were fired. The pace stepped up in speed and desperation. The circles of the boats became tighter, more constricted, and then came the long dash toward the cypress trees once more and the swerve toward the half-submerged sinker that was to be the launch ramp.

Like a shaft at the head of a giant arrow, the skiff sped straight and true in flat-out flight. Behind Julie, someone cursed in awed admiration. The Chapman crane creaked as the master camera swung to follow the dazzling passage through the trees. Julie's heart pounded with resounding strokes. Her lips parted, but no sound came.

Faster the skiff went and faster still, tearing down upon the great sinker that lay shining darkly with the opalescent slime of decay and the wet wash of decades of boat wakes and inland tides. Throttle wide open, motor straining, water churning, Rey held the wheel rock steady.

The aluminum skiff hit the sinker with a hard metallic jolt that had the sound of tornado-whipped tin. It skimmed upward, soaring, airborne with motor revving in a sudden whine and propeller spinning. In a rough yet powerful parabola, it cleared the nest of cypress knees beyond and descended with a slithering splash in open water. It fishtailed as Rey throttled it forward, driving through its own splattering rainfall of thrown-up spray to sprint clean and free of pursuit upriver toward the further reaches of the waterway.

There was silence while the cameras filmed the abrupt throttling down of the pursuing speedboat as it swung away from the sinker, and also the frustrated and enraged reactions of the two actors playing the goons in pursuit. Then cheers broke out, yells and shouts and whistles of approbation that rang over the water as Rey slowed the skiff and turned it in a neat circle, then brought it at little more than an idle back toward the shooting platform.

Julie applauded with the rest. Yet as she watched Rey stand up in the idling boat, pull off the wig he wore, and shake his head to loosen his own hair, watched him play to the crowd in the boats near the shooting platform and to those upon it with a grin and wave, she was aware of a growing rage.

She was enraged at the way Rey had risked his life, enraged at the way he had worked with Stan on the stunt without consulting her, enraged at the disarmingly casual, even diffident, smiles he gave to the coterie of females who had gathered to watch him. She was enraged at the way he had made it look so easy when she had been so afraid.

Most of all, she was enraged because of the fear he had made her feel.

Chapter 9

Julie closed down the location for Sunday. Many directors worked straight through the weekends, as had she on occasion, but it had been a long, hard week for them all, with several late nights on the swimming scene, and they needed the time to rest and recuperate. Besides that, Aunt Tine had been hinting that Julie should go to Mass with her, and Julie hated to disappoint her.

The three of them, with Rey, went to the midmorning service, then came home to lunch on gumbo and potato salad with French bread warm from the bakery. Afterward, Aunt Tine went to lie down for a nap, leaving Julie and Rey to clean up the kitchen. She was gone only a few seconds before they heard the pad of the house shoes she had changed into from her Sunday heels.

"I forgot to tell you, Julie," she said as she popped her head in at the door again. "You are invited to a wedding this Friday night; my great-niece, Rey's cousin, the daughter of my husband's oldest sister's third child, is getting married at St. Joseph's. It should be a big deal, yes; she's caught herself a doctor and her mother means to show the new in-laws she's as good as they are."

Julie grinned at the older woman's droll tone. "Sounds like something not to be missed."

"For true. There will be a jambalaya and the wine will flow from a fountain—who could ask for more? Then there will be the money dance, where all the men pin money to the girl's dress and veil. Who knows," the old lady finished with a wink, "you might even get some idea for having a Cajun wedding in your movie, 'stead of that crazy mix-up mess like in that other one. That would show them."

Julie laughed and agreed, though she thought there was little chance. When Aunt Tine had gone away again, she wiped the last of the cabinet tops and rinsed out her dishcloth while Rey took the leftover scraps of food out to feed to the chickens and peacocks. Julie glanced around the kitchen a final time to be sure everything was done, then walked out into the dining room.

Rey, coming back into the house from outside, let the screen door slam behind him. He said, "I've been thinking about the ending of the stunt scene we did yesterday."

She paused warily. "Yes?"

"According to the script, after Jean-Pierre jumps the cypress knees and loses his pursuers, he disappears down a bayou. That last part, his disappearance, hasn't been filmed yet. Am I right?"

Julie rubbed with two fingers at the frown between her brows. "Actually, it has, in part. We filmed it with Vance the day of the accident. But it only shows Jean-Pierre swerving into the bayou's mouth and cutting his engine, then waiting while the other guys chasing him go on past. After what you said about the bubbles of his wake showing his trail, I'm not sure it works."

"I know a great place for the trick with the two bayous, if you'd like to see it."

"Today?" she asked. Julie had visions of an afternoon nap to make up for her long night hours spent working.

"It won't take long. I can show you from the air, if you like, instead of by boat."

"You don't have to do that; it's too much trouble." Julie had almost forgotten that he was supposed to have his own plane.

"No trouble. I need to check out the plane and take it up anyway. It's been too long since I had it in the air."

"But you have to drive to New Orleans to do it, don't you?"

"It's only forty-five minutes away, maybe less since it's Sunday."

Duty was a hard thing to fight, especially when the deadline for ending the movie was looming closer each day. "If I go with you," she said, "that doesn't mean that I will agree with your choice of location."

"I know that," he answered, his face grave though his eyes were not. "It's just a suggestion."

Julie was sure that it would be a good one. Rey seemed to have an instinct for what she wanted in the way of screen images. More than likely, she would agree to it. She thought about Stan's claim that she was letting Rey run the movie, thought about what he and the others on the set might say if they discovered Rey had influenced her decision over this particular scene. She could face them down, of course. But with any luck they wouldn't find out about it.

"Can you wait while I change?" she said.

She had on what she had worn to church, a simple shirtwaist dress of cream silk with a wide taupe belt. Since Rey was still in his dress slacks and a pale blue dress shirt with the sleeves rolled to the elbows and the neck open, she half expected him to say that he would put on something more casual, too.

"Don't bother," he said instead. "You never can tell what we may decide to do afterward."

"I can. I'm coming back here and taking a nap!"

"It's a waste of fine weather, but whatever you want."

It really was a beautiful afternoon. The mellow Indian summer continued with days warm enough to be certain you were in the south, yet cool enough to be comfortable. The humidity, which could at times hover in the nineties for days, was a fairly reasonable fifty percent. The leaves fell gently from the trees, unhurried by wind. They lay in a light sprinkling on the road, blowing up in sudden brown and gold flurries with the passing of the Cherokee. There was little red or orange color among them; except for sumac and poison ivy and an occasional sweet gum, the autumn colors in this subtropical clime were subdued. Fall was no last bright hurrah before the deep sleep of winter here as it was in the north, but rather the gradual somnolence before a brief winter's nap.

She had naps on the brain, Julie thought wryly, and struggled through a few desultory remarks to try to keep herself awake.

The plane, a Cessna 310, was ready and waiting; Rey had called ahead to notify the mechanics at the hangar that he was coming. Still, they sat on the ground with the sun glaring through the windshield, raising the inside temperature approximately ten degrees per minute, while Rey went through an interminable checklist. At last he put aside his clipboard and increased the speed of the engines to a nice powerful roar. They began to taxi out onto the runway, mingling in alarming proximity with the huge planes of the airlines that made the Cessna seem like a toy. They threaded through the traffic with panache, however, and a short time later they were airborne.

They banked and turned, back over Lake Pontchartrain and the long causeway that bisected it, back over the Bonne Carré Spillway and the swamp that led up to the edge of the airport at the back door of New Orleans. Julie saw I-10 stretched out below, the cars creeping insectlike along it. Moments later, they were skimming lower, making a wide circle over the looping twists and turns of the Mississippi River and the small towns, chemical plants, and old plantation houses strung along it like charms on a bracelet. They flew over the Sunshine Bridge, that monument to former governor Jimmie Davis and to Louisiana's modern glory days when it seemed that oil money could do anything, even turn a swamp into gold.

The movie location went by so fast Julie wasn't sure she had seen it. Then they were following the twists and turns of Blind River, dropping low enough to scan the camps and houseboats that lined its upper coils and the canals and bayous that ran into it. They stayed with it, chasing their own shadow over the surrounding swampland, flushing great white swamp birds from the tall cypress trees and into flapping, silver-winged races. Reaching the river's end, they zoomed out over tree-lined Lake Maurepas, joining the flights of gulls, then turned back, squinting, into the sun.

Julie was glad she had come. The freewheeling flight was exhilarating. Watching the land below zipping past under the plane, she was able to form a much clearer picture of the swamp and how the portion of it she was shooting lay in relation to the Mississippi and the two big lakes. The plane's air system worked well in the air, so the only discomfort was the sun's brightness as it glinted on the plane's nose and windshield. The cockpit's interior smelled faintly of leather and oil and the warm spice and lime of Rey's after-shave. He had insisted that she sit in the co-pilot's seat though there were others available in the cabin behind them. The view was better, he said, and no doubt he was right.

Julie had no particular fear of flying, but her experience had been mainly with commercial airlines and the occasional corporate jet. She had felt a qualm or two about going up with Rey, since owning a plane did not automatically make a man a good pilot. She need not have worried. He handled the plane with the same competence that he had shown with a boat. His hands on the controls were steady, his attention concentrated, yet relaxed. He seemed to have almost forgotten that Julie was there as he leaned to gaze out the window at the swamp below.

"It looks like some ancient Eden from up here," Julie said. "One that stretches forever, even past the horizon."

"It's one of the last intact ecosystems in the country. Otters still breed in the wild down there and otters can't take pollution. It's part of one of the great migratory-bird flyways; ducks and geese congregate in the fall and winter in the millions. But it's changing, has been changing by slow degrees for decades. There's chemical pollution now, both from industrial sources and from farming runoff, plus the developers encroach a little more every month, draining a few hundred acres here, a few hundred there. The wetlands are disappearing, drying up."

"Surely somebody is doing something about it?"

"They are trying, the conservation groups, civic organizations, and many of the state and local senators and representatives. It's an uphill fight."

"It might be interesting to give our Jean-Pierre a few lines about it on-screen. It seems like an issue that would concern him."

The smile he turned on her was bright with surprise and something more that made his gaze linger on her face. "That would be great, it really would." He turned away with every appearance of reluctance. An instant later, he said, "There, that's the place I was talking about."

By the time he had finished speaking, they were flashing over the spot, and Julie had to turn her head quickly to keep it in view. The Blind River was more narrow at that point, more closed in with rotted logs and dark green palmetto. The two bayous lay within a few hundred feet of each other, the mouth of one nearly choked with debris. It would be fairly easy for a man with enough of a lead to run his boat into one in a flurry of foam, then quietly paddle out and wend his way into the other.

"The larger bayou is a dead end," she pointed out.

"So it will appear that your swamp hero vanished into thin air."

"Shades of a B western."

He glanced at her with a grin. "Think it's too corny?"

"Not," she said slowly, "if about the time the bad guys are deciding Jean-Pierre has turned into a ghost he cranks up his motor and speeds away. They hear him, but don't know where he is or how he escaped them."

"They curse him, which with the other assorted violence and nudity, will give you the requisite PG rating instead of the G that is box-office death or the X that you don't want."

"I didn't make the system," she said defensively.

"I didn't say you did. Summer was telling me more about it yesterday, calling G-rated movies baby pictures. I was more or less checking for accuracy."

"She has a fair grasp on the subject, if that's what you mean."

"She's a smart kid. There isn't much she misses."

Julie made no reply, her attention caught by a boat moving along the waterway just below them. White and sleek, it was running at high speed, almost as if it was racing them. There was only one person on board, the driver, who was dressed from head to toe in white so that he was no more than a blur in the brilliance of the afternoon. Then the plane overtook the boat, surging ahead, leaving it behind.

"Wasn't that the cabin cruiser from the location?" Julie asked as she craned her neck backward to see.

"Was it?"

"I thought I saw the camera mount. But I don't know why anyone would have it out on the water."

"Probably just joyriding."

"It's supposed to be under lock and key unless it's being used for filming, since it's part of the lease agreement."

"We can take another look," Rey said, and banked for a turn.

They dropped lower as they came back around, skimming the treetops. Rey did not make a complete turn to follow the river, but rather came at it from a right angle to cut across the water. They saw the boat ahead of them. It was nearing a canal at the juncture in which lay a number of camps with boat docks reaching out into the water from them. As the plane neared, the boat swerved toward a dock with a boat house attached. Its forward motion dropped off sharply, as if the engine had been cut to idling speed. Seconds before the plane passed over, the boat slid under the roof of the boat house, as if it had reached its home dock.

"My mistake," Julie said with a shake of her head as they flitted past. "Sorry."

"No problem," Rey answered, and eased the plane's nose up again, regaining altitude.

The maneuver they had made set off a jangling reminder in Julie's mind. After a moment, she said, "You remember the night we met, and the plane that came over just before we—ran into each other?"

He gave a brief nod. "What about it?"

"I understand planes like that sometimes drop drugs into the swamp to be picked up by boats. Since you were once with the DEA, I thought I might—check the accuracy."

"It happens," he agreed. "A few years back, they also landed a stripped-down four-engine DC-4 on a road not far from here, near Grand Point, one that was blocked off, under construction. They were unloading some eight or nine tons of marijuana and a half-million Quaaludes into trucks when they were interrupted by police acting on a tip from a Grand Point resident. Three of the men were chased down through half the backyards in the area."

"Must have been exciting."

"People still talk about it. But I'd say most of the stuff is brought in by boat these days. It comes up through the barrier islands and bays along the coast, just as they used to bring in liquor during Prohibition or pirated goods during the days of Lafitte."

"Whoever did it would have to know the coast and the waterways well."

"Or hire themselves somebody who did," he agreed, and turned his head to give her a level look.

She had not been suggesting anything—or had she? Holding his gaze with an effort, she said, "Is there really that much traffic, compared, say, to Florida?"

"It gets bigger every month. The more the government's drug task forces concentrate on places like New York and Miami, Houston and L.A., the worse it gets. Drug dealers are guerrilla fighters. They don't stand and trade fire; they fade away and make another beachhead somewhere else, in this case the bayou country. Another factor is that Louisiana is centrally located. It makes a good crossroad for traffic headed to points both east and west."

There was something forbidding about his face as he spoke. On impulse, Julie said, "Do you ever regret it, leaving the agency, I mean?"

He shifted a shoulder under the taut material of his shirt. "By the time I left, I was a little tired of the idea that throwing men and money into a war on drugs was going to defeat the problem. Before we conquer drugs, we're going to have to take away addiction as a crutch or an escape. People who abuse drugs or any other substance, even food, are going to have to accept responsibility for what they are doing to themselves. As another swamp dweller put it, 'We have met the enemy, and it is us.' I'm not sure the quote is completely accurate, but Pogo had the right idea."

"Not a very sympathetic attitude."

"I didn't mean to offend your liberal California sensibilities," he said, his voice even. "But there has been sympathy in plenty for drug users for twenty years and more. The results can be seen on the news practically any evening."

"What's your solution? Throwing all the addicts in jail?"

"Forcible detoxification for one to five years for anyone arrested in connection with a drug-related crime or who gives birth to a drug-addicted baby. Public education to such a saturation point—and depicting addiction in such raw realism—that any child or adult exposed to it would as soon pick up a knife and stab themselves as become a user. Stop the demand and you stop the supply, and the suppliers."

"Do you honestly think it would work?" She was as curious about his ideas, his attitudes, as about his ideas on drug trafficking.

"Who knows? It has to work as well as stopping maybe one kilo of coke in every thousand, one ton of marijuana out of every hundred that comes ashore."

She made no answer, though she wondered if many of the men who worked with the DEA felt as Rey did. And how they were able to do the jobs they were assigned if they had such doubts.

They were flying west again, and the sun in her eyes made her close them for long moments before the plane began to circle back again. The droning of the engines and the steady movement were relaxing, and she stifled a sudden yawn.

"Listen," Rey said with quiet humor, "why don't you go back and take one of the seats that recline? You can catch that nap while I check out a rattle or two and put in some flying time."

"Rattle?" she asked with a shading of doubt.

"Nothing major and nothing for you to worry about, though I'd like a few minutes to trace it down. I promise to let you know well ahead of time if we have to bail out."

"Thanks a bunch, but couldn't the airport mechanics take care of it."

"They could, but since it's my neck on the line, not to mention other parts of my anatomy, I prefer to do it myself."

"I do see your point," she said on a laugh, and unfastened her seat belt in order to move back into the cabin.

It occurred to her as she lay back, listening to the soft hissing of the air system and drifting on the edge of sleep, that it was odd how easily she had accepted Rey's word that nothing was wrong. She was not usually so trusting. It was also strange that she had not taken offense at his gibe about her liberal California sensibilities. It may have been that she was too sleepy for indignation, or else that she had not wanted to spoil the afternoon with useless animosity. She had no cut-and-dried position on drug use anyway. It was her personal belief that it was stupid to put anything so potentially lethal into the only body you were ever going to have, but she felt no righteous wrath at what anyone else might choose to do. She was aware that there was a certain amount of drug use among the cast and crew on her movie; the evidence would have been hard to miss. She had no right, felt no need, to interfere unless it affected job performance.

Job performance. Was it possible that someone had not done their job on the day Paul Lislet had died? The idea was not a comfortable one. She shied away from it in her mind.

She opened her eyes, her gaze moving to the cockpit beyond the small open doorway with its swaying curtain pulled to one side. Rey was a solid figure at the controls, his hands firm, his attention close on the bank of switches and dials and digital indicators. His profile against the light was strong, well molded, trustworthy. Surely trustworthy. She closed her eyes again. She really was tired. It wouldn't be hard to drift off.

Somewhere in the haze of a dream, she felt the plane bank into a turn, heard the crackle of a voice on a radio and the steady, even tone of Rey's reply. She turned her head on the headrest, frowning slightly in her sleep, but did not waken.

A jolt roused her. She recognized it a moment later as turbulence; it had that soft compression. Her neck was stiff, and she felt sluggish and disoriented. She could not have been asleep as long as it seemed, yet the light was dim, as if someone had closed all the side windows of the cabin. They had not; they were open. She leaned to look out.

Far below, there was a broken layer of puffy clouds. Beneath it, water sparkled and shone, an undulating edge of aqua blue against beige, the colors fast turning gray in the twilight. It was a beach.

She sat up so fast the seat belt snapped taut across her abdomen, making her gasp. As she opened it with a sharp click she saw Rey, shadowy in the lights from the instrument panel, turn his head to glance over his shoulder. She sprang to her feet, taking the two swift steps into the cockpit.

"What," she asked in carefully controlled tones as she dropped into the seat beside him, "is going on?"

"You'd better see to your seat belt. It may get bumpy when we turn out over the ocean." His gaze rested on her face, as if to assess her mood, though his own expression gave nothing away.

"The ocean!" she exclaimed as she jerked her belt around her. "If this is some kind of joke, I warn you it isn't funny."

"The coast of Florida. If I told you it was a mechanical problem, would you go all hysterical on me?"

Her movements stilled. "Is it?"

"As a matter of fact," he said, glancing at the gauges in front of him, then looking back at her once more, "it isn't."

"Precisely what kind of problem is it?"

"Physical. I was hungry for lobster."

She looked at him for long seconds before she said with exactness, "You have two minutes to tell me where we are and where we are going before I become violent."

"Only violent? I was afraid you would be murderous."

"The thought has appeal, but I'm not also suicidal."

He rewarded that piece of logic with a wry smile and a single word.

"Nassau," he said.

"Nassau. As in Nassau in the Bahamas?"

"Unless they've moved it."

"You're going there without asking me or giving me so much as a hint?"

"Would you have come with me?"

She ignored the question. "All that stuff about rattles and airtime was so much hot air, wasn't it?"

The look in his dark eyes was impenetrable.

"And I suppose you could have shown me those two bayous in half the time, and much better, in your air boat?"

"The view would have been different, not necessarily better."

She sat back in the seat, crossing her arms over her chest as she gazed straight ahead. "Wonderful. I hope you enjoy eating your lobster, by yourself."

"You don't like lobster?" The question was tentative.

She loved it, but she wasn't going to admit it. She only looked at him without answering.

"I should point out, before you say something you'll regret," he told her in tones of extreme reasonableness, "that it may be late, very late, before we get home. You just might get hungry."

She opened her lips, then shut them again. She was already hungry. "Why did you do this?" she inquired, trying to keep her voice calm, though it became more agitated with every phrase. "There may be some women who would be thrilled to be kidnapped and carried away to some exotic place for the evening, but I'm not one of them. I can't imagine why you ever expected I would be. I thought I had made it clear that I despise being forced into anything against my will, that I hate these kind of cowboy tactics, as if I have to be roped into doing something because I don't really know what I want or what's good for me."

"But you do know?" he said, the pitch of his voice low yet edged with roughness. "You know exactly what you want and what's best for you, and this isn't it. It must be nice to always be so certain. And just think—you haven't even sampled the lobster."

She turned her head to stare at him as she registered the emphasis of his last words. The heat of a flush rose slowly to her cheekbones in the semidarkness as she wondered if he could possibly mean what she thought, mean that she had been sure she didn't want him. He gazed back at her, his eyes as opaque and shining as Cajun coffee. For an instant they also appeared just as hot, then the radio crackled and began to issue a staccato stream of questions and instructions. He turned from her with his lashes lowered to shutter his expression. His voice was quiet, authoritative as he made his answers.

They did not speak again until they were on the ground at the Providence Island airport.

Passport control was a formality quickly settled with a minimum of identification. The rental car Rey had arranged for by radio was waiting. In less than an hour, they had made the drive along the coast road past sighing, moon-sparkled waves and whispering casuarina trees, and were sitting at an outdoor restaurant with lobsters steaming gently in front of them.

The air was soft and warm, and scented with salt and flowers and the smell of fried conch made sharper by a hint of drying fishing nets. The offshore wind fluttered the fat citron candle in its hurricane globe in the center of their table, rustled the palm thatch of the small shelter above their heads, and swayed the strings of fairy lights in the potted shrubs set about the restaurant perimeter. Far out on the horizon, the sea shifted under the moon like the back of some shiny-scaled monster, while nearer at hand yachts with furled sails, schooners waiting for guests on shore leave, and fishing boats in various stages of dilapidation rocked in peculiar synchronization with the beat of reggae music from a boom box on the beach.

Rey had offered to take Julie to Graycliffs, a restaurant in an old Georgian Colonial inn, the only five-star restaurant in the Bahamas. She had declined. If she was going to eat dinner on an island, she wanted it to feel like an island, wanted to smell the sea and feel its breeze in her face.

The lobster was sweet and delicately flavored, the lemon butter fresh and hot, the bread thick and crusty and sprinkled with sesame seeds for a nice nutty flavor. The jug of Chablis that was the best the restaurant had to offer had a peach-pear scent and slight astringency that went well with the food.

It was difficult to remain angry with someone while watching them eat a whole lobster. Stiffness and fastidious gestures were as ridiculous as would have been a delicate nouvelle cuisine–type garnish of edible flowers and decorative grass. It was heavy, messy work, with claw crackers and picks and the quick flick of a napkin to catch butter drips. It was impossible not to exchange murmurs of enjoyment and triumph and muttered comments on difficulties.

A replete stomach also engendered feelings of charity, Julie discovered. She still resented the way she had been tricked, but was considerably less militant about it. In any case, it was impossible to remain suitably furious with a man who had such a capacity for savoring the moment. Rey Tabary made no attempt to hide his pleasure in the meal, the company, or the place. He seemed not to mind her mood or the effort it had taken to reach the island and the restaurant. He was attentive to her needs of the given moment, supplying more wine, help with an uncooperative lobster claw, or a lemon slice to rub on her fingers to remove the seafood smell, each as required. He was careful not to overstep the boundary between good manners and familiarity, careful to maintain a mental distance of his own, yet his concentration upon her was total.

It was also, in its way, unnerving.

They drank their coffee while watching the water, and also the tourists in various stages of dress and undress, intoxication and sobriety, joviality and moroseness, who came and went along the beach in front of them. Afterward, they joined the parade, looking into shop windows, bargaining for Julie a straw hat with one of the few straw market women who still had wares for sale this late in the day. When they had made their way back to where the car was parked, they got in and headed toward the airport.

They were well out of town when Rey slowed the car and turned into a parking area that lay on a headland overlooking the ocean. He sat for a moment with his hands on the steering wheel, then opened the door and got out.

"Let's walk on the beach," he said, "just for a little while before we start back."

There was nothing in his voice except polite suggestion, still Julie was reluctant to step out of the car. The combination of wine and sea and moonlit beach was a potent one, and no one was more of aware of it than she, who had spent a great number of nights watching the waves come rolling shoreward. There was no deep surf here; the waves were broken by a coral reef that tamed them into lapping calm. Still, Julie knew her susceptibility.

She was susceptible to Rey, too. He wasn't her type, they had no shared interests or aspirations, no common background, the places they lived and their ways of thinking were miles apart, yet there it was.

He was walking away. She could sit in the car like a surly child, feeling abandoned, or she could join him on a slow prowl along the sea-wet sand with the wind blowing in her hair and the ocean's murmur sounding in her ears. There was really no choice.

He was waiting for her at the top of the headland. He gave her his hand down the steep path that led over limestone boulders and under clattering sea-grape trees before it shelved onto the sand. Releasing her, he walked over the powdered coral to the water's edge, where he stood looking out to sea with the waves making wet lace frills around his feet.

The beach was a wide crescent stretching away on both sides into the darkness. Behind them rose the headland, cutting off view of the road above and the parking area. The air was moist with blown spume from where the ocean foamed around the coral reef several hundred yards out. The surface of the ocean was like dark blue satin sewn with silver spangles. The moon was a pewter dish muffled in a dirty polishing cloth of cloud. Far out in the darkness was the square shape of a container freighter, blinking with slow diligence, trailing a smudge of black diesel smoke against the night sky as it headed toward the edge of the world.

Rey turned his head to look down at Julie as she advanced over the sand to pause at his side. When she began to move down the beach, he swung around to keep step, matching his stride to hers.

The wind lifted and swirled Julie's light silk skirt, blowing it about his long legs. It clung to the material of his dress slacks, but he made no attempt to move away. He pushed his hands deep into his pockets, and his words as he spoke matched his steady, even pace.

"I never meant to treat you as if you didn't know your own mind. I only thought—it seemed to me that you needed to get away from everything for a little while. You've been working practically night and day—you were strung out, not getting enough sleep, had dark circles under your eyes. It seemed likely that you would find a thousand reasons not to come with me if I asked you, so I didn't ask."

"For my own good."

"And mine. I had had enough of things, too."

"Did you expect me to be happy about it, especially after our agreement the other night?"

"I don't remember agreeing to anything."

"Oh, please. At least you'll admit you didn't disagree."

"Maybe I had second thoughts. Anyway, what I expected tonight was that you would recognize a fait accompli and give in gracefully."

"Or maybe gratefully."

"My dreams weren't that wild."

The dry sound of his voice rasped on her nerves. The power of the man to disconcert her was maddening. She considered herself not unskilled at the sexual repartee that passed for flirtation in L.A. Certainly, it was not often that she was at a loss. The reason might be that in California, she and her partners were seldom emotionally involved; it was all an exercise in mental quickness and unblushing sangfroid. This was different. The levels and degrees of feeling between Rey Tabary and herself shifted as constantly as the sea, and with less explanation.

On the road high above them a car passed, its headlights sweeping over the beach. Another followed more slowly, almost at a crawl. Julie waited until the sound of both cars had faded before she spoke.

"I can't speak for your dreams, but I have to tell you that your speculations about my reasons for breaking off our relationship were certainly wild."

"What do you know about my speculations?" The question was more than curious.

"I can only judge from what you said."

"And that was?"

She wished she had kept her mouth shut. She wasn't sure what impulse had made her bring up the subject anyway, unless it was in return for his determination to remove any misconceptions she might have about his motives. However, she refused to back down now.

"You seem to think I was dissatisfied with the sample of your lovemaking. That wasn't it at all; I told you my reasons as plainly as I was able. And don't, please, tell me that I've now left myself wide open for some unholy comment because I know it, and if you take advantage of it, I refuse to be—"

"I wouldn't dare," he said in soft interruption. "The reply might be dangerous to my sanity."

She was lost in that instant, while she stood with her hair blowing around her face, with her lips parted and the irritation of anger dying slowly from her eyes. The quicksilver movement of his mind in meeting hers, in taking her meaning, accepting it and stretching a pace beyond was as seductive as the wind and the sea, the night, and their isolation. It touched some deep inner emptiness, filling it, combining with his humor, his concern, and his firm removal of the barriers to understanding that lay between them to create a resonance that rose inside her like a shout.

She could love him. It was unwise, improbable, but she knew it was possible. It could never work out, but the attraction was there. It hurt to admit it, but she was susceptible, ripe for his love. Another time, if things had been different, she could have loved him.

"Oh, Rey," she whispered, and it had the sound of loss.

One moment they were gazing at each other, stunned by the reflections the moonlight found in their eyes, the next they were moving together in a smooth and perfect blending.

His kiss tasted of salt from the windblown spray, but was also sweetly beguiling, tender in its firm command. Julie met and matched his ardor, twining her tongue with his, giving him her own salt sweetness. She traced the faintly ridged edges of his lips and the polished sharpness of his teeth, and explored the warm resilience of his inner mouth. She pressed her breasts against his chest as if to imprint the memory of his body upon hers, and felt his arms tighten around her, gathering her closer still.

The steady surge of the waves was in her ears, a counterpoint to the thudding of her heart. The wind that touched her heated skin had the feel of a caress, one that fueled her desire. The open sky above granted unlimited freedom, timeless benediction. The night was a soft covering, one that shimmered with the pale light of the half-hidden moon.

There was a dark wedge of shadow in the lee of the headland. They moved toward it of one accord. He slipped the buttons of her dress free of their holes, while she performed the same service for him on his shirt. The cream silk of her shirtwaist slithered to the sand, spreading in small billows. They knelt upon it, their mouths clinging, while she slid the shirt down the rigid musculature of his back, pinning his elbows until she could draw the sleeves from his arms. His mouth moved gently upon hers as he waited without impatience to regain the use of his hands.

He cupped her breasts then, flicking the nipples under their thin covering of silk and lace with his thumbs before sliding his fingers along her rib cage to the back to unfasten the bra hook. He bent his head to taste the smooth, blue-veined globes he had uncovered, inhaling the warm female scent of her, closing his eyes so she felt the tickling sweep of his lashes against her skin.

There was silk and sand against their naked flesh as, stripping away their remaining clothing, they eased down upon the ground. The powdered coral shifted under them as they moved together, touching, holding, tasting in a slow and rapturous quest for mutual delight, mutual joy.

They found more than they sought. It was a ravishment of the senses, a gathering of glory that began in the mind and spread to the heart. Joined indissolubly, vulnerable in their tenderness, they moved in a union of pounding power and rare grace, of breathless fervor and a delicate passion made poignant by terror. Afraid to feel, they were caught in a fiery, consuming enchantment of feeling. It took them unaware and made them one, bound them in a brilliant, bursting transfiguration forever encapsulated in a memory of sand and moonlit sea.

Later, when they had put their clothes back on and climbed to the headland, they discovered that the battery of their rental car had been stolen, taken while they lay oblivious down below. They looked at each other and burst out laughing. They shared the joke with faint grins while they waited for a jitney to take them to the airport, while they saw that the rental-car company was informed as to where someone could pick up their car, and later, on the long flight home.

Their humor vanished when they reached Aunt Tine's house. A man rose from a rocking chair on the gallery as they climbed out of the Cherokee. He moved to the steps to watch them walk toward him, his gaze austere as he surveyed their wrinkled clothing, the straw hat Julie carried, and the way Rey walked with a protective arm about her waist. The man was slender, with gray-brown hair and an air of refinement. His voice held the cultured twang of Boston as he spoke, though its undertone was incisive, as slicing as fine English steel.

"Good evening, Julie," he said, "or rather good morning; you'll forgive my confusion since I've been waiting for you for some time. I would ask where you've been, but the question seems indiscreet, not to say futile, given the circumstances."

It was Allen.

Chapter 10

"I apologize for my ill humor earlier this morning," Allen said as he turned from the window of Ofelia's trailer office that the assistant director had given up temporarily for his use. "My excuse is that I was tired and concerned. If I said anything that upset you, I want you to know that I sincerely regret it."

Julie had barely entered before Allen began to speak, as if he had been rehearsing his lines while he waited for her to answer his summons this morning. She stared at the man who was her fiancé, the producer of her movies. She was as disconcerted by this about-face and by the weariness she heard in his voice as she was by the formal nature of the interview. Allen's manner was absurdly stilted considering their past relationship. Or maybe it wasn't, maybe it only seemed that way, she thought, because she had grown used to Rey's informality, his deliberate obliteration of the distance that people usually kept between themselves and others. She could not imagine him permitting so much physical space to separate them if the two of them, like Allen and herself, had been apart for weeks, nor could she feature him speaking to her in that excessively polite tone as if she were no more than a business associate. Of course, Allen had never been what might be called a casual man. Having something of a mania for things British, he patterned his behavior both public and private after that of a civilized English gentleman. He was, accordingly, correct, fair and pleasant, but reserved. She had never thought that strange before; apparently her ideas of personal closeness in both territory and relationships had undergone a change.

Never had Allen looked more the aristocrat as he stood there in his impeccable gray trousers and Turnbull and Asser shirt worn with a burgundy and gray ascot, with his silver-touched sandy-brown hair brushed carefully back at the temples and his face bronzed by the sun's reflection off countless tennis courts. She wondered where he had found the china cup for the Earl Grey tea that steamed on the desk, and who had laid out the onyx desk set and plugged in the streamlined black telephone that he preferred. Perhaps it had been Ofelia. The assistant director mocked Allen's whims but seemed to take perverse pleasure in satisfying them to the last detail.

Finally she said in quiet tones, "You're very generous."

"Not at all. I had no right to rant at you in that way. I offer as excuse the fact that no one seemed to know exactly where you were, only that you had, presumably, gone off somewhere with Tabary. While I will grant that his aunt tried to be helpful, she was maddeningly vague about what you could be doing or how long you might be absent. I had been envisioning all manner of disasters, and had decided to contact the police if you weren't back by daylight."

"I would have left word if I had known you would be there to be concerned—and if I had known where I would be. The flight to Nassau was an impulse, definitely not something planned."

Julie had given her fiancé the briefest of explanations the night before. She had not told him then, any more than she had just now, that she had been kidnapped. Somehow that piece of information seemed likely to call for a more detailed description of the outing than she was willing to undertake. There had been no repercussions over the news beyond Allen's first bitter remarks. Rey had stepped in at that moment, suggesting that morning would be a better time for this dramatic reunion, when Julie was rested and Allen's temper had had time to cool. Rey had then reinforced the recommendation by taking Julie's arm and guiding her past Allen to the outside door to her room. Julie had walked inside and closed the door with relief. A moment later, she had heard the voices of the two men in a curt exchange followed by the sound of Allen's footsteps retreating down the steps and his car driving way. She had thought that Rey might return to talk about Allen's sudden appearance, or at least to say good night. He had not, nor had Julie seen any sign of him this morning.

"I would really rather not talk about your outing with Tabary, if you don't mind." Allen turned to face her as he spoke, a faint smile curving his mouth, clashing with the distress in his gray eyes. "I've had time to think about it, and about my reactions, and I realize I'm probably as much to blame as you. I've neglected you, left you here to do this job by yourself. I've taken it for granted that you were happy in our arrangement."

"I have been," Julie said, her voice defensive. She had not wanted to hurt him, and the knowledge that she had was heavy inside her.

"Possibly. Still, we did agree in the beginning that each of us would have the right to have other friends, other relationships. I suppose that since the question had never come up again for you, I thought it never would."

"I didn't intend to become involved with Rey. It just—happened that way."

"It usually does. I won't pretend that I don't understand or that I've never been involved with someone else during our time together, because it would be untrue—and I think you know it. I've always disdained the double standard that allows men to become irate when the shoe is on the other foot, but now I find that instinct hard to overcome. Still, I'm trying."

His wry self-disparagement was moving in a man who normally had so much dignity. Julie, feeling the slow rise of old affection, stepped to place her fingers on his arm. "That makes you an unusual man."

"I doubt I qualify for sainthood yet. But I wanted to make things right between us. I wanted you to know that I won't let this make a difference, not if I can help it. When we are back in L.A., everything will be the same again. I don't want to lose you."

There was something in what he was saying, or perhaps the way he said it, that troubled her, though she couldn't quite put her finger on it. Regardless, the warm attachment of years was strong, and so was the habit of reassurance. "I tried to break it off with Rey before—I can see as well as anyone how hard it would be to maintain a relationship when my interests and his are so far apart. More than that, he has not mentioned the future. It seems . . . unlikely that whatever is between us will be a factor once the movie is finished."

"That is, of course, a relief to hear. But in the meantime?" The words were gentle.

"I don't know," she told him, her green gaze earnest yet somber with the weight of the depression inside her. "I may need a little time to adjust. But you needn't worry about being embarrassed while you're here. I'm not the kind of woman who is comfortable doing a balancing act between two different men."

"There was no need for you to tell me that," he said with a shading of reproof.

"Maybe I needed to say it," she answered with a soft sigh. "Anyway, I'm sorry if you were upset. I didn't mean it to happen."

He watched her for a long moment before he moved to seat himself behind the desk. "No, you didn't know I would be arriving so soon, did you. There was a reason why I came, something I thought I should tell you in person, before the rumors had a chance to reach you."

There was such a grave look on his face that Julie felt a tremor of doubt. She stepped to one of the chairs facing his desk and sank into it. "Rumors?"

"I have taken a step that I have been considering for some time, from the moment work began on this project, actually. Please don't think the decision was hasty or made without a thorough analysis of all aspects of the problem—or without concern for your feelings in the matter. You know that I have every respect for your talent and ability. I have always been proud of your accomplishments, and more than satisfied with the monetary returns from the projects we have undertaken together. You are a director of exceptional vision and sensitivity, and your feel for story and what will move an audience is phenomenal."

"Allen," she said tightly, "it's beginning to snow in here. Could you cut the buildup and tell me what you've done?"

"It's important to me that you understand my position. I have a responsibility to my backers to see that *Swamp Kingdom* retains its image as a quality product. At the same time, it must be completed at a figure near enough to the projected cost to guarantee a reasonable profit."

"I thought that was my responsibility."

"You certainly share it," he agreed with a direct look before he went quickly on. "As the director, and also the initiator of this project, I'm sure you also share the concern of all of us that this movie be well received by the public, in a financial sense as well as in a critical one. The chances of this happening have been seriously compromised by the unfortunate death on the set and the publicity that has come from it. Sensationalism can always overcome quality."

"I'm sure that when people see the movie—"

"To wait until it's in the theaters would be to take an enormous chance. I prefer to do everything possible to ensure the desired outcome well before that time. What I propose will not only increase the chances a hundredfold, it will also give you an opportunity that many young directors would give their souls to attain. The game plan is so perfect, so natural, that I'm astonished it didn't occur to me at the beginning, or to you for that matter."

"What in heaven's name—" Julie began, then stopped abruptly as a possible explanation struck her, one so devastating that she felt the blood recede from her face. She sat back in her chair, her hands lax upon the arms. There was the timbre of her incredulity in her voice as she said, "You have hired Bull!"

"Just think what it will mean, a father-daughter directing team, a joint effort showing the best of the old and the new in L.A. The publicity will be stupendous; every talk-show host in the country will be drooling to have the two of you on. You'll be as hot a topic as Kirk and Michael Douglas, or Martin and Charlie Sheen."

"Bull and I aren't actors, Allen. Anyway, that part of it isn't important. It's the movie that matters, and you can't do this to *Swamp Kingdom*—or to me."

"The only thing I'm doing is improving the prospects for the movie and giving you the boon of this joint effort."

"Joint effort?" she exclaimed in pained disbelief. "You don't know my father. I know you've always admired him, enjoyed his work, but you've never lived with him, not as a daughter. He will take over this movie; it will become his. He may not mean to do it—he may not even realize he's doing it—but it's not in his nature to work any other way."

"Will that be so bad? I mean, you've done so much already, it surely can't matter what happens with Bull."

She stared at him, then gave a short laugh. "I can't believe you said that. Bull is an action-oriented director. He has wonderful pace and suspense and great male camaraderie and humor in his films, but there's little subtlety and no scenes that can be remotely described as delicate. By the time he gets through editing out the nuances and putting in action, what I've done will be totally unrecognizable."

"His films are, and always have been, box-office successes."

"Meaning *Swamp Kingdom* might be better for the Bull Bullard touch?"

"I didn't say that. But surely there is some compromise that can be made, some way that the two of you can work together."

"Oh, there's a way, if I do all the compromising!"

"I refuse to believe that you're that weak. In fact, I know differently."

"You don't understand. Bull is simply the way he is; fighting him is like fighting a stone wall. You either do it his way, or you leave. And I can't do it, Allen, not on this movie."

"You may have to, Julie." His voice was firm in its finality.

She sat staring at him for long moments, then leaned forward with her hands clasped in front of her and her eyes narrowed. "Why are you doing this, Allen? When did you decide? Are you sure there isn't something in it that smacks, just a tiny bit, of revenge?"

"Julie! I hope I'm not so petty."

"So do I," she said, her gaze never leaving his, "because I don't think I could stand knowing that you would deliberately strike at me through this movie. I don't think I could bear to be near someone who would do that. And I will tell you something else. I will never work with Bull on *Swamp Kingdom*. I found this story, I wrote the screenplay, it's *my* movie."

"It can be arranged that it's Bull's movie," he said with measured emphasis.

"I would prefer that to becoming a mere assistant director in the credits." She did not raise her voice or permit her gaze to waver even a fraction, though it occurred to her briefly that directors such as Spielberg, Friedkin, Robert Benton, or Oliver Stone were more likely to fire their producers than to be fired by them. The difference, of course, was the money they commanded at the box office, and the power.

"If it's credit you want—"

"You know it isn't!" she cried, slamming a fist on the arm of her chair. "I want to put the story I see in my mind on film, my story. Either I make it my way, or not at all."

His eyes widened. "Are you actually threatening to walk out and leave the project hanging?"

"You'll have the great Bull Bullard. A minute ago, that was enough."

There was a small silence while he searched her face. The sounds of the location filtered into the trailer: generator motors humming, a truck pulling into the parking lot, the mutter of voices.

Allen ran a hand over his face in a gesture of exasperation. His tone grudging, he said, "It won't be the same."

"That's what I've been trying to tell you."

"That may be, but I can't stop Bull from coming. He's already on his way."

Julie lifted an ironic brow at the length of Allen's advance notice to her. "Then I suppose you'll have to tell him to turn around and go back."

"I don't know if I can do that to him. He was so excited at the idea of working with you."

Julie took a deep breath and let it out again. "So far, Allen," she said, her voice tight, "you have tried flattery, bullying, pathos, and now blackmail. All that remains is for you to offer me more money."

"I wouldn't insult you like that."

"If you would show as much respect for my intelligence as for my integrity, then we might get somewhere."

He sat back, reaching for his tepid tea. Taking a sip, he made a face. As he put the cup down and pushed it aside he looked across at Julie with frank appeal in his eyes. "All right, maybe I should have consulted you first, maybe I should have sounded you out as to how you felt about working with your father. I didn't, and there's not much that can be done about it now. The thing is, Bull will be here tonight or tomorrow, and I can't just say to him, 'Look, the deal is off.'"

"I assume you want me to say it for you."

He went still with one hand frozen in the air in the gesture of repudiation he had been making. At last he lowered it by slow degrees.

"God, Julie, when did you get so cynical?" he said, the look on his face perplexed before he added almost as an afterthought, "or so discontented that you decided to shop around, for that matter? Where have I been that I didn't notice?"

She wished she knew the answers herself. She thought it had been coming on for a long time. Allen hadn't noticed because, until now, the two of them had seldom clashed on matters of importance, seldom been apart for long.

"Let's leave personalities out of this, if you don't mind," she answered.

"Very well," he said after an instant. "What I wanted to ask was that you talk to Bull, yes, but just to see if there isn't some way this thing can be made to work. There's bound to be a way. After all, the man's your father!"

"That's the problem." The words seemed to make no impression on Allen, who only sat waiting for her answer. "All right, I'll talk to him, though I warn you it will make no difference."

Allen sprang to his feet and rounded the desk to take her hands and draw her up in front of him. "Bless you, darling, I knew I could depend on you to see reason. Come now and give me a kiss to show there's no hard feelings; you know I hate petty squabbling. Besides, you haven't given me a proper welcome."

She tipped her head to meet his lips as much from habit as willingness. His mouth was warm and mildly pleasant, the contact brief. There ran through her mind a fleeting, guilty comparison to the kisses she had shared with Rey. Where was the heat, the tingling adhesion, the sensual elation, the sweetness? A moment later, she forced the images aside to concentrate on what Allen was saying.

"As a reward for being so cooperative, I have some news for you. What would you say if I told you that your last picture, *Dangerous Times,* has been chosen to open this year's Women in Film Festival?"

"Are you serious?" She drew away from him to see his face.

"The news came last week. You're in the running for their Crystal Award for Best Director. If you win it, that will put you up there with the other female greats like Amy Heckerling and Martha Coolidge."

"Last week? You knew about it last week, and you're only telling me now?"

"I wanted to save it as a surprise when I saw you."

"The festival is this coming weekend. You might have given me a little more warning so I could make arrangements."

"You didn't intend to go before, did you? I thought you would be so involved here that you wouldn't leave everything just to be applauded for a few minutes. It's a nice honor, yes, but it isn't the Directors Guild Awards."

She stared at him, unable to decide if the disparagement was for her and her film, or just for women's films in general; whether it was unconscious, or made for a purpose, which was to keep her from leaving the location, delaying the movie. In any case, she was too tired of arguing, too distracted by the surprises and ultimatums Allen had given her, to make an issue of it. Her voice cool, she said, "Honors are hard enough to come by in this business; I'll accept anything I can get."

"It's up to you, of course."

"Yes," she agreed with precision, then stepped away from him. "Now I had better get back to work. I still have a movie to make, at least for the moment."

"Julie—wait!"

She heard him calling after her as she walked to the door, but she did not look back.

Concentrating on the paperwork stacked in her office would be impossible, Julie knew. She needed the distraction and comfort of other people, needed the noise and bustle of the location around her. She passed directly through the reception area and out the trailer door, descending the concrete steps with a tread so quick it was almost like running away. Realizing it, she slowed, then glanced around her.

Vance was holding court under the big cypress tree near the boat pier, lying back in one of a pair of lounge chairs as he talked to a circle of women of all ages. A second look showed that he was giving an interview; there was a young woman with a wild mop of hair and horn-rim glasses scribbling on a pad as she sat in the opposite chair, and reaching out now and then to check the small tape recorder on the low table between her and the actor.

Ofelia was coming across the parking lot. She had a jaunty air this morning, caused in part by the bright orange of the cotton jump suit she wore and the enormous long earrings made of turquoise and wood and orange glass beads strung on leather strips that hung from her ears. In her hand was a sheaf of forms with Polaroid mug shots stapled to them.

"Morning," she called, "I have the possibilities for the extras needed for the town shots when you get the time to look at them. Also some just wonderful news. Summer's teacher-welfare lady has jumped ship. Seems the woman's pregnant daughter went into early labor, and the grandmother-to-be took the red-eye flight back to L.A. last night."

"Wonderful," Julie echoed in laconic agreement. She took a deep breath and let it out with a puffing sigh of frustration. The licensed teacher-welfare worker was a requirement of the California labor laws regarding child actors. As a California-based movie company, they were not supposed to employ Summer without such a person on the set to see to her education, health, safety, and moral well-being. The lady who had departed had been excellent, doing her job unobtrusively and with a minimum of disruption to the filming or difficulty in getting along with Summer.

"I can call the local school-board office, see who they can dig up for us."

"No, wait," Julie said as an idea struck her. "When Rey gets here, ask him if he thinks Donna Lislet might be interested. I know he said she's a teacher, and maybe the rest of it can be worked out with the child welfare office if she wants the job."

"Rey's here somewhere already," Ofelia said as she scribbled herself a note on the edge of a form, "at least, his Cherokee's over there."

Julie felt the muscles of her lower abdomen grow taut. She had no idea how he felt about Allen's arrival, or where she was with him after their night on the beach. At the thought of seeing him now, in front of so many people, the tension that had been slowly building inside her all morning tightened another notch. She clasped her hands together as she felt a tremor run along her nerves.

Glancing up from her note, Ofelia said, "Hey, what's this I hear about the Bull blowing in?"

"You mean the news is out already?"

"Circulating like a hurricane. Half the crew says he's visiting his dearest and only daughter, and the other half are betting he's taking over. Anything I should know?"

"Not at the moment."

"Good. But you might have warned me, given me a head start on finding him a room, maybe an office if he wants one."

"I'd have been glad to," Julie said dryly, "if I had known. I just found out myself."

"Men. Don't they just kill you?" Ofelia put a hand on an ample hip as she nodded toward Vance. "Just take a look at the potentate over there. He's eating it up, all the sewing circle ladies and Lois Lane oohing and ahhing over every jewel of wisdom that falls past his pearly caps."

"Sewing circle?"

"Home demonstration club, something like that. They called a couple of days ago and asked if they could visit the set. Vance was in the office when the call came in, and since they mentioned how they never missed an episode of his soap when he was on, he decided to give them a charge. Where the reporter came from, I don't know. I hope she's legit."

It was not unknown for people to pretend to be with the media in order to have a few minutes alone with a star. All possible efforts were made to prevent such breaches of security, but sometimes publicity-hungry actors were hard to protect.

"I have no idea," Julie said.

"Did Vance ever tell you about the reporter who got his pants down? No? It was on another picture, on location in New Mexico or someplace. This good-looking girl comes out to the set, says she's with a college paper and also in the process of setting up a fan club, and can she do a special piece. They talk, and it gets a little sexy—you know Vance. Then the girl says how great it would be if she could tell the fan club what kind of underwear he buys. He tells her, and she pretends not to believe it, says it's the same brand her grandfather wears. Well, the upshot is, he drops his pants to show her—probably hoping for further developments. She has a good look at the label in the back, also his buns, then says thank you and goes away. Come to find out, there was no such college paper."

Julie smiled with a shake of her head. "Poor Vance. So that's why he's protective of his backside."

"Poor Vance, my eye! He deserved whatever he got, I'd bet money on it. I'd also bet that if he thought it would make him a superstar, he'd shuck his pants for the camera faster than you can say zipper. It never ceases to amaze me what people will do. Look at you, anything for your art, anything at all!"

Ofelia's voice, never exactly soft, had a ringing quality as she spoke that made Vance glance in their direction, then frown. Watching him, wondering if he could possibly have caught a part of what they were saying, Julie almost missed the other woman's last comment. Now she swung back. "What are you talking about?"

"As if you didn't know." Ofelia rolled her eyes, then blinked as she looked beyond Julie's right shoulder. "Morning, Rey. How's it going? Hey there, Summer, honey. Found yourself a new teacher?"

"Rey and I were having breakfast," the child actress said, holding her head so high she almost seemed to be looking down her nose at the assistant director, though at the same time she gripped Rey's right hand as if she thought someone meant to take it away.

"Her mother isn't feeling too well this morning," Rey said.

"She has a headache," Summer added. "She had to lie down, because she says she doesn't know how she's going to cope until I get somebody new to help with my lessons."

"We're working on it," Ofelia told her, then winked at Julie. "I'd better run. Talk to you later."

As Ofelia walked away toward the trailer office Rey looked down at Summer. "You might want to check on your mom, see if she needs anything. While you're at it, ask her if you can ride down the river with me for an hour or so."

The girl's smile was beatific. "I'll be right back!"

Rey watched the girl run toward her motor home with her blue-jean-clad legs pumping and her hair like fine sandy-blonde silk shifting on her back. When she was well out of hearing, he looked down at Julie with the same warmth in his dark brown eyes that he had shown Summer. "How are you feeling this morning? Still need a nap?"

"It wouldn't hurt." She put her hand on the back of her neck as she stretched her back a little.

"I wasn't exactly anxious to get up either," he said.

"I'm sorry about Allen. He isn't usually so obnoxious."

"I suspect that in his place I would have been ready to murder someone, and it wouldn't have been you."

She gave him a brief glance, thinking of his size compared to her fiancé. "Physical violence isn't Allen's style. He's much more likely to cut you down with words."

"Civilized, but maybe not as satisfying," he commented with dry humor, then went on quickly as Summer came slamming out of her motor home again, running toward them. "Did you know that Annette Davett is an alcoholic?"

"Not really, but I can't say I'm surprised."

"She was drunk this morning—or else high on something—and it isn't the first time. Summer does her best to cover for her, but she did tell me that her mother takes handfuls of pills at all hours."

"About a new teacher-welfare person, I was wondering if Donna might—"

"Julie! I'm glad I caught you before I had to leave."

It was Allen, calling to her from the steps of the trailer office. He came down them quickly with his briefcase in his hand, ignoring Rey as he walked toward Julie. He went on as he drew closer.

"I just had a call from L.A. to say that Bull left early this morning on his way to New Orleans. He wants to meet with me at my hotel, so I'm going on back. I think we should all get together tonight, have dinner, so I told Ofelia to have a bunch of limos sent out, bring everybody into town for a few drinks, some decent food, a chance to really talk away from the set."

"Everybody?" she said, her voice stiff.

"You know, Vance, Madelyn, Summer and her mother, the head people. Whoever you like."

"I thought Bull and I were supposed to talk privately first."

"That can come later this evening, after everybody else leaves. You'll be staying at the Windsor Court Hotel with me for the time being, of course. Just remember to pack a bag, bring it with you."

Allen looked beyond Julie, then, locking his gaze with that of the man who stood beside her. Rey returned the cool and deliberate regard for long seconds before he shifted slowly to face Julie. His mouth curving with humor that did not quite reach his eyes, he told her, "Thanks for the warning. You will tell me if I start to bleed?"

Rage and embarrassment warred in Julie's face as she looked from Allen to Rey and then back again to her movie's producer. "If I come with you now, Allen," she said with precision, "I can talk to Bull before the others get there, then come back here with them later. I don't believe I'll be staying; New Orleans is a little too far from the location for convenience, or for comfort."

Allen reached out to take her arm. "I'm sure we can work something out. We'll talk about it on the way."

At that moment, the office trailer door banged open. Ofelia came running out with her earrings jangling, her face flushed, and her eyes like plates.

"Allen, wait, don't go! Listen everybody!"

Her voice boomeranged in harsh echoes from against the river's far tree line as she stopped at the top of the steps, standing with her hands on her hips and feet spread. Allen turned back to face her with one brow lifted.

"We've got to clear the parking lot right now!" Ofelia cried. "Move the cars, move the trucks, move every single vehicle out of here! We just had a call from Dallas. Bull Bullard's on his way straight here, arriving in fifteen minutes!"

"It's good news about Bull," Allen said, "but why the excitement?"

"There's no landing pad, and we have just fifteen damned minutes to make one! He's coming by helicopter!"

Chapter 11

Dirt and gravel swirled in a stinging cloud. The treetops whipped back and forth and the grass verging the parking lot flattened, shivering. The surface of the river quivered in a thousand tiny wavelets while the boats tied up at the pier sidled and strained at their ropes. The roar of the helicopter engine and beat of its rotor blade made it impossible to talk. Squinting, holding her flying hair out of her eyes, Julie leaned into the whirling vortex. Around her the cast and crew who had gathered did the same.

The helicopter bearing Bull descended like some deus ex machina on a stage. It hovered above the area that had been cleared at such speed that the vehicles from the parking lot were scattered everywhere, behind the trailers and motor homes and the boat club, or else strewn up and down the highway at odd angles. Descending with slow precision, it settled to the ground with its engine winding down and the whip of the rotors slowing as they lost speed.

Near where Julie stood, the reporter who had been interviewing Vance was bouncing up and down with excitement. Leaning close to the actor, she yelled, "I can't believe it! I can't believe it's Bullard himself. Do you think I could get a comment from him?"

"Go for it. No harm in trying," Vance said with his crooked grin.

"You think so? I can't thank you enough for talking the guard into letting me stay after I moved my car, Mr. Stuart. You've really been wonderful."

"Just remember to say nice things when you're writing your piece."

"Oh, I will," the girl cried, "I will!"

Madelyn, who was standing next to Rey on Julie's other side, glanced over at Vance and the girl with a pitying smile. "I do believe Vance has wrangled himself another puff piece. Isn't it touching?"

"It's all part of being a star, isn't it?" Julie's attention was on Bull, who was unfolding his large frame from the helicopter seat. He looked well, his craggy face a healthy brown, his thinning hair that had gone gray combed straight back, his hazel eyes alert.

Madelyn shrugged. "I prefer it in carefully controlled amounts, myself. Fame is fine, but it doesn't do much for your retirement plan."

"That can't be a great worry for you."

"I've been around awhile, my dear. Not quite as long as your father, though he gave me my first break. We were an item once. Did you know?"

Julie gave the actress a quick glance. "You and Bull?"

"Don't sound so shocked; there was very little danger of you having me for a stepmother. I wasn't really his type."

"I wouldn't have thought that he was yours, either."

"Oh, Bull can be quite charming in his fashion, so uncomplicated. You know: Me man, you woman. I enjoy paying my own way, but it's sometimes nice to have a man around who picks up checks, not to mention opening doors."

Bull was shaking hands with the helicopter pilot who had unloaded an overnight bag. With his head bent in a half crouch to avoid the still-turning rotor, Julie's father swung around to scan the crowd. As Allen stepped forward and called a greeting he moved toward him. The two men shook hands as Bull straightened. Bull said something to the producer and Allen gestured toward where Julie stood. Smiling broadly, Bull Bullard started toward her.

The young reporter stepped into his path, tape recorder in hand, her long, curling hair flying wildly around her face, and eyes wide with excitement. "Mr. Bullard, it's my great privilege to be the first to welcome you to Louisiana. I would appreciate it if I could get a few words for my paper."

"Later, maybe," Bull said, "not just now."

"It will only take a second. Could you tell me what brings you here? Is it true that you'll be taking over as the new director of *Swamp Kingdom?*"

Bull gave the girl a sharp look. "I have nothing to say about that. All I'm doing—or at least trying to do—is visiting my daughter on the set of her picture."

He brushed aside the tape recorder and the young woman who held it, spreading his arms wide as he approached Julie. She stepped to meet him with relief flooding through her and a tremulous smile on her lips. He was Bull, her father, in spite of everything. His hug was warm and tight and loving, carrying with it intimations of distant but well-remembered security.

Drawing back with a laugh and a quick blink to banish the moistness from her eyes, Julie turned to introduce Bull to Rey. Their handshake was firm, the looks they exchanged intent, measuring.

"A pleasure, sir," Rey said.

Bull grunted. "I've been hearing about you and the job you've been doing. I'd like to find out more about it later."

Rey inclined his head in agreement, but before he could answer, Madelyn pushed forward.

"What a show-off you are, Bull," she said, her voice drawling. "A helicopter, for crying out loud. This isn't darkest Africa."

"Madelyn, dear heart, you know me, always in a hurry." He laughed deep in his belly, then reached to give her a swift kiss that the actress prolonged a few seconds by placing one hand tipped with bloodred nails in a French manicure on the back of his neck.

Behind them, the helicopter was taking off again, kicking up sand and pea gravel and once more drowning all sound. Julie leaned close to Bull, yelling in his ear. "We need to talk, alone, as soon as we have a chance."

"That we do," he called back, nodding his massive head. "But first let me say hello to everybody."

He moved up and down, shaking hands with the cameramen and sound technicians, the electricians and gaffers and gofers and catering people as well as the cinematographer, the editor, and Ofelia. Stan,

Julie noticed, stayed well back, giving Bull a short nod as their eyes met, but not coming forward like the rest for a personal hello.

Before Julie knew it, her father had gathered a number of people around him and was encouraging them to talk about the production, about some of the wild and funny things that had happened, the problems and the successes. Not long afterward, while she was in a discussion with Ofelia about where exactly to set up Bull's office, she heard a boat motor start. Looking around, she saw Bull and Rey, with Summer between them, heading off down the river in Rey's air boat. Julie put her hands on her hips, staring after them with her lips set in a straight line.

It was the middle of the afternoon before the trio returned. Bull and Summer were sunburned, but full of everything they had seen. They had been as far as Pass Manchac, and had tied up the boat long enough for lunch at Middendorf's, a treat that Bull pronounced mighty fine eating. Bull had some ideas he wanted to discuss with Julie, maybe compare with what she had already done, he said, but first they ought to freshen up, get ready for his ride into New Orleans that Allen had promised. Rey had suggested that they all go back to his aunt's house, have a drink, take a shower, sit on the gallery, and unwind. Bull was ready for all three, but especially the drink.

Julie fumed silently as she bathed and dressed for dinner. So far, Rey had seen more of her father than she had, and she was sure it was no accident. Bull could be cagey. For a moment there, when he had first arrived, she had allowed herself to hope that he had no part in Allen's plans. That hope was fast receding.

She stopped and stood listening as she took a dress of close-fitting peach silk crinkled into tiny pleats from the armoire. Rey and her father were still at it out on the gallery. If Bull had one more beer and unwound an iota further, they were going to have to put him in the limo in a bucket. She had stayed with the two men long enough to sip a glass of wine and watch the peacocks at their evening promenade across the lawn. But she had heard the stories Bull was holding forth on a few dozen times, and was in no mood for the latest embellishments.

If it didn't seem so unlikely, she would suspect Rey of encouraging her father to expound on the more outrageous of his exploits. He seemed to be offering stories of his own by way of encouragement, or possibly competition. She couldn't imagine what reason he might have, however. Whatever was going on, they both seemed to be enjoying it from the accompanying rumble of their laughter.

Julie tried, briefly, to picture her father and Allen in such a session and failed. In the first place, Allen didn't talk about his own frailties or tell jokes on himself. Secondly, he was particular about what he drank. He didn't care for beer, preferred his wine with pedigree attached, and wanted his hard liquor at least twelve years old and from the more remote reaches of the Scots highlands. He had been known, on occasion, to take his own bottle of Glenfiddich to places where he feared only inferior brands might be offered. He was most definitely not one of the boys.

Allen's dealings with Bull had a surface cordiality, but the two seldom discussed anything beyond the business of making movies. It would have been difficult to find two men with less in common. Julie had come to admit, after so long a time, that this was something less than a coincidence. She had chosen Allen all those years ago because he was the opposite in all ways of Bull.

There was also the fact that Bull had never come to terms with the idea that his daughter was living with a man. He and Julie had had some ferocious arguments about it in the early days. When Bull discovered that she could not be browbeaten, he had finally stopped ranting and raving, but he had never accepted it. He handled it now by acting as if that part of her life did not exist. Since he had begun his career in Hollywood as an actor playing bit parts in B movies, he made a fair job of the pretense.

The irony was that Allen admired Bull tremendously and would have liked to be closer to him. It was not the usual homage to the point of worship paid these days to directors whose films grossed fantastic sums, but rather a real appreciation for Bull's work. Bull had always stressed action and adventure in his films, but the themes he explored had a grandeur that could be traced back to the Bible and Shakespeare, Chekhov and Ibsen. This put him head and shoulders, in Allen's opinion, above the so-called brat directors with their simplistic gee-whiz observations, a group who proudly admitted taking their inspiration from television sit-coms and cartoons. Allen said, not entirely facetiously, that he couldn't wait until the baby-boom directors discovered that life was not always fair, that the good don't always win, and other such verities. These judgments and observations were made for Julie's ears alone, of course, not for public consumption.

Julie would have suspected Allen of arranging the convoy of limousines this evening to satisfy Bull's sense of self-importance if he had not mentioned them before her father's arrival. On the other hand, the chauffeured cars might be for her benefit, like some public vote of confidence to show the cast and crew that she was not being shunted aside but was still important enough to warrant special treatment. Julie would have been more appreciative if she had not been fairly sure that the cost of the evening would be charged to the budget of her movie, or if she didn't suspect that the gesture was also to satisfy Allen's sense of what was fitting for himself.

She still could not believe what Allen had done. Staring at herself in the mirror as she picked up a bottle of makeup and small application sponge, she thought of how little he seemed to realize the sacrifice he was asking of her, how little he seemed to understand how she felt. She had accused him in the heat of the moment of bringing in her father out of vindictiveness, but considering how far in advance Allen must have spoken to Bull for him to show up today, that wasn't possible.

Or rather, it was only possible if someone was keeping Allen informed.

She had suspected before that there might be a snitch among her people, someone running to Allen with every detail of the problems that arose. The thought was distressing. As Stan had said, a movie crew was a family. For the duration of the filming, loyalty to the project, to the director and the others working on it was a given. Gossip was one thing, but for someone to violate the ties of the set by passing on information was a serious betrayal, a pathetic case of pandering to their own self-interest, trying to get in good with the producer. It might be argued that Allen, as the producer, should be kept informed. It didn't follow, not when he aligned himself so plainly with interests of the bonding company and the studio.

Julie found the gallery deserted except for Aunt Tine when she emerged from her room. The men, it seemed, had finally headed for the shower. Aunt Tine had no need to dress since she would not be going with them. Julie had invited her, but she had declined. The older woman would be spending the evening getting everything ready to make the jambalaya that would be served at the wedding on Friday, a jambalaya big enough to serve four hundred people. The restaurant at the Cabin, where the reception would be held, would be catering the rest of the food, but the jambalaya would be a gift from the bride's friends and neighbors.

Julie and the older woman talked in an idle fashion about this and that. Aunt Tine told Julie a few details about the wedding coming up, and also about the wedding of a friend's granddaughter that had taken place at the small wooden chapel on the river known as Our Lady of Blind River, a place Julie had noticed in passing without realizing its significance. In true Cajun fashion, it seemed, the men and women who spent their Sunday's fishing, hunting, and relaxing at their camps on the river had felt the need for worship. Rather than curtailing their pleasures on the water in order to attend church, they had simply built a place to thank God for the opportunity to enjoy them. Aunt Tine spoke also of her friends who had camps on the river and on the lakes, and the bounty of fish and shrimp they brought her, especially the son of a friend who worked in the surrounding swamplands as a game warden.

In return, Julie found herself talking about California and her days as a beach bum and neophyte filmmaker. It occurred to Julie after a while that Aunt Tine had extracted an amazing amount of information about her life with Bull over the years. The older woman's concern was so real that it was disarming, making the inquisition a painless one. Julie was saved from total confession, however, by the return of Bull and Rey.

Bull had changed into a pair of slacks and a nice jacket that, with his shirt and tie, made a harmonious blend of brown shades. His clothing was serviceable and of good quality, but nothing more. Clothes to him were a matter of necessity and practicality having nothing to do with style. All efforts to change him had always been useless.

It was Rey's appearance that made Julie's eyes widen. The lightweight suit he was wearing had the fluid lines and graceful detail found in men's clothing from the house of Caraceni on the Via Campagna in Rome. His shirt was silk and the links in the cuffs had the subdued sheen of eighteen-karat gold.

That he could surprise her again was irritating. She knew well enough by now that he was not poor, yet she had difficulty accepting the evidence of his wealth. It was the fault of the way they had met, which, by extension, made it his fault. Why in heaven's name had a man of his background been speeding through the swamp at night? The question had begun to haunt her, but it was not one she was sure she wanted answered.

Within a few moments, the cortege of limousines appeared from the direction of town, moving in stately slowness as they turned into the drive and drew to a stop at the side of the house.

"Tiens," Aunt Tine, who had bridal affairs on the brain, exclaimed, "it looks to me like a wedding party—or maybe a funeral."

She was right. There were five pearl-gray limousines, each waxed and buffed to such a high sheen that, as Bull said in mock awe, even a fly couldn't land on them. Watching them pull up one by one, Julie felt her cheeks burn. In L.A. or Las Vegas or New York, they might have seemed natural, but there before the faded simplicity of Aunt Tine's house, they seemed vulgar, a typical ostentatious Hollywood display of tastelessness.

There was, in theory, a limousine for each of the three principal actors in the film, Vance, Madelyn, and Summer. The fourth should have been for Julie and Allen, while the fifth had undoubtedly been added at the last moment for Bull. Actually, three of the limos were packed with people while Madelyn rode with Allen and one was empty. Allen, climbing out as the driver opened the door for him, moved to the foot of the gallery steps where Julie and her father stood with Aunt Tine and Rey. He shook hands and said everything that was appropriate to the older woman as they were introduced, then turned to Julie.

"Shall we?" he said. "Madelyn will take Bull and Tabary with her. That will give the two of us a little more time to catch up on things."

His obvious assumption that she would fall in with his arrangements, that everything was perfectly fine between them since he had made his public claim of her, rubbed Julie the wrong way. Keeping her voice as pleasant as possible, she said, "I'm sorry, Allen, but I really wanted to talk to Bull on the drive in to town. Why don't you and Rey go with Madelyn. I'm sure she won't mind the change."

The skin around the producer's eyes tightened. He glanced beyond her, his gaze scanning the gallery floor. Failing to find the overnight bag he had so obviously expected, he returned his gaze to Julie with accusation in its cool gray depths.

"As you prefer," he said shortly. "I'll see you in New Orleans, then."

"Hold on there a minute," Bull said in hearty tones. "Rey's been telling me about shrimping on Lake Pontchartrain, and how he can fix me up with a trip with some of his buddies. He can come along with me and Julie while he fills me in on a few more of the details."

It was the first Julie had heard about a shrimping trip. She opened her mouth to object, then shut it again. Rey as an audience for what she had to say was not what she had wanted, but was better than speaking in front of Allen. At least Rey was not directly concerned in the outcome.

With the seating arrangements settled, the limousines got under way again. Children waved and older people turned to stare as the convoy wended its way along the river road. The vehicles moved at a steady clip past miles of snaking river levee and spreading acres of waving green sugarcane, past chemical plants and bins where grain was stored before being loaded on freighters, past the neatly laid-out streets of the residential section of the town of Lutcher. They made a left turn then, heading for the Airline Highway for the quiet route to New Orleans.

Julie sat looking out the opaque window glass that hid her from view and listening to the drone of her father's voice. There was, apparently, no question too involved, no detail of shrimping too minute for him to pass it by. He hardly waited for Rey's answers before bringing out his next probing comment.

He was doing it on purpose. What Bull hoped to gain by putting off their discussion, Julie didn't know, but finally she had had enough.

"What I wanted to ask, Bull," she said firmly at the first sign of a pause, "was whether Allen really discussed with you the possibility of working with me on this movie."

Bull turned slowly from Rey to face Julie. There was a measuring look in his eyes as he leaned back on the seat and placed his big hands on his knees. "You don't seem happy at the idea."

"Would you be, in my place?" she said with quiet reason. "I don't see the necessity at all. To my knowledge, the director's name in the credits has never sold a single movie ticket."

Her father pursed his lips. "I don't think that was Allen's main concern."

"Are you saying he thinks I might not be able to complete the film? I know there have been problems, but nothing other directors haven't faced."

"That could be, but Allen may feel more confident—"

Keeping her voice steady with an effort, she interrupted him. "I don't want you on this picture, Bull."

"I hate that you feel that way." He gave a heavy sigh. "I was looking forward to it, myself."

"You wouldn't be if I was coming in to take over your project."

"I didn't intend to take over. I only wanted to help."

The defenseless sound of his voice was painful to hear. "You don't know how to help," she said in desperation. "Remember the time in eighth grade when I had to have a presentation for a science fair? I made the mistake of asking you for last-minute help—and you brought in a production designer, an artist, and an engineer to work all weekend on it!"

"It got the job done, didn't it?"

"Oh, yes, but it wasn't my presentation anymore. It was nothing like the idea I started out to do."

"Ahuh," he said.

"Exactly. Why can't you and Allen see that I know what I'm doing, know what I want to accomplish? Why can't you leave me alone to do it?"

"Maybe we're afraid."

"Afraid of what? That I'll blow the money and have nothing to show for it? Thanks a lot."

He shook his head. "Afraid you'll get hurt, that if things don't work out this time, you'll lose the opportunity for another chance, or else that the critics will give you such a going-over you won't dare try again."

"That's the kind of reasoning that has done more to keep women from trying things than all the prohibitions against them put together. I'm not that fragile, I promise. I don't need somebody to prevent my lumps, or to share them."

"If we worked together, there might not be any lumps."

"Meaning you think I can't cut it on my own? Dear God, Bull, what does it take to convince you?"

"Allen is the one to convince."

The look she gave him was unflinching. "No, he isn't. He can't do a thing if you don't agree."

"I'm not the only director he could bring in, just the one he thought you would be more likely to accept."

"He was wrong."

"So tell him, not me. Now, where is it we're going to eat? I'm starving."

There was nothing more to be said. Julie, avoiding Rey's thoughtful gaze, turned away to stare out the window once more.

Their reservations were at Brennan's on Royal Street in the heart of the French Quarter. The limousines pulled up before the three-story building with its plastered facade glowing a soft rose-pink in the last light of evening. The flickering light from gas lamps threw the shadow of the wrought-iron balcony railing against the old walls, making a soft gray tracery of its intricate design. Across the street, the magnolia trees around the Victorian building that had once been the city hall stood somber and still in the dusk.

The maître d' appeared as the party crowded through the heavy double doors. They were greeted and welcomed with smiling ease, then shown to a special table on one end of the second-floor gallery that overlooked the walled courtyard.

A night wind, gentle and pleasantly cool, rustled the leaves of the bananas and magnolias in the flagstoned courtyard below and waved the edges of the rose-pink cloth on the long table. The scent of the centerpiece of old roses, stock, and fern in a low silver bowl wafted on the air, combining with the wonderful aromas of fresh baked bread and caramelizing sugar with just a whiff of brandy. Their waiter was attentive and informative, his manner polished and with just a shading of gallantry toward the ladies. As the first round of drinks were brought and menus given serious study Julie could feel the tension inside her recede a fraction. It began to seem as if Allen's idea might not be so bad after all.

Julie ordered a Jackson salad with its wonderful blue-cheese dressing, turtle soup that was guaranteed to be the best in the city, and a filet Stanley with an interesting-sounding sauce of horseradish with banana. The others chose various meat and seafood dishes, so that Allen, after much consultation with the sommelier, ordered several bottles of both a fine old Bordeaux and a pleasant Alsatian Reisling for the table.

When the wine was brought and poured, Bull picked up his glass and got to his feet. "I'd like to propose a toast on this occasion to a director of note. To my daughter," he said, "whose film *Dangerous Times* has been selected for viewing at the Women in Film Festival. To Julie, who knows better than most what she's doing."

He smiled at her over his glass as he drank. Julie could not prevent herself from smiling in return. There was pride in his voice, and love, she thought. She was warmed by it, moved by it. At the same time, she was saddened by the hint of flattery and cajolery that she caught in his words. As the others drank, then applauded, and offered congratulations she smiled and responded. Still, she could not help thinking that Bull's generous gesture was going to make her seem stingy and uncooperative when it became known she had refused to allow him to join her on the picture.

The party began to pick up momentum as the French bread was broken and chilled butter passed around. Shoptalk was inevitable, but was accompanied by much good-natured banter and friendly insults. Laughter was a constant undertone, until a short time after the entrée was served. It was then that Vance, sitting on Julie's right, began a conversation across the table with Stan and the cinematographer Andy Russell about the accidents and deaths of various stuntmen during the making of movies.

"One of the first I remember hearing about," Stan said, "was the poor guy driving the chariot during the making of the old silent version of *Ben-Hur;* flimsy rig lost a wheel, threw the guy thirty feet in the air. He didn't make it."

Andy Russell nodded. "I always heard making the *Perils of Pauline* with Pearl White back in the twenties was no picnic. One of the men doubling for her bought it."

"Jimmy Stewart's stunt double in that desert survival picture— what was the name of it?—is suppose to have died in a simulated plane crash."

"That would be *Flight of the Phoenix,*" Stan said. "But the one that really got to me was the guy doubling for Clint Eastwood in *The Eiger Sanction,* lost his footing during a mountain-climbing sequence."

"I wonder if Stewart or Eastwood felt responsible," Vance said, "or if they were only relieved it wasn't them."

"Both, I would imagine," Julie said, her tone abrupt. "Do you think you three rays of sunshine could talk about something else?"

"Sorry," Vance said with his famous grin, but he didn't sound sorry.

"I was thinking this afternoon about Madelyn," Bull said, his expression pensive, yet droll.

"Were you indeed?" Madelyn drawled, giving him a sultry look from under her lashes.

"There was the incident of the red wig, do you remember?" Julie's father met the actress's gaze, his own kindling to humor.

"You miserable pig of a man," Madelyn said, sitting up straight in her chair. "You wouldn't!"

"Oh, I think I would," he assured her before turning to speak to the whole group, which had fallen silent to listen. "We were making this marvelous picture called *Dawn of Evil* down in Mexico a good while back. We were in the back boondocks; the closest town was an Indian village twenty miles away. It was hot as hell's hinges. Madelyn was playing this red-haired siren who is doing her best to tempt a priest—the priest manfully resisting, of course, in spite of the fact that he's a con man in disguise. Comes the big scene to be played out beside a lake at dusk. The passion is waxing hot, when all at once an ocelot comes bounding out of the bushes and makes straight for our Madelyn. Panic time, I kid you not. Nobody had a gun; hell, nobody had any idea there was an ocelot within a hundred miles!"

"This story," Madelyn said with indignation, "isn't funny."

"Well, the priest/actor takes to his heels," Bull went on without pausing, "while our Madelyn dives into the lake. Trooper that she is, she even manages to take refuge without getting her wig wet. Then we all discover that ocelots can swim, if they want. This one wanted. You should have seen Madelyn backing up. She lost her balance and went under. The wig came off, and you know what? The cat attacks the wig, flails the thing around until he thinks its dead, then runs off with it. That's when we find out that Madelyn had cut her hair off about an inch long all over, that she had been wearing a wig of some kind night and day, even off the set, because she didn't want anyone to see that her roots were definitely not black."

"For this, my dear Bull," Madelyn said with dangerous calm, "you will pay dearly, painfully, and at great length."

"Do you deny it?" he asked.

The actress ignored the question. "I'll have you know that premature gray hair runs in my family. I can't help it if the moviegoing public equates it with age. Men can get by with being silver-haired— look at Sam Elliott—so why not women?"

"Life and the motion-picture business are not always kind," Allen said from his seat at the head of the table. "I remember one of Julie's last surfing movies. She needed people for a beach volleyball scene and the number of extras casting sent out didn't begin to look right for the fun-in-the-sun hot competition Julie wanted. She filled in by sending out for bathing suits and putting everybody not directly involved with filming out on the sand."

Julie, beginning to see where Allen's story could be leading, tried to head it off. "Needless to say, it was a disaster. You never saw such an awkward bunch of beach bums."

"Yes, but the prime example was Ofelia. She was issued this red-, white-, and blue-striped suit that made her look like a circus tent, then was shoved into a game. She goes back for a deep volley, stumbles backward, and winds up in the surf. Her feet get knocked out from under her, and she wallows and rolls and rolls and wallows until first thing you know, she's losing her tent. It was the great white whale all over again."

Ofelia laughed with the rest, though the color that mottled her face was not entirely from the wine. With a touch of strain in her voice, she said, "The whole thing was so hilarious that Julie kept the more decent parts in the final cut."

"It was my idea," Allen admitted. "Julie thought it was too slapstick, that it cheapened the production, but I felt it added comic relief."

Julie still wished she had not left the scene in her movie, still blamed herself for not standing up to Allen and excising the footage. She had been younger then, and more willing to listen to the opinions of others.

Down the table from where she sat, Julie saw Ofelia lift her glass and empty it, then refill it again without waiting for the services of the waiter. There was a suspicious sheen to the other girl's eyes, and she kept them lowered, as if to avoid eye contact with anyone else at the table. Ofelia, Julie knew, was more easily hurt than her brash manner would indicate. She was hurting now.

Allen, his narrowed gaze on the assistant director, spoke quietly. "Did I say the wrong thing, Ofelia? I didn't mean to upset you."

Ofelia set her glass down with a solid thud that was a serious threat to the crystal stem. "God, Allen, do I look like such a namby-pamby? I can take a joke with the best of 'em."

"It did bother you. I'm such a clod sometimes."

"Yes, you are," she answered with blunt forthrightness, "but I forgive you, anyway." She rounded suddenly on Vance, who was still grinning. "I don't see what you think is so funny. I seem to remember a time when you were caught with your britches down, too, or was it just your underwear? Not to mention the day on a circus set when you were so stoned you tried to do a double back flip from a trapeze that was a painted backdrop."

Vance flushed, looking around the table. His gaze stopped on Annette, who was staring at him with wide, shocked eyes. "Yeah, well, at least I never got so high or so desperate for dough that I danced naked with a big damned python crawling all over me."

Annette's gasp was harsh. The color receded from her face.

Summer, frowning at her mother, said, "A python's a snake, isn't it?"

"It's a stupid joke is what it is," Ofelia said brusquely, "and I'm tired of it. So what's everybody having for dessert?"

"I can recommend the house specialty, Bananas Foster," Rey said, directing a quick smile at Summer. "The bananas are fresh off the boat, the flaming brandy sauce is heartwarming to say the least, and the ice cream is dairy decadence."

"I want it," Summer said, grinning.

"With brandy?" Annette asked doubtfully.

"The alcohol burns away; all that's left is the taste," Rey told her.

"Too bad," Ofelia said, "but I'll take it, too."

"Thatagirl," Bull said, before cocking an eyebrow at Rey. "I don't suppose they could dribble a bit of chocolate syrup around over this concoction?"

Rey shook his head. "Sacrilege. Taste it first, and I don't think you'll want chocolate syrup."

Julie, watching the byplay, was intensely grateful to Rey for his intervention. She felt her tension returning with renewed force, and along with it an immense weariness. She was so tired of this game, the movie game, with its jealousy and petty revenge, its intricate little tricks and bits of playacting for effect.

Nothing was ever quite as simple as it seemed. Vance, Julie suspected, had begun the conversation about stunt deaths in a sly attempt to sabotage her evening. Bull had recognized it and told the story about Madelyn to distract attention from his daughter, but also, it seemed likely, to deflect the actress from any overt invitation to intimacy. Allen had brought up the incident concerning Ofelia to suggest, apparently, that things had not always gone as Julie expected or wanted in the past, and also as a reminder that he had influenced her before and could do it again. The other tales had sprung from hurt feelings, probably, but also from the need to settle old debts. Actors had long memories.

"After dessert," Allen said, surveying the table with an expansive and satisfied air, "I thought we would walk down Bourbon Street, listen to some jazz and maybe a little of this zydeco I've been hearing about, then hit a few of the clubs, see what kind of nightlife New Orleans really has to offer. Everything on me, of course. What do you say?"

"I say thank you, it sounds lovely," Madelyn answered in firm tones.

"Summer and I will join you for the jazz, but after that we'll have to go back to the motel," Annette said.

"Oh, Mother!"

"You're underage, sweetheart; I don't make the rules."

The others assented with varying degrees of enthusiasm, except for Rey, who sat turning his wineglass in one spot on the soft rose-pink linen of the cloth.

"Well, Julie," Allen said, "are you with us?"

Julie stirred in her chair. "I don't think so." She turned to Rey with appeal in her eyes. "I believe someone said you have a car here in town. Could you—would you drive me back to Aunt Tine's?"

"Of course," he answered. His gaze holding hers gleamed with the light of surprise and something more.

"Really, Julie!" Allen exclaimed, "I planned this for you."

"Did you?" she said without looking at him. She got to her feet, picking up her small silk evening bag from beside her plate. Rey rose at once and moved to draw out her heavy chair.

Allen flung down his napkin as he stood up. "I had thought we, you and your father and I, could go back to the hotel later to talk."

"You and Bull can talk," she said. "I've already said everything I intend to say."

Turning, she walked away. Rey nodded to the table at large with a quiet good-night, then moved to keep pace at her side.

Chapter 12

"Would you like to walk for a while before we start back?"

Julie agreed to Rey's suggestion almost automatically. She was so disturbed that it made no real difference what she did, so long as she was away from Allen and the others.

It was difficult to accept, after all these years, how remote she felt from Allen. It was as if she were seeing him with different eyes. He had many fine qualities, she knew; he could be, and usually was, a caring human being. He was an inveterate supporter of museums and art galleries, the symphony, opera, and theater. He enjoyed improvisational theater and brickwall-comedy places, fine old churches, flower shows, and rare coin displays. He was well read, articulate, and could be a relaxed and comfortable companion. She knew all these things, and yet it seemed she hardly knew Allen at all.

How was it possible that she had lived with a man, cooked for him, shared Sunday-morning newspaper comics with him, bought his underwear, and had his favorite Old English sheepdog put to sleep when the time came, and still not recognize the limitations of his personality? How had it happened that she understood him so little, or he her? What had happened to her that she could sit at the same table with him, look at his face that should be so familiar, and feel as if he were a stranger? Feel, moreover, that he was someone she really didn't care to know.

It wasn't simply that she was angry with Allen for trying to supplant her as director of the picture, or hurt because it seemed that money was more important to him than her feelings and needs. It was as if the feelings she had once had for him had seeped away without her knowing it, disappearing so slowly that she hadn't known they were going until suddenly they were gone.

She couldn't remember the last time they had made love.

Surely it must have been the night before she had left to come to Louisiana, but she could not recall where or what time or how. It might just as easily have been a month before, or longer. When she tried to bring the details into focus, her mind was filled with images of the man who strolled beside her, of Rey with moonlight on water reflected in his eyes, of the thudding of his heart mingling with the thunder of her own, of soaring flight and gentle landings.

She glanced at Rey, a quick, almost furtive look. The width of his shoulders, the memory of them beneath her hands, sent a small shiver along her spine. Aware of her slightest movement as always, he turned his head to smile down at her, then reached to catch her hand as they neared a cross street where traffic rolled in a steady stream.

As she shivered again he asked, "Cold?"

"No, not really."

"Why didn't you tell me about being honored by this women's film festival?"

"Allen just gave me the news this morning," she answered.

"Will you attend?"

She had not fully made up her mind. However his calm assumption that she might seemed to reinstate some of the legitimacy of the trip that Allen had taken away with his disparagement. She said quietly, "It's possible."

"You won't have to worry about Summer if you do. I spoke to Donna, and she'll be happy to have the job teaching her."

"She did understand that she can still be an extra for the town scenes?"

He nodded. "She'll report Monday for Summer, if that's agreeable with you."

"Couldn't be better," Julie answered. It was good to have at least one problem solved.

The street ahead was narrow and overshadowed with balconies, and congested with cars and foot traffic. Rey paused briefly to look both ways, then increased their pace by a half step to avoid a horse-drawn tourist carriage, one of the many that plied the quarter. On the opposite corner, they threaded their way through a small crowd gathered to listen to a guitar player. The guitarist was young, hardly more than a teenager, but his fingers were nimble, his music soft and sweet. The guitar case that stood open at his feet had accumulated a substantial number of greenbacks, while the hot-dog vendor with his wiener-and-bun-shaped cart a little further along was doing a brisk spillover business.

The music followed Julie and Rey down the street, blending without a break into the mellow wail of a trumpet coming from a bar a block over on Bourbon. Unconsciously, Julie slowed her steps to the gliding, sensual rhythm of the music. Rey, noticing, looked down at her. Once more, her lips curved in slow answer to his smile, while inside she felt a quick lilt in her heart, as if the rhythm of its beat had changed also.

Partly as camouflage for her reaction to him, partly from real curiosity, she asked, "What is that I smell?"

He inhaled and breathed out again. "Let's see, hot dogs and mustard, Ol' Man River, crab cakes from the restaurant over there, rum and bourbon, onions frying for some apartment dweller's supper, perfume from the shop down the street—have I hit it yet?"

"I don't think so. This is sweet and flowery, but not quite like anything I've ever come across. I noticed it when we were filming here before, but couldn't pin it down."

"Ah. That's the sweet olive from St. Anthony's garden, behind the cathedral—or maybe from my grandmother's garden."

"Your grandmother's?"

"That's right. She lives here."

They were standing in front of an enormously wide and tall door set into a plastered wall between two shops. As Rey spoke he rang a buzzer set into the wall, then stood back to wait.

Julie moistened her lips. "Are you sure you want to do this? She isn't expecting us."

"She'll be delighted to have visitors, though we won't stay long if you would rather not. It's just such a good place to use the phone and have my car brought around. My apartment is too far to walk in evening shoes."

Before she could answer, the door opened. A tall black man with grizzled hair and a gentle smile bid them a cheerful good evening, then stepped back to allow them to enter. They followed him down a long, narrow corridor with an arched ceiling dimly seen in the glow of electrified antique gas lamps. At the end was a small anteroom with a mural of Versailles in pastel gold, green, and blue around two full walls and also surrounding the tall French doors in the third wall, which led into a courtyard in the darkness beyond the glass. A pair of giant ceramic vases sat on either side of the doors, and a circular mahogany staircase swept upward just above them, spiraling into a lofty inverted well of light.

They ascended the treads of the stair, stepping on concave places worn by countless footsteps. There was a faint coolness in the air, and also a smell of ancient dust overlaid with lemon-oil polish, like the scent of better antique shops. The closed-in feeling of the lower corridor gave way as they climbed into spacious airiness and gracious comfort. Passing through another arched opening fitted with French doors that were flung wide and hung with heavy brocade portieres in a rich French blue, they stepped into what could only be called a parlor.

There were three floor-to-ceiling windows overlooking the street, one of which was open to the night air, though the solid shutters that closed the others were fastened tight. Through the open window could be seen the wrought-iron railing of a balcony that Julie had hardly noticed from below. The floor was highly polished random-width planking covered by a thin and softly worn Old Serapi carpet in blue and cream, coral and terra-cotta. The walls were painted a soft coral, and occasional chairs, most of them from the Louis Quinze and Direc- toire periods, were covered in cream and blue silk in a variety of stripes and florals. There was an enormous bouquet of coral lilies, chrysan- themums, and wild grasses on a side table, while a deeply cushioned sofa of cream linen sat before a coal-burning fireplace fitted with a white marble mantel.

An older woman as elegant as the room she inhabited rose from the sofa and came forward with outstretched hands. "Rey, *mon cher,* what a nice surprise."

Rey took his grandmother in a gentle embrace, then turned with his arm still encircling her waist while he introduced her to Julie as Madame Villars. The older woman's welcome was warm, though her regard was penetrating as she gave Julie her hand. Julie was captivated at once. In spite of the beautifully cut hair the texture and color of smoke and the expensively simple style of the gray silk dress the other woman wore, Rey's grandmother reminded her very much of his aunt Tine. They had the same animation in their voices, the same intense interest shining from their eyes.

"I suppose you have eaten?" Madame Villars said. "Yes? Then come and have coffee and Armagnac with me."

The coffee was served in Old Paris china, the cups dauntingly thin, almost too delicate for the strong, hot brew. Rey's grandmother had neglected to mention the Lane cake that was served with it, a sumptuous dessert made of four layers of white cake filled with a caramellike frosting thick with pecans, raisins, coconut, and candied cherries, and flavored with butter and bourbon.

Julie sat on one end of the sofa with Madame Villars on the other. Rey stood with his back to the fireplace, sipping his brandy-laced coffee with no more concern for the piece of fragile old china he held than if it had been a cheap Styrofoam cup. Watching him, seeing how well he blended with the opulent, antique furnishings of the room, Julie was bemused by a fleeting thought of what a fine antebellum gentlemen he would have made. She could see him bowing before the ladies in their salons, gracefully accepting a challenge for pistols at dawn. And she was annoyed all over again with herself for being taken in by his act as a back-country-swamp man.

"I have heard a great deal about you and your movie, Miss Bullard," Madame Villars was saying. "Yours must be an exciting occupation."

Julie replied suitably, adding, "It's been a great help having your grandson near for technical advice."

"I'm sure he's enjoying it; the swamp has been his passion since he was old enough to walk. It used to terrify me, that intense interest, but no longer. I've accepted so many things, the world has changed so much since I was girl."

"Don't let her fool you," Rey said, his tone dry. "She might like us to believe that she is a pillar of old Creole aristocracy, but I happen to know that she led a wild Bohemian life in Paris during the twenties and only came home to marry my grandfather under protest."

"The very late twenties, if you please; don't make me out to be more ancient than I am." The older woman sent him a smile half-chiding, half-amused. To Julie, she explained, "I thought I wanted to be an artist, you see."

"She is an artist, and a fine one."

"Portraits of fragile children and nurturing mothers in the style of Mary Cassatt, safe women's subjects. If I had stayed in Paris, I might have gone off in some mad direction like Dali."

"You know you have your own style."

"Possibly," the older woman admitted. "At any rate, it gives me pleasure and my regrets are few, so perhaps I wasn't meant to be a female Dali after all."

"Grand-mère's marriage was arranged by her parents," Rey said to Julie, "though it must have been one of the last of its kind. My grandfather always pretended to be immensely grateful for the sacrifice she made in accepting him."

"He was full of charm and devilment, may the good God and Our Holy Mother rest his soul. He allowed me to paint so long as I looked the other way while he dabbled in business with his American friends. Commerce, you see, Julie, was dishonorable. A man might have a profession, be a doctor or preferably a lawyer, but he could not be in trade."

"And a Creole girl must not marry out of her class, must not look at an American or a Cajun." Rey set his coffee cup aside as he spoke.

"I've read enough to understand the problem with marriage to an American, but what could be wrong with a Cajun?" Julie asked.

Madame Villars shook her head. "They were, rightly or wrongly, perceived to be of a different class, farmers rather than aristocrats. It was all foolishness, I suppose, since many of the old Creole families, if they would admit it, trace their ancestry back to the scrapings of the prisons of Paris. The women sent first as wives to the colonists were petty thieves and former prostitutes, while the *filles à cassette,* poor girls of good family brought out by the nuns with a few belongings in a trunk, or casket, given to them by the king, came some five or six years later. A favorite joke among Louisiana historians is that by some strange quirk of fate or anatomy, not one of those first wives ever had a child, while the casket girls were amazingly prolific!"

"My grandmother and grandfather," Rey said, his gravity complete, "were, naturally, from two families which could claim rightful descent from casket girls."

"Naturally." His grandmother gave him a look of mock hauteur before she sighed. "It sounds ridiculous now, does it not? But the standards were there and had been followed for generations with good results; how could they be challenged? Except that my daughter was as headstrong as I ever dreamed of being, and Rey's father was beguiling and incredibly persistent. I regret now only that my husband and I kept them apart for so long."

They went on to talk of the large number of movies being made in New Orleans, and of the apparent renaissance of the city as a haven and inspiration for writers as it had been in the twenties, thirties, and forties when Sherwood Anderson, William Faulkner, F. Scott Fitzgerald, Tennessee Williams, and Truman Capote had spent time there. They touched briefly on the liking of the literary muse for the scent of magnolias, as someone had once explained the proliferation of writers from the south. They could not, however, come any nearer to an explanation for the phenomenon than had anyone else in its long history.

A short time later, Rey excused himself to make his phone call. During his absence, Julie asked directions to a bathroom. She was shown through the connecting dining room and out onto the back gallery, then sent along it to a bedroom with adjoining bath.

As she made her way back once more toward the parlor she paused for a moment on the gallery overlooking the courtyard garden. It was dark and still below, illuminated only by the glow of lights from the house. Beds of what appeared to be white vinca made pale knot patterns around the edges of the flagstoned floor, while the shadows of tree limbs laid black lacework over the brick walls. There was something secret about it, hidden away there behind the house, concealed from the passersby outside. It hinted at secluded lives, private pleasures.

Just behind Julie, there was the sound of quiet, strolling footfalls accompanied by a soft tinkling noise. She turned, expecting to see Rey or the man who had let them in the house. There was no one there, yet at the very edge of vision, she thought she saw the last vestige of a fleeting shadow.

"Rey?" she said softly.

For long moments, there was no sound, then Rey stepped from the dining room in the opposite direction from which she was looking. "What is it?" he asked.

The light falling from the parlor silhouetted his tall form in the doorway while leaving his face in the dark. The trace of amusement she thought she heard in his voice was suspicious, though Julie knew he could not possibly have moved fast enough to have left the spot where she thought she had heard him and still have reached the point where he stood in time to answer her.

"There was someone there," she said. "I heard him walking."

"How do you know it was a man?"

She gave him a look of exasperation. "It sounded like a man. I thought it was you."

"You must have heard the chevalier."

"I heard who?"

"Our resident ghost. Some claim to have seen him, a man wearing a sword with a frock coat and breeches of the sort dating from shortly after the house was built."

"Oh, I see," she said, not believing a word of it. "Does he have a name, and did he come to an untimely end?"

"Nobody knows. He simply likes to look at any lovely woman who walks along the gallery after dark."

"Fine, so long as he stays out of the bathrooms."

"There's no guarantee of that."

Madame Villars appeared behind her grandson. "Did you say Julie saw the chevalier?"

"Heard him," Rey replied as he made room for his grandmother to stand beside him.

"How fascinating, so nearly an omen." The older woman came closer, gazing at Julie with warm speculation in her eyes and more than one glance into the shadows behind her.

"An omen," Julie repeated, her tone carefully neutral.

"Never mind," Rey said, "it's only a superstition. We are, you'll discover, a superstitious lot."

Julie was willing to be amused. "Yes, but an omen of what, not something terrible like the fall of the house of Villars?"

"Nothing like that. If you had seen him, it would only have meant that you belong."

"To what, the house?"

"No," he said, half turning, so that the light caught the teasing look in his eyes, "to the family."

The moment passed as Madame Villars chided her grandson for inflicting ridiculous family myths on Julie. Talking volubly about the strange ways that sound traveled in old houses, the older woman drew them both inside with an offer of more coffee.

A short time later, the butler announced the arrival of Rey's car.

It was dark blue, low-slung, and obviously powerful, the infamous Maserati Madelyn had mentioned. At the wheel was a young black man with laughing eyes and a goatee. He got out wearing a dark blue turtleneck and jeans, but in spite of his informality, came around to stand beside the back door of the car as Julie and Rey emerged onto the street.

"What's it going to be, boss?" he asked with a grin. "Shall I drive, or am I supposed to walk?"

"You get to drive, at least as far as the apartment," Rey answered before turning to Julie. "Meet Greg Leonard, Julie. He studies law at Tulane when he's not taking care of things for me. Greg, Julie Bullard, the lady director of *Swamp Kingdom.*"

As Julie and Greg shook hands Rey went on, "I hope you don't mind if we run by my apartment a few minutes, Julie. I'd like to check my messages."

"Not at all," Julie said as she stepped to enter the car door Greg held open.

He asked so nicely, it hadn't seemed possible to object, especially with Greg standing listening. Still, Julie felt tension gathering once more in the muscles at the back of her neck. She was in no mood for intimacy. She couldn't believe that Rey, and with his knowledge of her refusal to submit to the same kind of ploy by Allen, would use such a blatant maneuver to try to get her into his bed again. It was, of course, impossible to be sure.

They threaded the narrow one-way streets, stopping at nearly every cross street for pedestrians who were dressed in everything from designer silks and evening clothes to scruffy shorts. Greg drove with wary skill and only a few scathing comments for the meandering drunks, reckless cabdrivers, and street-hogging tour buses that crossed his way.

Julie, in a pretense of ease, turned to Rey. "All that stuff about your family ghost, you don't really believe it, do you?"

"Don't I?" he said, smiling down at her as his shoulder pressed against hers while they rounded a corner. "I can imagine how it must have sounded to you, like something out of a Victorian gothic novel. At least you didn't laugh when Grand-mère mentioned our legend. I do appreciate that."

"But you can't really think—"

"No, no. Or only on stormy nights."

She gave him a look of humorous irritation. "I should have known better than to expect a serious answer."

"It's serious you want? All right. The logical left side of my brain says, 'Nah, impossible, there's no such thing as ghosts.' But then the mystical right side says, 'Yes, dear, and what shall we name the children?'"

She shook her head in despair as she recognized yet another diversion. Accepting it, she said, "Children, as in plural?"

"At least four, two boys and two girls."

"How nice. And you would come home at the end of the day and play touch football with the boys and dandle the girls on your knee while your wife cooks dinner."

"Or the other way around, depending on their ages."

"Lovely, but your wife is stuck in the kitchen."

"I also cook, and enjoy it."

"What a paragon!" she said in mock appreciation.

"You've no idea," he answered, and hesitated as if he would add something more. Instead, he turned his head abruptly, instructing Greg, unnecessarily, to turn to avoid a street barrier that lay ahead.

One River Place was a high rise of stone and reflective glass with wraparound balconies overlooking the Mississippi River. Located near the Riverwalk, where the World's Fair of 1984 had been held, it was actually an ultramodern residential tower rather than an apartment building. The only one of its kind in the city, it was also the only one there would ever be on the riverfront due to changes in the building codes.

Rey's suite of rooms was furnished with an eclectic blend of overstuffed pieces in dark gray-blue leather paired with sturdy country French antiques, with lighting fixtures and lamps of polished steel side by side with candlesticks and sconces of rococo ormolu. The rug on the polished living-room floor bore a strong resemblance to the one Julie had noticed in his grandmother's parlor, and probably, she thought, came from a bedroom or attic storeroom of the French Quarter house.

She had suggested that she stay in the car, but had been overruled. Security was excellent in the building and its parking amenities, Rey said, but he preferred not to test it, not at that hour. He dismissed Greg for the night, saying he would drive Julie home himself. She was left alone with him.

He did actually check his messages, leafing through the pile of notes left beside the phone, sifting quickly through his accumulated mail, playing back at low volume the recordings on an answering machine. Julie stood staring out a wall of windows at the river, which lay coiled below like a giant black snake nestled among jewels of light, keeping her back turned to allow him privacy.

There was a steamboat on the river, easing along at half speed past the freighters tied up along the docks, its lights reflecting red-gold gleams on the water. It looked like a phantom from another time, moving so silently without smoke from its stacks or the turning of its paddle wheel, and with its progress so slow that it scarcely left a wake.

Ghosts. She should really stop letting her imagination run away with her. It had played a trick on her once this evening already, or perhaps more than once. There had been no one there behind her on the gallery; it had no doubt been as Madame Villars suggested, a trick of acoustics in an old house. Rey's comments on the incident had been only another example of his quirky sense of fun.

His footsteps behind her were so silent on the old rug that she jerked, startled, as he placed his hands on her shoulders.

"Relax," he said quietly as he began to knead the muscles under his warm grasp. "I promise I'm not going to pounce on you."

The sudden drain of stress brought the rise of gooseflesh along her arms and down her spine. She leaned into his hold ever so slightly. "I never thought you were."

"Good. I'm also not going to ask you to stay here with me tonight, as much as I might want it."

She turned her head as she felt his warm breath against the back of her neck. "Aren't you? Why?"

He moved so she was held close against his side. Placing his temple against hers, his lips almost touching the corner of her mouth, he said, "I'm a very selfish man. I prefer your full attention."

She sighed as she turned and slid her arms around his waist, resting her head against his shoulder. "You're also a very considerate one, and I'm grateful."

His arms closed around her, a warm, gentle hold. She lowered her lashes, her senses awash in the strength of him, the faint scent of warm silk and spice and lime after-shave. She thought of how easy it would be to sink into his arms, into the sort of domesticity he had described earlier as a joke, becoming a wife and mother with no more on her mind than grocery lists and car pools, disposable diapers and Little League and satin dancing shoes in small sizes. How satisfying it would be to lie with him in a king-size bed with their bodies curled around a sleeping baby, to tiptoe beside him from a nursery and sleep, exhausted, in his arms, waking to love in the dawn.

Oh, God, but what hormonal betrayal had brought her to this? What trick of nature had made her suppose that marriage and children would be enough. It wouldn't, and she knew it. She could never be a dutiful wife, submerging her dreams in a welter of family duties. It wouldn't work, at least not for long. She would either go mad or drive someone else crazy.

But she was safe. Rey hadn't offered marriage, had retreated from the suggestion into humor just as he had retreated from intimacy this evening. It was highly probable that he did not see her in that light at all. He was a traditional man and would expect a traditional wife. For all his talk of helping to cook, he would expect the woman he married to give up everything like his grandmother, to devote herself to him, to hearth and home. Donna Lislet was the kind of woman he would think of as the mother for his children, a woman soft and emotional and easily swayed, a woman of small dreams.

Julie thought that, to Rey, she herself represented a challenge, a distraction, a physical attraction of varying degrees of power, but hardly more. She was different, and intriguing because of it; he enjoyed her mind, her spirit, her body; still, he was not totally enraptured.

Or was he? It was difficult to tell. For all his quick personal observations and good-humored conversation, he was not an easy man to know. There was a deep reserve inside him, almost as if there were thoughts and emotions he held in abeyance by stringent will and for some purpose known only to himself. He was not what he seemed. She had uncovered layers of identity that he had kept hidden from her, but was still troubled by the layers she might yet discover.

"I'm human, too," he said, his voice strained as he put his hands on her arms in a gentle caress before moving them to her shoulders and setting her from him. "I have good intentions, but they can be overcome."

"I wouldn't want to do that," she said slowly.

"No, I was afraid you wouldn't," he answered, and turning, went to open the door and hold it for her.

Chapter 13

The location was buzzing with talk about the arrival of Bull and the wild progress he and the L.A. contingent had made through the clubs and joints of New Orleans the night before. The speculation about Bull taking over the movie was still rife; Julie could tell by the way people stopped in the middle of their conversations as she passed. There was not much getting done—not that Julie was surprised. The crew couldn't be expected to break their backs on a job that might have to be done again if the new director didn't like it. Something would have to be decided one way or another, or the whole operation would soon go to pieces.

Julie had left the house early, before anyone was stirring. She worked in her office until hunger overtook her. She thought about seeing if Ofelia wanted to go over to the boat club for coffee and doughnuts; she had heard her come in nearly a half hour before. On second thought, she wasn't anxious to face all the sly looks and whispers. She would go to the motor home, maybe cook a piece or two of bacon and an egg in the microwave, make a piece of toast. It would be better than all that sugar and caffeine. The upsets recently along with the rich food and drink the night before had left her stomach feeling something less than settled.

She waved at Stan as she crossed toward the motor home. He was huddled with Rey and the special-effects man, probably working out the final details of the new stunt they would be doing this morning. At least someone was still trying to get something accomplished. Madelyn's car was in the parking lot, so she was around somewhere. Vance was leaning in careful negligence against the cypress tree beside the river, his accustomed place, while he talked to the script coordinator. Annette Davett's querulous voice could be heard coming from the next motor home, so apparently Summer had arrived. Of Allen and Bull, there was no sign, a small mercy Julie accepted with suitable gratitude.

Closing the metal door of the motor home behind her felt remarkably like entering a haven, and Julie sighed with relief as she locked it. The sun on the metal-and-glass structure had raised the temperature considerably, however, and brought out the nose-stinging smells of the synthetic fabrics and wood glue. Julie flipped the air-conditioning on as she moved toward the small bathroom to wash her hands.

She heard the dry, clattering sound first as she was holding her hands under the running water in the basin. She glanced up, thinking it might be air coming through an air-conditioning vent. It would be about par if the cooling unit was on the blink.

She took a half step as she reached for a towel. The rattling came again. It was closer, and lower, than before. Something about it made the hair rise on the back of her neck. She went still. Slowly, by minute degrees, she bent her head to look down at her feet.

The snake was shining black mottled with gray. It was coiled in the corner made by the wall and the shower stall, just in front of the commode. Its head was raised, weaving gently from side to side, while its thin tail of rattles was held stiff and straight above its back.

A swamp rattler.

The identification reverberated in her mind, gleaned from the books about the swamp she had read and descriptions Rey had given in his lectures on how to protect oneself in the swamp.

Her bare legs beneath the slim skirt she wore felt achingly vulnerable. Her heart beat in double time against the wall of her chest. Her muscles stiffened with the paralysis of mindless, primitive horror.

If she called out for help, the snake might strike. If she moved, it could strike. If she stayed where she was, the very heat of her body and motion of her breathing might cause it to strike.

Its fangs gleamed with pinpoints of light. Its tongue flickered in and out, as if tasting the air. The rattle at the end of its tail whispered.

She could not stay frozen where she stood forever. The snake was not going to leave. It had nowhere to go; it was cornered, trapped by her presence. The two of them were holding each other in a stiff tableau of fear.

The snake might strike; then again it might not. In any case, there was such a thing as antivenin.

It was this last fact, penetrating to her rational mind, that released Julie. She flung herself backward through the bathroom doorway, crashing against the hallway wall opposite with a jarring thud. Careening off it, she grabbed the narrow bathroom door and slammed it shut.

Convulsive shudders shook her as she backed away from the door. Coming up against the table in the kitchen–dining area, she wrapped her arms around her upper body, holding tight. Her reaction was not rational, she knew; it was instinctive, therefore uncontrollable.

It was at that moment, while she bent her head and closed her eyes, trying to stop shaking, that it occurred to her to wonder how the snake had gotten into the motor home.

The outer door had been locked; she had opened it with her own key when she entered just now. It was always locked at night, though not during the day. Even when the motor home was left open for easy daytime access, however, the door was kept shut because the air-conditioning was usually left running to keep the interior comfortable. If the metal door itself was left open, there was still an inside screen door that fit tightly against the high metal threshold across the entrance.

More than that, the outside doorway was several feet above the ground. There was a set of metal steps which swung down for entry, but which did not reach ground level, hanging instead nearly a foot above it.

Motor homes, travel trailers, truck campers, and other such vehicles built for camping in out-of-the-way places and wilderness areas were specifically constructed to discourage wildlife visitors. The chances of the swamp rattler having gotten into the motor home by itself were almost nonexistent.

It was still barely possible, of course. Snakes could climb, and also pass through small openings. But they had to have good reason to do it, one usually associated with food. There was little to eat available in the motor home, and nothing of the warm and moving variety that snakes preferred, unless it was a stray mouse.

It appeared, then, that someone must have put the snake in the motor home.

Who would do that, and for what reason?

The first thing that came to mind was a practical joke. True, using a swamp rattler was somewhat drastic, but someone from California, say, might not realize the danger. It wasn't too unusual for such jokes and tricks to sweep through a movie company on location in cycles. That they could get out of hand, erring on the dangerous side, was also true.

If it was a practical joke, who had been the target? She or Ofelia? Or had somebody figured, perhaps, that Bull might now be using the motor home?

If it was not a practical joke, what then?

She had no answer to that one. She could think of no one who would want to harm Ofelia; her assistant director got on well with most everybody. Bull had not been around long enough to stir up resentment. As for herself, there might be people who didn't care for her particularly or who were annoyed with her, but she could think of no one who would deliberately try to injure her. If there were a member of the cast or crew who wanted to encourage her to allow Bull to take her place, they would discover they needed to use more forceful measures.

None of that mattered much at the moment. The question was, what was she going to do about the snake? She could go for help, but that would only advertise that she had found the thing, not to mention signaling her own terror and helplessness. She refused to give anyone the satisfaction of knowing they had frightened her. She preferred to have it appear that the joke, if that was what it was, had backfired. It would be best, then, as much as she disliked the idea, to do away with the thing quietly herself. That way, whoever had put it in the motor home would have to wonder what had happened to it, wonder why there were no screams and panic—maybe even wonder where it would turn up next.

But how was she going to get rid of it?

She didn't want to kill it; the snake had done nothing to her except scare her. On the other hand, someone had upset it, so it was not likely to go quietly. Unless she wanted a permanent crawling resident, she had no alternative except to try to kill it.

How?

Growing up, she had seen her mother dispatch several snakes who were unwise enough to invade her flower beds. Julie herself had even killed one or two that crossed her path. The weapon of choice was a garden hoe. Since there was not one handy, any sharp instrument on a long stout pole would do.

Julie stood up straight and walked to the small pantry beside the refrigerator. Inside, she found a Fuller broom with a fairly heavy metal handle and also a wedge-shaped metal cover over the plastic broom straws that was near the size of a small hoe blade. She picked it up, hefting it in her hands. It would work.

Holding the broom by the end of the handle like a club, she eased back down the hallway toward the bathroom door. She put her hand on the handle, turning it with slow care. Inch by inch, she pulled it open.

A few moments later, it was over. The snake was stunned from her blows, but she had no real idea if it was dead. With clenched teeth, she used her broom to push the long, unwieldy body into a plastic garbage pail. She dropped a hand towel in on top to cover it, then paused to consider how to dispose of it. She decided at last to take it to the edge of the swamp that lay a few feet behind the line of motor homes and fling it into a palmetto thicket. She might be seen while she was doing it, but that was a chance she would have to take.

No one paid any attention to her, no one called out or followed as she left her motor home and eased between it and the one being used by Summer that stood next to it. Stopping at the edge of the swamp where the undergrowth began past the parking-lot pavement, she drew back her pail and threw the contents as far as she could. The snake made a heavy flopping sound as it landed on the ground among the dense palmetto. Julie turned and walked away quickly without waiting to see if it revived.

As she rounded the end of the motor home again Julie saw that Allen and Bull had arrived. She set the garbage pail beside the metal steps and moved toward them. Somehow, she was no longer interested in returning to the motor home, and not at all hungry.

Bull was in fine form; he had taken over Vance's chair under the cypress tree and was holding forth with some long and involved tale about a film shot in Africa. A raconteur of no mean skill on top of being a Hollywood luminary, he had gathered quite an audience. Allen sat in a director's chair nearby, pouring tea from a silver-plated thermos into a china cup.

Vance was also there, sharing a lounge chair with Madelyn, who was sitting on the footrest and leaning her back cozily against his upraised knee. Nearby was the female reporter who had been there the day before. Summer sat on Bull's other side with her legs folded like an Indian, looking enthralled. Her mother, Annette, was not present, but Donna Lislet occupied a stool not far from Summer, next to Rey, who sat on the ground with his back against the cypress tree. The young girl sometimes sent the widow an appraising glance from the corners of her eyes, so it seemed likely that Donna had been introduced as her new teacher-welfare person.

Julie wondered what would happen if she announced her recent visitor to the assembly. It might be interesting to see the reactions, see if anyone behaved at all strangely. However, she didn't want to spoil the story Bull was telling, nor did she want to be the target of questions she could not answer. She let it go.

Ofelia was not far away, exchanging quick, scurrilous asides on Bull's story with Stan and a group of cameramen and sound people. Seeing Julie approaching, the assistant director broke off and came toward her with storyboard and shooting schedule in hand. Stan ambled after her to join Julie also.

They were all still waiting for the special-effects people to get their equipment ready to go, Ofelia said. As soon as that was done they could proceed to the open area downriver and run through the complete rehearsal Julie had scheduled. Until then, there was nothing to do except listen to Bull—both literally and figuratively.

The stunt planned was one of the most important in the movie. Rey would not be playing Vance this time, but would be standing in for one of the actors playing the villainous type hired by Jean-Pierre's wife, Dorothea. According to the script, while Dorothea seduces Jean-Pierre, keeping him busy, one of her hired goons kidnaps Alicia. Discovering the loss, Jean-Pierre gives chase. In his bitter anger at having been betrayed once more by his wife, he endangers his daughter's life by causing the speedboat to crash. There is a fiery explosion. The Cajun saves his daughter from drowning after she is thrown out of the boat. Recognizing the danger he has placed her in by bringing her into the swamp and accepting the responsibility for her injuries, he is overcome with remorse.

Summer had no part in the shooting; for the sake of safety, her role was being played by a stunt dummy wearing a sandy-blonde wig and wrapped in a blanket. The stunt was too dangerous even for a child double to take her place. Her supposed rescue from the wreckage by her father would be filmed another day, as would a few other scenes of father-daughter interaction that would take place in and around the dilapidated fishing camp where the seduction scene had been filmed.

Vance had insisted on running his own boat for the explosion sequence, dispensing with a stunt double. He was tired of letting somebody else take the glory, he said. Besides, this business with the speedboat crash was a piece of cake, nothing to it, at least for him. He was at least partially correct. Vance would need to do some fast driving and a few tight turns as he pursued the speedboat, but would be in no serious danger; it was Rey who would be at risk as he jumped from the speedboat at the instant of impact, scant milliseconds before it was timed to disintegrate in a burst of flames. All Vance had to do was hold his boat steady through the smoke and debris and the wash of the explosion. Since they lacked another stuntman of Rey's caliber, Julie had, finally, agreed to let the actor have his way.

The story Bull had been telling came to an end. Donna got to her feet. "It must be about time I began to earn my keep," she said with a warm smile for Summer as she held out her hand to the girl. "Why don't you show me the books your other teacher was using, let me see what progress you've made in them?"

"Just one more story, please!" Summer said, her eyes huge with appeal as she looked up at the widow. "Then I'll go, I promise."

"There may not be another story."

"Oh, yes, there will be," the girl said confidently.

Bull gave a shake of his head. "I did mention I might tell about my first job in Hollywood, playing Billy the Kid in a singing-cowboy picture."

"You are kidding?" Donna said, looking skeptical yet not unwilling to be beguiled.

"Not quite!" Bull let out his deep laugh and launched into yet another yarn.

Julie retreated to the boat club, where she picked up a piece of toast and a cup of coffee. She was sitting, thinking of what was going to have to be done in the upcoming stunt and stirring cream into the chicory-flavored black brew served by the catering service when Madelyn sauntered in. The actress picked up a cup of coffee for herself and came to join Julie.

"So," Madelyn said when she had seated herself and settled the skirt of her red silk dress around her so it wouldn't wrinkle. "Are you going to let Bull help you or not?"

Julie gave her a straight look. "Did he send you to find out?"

"You should know better than that. Bull never mentioned it, as a matter of fact; I just wondered."

"I don't know why you care, unless you would prefer to be directed by Bull."

"In other words, mind my own business?" Madelyn laughed without humor. "Actually, I'm concerned about Bull."

"Are you? Now why?"

"Would you believe for old times' sake? He looks bad to me, tired, worried. Maybe worried about you and what you're going to do."

"I can't help that."

"No? You might remember he's not as young as he used to be—none of us are. He's big and rough and as self-sufficient as they come, but he can still be hurt."

"I know all that, but am I supposed to sacrifice everything I've worked for because of it?"

"He sacrificed as much for you."

"What are you talking about?" Julie stared at the other woman with a frown between her eyes.

"He threw me out when you came to live with him in L.A. years ago; we had been living together for nearly a year by then but it didn't make any difference. He was sorry, he told me, but he had to do it. You had never forgiven him for the breakup between him and your mother, and he had to make it up to you. He wanted no emotional entanglements, no other ties, while he persuaded you to like him again."

"I never knew that." Julie's gaze was intent on the other woman's flushed face.

"That isn't all. Bull turned down dozens of films, important properties that any director would have given his eyeteeth to do, because they would take him out of the country, away from you."

A shade of defensiveness crept into Julie's tone as she said, "I didn't ask him to do it."

"You didn't have to. He thought you needed him and so he made certain he was there."

"It would have been more to the point if he had been there for my mother."

"Dear Julie, I'd have thought you had been around the motion-picture business long enough to know that the people who work in it are human beings, no more, no less. There are no heroes and villains: the superstars and movie legends bleed and sweat and have heartaches like everybody else. They make mistakes, but seldom make them alone. Even Bull."

"Very profound," Julie said with a sigh. "I suppose you are trying to say something?"

"It takes two to make a child, or a divorce."

Julie waited until she could speak evenly. "Look, Madelyn, what's going on has very little to do with what I feel about Bull or what he feels about me. Mainly, it's a business matter. There's no need to plead for him, or pity him."

The other woman's red lips curved in an ironic smile. "He was right, wasn't he? You haven't forgiven him."

The actress rose to her feet and picked up her coffee cup. Julie sat where she was as Madelyn walked away. She didn't watch her go, but sat making rings on the Formica tabletop with the bottom of her cup. She was still there with her cold coffee and uneaten toast before her when they came at last to tell her everything was in order and the boats were ready to go.

Allen had emerged from his borrowed office and was standing with Bull and Ofelia at the pier beside one of the cabin cruisers. He turned as Julie approached. Before he could speak, her father said, "Allen and I thought we might go out with you—strictly as observers—if you don't mind?"

"Why should I mind?" Julie said pleasantly. "I'll join you in a minute." She touched her father's shoulder in passing as she indicated that the two of them should go aboard the boat waiting for her. She stood for a moment settling the last details of the stunt with Stan. That out of the way, she leaped lightly down onto the cabin cruiser's deck. Without further delay, they headed down the river.

Rey had already left in the speedboat, the boat he would be using for the stunt today. He was at the spot chosen for the day's shooting when they arrived. It was the same open stretch of water where the other stunt had been filmed, one of the few wide enough for fast maneuvering on the river. They had moved the shooting platform to the opposite bank for a different filming angle and would use a different direction of approach so the shorelines would not appear the same.

The run-through of the stunt went well. There was, as before, a few small explosions set up to simulate gunfire hitting the water. The rehearsal showed exactly where they would be so Rey and Vance could drive past them at the correct pace while using them for the best effect. They could not, of course, simulate the bigger explosion or rehearse Rey leaving the speedboat, since the boat would be destroyed by the stunt, but he and Stan worked together on the timing until they were both satisfied.

Julie tried to close her mind to the danger, to pretend that this was just another shot, another stunt with a man who was being paid to put life and limb on the line and was doing it with his eyes open. It didn't work. She watched the speedboat, Vance's skiff, and the camera boat as they sped over the water or circled each other, or else lay idling, wallowing in their own and each other's wakes. Her gaze behind her dark glasses returned again and again to Rey. His dark head shone in the sun and his shoulders were made broader by the bulky dark suit that he wore. His movements seemed confident and purposeful, yet careful.

She wanted to be just as confident, just as purposeful and careful. Instead, she felt sick. That sickness gave her voice an edge as she spoke to the men out on the water over her walkie-talkie. She thought her voice, echoing thin and raspy with static in her own ears, sounded impatient, irritable at the delay caused by the rehearsal. There was good reason for it. She wanted desperately for this stunt to be over. In fact, she wanted this movie to be over, the sooner, the better.

Or did she?

Did she, perhaps, want to make it last forever? She didn't know. She really didn't.

The boats were circling once more, taking up their starting positions for the scene. The Chapman crane overhead creaked as the master camera swung into position. The murmuring of voices on the shooting platform began to die down as it appeared action was about to start.

The putt-putt of a boat engine, one different from any they were using for the stunt, made the sound man next to Julie squint with a pained expression. They had a local coming to visit their set, or else a fisherman moving through it on his way downriver; there was an ancient motorboat just appearing at the end of the dim tunnel that led back toward the location.

Then the boat moved into the sun. It was beat-up and dingy and unbelievably decrepit, but the person guiding the smoking outboard motor without a cover that was attached to the back was no fisherman or idle visitor. It was Donna.

The young widow waved and shouted something across the water, but she could not be heard above the idling of the other boat motors or the noise of her own sputtering motor. Julie waved her on in. The minute Donna cut her motor to glide up to the platform, Julie made a final visual check, then nodded at Ofelia.

"Right. Here we go," the assistant director called into the bullhorn she held. "Action!"

"I'm sorry," Donna said, in a breathless whisper as she came up the platform's ladder. "I didn't mean to upset things."

She was shushed by a half-dozen people. She reddened, but was silent until she had reached Julie's side. "I'm sorry," she said again with soft sibilance, "but I had to come. I can't find Summer."

"Quiet!" Ofelia glared at the other woman, starting to move toward her, but Julie held up her hand.

"Go on," she said to Donna.

"Summer told me she was going to have a late breakfast with her mother, but when I went to find her after a half hour, Annette hadn't seen her. I've looked everywhere, but she's not at the location. I thought maybe she begged a ride out here. All the boats were gone, so I drove around the canal to the camp of some people I know and borrowed their boat. Is—is she here?"

Out on the water, the boats were gaining speed, circling, getting ready to make their long, weaving run that would end at an old, partially submerged railroad trestle, an artistically rebuilt copy of one existing elsewhere on the river, that lay some two hundred feet past where they all stood. Julie felt as if her mind had become compartmentalized, dealing with the two problems presented to her as if they were separate parts of a whole, if only she could make them mesh. Concern for Rey and what he was about to do ran parallel with anxiety for Summer.

"Has anyone seen her?" she mouthed soundlessly, turning this way and that to take a consensus of those around her. But there were only shrugs and shaking heads.

"Not since just before we left," Bull whispered, stepping up close beside Julie.

They were interrupted by the roar of engines at full throttle as the boats began their run. Then came the crack of shots as Rey, in the lead boat, fired back at Vance and the special effects in the water went off in a perfect series. Vance, in his boat, made a ducking movement, swerving so his wake made a zigzag curve.

Julie, watching the speeding action, had a fleeting memory of

Summer sitting at Bull's feet and listening to his deep voice, just as she used to do so long ago. A lonely child, wanting so much to do exciting, wonderful things like him, wanting to do them to impress him. At the same time, Julie's gaze was fastened on Rey in his dark suit, turning, firing, controlling the speedboat while pretending to let it drift, seemingly oblivious of the half-sunken railroad trestle looming ahead as Vance gained on him, pushing him toward it. Behind him in the narrow backseat lay the child dummy with its sandy-blonde wig shining, streaming in the wind.

The dummy was moving.

The dummy was sitting up, pushing back the blanket as if in a daze. A pale face appeared with open, staring eyes. A small hand reached from the blanket folds to clutch the gunwale of the hurtling boat.

Julie brought her walkie-talkie up by purest reflex. It couldn't be happening, not like this. Not again. Her mind wavered with the disorienting unreality of déjà vu even as she screamed into the mechanical radio in fear and rage.

"The dummy is Summer! Rey, the dummy is really . . . !"

The last word was lost in the booming roar of the explosion. Rey's dark form was thrown into the air, catapulting from the boat in a billowing wall of flame.

Chapter 14

"I don't know how Tabary did it."

Bull said the words again for at least the hundredth time in the past three days, said them with a wondering admiration that was shared by them all. He was sitting in the schoolroom, a reception room attached to the Cabin restaurant, which was located, in part, in what had once been a plantation slave cabin. The wedding reception of Aunt Tine's great-niece was well under way around him. Reared back in his chair with a glass of champagne in one hand and a bowl of jambalaya in the other, he was holding forth in his best style. Some of the fellow wedding guests, friends of Aunt Tine's, were gathered around, hearing yet again about the accident out on the river.

Julie knew how Rey had done it.

She knew exactly what had happened, because she had watched it with her heart in her throat and anguish caught tight in her chest. She knew because she had seen it at least five times since on rough-cut film.

As she sat at the table beside her father, watching the beautiful dark-haired bride in her white silk and lace sewn with pearls posing for pictures with her bridesmaids, Julie could see the scene replayed yet again in her mind.

Even as she had screamed at him Rey had already been turning, had seen the hint of movement in the figure on the backseat of the boat. He had leaned over the seat and scooped Summer up, then hurled himself over the side of the boat as a fireball of orange and red ballooned overhead and booming thunder shook the trees hard enough to make the gray moss on their limbs dance. His suit coat had trailed flame as he and Summer hit the water. The boat had been a pyre with

205

an iridescent slick of burning oil spreading outward from it for twenty feet before the two of them broke the surface again. It had been the longest wait of Julie's life.

Vance, in the other boat, had been the first one to reach Rey and Summer. He had dragged them into the skiff and brought them to the shooting platform. Summer, still wrapped in her blackened blanket, had been fine except for having singed hair and swallowing a fair part of the Blind River. Rey's coat had been charred and his shoulder extending well down his back burned like seared beef. In delaying to snatch up Summer, he had almost made his jump too late.

Donna's hysteria had been understandable but trying, as she sobbed over and over that it was her fault. Summer's distress and the shock had thrown her into a bout of weeping that seemed endless as she realized she had nearly gotten Rey killed as well as herself. It had been some time before the young girl could be comforted or persuaded that Rey did not require her help with his wounds.

Rey had needed a doctor, and it seemed best to have Summer checked to be sure she had not breathed any of the oily river water into her lungs. It was not until they were all in the cabin cruiser, Rey and Summer, Donna and Julie, Allen and Bull, speeding back toward the location on their way to the hospital emergency room, that anything could be learned about why the young girl had stowed away on the speedboat.

Finally, Summer could be understood to say that she had the idea from a story she had overheard Bull telling about a brave young Mexican boy who became a star after he sneaked in a bullring and fought a bull with a cape instead of letting his dwarf stunt double do it during the making of a movie. This morning, she had heard somebody—she didn't know who—saying what a shame it was that Summer couldn't play her own part in the boat-explosion stunt. It had seemed like a good idea, one that would make her famous. She knew Rey wouldn't let anything happen to her.

But then, when she had hidden the dummy and taken its place, somebody had come along and she had felt a sting in her arm. She had gone to sleep and not woken up until she heard the sound of the gunshots going off for the stunt.

Bull, profane and apologetic by turns, was aghast that it was his story about the boy and the bullring that Summer had heard. No one could make a guess, however, at who might have suggested that Summer do her own stunt.

"Are you sure," Bull said to Summer, "that you heard somebody say that? Are you absolutely certain you didn't get the idea all on your own?"

Summer twisted her lips and bit the insides of them while she knit her brows. "I think I heard it. I'm almost sure I did."

"You're sure you felt a sting, too? It couldn't have just been—oh, a scratch from the blanket because it was hot?"

"You think I just went to sleep?" Summer said in indignation. "I never sleep that good! I could never sleep through that motor being cranked and all that driving."

Nothing could shake her story, not even questioning by the St. James Parish sheriff's deputies. No one could get any further details out of her, either. There was what might have been a pinprick on her upper arm, but a blood test showed nothing unusual. After a thorough examination, she was released.

It was not surprising that a canvas of the movie crew turned up not a single person who had seen Summer climb into the boat or what happened afterward. Anyone who had seen it would most likely have told the girl to get away from there or else called attention to her in some fashion. There were several people who voiced the suspicion that Summer was dramatizing the situation, or maybe making up excuses for herself. The deputies were too polite to agree. However, lacking any evidence of foul play, the investigation was conducted with dispatch and as quickly dropped.

Summer appeared unaffected by the accident. Dressed this evening in pink and white with an iridescent pink bow in her hair, she had watched the wedding in the old church on the River Road with the light of pure pleasure in her thin face. She had made serious inroads on the plate of food Aunt Tine had helped her fill from the bounty spread for the reception, and was sitting watching the other guests with an intent expression, as if storing gestures and speech patterns in her agile young actor's mind.

Everyone seemed to be having a marvelous time, eating, drinking, laughing, and talking all at once. There was nothing staid, nothing formal about the proceedings; the reception was simply a warm and convivial welcome into adulthood and the community for the young couple, with family and friends, neighbors and acquaintances rejoicing in their happiness.

The smiles of the bride were touchingly happy, those of the groom, wearing a white tuxedo to match his bride, loving and proud. There was between them the wildest of anticipation held in check by decorum, but bubbling up in snatched kisses and long looks of smiling promise.

The air was scented with rich food and wine, with the sugar icing on the tall white cake crowned with gum-paste orchids and decorated with cupids and columns and swags of sweet ribbon; and with the spice smells of "rice bags" filled with the birdseed and potpourri that had taken the place of rice these days. The bridesmaids flitted here and there and the groomsmen followed. The mother of the bride stood looking dazed, looking also as if her feet hurt and she was wondering when she would get something to eat from the bounty she had arranged.

The guests flowed from one buffet table to another, laughing, talking in a murmurous cacophony, exclaiming over the beauty of the flowers in the church, the words said by the priest, and the five white Lincoln Town Cars that had brought the wedding party to the reception from the church. In the corner was a man with a video camera, recording it all for posterity.

"Are you having a good time, getting enough to eat?" Aunt Tine asked as she paused beside Julie with a glass of wine in one hand and a barbecued sausage on a fork in the other.

"I certainly am, especially the eating part," Julie answered with a hand held to her stomach. "But tell me something? What's the secret? What causes the Cajun *joie de vivre*, all this pleasure in a party?"

The old lady eyed Julie with bright eyes and a whimsical smile. Waving her fork and sausage for emphasis, she said. "Well, *chère*, it's like this. When the Acadians were forced to leave Nova Scotia, they left everything behind, food, furniture, homes, everything except the clothes they wore. They were herded on ships, families separated never to see each other again, sent first one place, then another. It was many years before the few who did not die of cold and starvation and grief made their way to Louisiana. Only those with a lust for life made it. But from this great loss and long journey they learned one thing for sure. They learned that life is short and death is long, and all we are promised is the minute in our hands. This minute can be hateful or full of joy. Joy is better."

Julie, her gaze returning to the people around her, said slowly, "I think you have something there."

"Believe it, *chère,*" Aunt Tine said. "And have a sausage. They are so good!"

After a time, the four-piece band that had been tuning up and adjusting its speakers out on the side gallery began to play. The bride and groom descended to the brick-floored courtyard to drift slowly about in a waltz. Afterward the bride took the floor with her father while the groom led out his mother—and nearby the flower girl and the ring bearer steered each other around and around in a circle while the guests smiled from the gallery above. The entire wedding party, including the best man and maid of honor plus five bridesmaids and groomsmen, gyrated to a reggae piece as the long gray-blue twilight faded into torch-lit darkness. Finally, with the dancing officially opened, the floor was turned over to the guests.

The only members of the movie company in attendance besides Julie and Bull were Summer and her mother. The invitation had not been a blanket one; it was a private wedding after all, with a limited budget for the reception. It was Donna who had insisted that Summer come, perhaps as a treat to help banish the accident from her mind. It was also Donna who had given the girl a glass with a few drops of champagne in it. It would not hurt her, she said, and it was better to let her try it as a public ritual than have it become a secret addiction. Summer, at first less than pleased to have a new teacher, was becoming more reconciled to Donna with every passing hour.

Rey danced with Summer. Julie had seen him from time to time through the evening, saying pleasant things to the wedding couple, helping an older friend of his aunt to refreshments, talking in a quiet corner with one or two friends. He did not lean against anything,

especially not a chair back, and he made no sudden moves. It was
possible to see, if you looked closely, that the bulge of the bandaging
on his back disturbed the line of his suit. Still, he bent to listen to
Summer's chatter without a sign of strain, and he twirled her through
the Cajun waltz until her skirts flew around her, teaching her how to
whirl backward with one hand held gracefully at the small of her back.
He appeared from a distance to be gravely attentive, though with quick
flashes of humor. Summer laughed up at him in transparent delight,
and with worship shining in her eyes. He was, it was easy to see, her
hero. Julie, watching, found herself wishing fervently that his image
might never be tarnished, or if it must be, that Summer never learn
of it.

Donna, carrying around a towheaded toddler on her hip, hugging
the groom who was related in some way, answering the many expressions of sympathy extended to her with grace and composure, seemed
to be having a good time in a quiet fashion. Nobody frowned when
she went with Rey to the dance floor, though the toddler was inclined
to be upset at her loss. The baby's frowns turned to chortles, however,
as the bride handed him the loop to her train to hold in his plump little
hand and waltzed him around and around down the gallery.

A few minutes later, the bride was on the dance floor again, this
time dancing with her grandfather, who was pinning a hundred-dollar
bill to her veil while shuffling happily to the music. It was time for
the money dance, where the men, most of them friends and neighbors
if not relatives, danced with the bride and left a monetary token of
affection pinned to the more accessible parts of her wedding costume,
sometimes the sleeves of her gown, but most often the veil. The
money, so Aunt Tine said, was usually used to help with the expenses
of the honeymoon.

The couple would be going to a plantation house, Tezcuco, for
the night, one that had been turned into a bed-and-breakfast inn. From
there, they would be heading for a week on the Florida gulf coast.
When they returned, Julie thought, they would take up their lives as
man and wife, have children, live and work, and quite probably die
without ever moving more than a few miles from the lovely Victorian
church where they had been married. The bride would become a wife

and mother, aunt and godmother, great-aunt and grandmother in inevitable progression. She would not complain and she would, most likely, be happy.

Contemplating that existence, Julie shook her head. How simple it sounded, and how impossibly idyllic.

It wasn't for her.

Four children, two boys and two girls—

No, it wasn't for her. Her dreams could never be made to fit. They were too big, too wide, for so narrow a life.

"Shall we?"

Rey was standing before her with his hand held out in invitation while the band struck up another Cajun waltz. Julie placed her fingers in his. Rising, she moved with him along the gallery and down the wooden steps to the courtyard dance floor.

She had watched the others, and knew a modicum of ballroom dancing; she was soon whirling with Rey around the brick floor, swinging in and out of his arms, turning with him in perfect rhythm with his hand held against the arched small of her back. And there was joy rising inside her, a sweet, fearsome joy.

It could not be contained, that joy, but it must; it should not end, but it would. And so she set herself to make of it a personal memory held inside her, one that would sustain her because of its strength.

"So, have you decided to put a Cajun wedding in your movie?" he asked, his gaze warm yet darkly opaque as he smiled down at her.

"I think I just may. There seems no better way to show some aspects of Jean-Pierre's life and beliefs, or of the emotional development of his Alicia."

"Aunt Tine will be happy."

"Will she?"

"She'll enjoy thinking she contributed something."

"She contributed a lot," Julie said. "I picked up all kinds of nuances from talking to her."

She was grateful to him for the introduction of a neutral subject. She wondered briefly if he did it from politeness, for his own comfort, or if he was concerned for her. Whatever the reason, she was pleased to allow her thoughts to move on one level while her emotions ran in wanton unrestraint on another. It was disturbing, to say the least, to be in his arms again.

"How is your shoulder?" she said, and was afraid for an instant that he would be able to make the same sequence of mental connections that she had in order to come to that question.

"Sore," he answered, "but not totally useless."

He caught her close, whirling her suddenly into a series of turns that melded their bodies together from breasts to thighs, and left her breathless and clinging. Then gently he returned her to arm's length while his eyes, unbearably lucid, held hers.

It was plain he understood her much too well, and was dangerous precisely because he wasn't afraid to let her know it. If he had said to her then, at that moment, "Come with me," she would have gone. He did not. That he had his reasons, she did not doubt. She was, of course, free to guess what they were, but was not sure she wanted to know.

She was going to miss him, miss the bright flash of laughter in his eyes, the warm depth of caring in his voice. She would feel the loss of his febrile intelligence that reached out to meet and support her own, and also the delicacy of the understanding he extended without expectation of return. She would miss, already missed, the touch and taste and feel of him, his inventive caresses, his controlled power. She would even miss his strength, both of body and will. Realizing the last, she knew, too, that it was a good thing she was going.

The bride threw her bouquet, the groom threw the garter, and there was much teasing of the young woman and man who caught these tokens. The pair left them in a hail of birdseed and potpourri, and good wishes.

The band packed up and left and the guests straggled out to their cars. Bull and Rey left together, giving no destination, though Rey told his aunt not to wait up as he kissed her good night on the cheek. Bull would be staying in the same motel in Gonzales where the rest of the crew was registered, so said only that he would see Julie on the set.

Julie was left behind with Aunt Tine, helping the mother of the bride and her friends and relatives to clear some of the mess left behind, though the final cleanup would be done by the staff from the Cabin restaurant. Julie didn't mind; there was something relaxing, even satisfying, about being there for the end of the evening.

Aunt Tine insisted that Julie drive on the way home, claiming she was tipsy from champagne. Once there, they sat for a while on the gallery, talking about the wedding and the people who had been there, wondering what Bull and Rey were up to in the middle of the night. It wasn't actually that late, of course, only a little after eleven.

Regardless, Julie began to yawn. She had been too wrought up since the accident, too plagued with questions and fears to rest. She woke often and could not go back to sleep, instead lying staring into the darkness, thinking, endlessly thinking. Maybe tonight would be different.

It wasn't. She dozed for perhaps an hour, then woke with a jangling start as if at some silent alarm. She sighed, turning to her stomach, running her fingers through her hair as she raised on her elbows. She reached for her small travel clock and punched the button to light the numbers. One o'clock.

Lying back down again, she put her arms around her pillow and nestled her face into it. She tried to keep the tired round of questions at bay, but it was no use.

The one that stood out, that troubled her the most, was whether the accident with Summer had anything to do with the death of Paul Lislet. It didn't seem possible that it could, and yet it was too much of a coincidence that there had been dangerous problems with two separate stunts. If Rey had not noticed Summer's first tentative movements, there would have been two deaths. And the second, that of a helpless child who should have been nowhere near that boat, would have been hard indeed to explain.

It would have been even harder to live with. It was this that had brought Julie awake night after night, sweating with terror. She might have been to blame for Summer's death.

Still, there was more to it than that. Julie had to question whether the girl had nearly been the victim of some peculiar plot that was directed against her and her movie. There was the snake. Had it been

meant to frighten or injure her? Or had it been a warning, a sign that
someone did not want her to direct *Swamp Kingdom,* did not intend
that she complete the picture.

Why? Who would care whether she succeeded or failed? Who
could hate her enough to want to stop her? Who was demented enough
to kill a man and nearly kill a child simply to prevent her from putting
a story on film?

Maybe she was wrong. Maybe she was being paranoid, or else
supremely egocentric to think that the things that had taken place
revolved around her. Accidents happened, especially where stunts were
concerned. Snakes lived in swamps; there was nothing strange about
one appearing at the location. As a matter of fact, several had been
killed while the motor homes were being moved in and while the
shooting platform downriver was being built. According to Rey, men
in the area sometimes went out with guns in the high water during
the spring runoff strictly to thin the population; it was nothing to see
snakes of all kinds draping the tree limbs then in swags and loops and
knots like living decorator cords.

It was also possible, Julie thought, that she was letting her distress
over what was happening with the people concerned with this film
color her reactions. Allen's defection, his insistence that she turn her
film over to Bull, was depressing. So was the realization that so many
on the set had reasons, some stretching back years, to be unhappy with
her. She was used to a more relaxed, trusting relationship with her
co-workers, one where the main concern was the film, not jealousy and
ancient resentment.

She was so tired of all the doubts and delays. She wanted to get
on with her movie, but there was a place somewhere inside her that
was braced, waiting for what would happen next.

The yellow sweep of light around her room, the kind caused by
the headlights of a car, deflected her attention. A moment later, she
heard the purr of Rey's Maserati as it pulled up beside the house, then
the dying rumble of its engine as the ignition was turned off.

Nothing else happened for so long that she turned to her back and
propped herself up on her elbows to listen. She expected to hear Rey
enter the house from the front gallery; she had grown adept in the past

weeks at deciphering the sounds of the house, and also his comings and goings. Instead, she heard his footsteps, cautious and slow, on the steps to the back gallery. There came then a dull, clattering thud and a soft curse. Julie raised a brow as she recognized that Rey had knocked over one of the rocking chairs.

His footsteps continued along the gallery, nearing her door. They stopped outside. Silence descended.

After a time, the footsteps retreated slightly. Julie heard a soft, off-key singing in Cajun patois, so quiet it was plain the song was not meant for public hearing, that he was singing to himself. The words were not clear, and as she caught the slight slurring of the syllables Julie shook her head with a laconic smile.

It did not seem likely, but she would swear that Rey Tabary was drunk. This might, just possibly, be a sight to see.

She got out of bed, reaching for her thin silk robe, tying the belt about her waist as she felt for her slippers. She didn't turn on a light, but moved in the dark to her bedroom door. She turned the key in the old lock, then eased it open. Putting her head out, she looked up and down the gallery. Rey was nowhere to be seen. Then a slight sound like an indrawn breath made her look up toward the railing to her right at the end of the gallery.

He was walking it. Wearing only a pair of slacks and a shirt with the sleeves rolled to the elbows and button undone so it hung open, he was treading the rail like a high wire at a circus. His bare toes gripped the wooden top board, and his arms were spread wide for balance. There was unconscious grace in his movements, though his progress was somewhat wobbly. He reached the end of the space between the square columns and turned, walking back.

There was no sign of Bull. Julie supposed Rey had dropped him at his motel. She stood waiting until Rey was nearly opposite her, well within reach of the next column supporting the railing, before she spoke.

"What do you think you're doing?"

He started, wavered, then lunged for the near column. Hugging it to his chest, he turned to face her.

"What did you do that for?" he asked in plaintive accusation.

"Curiosity," she answered.

He looked down at her in the faint light from the starshine and a security light somewhere toward the front of the house. If the word she had spoken had any meaning for him, he did not show it. His eyes gleamed with appreciation overlaid with melancholy, and something more serious than either one.

After long seconds of contemplation, he said, "I can't surf."

"Is *that* what you were doing?" she said as if in enlightenment.

"There's no ocean." The words were solemn.

"You're right. I suppose you could, otherwise."

He shook his head. "I can't act, either."

"I think you may be wrong there, but I'll take it as gospel."

"Do," he said.

She moved closer in order to see his face, wondering if he was as drunk as he seemed. "It isn't necessary for you to act."

"You like actors. And surfers."

She blinked, in part because of the sadness of his tone. Her reply was flip because she could think of no other way to take what he said. "It's a defect, I know."

"L.A. people. Sunglasses and suntans. Bel Air and Rodeo Drive."

"Well, yes," she agreed, intrigued.

"Producers. Ass—aesthetes."

Was the last word proceeded by a slip of the tongue? If so, he seemed to find it humorous, for a grin crossed his face and was extinguished before he went on.

"That's not me," he went on. "All I know about movies is how to watch them."

"You underestimate yourself," she said.

He eyed her with solemnity, as if he suspected her of answering more than his last comment. His voice softer, he said, "I'm not Jean, either."

"That's certainly true."

"And you're not his Dorothea."

He said the name with significance, as if there were meaning there he expected her to grasp. She didn't, though she was willing to try. "No?"

"They only know how to hate and to pretend to love. There's more to marriage than that."

"I should hope so." She was still at a loss, though one thing was plain to her. Beneath his strength were levels of vulnerability she had never suspected.

"I'm not a rat," he said.

Her tone gentle, tentative, she answered, "You're the Swamp Rat."

He shook his head. "No."

"What are you then?"

"A man. Just a man." He let go of the column and swung down then, landing on his feet with a dull jar. Still crouching, he grimaced, putting one hand to his head and the other to the bandaging across his left shoulder while he slowly eased erect. He swayed a moment, then backed to lean against the railing, weaving back and forth as if in intolerable pain.

She stepped quickly to put her arms around him, holding him steady. Her voice sharp, she said, "You shouldn't have had so much to drink."

He bent his head to rest it on her shoulder, while the ghost of a laugh shook him. "Percodan and Jack Daniel's don't mix."

"Is that it?" Her relief was excessive, and she knew it. It was just that she had not expected overindulgence from him. Regardless, the combination of whiskey and pain medication could be lethal. She went on, "You should have known better."

"Bull insisted on the Jack Daniel's."

"What's he got to do with it?"

He chuckled again, a warm sound that wafted his breath downward over the nipple of her breast under her silk robe, so that it tightened. "Asked my intentions. Very words."

"You have to be kidding," Julie said in indignation. Then added against her better judgment, "What did you say?"

"Said, 'Good or bad?' "

"Very funny. And was that all?"

"Told him, wasn't his business. Didn't like that. Bought 'nother round of drinks."

"You stuck to your guns anyway, I hope."

"Humm." He shifted and lowered his arms to wrap them around her waist, pulling her closer. "This is nice."

Since he had not precisely answered her question, she could only assume the answer to it was affirmative. As for the current moment, she might as well get whatever she could out of it. She asked, "Only nice?"

"Comfortable."

"I'm glad you like it," she said in mingled amusement and exasperation. "And was that the whole reason my father plied you with alcohol."

"Two drinks. I swear. Only took two."

"Good for you."

His silent laugh shook his body. "Bull was surprised."

Thinking of her father's legendary ability to drink most men under the table, she said, "I imagine so."

"I told him. Love."

She bent her head, trying to see his face. "You told him what?"

"Love. And com—compassion. Way to reach you."

"He asked you how to reach me? What made him think you would know?"

"I don't know."

Was that a lie, or was his understanding so instinctive that he had no idea himself how deep it went?

"You think compassion is the way to my heart, then?"

"Bull's way. Not mine."

"What is yours, then?"

He sighed. "Nothing."

Nothing. Did he mean that there was nothing he could do, or that he meant to do nothing—that he had no use for a way to her heart?

"I'm not Jean-Pierre," he said, when she made no reply.

"I know that," she answered, her voice thick.

"Then it's all right."

They could not stay where they were. The night had grown cool, there was a chill wind blowing out of the north. Her feet were freezing. To get him through the house to his own bedroom without waking Aunt Tine seemed an impossible task. Besides, she didn't feel up to it just now. Her own room was much closer, and it would not be the first time he had slept beside her.

"Come on," she said, "let's get you to bed."

He made no protest, but straightened docilely enough, allowing her to drape his arm over her shoulders. Julie maneuvered him through the doorway, then walked him to the bed. She made certain that it was his good shoulder that would hit the mattress when she sat him down then pushed him over onto it. Tugging the blanket and sheet out from under him, she covered him with them, then went back to close and lock the door.

She stood there for a moment, wondering at herself, wondering if she was being humane or simply stupid. It didn't matter, not really; she was doing what she wanted. Slipping out of her robe, she threw it across the foot of the bed and eased under the covers beside Rey.

"Feet are cold," he said as her toes brushed his ankle.

Deliberately, she moved nearer, pressing them against him as she told him, "You deserve it."

He turned to put his hand on her bare waist, spreading his fingers in a possessive caress, drawing her nearer still. "I know," he said.

Chapter 15

Why was it that hotel telephones always had a ring like a fire-alarm bell? Julie, startled by the harsh sound as she was putting an earring in her ear, exclaimed in irritation as she dropped the sapphire cluster. She considered ignoring the summons. She couldn't think of anyone who would be phoning her here anyway. The only person who knew where she was staying in L.A., as far as she was aware, was her secretary, who had made the reservation. If the girl was calling to report some further disaster on the location back in Louisiana, Julie wasn't sure she wanted the news.

Listening to the ring was worse than answering. She picked up the receiver, her voice less than cordial as she spoke into it.

"Miss Bullard?" came the voice at the other end. "This is your driver. Your limousine is waiting, at your convenience."

"But I didn't order a limo," Julie objected.

"Somebody did. I'll be waiting for you outside, Miss Bullard."

It was possible the film-festival committee had arranged for the car. It was a nice gesture. Julie said, "I'll be right down."

She found her earring and fastened it, checked her evening bag to be sure she had her key, lipstick, a little cash, and a credit card in case of emergency, then took a last look at herself in the full-length mirror on the closet door. Her hair, woven in a simple French plait down the back, was classically neat. Her formal gown of iridescent silk shading from gold to cobalt blue had a somber medieval drama in its square neck and large sleeves that suited her mood. The hem of her long full skirt was even and her underskirt wasn't showing. She would do.

The doorman opened the bronze doors as she crossed the lobby toward them. She passed under the hotel's canopied entranceway and over the bridge to where the limousine waited with the driver in his black uniform on guard near the rear door. As she neared, the man moved forward, touching the narrow bill of his cap.

"Miss Bullard? Good evening." He reached to get the door for her. "Step right inside."

She had already bent her head to enter when she saw that the limo was not empty. A man sat on the backseat, a man startlingly handsome in evening dress.

"Hello, Julie," Rey said.

She took the hand he held out to her in a reflex response, allowing him to draw her inside and settle her on the seat beside him. The driver had closed the door and moved to set the car in motion before she could sort out the jumble of surprise and confusion that were her thoughts enough to speak.

"You didn't have to do this," she said.

Amusement glinted in his eyes. "I know, but it seemed a little ostentatious to ship the Maserati out for just one evening. Besides, I wanted to be able to talk to you instead of watching traffic."

"You know what I mean."

"Yes, well, the suspense was too much for me."

Warily, she said, "Suspense?"

"About what I missed before I fell asleep in your bed."

"Not a great deal," she said shortly.

He searched her face in the passing gleam of street and traffic lights. "I have a feeling I may have said a lot of dumb things."

"You didn't seem to think they were dumb at the time."

He let out a deep breath, slouching down in the seat as he stared straight ahead. "I knew it. Tell me the worst."

"You said my feet were cold."

"Was that before or after I tried to fly off the gallery railing?"

He was embarrassed and contrite, she realized in amazement, but able to make a joke of it. She said, "Does it matter? There was no harm done."

"Then why did you leave without saying good-bye?"

"You were sleeping so soundly it seemed a shame to wake you. Besides, I had a plane to catch."

"Something you failed to mention. Something I might not have found out at all if Bull hadn't managed to pry it out of your secretary then pass it on."

She tipped her head to one side. "I didn't know you would be interested."

"This is important to you, isn't it?" he answered, as if that explained everything.

Maybe it did. And again, maybe it didn't. She was touched, incredibly so, and that was frightening.

He was too handsome, too rich, too strong, too intelligent, too sensitive, too attentive—too much of everything. With so much perfection, there had to be huge flaws also. And there were. She had had a great deal of time to think about it since the night before, a transcontinental-flight worth of time.

He had never really explained how he came to leave the DEA, never explained what a man like him was doing in the drug agency in the first place. His wife had died, he said, but no one else had mentioned how it happened, though Aunt Tine had referred briefly to the marriage one or twice. There were the rumors of a past affair with Donna—or one not so far in the past. There was his speeding progress along the Blind River on the night the seaplane had skimmed by overhead, and his undeniable interest in that plane's progress. And there was the day she had found him going through the files in her office.

More than that, he was everything that was perfect for everybody. Summer adored him. Donna depended on him. Ofelia thought he was awe-inspiring. Stan admired him. Even Bull liked him. Everybody except possibly Vance and Allen thought he was wonderful. He had gone to a lot of trouble to make it so.

Why?

What did he want?

There had to be something.

Suspicion. Cynicism. They came easily in L.A.; they were a part of the landscape, as ubiquitous as the palm trees and smog. They were a form of protection, often necessary, sometimes expedient.

She was afraid of Rey Tabary. He was the kind of man who could overwhelm her careful defenses so she became lost in his world, his life, the mind-numbing seduction of his lovemaking. She didn't want that. She liked her life the way it was, evenly divided between the personal and the artistic. If her personal life with Allen was sometimes rather impersonal—well, that was her choice. If her artistic life did not always satisfy, what did?

"Would you rather go alone?" Rey said quietly. "Just say so, and I'll get out anywhere along here."

Too sensitive.

"Don't be ridiculous," she said with a smile that felt brittle around the edges. "Having an escort will be lovely. I'd have ordered myself one if I had thought of it."

He looked at her a moment. "The tux and I do go well with the car, don't we?"

She had been trying to reduce the value of his presence and had succeeded. She did not feel victorious, however, only embarrassed.

"I'm sorry," she said, turning her head to look out of the window at the endless stream of seedy motels and liquor stores and Laundromats they were passing. "I don't understand why you went to so much trouble to come here, so I don't know what to say to you."

"You don't have to say anything," he answered in tired tones. "Just relax and enjoy your night."

The Women in Film Festival might not be the Directors' Guild Awards, still, it was a gala occasion. An annual event some six or seven years old, it had been conceived to honor the accomplishments of women in film from all over the world, including female filmmakers from countries such as Czechoslovakia, the USSR, and even Morocco. The infiltration of women into the upper echelons of this male-dominated industry was a slow process, though the numbers of women producers, screenwriters, and studio executives, as well as directors, were increasing. Since recognition of their achievements was even slower than their progress, they had banded together to celebrate themselves.

There were lights and cameras, speeches and applause. Julie's film *Dangerous Times* received a warm and enthusiastic reception. She

hardly knew what she said when she was called up on stage to receive
her reward, the award as Best Director; she only knew a wonderful
sense of confirmation of her work. Much more than the award, she
appreciated that jolting boost to her confidence in her methods and
herself. It was something she sorely needed at that moment.

Descending from the stage in the glare of the spotlight with the
crystal piece in her hands, she made her way back to where Rey stood
applauding with the others. She was aware of fierce elation, and also
gratitude that he was there to share her triumph. He had gone to a great
deal of effort to offer her his support, and she had been too busy
looking for base motives even to thank him.

Eyes sparkling, smile brilliant, feeling warm and joyous inside,
Julie opened her arms as she neared Rey and slid them around his neck.
Her voice husky with the exuberant pleasure of the moment, she said,
"I'm glad you're here; I really am."

"So am I," he said, smiling down at her as he held her loosely
clasped against him. "So am I."

When it was over, when the last photograph had been taken, the
last comment recorded for the television cameras, the last compliment
accepted, Julie and Rey made their way toward their limo. It was a
relief to sink into its soft quiet and be anonymous behind the dark glass
of its closed door, a pleasure to feel the car pulling away, joining the
flow of traffic, and know that the evening and its stresses were behind
her. Julie could feel the electric tension of the past few hours thrum-
ming along her nerves with painful intensity. She was happy, yet at
the same time too keyed up for her own comfort.

"Where do you want to go?" Rey asked. "Are you hungry? Is
there someplace special you would like to eat?"

Julie leaned her head back on the seat. "I don't know, really. I'm
a little hungry, but I don't particularly want to go to the Bistro or
Morton's or La Scala or any of the other places where—where the elite
always meet."

He noted the brief quote from an old New Orleans jazz tune made
famous by the great Satchmo Armstrong with a flickering smile.
"What?" he said. "No California nouvelle cuisine at a power table
with telephone?"

She turned her head on the seat back. "I'm not like that."

"I thought that in this town you had to be seen at the right places to look successful, and look successful to be successful."

"Some do, but that's the nice thing about being my father's daughter. He's already done all that, so I don't have to."

"Where to then?"

"Someplace private with a fire in the fireplace to take the dampness from the ocean air and excellent food. What do you think?"

"Nice, unless—"

"What?"

"Never mind. Where were you thinking of?"

"The Bel Air. Room service. My room." As he gave her a steady look that she could not interpret in the dim light from the street she said, "What now?"

"Not Gravesend's place? Or Bull's?"

"Oh, you wonder what I'm doing at the hotel in the first place? Simple. I decided to give myself a treat."

"And that's all?"

"I didn't feel like fighting traffic from Allen's house at San Marino, or braving the coast highway this time of night from Bull's Malibu colony place." Her voice had an edge to it that she wished she had controlled a little more carefully. Perhaps he would overlook it, she thought, though she should have known better.

He said, "Neutral ground then? Now, I wonder why?"

"Because I'm not feeling particularly cordial toward either of them. Is that what you wanted to know?"

"Yes," he answered.

She stared at him, and what she saw in his eyes caused her heart to jar against her ribs. Dear God, but how did he do it? He hadn't moved a muscle or so much as smiled, but she was suddenly breathless. To let him see, however, would be a serious mistake.

Keeping her voice carefully even, she said, "I have a suite at the hotel, very cozy, the direct result of using my father's name. You can do the honors with the fireplace, if you like, while I order dinner."

"I'm invited then?" he said dryly.

Her tact was wasted, and she wasn't sure whether to be amused or irritated by it. "You are, though I'm surprised you waited to find out."

"I'm trying my best not to use—what was the phrase from the Nassau trip?—cowboy tactics?"

Her lips twitched. "Yes, indeed, that's why you called and asked me if I wanted a limo!"

"I forgot. No games, no surprises."

He seemed to be in a strange mood this evening, distant, repressed, almost bleak except for rare moments. It was possible he was only responding to her own unsettled frame of mind, her lack of welcome.

"It was a nice gesture, and I do appreciate it," she said, "even if I have been less than gracious about it."

"Some surprises are acceptable?"

"Once in a great while," she said, her tone solemn.

"I'll remember it."

A short time later, the car turned into the canyon road leading to the hotel. They passed the pool where the famous swans, white blotches in the shadows, slept with their heads beneath their wings. The Bel Air loomed before them, a conglomeration of wings and towers. Rey dismissed the limousine and driver. A short time later, Julie opened the door to her suite and led the way inside.

It was expansive and luxurious, done in shades of green with rose accents and light-colored woods. The look was informal, with the armoire holding the television and the chest at the foot of the bed in pine, while the tables, large and small, were of antique brass and glass. The lamps had an Italian look in their heavy rose marble columns and bases. The sofa and chairs were modern, oversized and comfortable, done in a Canovas fabric that matched the fluffy duvet and pillow shams on the enormous bed. Natural stone faced the fireplace that was set in one wall. The balcony opening from the dining area was set with verdigris-colored wrought-iron furniture and great stone pots filled with rose geraniums and variegated English ivy.

She put the Crystal Award she still carried down in the center of the coffee table before the sofa, moving aside the painted china ashtray and ginger jar to make room. She offered Rey a drink from the wet bar and handed him the room-service menu while she went to change out of her heavy gown. When she returned, he was standing in front of the fireplace, where bright flames licked at the logs that had been laid there. He was in his shirtsleeves with a bottle of Heineken in one hand and her award in the other.

"You must be very good at what you do," he said.

She moved to the wet bar to pour herself a glass of wine. "Because of tonight, you mean?"

"And the way people were talking about your movie."

"I don't know whether I am or not," she said. "It's not something I think about a lot, though certainly I had a good teacher."

He looked up, his gaze resting for an appreciative second on the soft turquoise silk jump suit she had put on with turquoise Italian leather sandals. "You don't know?"

"I don't think anybody who does anything in the arts really knows when their work is good. It either satisfies them or it doesn't, and that's about it."

"The critics can't tell them, or the sales?"

"Critics are only people with a single viewpoint, their own. Schlock sells wonderfully, for brief periods. It seems only time can give a true judgment, and who can afford to sit around waiting for that?"

"I'm afraid I never gave the movie business much thought until these last weeks." He reached to replace the award on the glass coffee table where the crystal seemed to disappear on the glass top.

"It's a living," she said, and didn't smile.

"Have you ever thought what you would do if you couldn't make films?"

She stared into her wineglass as she considered the question. "Become a screenwriter maybe, though that must be one of the most frustrating jobs around when your vision and that of the director—or the star—doesn't match. Screenwriters have to have small egos."

"Or a greater love for money than for their ideas?"

"I don't know about that. I think maybe they fall in love with seeing the images they create come alive." She paused, then indicated the room-service menu lying on the sofa table. "Have you decided what you want?"

He looked at her, a faint smile tugging at one corner of his mouth. "Long ago."

She met his gaze for long moments, held by its openness and the teasing promise in its depths, met it until she felt the slow rise of heat under her skin, until she could bear it no longer. Her grasp was tight on the menu as she reached for it, but still it did not hide the tremor in her fingers.

They ordered salmon with garlic cream sauce and tarragon, which came with miniature vegetables, then followed it with white-chocolate cake with boysenberries for dessert. At their request, the food with its complementary California wine was served before the fire.

The lateness of the hour, the quiet crackle and warmth of the blaze, and its dancing reflection in silver and crystal, the blending of wood smoke, wine, and superb food flavors created such a sense of muted perfection that Julie could feel her tenseness unraveling like a piece of bad crochet. She and the man across from her said little, nor did speaking seem necessary. When they had finished their entrées, Julie set aside their dessert plates, then rolled the room-service cart from the suite while Rey made coffee using the sleek German pot in the kitchen. When it was made, they took their cups back to the fireplace, where Julie kicked off her sandals and curled into an armchair. Rey lowered himself to the carpeted floor, leaning his good shoulder against a chair and stretching his long legs out toward the fire. Julie handed him his dessert from where it sat on the coffee table, then picked up her own.

The last crumb was finally gone, the last sip of coffee swallowed. The fire had dwindled to its red heart. Julie, stretching in repletion and a curious half-acknowledged abandon, set aside her cup and plate. Leaning back in her chair again, she propped her elbow on the arm of her chair, supporting her head with her hand. Studying Rey, who lay watching the fire, she said, "You've been quiet this evening. Is your shoulder bothering you?"

He looked blank for an instant, as if his thoughts were occupied with a subject so different that it was difficult to understand what she was saying. He shook his head. "No, it's fine."

"Something else, then?"

He gave her a slow smile. "Nothing of importance."

She was not sure that was true. She wished, suddenly, that she could talk to him about what was happening at the location, could see what he thought about the ideas struggling in the back of her mind. It was impossible. He was too closely concerned with those ideas, too mixed up in them in ways she didn't understand.

"Actually," he said, his smile taking on a wry tinge, "that's not quite right. I've been concentrating hard on remembering my better intentions—what's so funny?"

"Nothing," she said, waving her hand palm out in a sign of innocence before using it to cover her grin of remembrance.

"I've also," he went on with narrowed eyes, "been trying to prevent the urge to read too much into your invitation to join you, or to search for hidden meaning in every word you say, such as your offer of the honor of tending your fire."

She blinked, then sat up straight, putting her feet on the floor. She should be annoyed, she thought, but was instead intrigued. "What a thing to say."

"The ramblings of desperation. I'm also having trouble with that silky thing you put on. From where I sit, it looks like purest provocation, but I could be wrong."

"You are. I think."

"Don't you know?" His voice as he asked it was shaded with despair.

"Why should I be any more certain than you are?"

"Because," he said, his gaze dark as it held hers across the space between them, "it's your room, your beautiful body, your inalienable birthright to tell me to go or stay."

The sound of his voice, the generosity of his concession, the restrained force of his presence were more provocation than anything she might have said or done. Desire, hovering at the outer edge of her consciousness for hours, rose inside her with the warm joy of gratitude and pleasure of remembrance, blending with the wine and the isolation of midnight and distance into certainty. And the only possible reply.

She said in soft entreaty, "Stay."

His face changed. He shifted positions then, rising with smooth and rigorous control to his one knee, then moving to kneel in front of her. "I didn't mean to force a decision," he said quietly.

"What did you mean to do?" she asked, reaching to place her fingers on his strong brown hand where it lay on the chair arm.

"To wait—this time—to see what you would like, what you would do."

"Now you know." She kept her gaze on her own slim fingers that lay so lightly on his own.

"Do I?"

Her gaze was clear when she looked up at him. "Do you think I could not say no?"

"I think you might decide it would be unfair."

"After leading you on? Or in the light of past actions? Either way, I'm not that noble."

"Then—"

"Then there's no need for you to be so noble, either," she said, and smiling, leaned to press her lips to his.

He insisted, however, making his need for consent into an erotic penance imposed with strength and guile and endless invention. She was required to say precisely what she was willing to allow, from the slide of every zipper and unfastening of every hook to the most delicate brush of his lips on any fragile skin surface. Relentless, ignoring protests, he continued, until she began to anticipate his moves and caresses, and turn her whispers of consent into demands.

Chest shaking with suppressed laughter then, he dragged her with him to the floor, rolling with her on the carpet in the dying light of the fire. And began to lure her into the rapturous game of pleasures asked and received in earnest.

Julie's heartbeat pounded with feathery warnings in her ears while her blood heated her veins and, turgid with yearning, concentrated in the lower part of her body. The muscles and planes of his chest against the pointed nipples of her breasts were a wild incitement. His thighs, hard-muscled, rough with curling hair against the smoothness of her own, made her aware of the enticing vulnerability at the center of her being. The lilt of his voice fueled the swift rise of her delight, while the feel of him under her hands, firm and resilient, was a sensation to be gently savored.

It was a physical enchantment without respite or remorse, a wondrous exploration of hollows and protuberances, of the heights of glad servility and the limits of endurance. And then, when the outermost boundaries of gallantry had been reached, he rose above her, poised, testing, and said, "Shall I?"

"Yes," she answered, and gasping at the shock of it, closed her eyes tightly while together they spiraled into oblivion.

And whispered again, afterward, after the striving, after the glory, after the fire beside them had died to ashes, "Yes."

She woke well covered but naked in the middle of the king-size bed. The French doors that opened onto the balcony stood wide and a fresh wind scented with the smell of pepper trees and new-mown grass was blowing inside, lifting the sheer curtain that hung beside it in a pale rose billow. Rey stood braced in the opening. His body, magnificent in its muscular sculpting, was outlined against slate-gray morning light. He wore a towel around his hips that flapped slowly back and forth in the wind. The white expanse of bandaging on his injured shoulder was smaller than it had been.

She watched him, absorbing the sight, enjoying it. Seen in repose, he seemed intent, alert, almost as if he was on guard, an impression she had noticed before. It was curious, since he was also one of the most relaxed men she had ever known.

She smiled, remembering his slow attention to the moment. At the same time, she wondered at the fact that he was there, with her. The answer to the question of why he had come tugged at her, not the facile, flattering reasons he had given, but the real ones. What did he hope to gain? What possible advantage could there be in it for him? There had to be something. There was always something.

She would think about it later. It was too early for suspicion, or cynicism.

"What is it?" she said sleepily. "Why are you up?"

He turned his head to smile back at her over his shoulder. "I was looking at the rain."

"Rain? In California?" She sat up, so that the sheet and duvet fell back, exposing her to the waist.

"Undeniably, with fog off the ocean. Thick fog. Not a good day for flying."

"Oh. What a pity," she said, catching his mood, and his intention.

"Isn't it?" he agreed. Removing his towel, he walked steadily toward the bed.

"Maybe tomorrow," she murmured as he slid in beside her, reaching for her with firm hands. His hair was damp from the shower and his skin smelled of fresh air and soap and clean male. She shivered a little with the chill of his fingers, and with expectation.

He said softly, "Maybe."

It was late afternoon of the following day when Julie and Rey reached the location. The sun was sliding toward the horizon, a great red ball of fire streaking the sky with the orange and rose-pink and gold of a swamp-country sunset, silhouetting the trees in a cinder-black edging against it. Julie, watching the changing colors in the last few miles of their homeward journey, had felt a pang of regret that she had missed it. It would have been perfect as the backdrop she wanted for the credits.

They turned into the parking lot. Everything was quiet, but Julie had expected nothing else. She had known nothing would be going on, but she wanted to stop by anyway on the way to Aunt Tine's house. She had to be sure that nothing had happened while she was gone.

The motor homes, the trailer offices, the catering vans near the boat club were deserted. Everybody would be at the motel or maybe in New Orleans, enjoying the unexpected hiatus caused by her absence, waiting for the callback. The guard on station, a local sheriff's deputy putting in a little extra off-duty time to supplement his pay, saluted Julie as she got out of the Cherokee, which they had picked up at the airport. She waited for Rey to join her before she walked toward the guard.

"What's going on?" she called.

"Just the usual," the man said, hitching at his belt and settling his gun as he stepped out of his small metal shelter and came toward them. "Everybody's out on the river, watching the great Bull Bullard do his stuff."

A chill moved over Julie; still, she kept her voice even and managed to hold on to her smile. "Bull? What's he up to now?"

"Got the crew out there taking pictures of the sunset, way I understand it."

"Is that so? Sounds like something I ought to see."

"Julie—" Rey said.

She swung to face him. "Will you take me out on the river? There must be a boat we can use here somewhere?"

"Don't you think you ought to wait until they come back. It can't be long now."

She saw what he meant. The sun-streaked sky would soon begin to fade. It made no difference. "No," she said, "I don't. If you would rather not go—"

"I'll take you," he said, his voice grim.

His air boat was still there, pulled up at the dock since the last day of filming when he had used it to run back and forth between the location and the shooting area. Within minutes, they were flying down the river with the wind in their faces and spray in their hair.

They didn't have far to go. Bull was filming in the nearest open canal, at a place where he could place his cameras to catch not only the sunset and tree line, but also the slow progress of a wooden pirogue with old Joseph in the stern, poling through the gathering shadows.

Pain and disbelief rose inside Julie's brain as she saw what was taking place, saw the careful angles of the set cameras, their filters that would catch the slanting gleams of fading sunlight, the pink and gold reflections, the wavering water-mirror images of man and boat and swamp. It was so familiar a vision, such a perfect reproduction of what she had seen so often in her head that she sat stunned by it, and by the implications of it.

Then from down the river came the roar of a boat motor. The skiff with Vance at the controls came skimming from around a bend. It shot toward the camera setup, whipping past the wooden boat. Vance sketched a salute toward the old man in the pirogue. Old Joseph merely nodded, turning his head to follow the progress of the skiff even as he rocked in its wake. And the cameras tracked to follow the swift-moving skiff also.

Julie turned slowly to face Rey as he decreased their speed, letting the air boat come to a wallowing idle. Her voice had the compressed sound of denied anguish as she spoke.

"You told him. You told Bull about the sunset."

He looked at her without answering, but there was regret in the darkness of his eyes.

Out in the cabin cruiser just ahead of them, Bull turned to glare at the air boat drifting so close to the cameras. He stiffened as he saw Julie. Reaching up, he whipped off the earphones he wore, and his voice rose, rough and hoarse, in a single shouted word.

"Cut!"

Chapter 16

Bull strode into Julie's office with his face purple red and set in a scowl. He slammed the door behind him so hard that the trailer shook. Crossing to her desk, he leaned toward her over its width with his fists on the edge. He stared at her for ten full seconds, his breathing harsh, before he spoke.

He said, "I'm sorry."

It was the last thing Julie expected. Her own anger, slowly rising since she had left the scene on the river, nurtured through her brusque leave-taking from Rey at the dock and in the quarter hour since she had taken refuge in her office, had been about to erupt at his intrusion. She felt disoriented, almost deprived, by having it blocked with an apology. At the same time, she was incensed all over again that Bull thought he could get around her over what he was doing so easily.

"For what?" she said. "Getting caught?"

"I shouldn't have taken over your crew and equipment without permission; it wasn't right. I know you're mad, and I don't blame you. I would be ready to kill anybody who did that on my set."

"Why did you do it then?" She threw down the pen she held and leaned back in her chair, clasping her hands at her waist.

"It was maybe the last chance to get the shot you wanted. This Indian summer they've been having down here was about done. Rey came to tell me just before he left that there was a cold front moving in with rain predicted for three or four days afterward. It was now or never."

"So the two of you cooked it up between you that you would do the scene while I was gone. And did Rey tell you that he might

235

see to it I was away an extra day, to be sure you got exactly what you wanted?"

Bull took a step backward, sinking into a chair. "Hell, no, Julie, nothing like that. We'd have got the scene yesterday, except old Joseph had to go to a domino tournament or some such thing."

She was not sure she believed him, still there was a slight easing of the tightness around her heart. "You could have called me, discussed it."

"Seemed to me you'd likely tell me to keep my paws off your cameras and mind my own business. The idea seemed too good to lose."

"And I was supposed to be so happy to have the film once the rain started that I would overlook how it came about. Is that it? Just when I did you intend to tell me about it? Was Rey supposed to do that for you—after he had softened me up, of course?"

Bull blinked at her suggestion but let it pass. "Well, we never thought you'd get back in the middle of the shooting, I can tell you that. I suppose in the back of my mind I did think maybe a good time to mention it would be when you thought it was too late to get the scene."

"Did you also think," she said slowly, "that this would be a good way to slide into taking over my job?"

"Julie," he began, then stopped as a spasm of what might have been pain crossed his face. He bent his head, staring down at the floor. Finally, he looked up again. "All right, maybe I thought you might be grateful enough to let me stay around. But I don't want your job; I wouldn't take that away from you if Allen offered it to me—not that I think he ever would. I really would like to work with you. Why can't we do that?"

"You know why!"

"I know what you say, but it doesn't have to be that way. All directors have assistants; that's all I'd be, another assistant."

"You expect me to believe that you would take that kind of billing in the credits?"

"Why not?"

"It's much more likely," Julie said tightly, "that I would become your assistant, both in the credits and on the set."

"I wouldn't do that to you."

"Allen might, if he thought it would make a more commercial film."

"You misjudge him, I think. He's just trying to do what's best for you, trying to save the picture."

"It doesn't need saving! There's nothing wrong with what I'm doing."

"Is that what's bothering you? You think bringing me in is some kind of comment on the job you're doing? It isn't, I can tell you that. There's not a soul here that doesn't know who's in charge; I've seen that in the past day or two. The production was set long ago, the film is two-thirds done. It's just a matter of finishing the last few reels so we can go home."

"That's right, which makes me wonder why in heaven's name you want to stay."

His eyes narrowed under bushy brows. "I could say I was concerned about you, about the accidents. I could say it looks to me like somebody doesn't much want you finishing this picture and I'd like to stick around to keep an eye on you, and maybe find out why. I could say all that, but it wouldn't be the exact truth."

"And what would?" she asked, ignoring the hollow feeling inside her chest.

"Well, it's like this." He stopped, clearing his throat as he stared over her left shoulder. "The fact is, I need a job. I need to be connected with a new project, a fresh project, need to rub up against some creative ideas for a change. I've lost it, Julie. I've dried up. I don't have what it takes anymore."

"Your last film did fine at the box office. What are you talking about?" She sat forward slowly, a frown pleating the skin between her brows.

"Oh, it was all right, but it wasn't great."

"The critics loved it."

"Critics don't finance many movies. The money boys want a

return on their investment, preferably a big one. But that's not the worst of it. I'm fresh out of ideas, Julie. I just—just don't have the juice for it, the vision, the mental images that flow and shine. Not like I used to. Not like you do."

"That's ridiculous," she said sharply, "of course you do."

"Not anymore." He wagged his big head as he answered. "I wouldn't say it to anybody but you, but I'm dried up, finished. The boys at the studio know it; they haven't returned my calls for months. Pretty soon the tabloids will get hold of it. Won't they have a field day."

"I can't believe it," Julie said. Somehow, she had thought of Bull as going on and on, making one movie after another until he dropped in his tracks. Other people might fall out of favor or even quit, but not Bull.

"I have a hard time with it, too," he said, so quietly she wasn't sure she understood him.

Julie swallowed and cleared her throat against the constriction that had lodged there. "Even so," she said, "I don't know what good it would do you to work with me. *Swamp Kingdom* isn't a guaranteed commercial success."

"Maybe, maybe not, though I happen to think it has a good chance. But it's being around the ideas, the fantastic things that are going on here that just may get me to moving again. You've got something, girl. I don't know where it came from, but you see visions and bring them to life. You feel things and are able to draw those feelings out of your actors, so people watching them melt in their seats. It's a gift, don't you ever think it's not. I used to be able to do it. I'd like to be able to do it again."

She was touched by his need and thrilled by what he said. Somewhere in the back of her mind was a voice that whispered that she was supposed to be, but she brushed it aside.

"You've seen the rushes?"

"Allen showed them to me. He's big on this picture, Julie; he thinks it's going to make a bundle if it ever gets done. He's just trying to safeguard that prospect."

"Funny he didn't say that to me."

"Maybe he thought it wasn't necessary, maybe he took it for granted you knew what you had—or maybe you just haven't given him the time since he got here."

There was enough truth in the last statement to make her uncomfortable, and enough censure to irritate her. "I might have given him more time if he had taken less for granted," she said in clipped tones.

"Yes, well, that's between you and him. Right now, I'm concerned about me and you. What do you say about working together? Could we at least give it a try?"

She lifted a hand to rub at her temple, running her fingers back through her hair and clasping the back of her neck. "I just don't know, Bull. You make it sound easy, but you and I both know it wouldn't be."

"If it wasn't, it wouldn't be my fault. I'd do my best to stand back until you told me what you needed me to do."

The earnestness in his face was painful. She had never in her life seen him so supplicating. How could she refuse? And yet she knew perfectly well that to agree would be wrong, all wrong.

She sighed. "Just let me think about it one more day, will you? Can you do that? I don't mean to sound hard-hearted, but this is a big step, one that will mean a lot of changes no matter how simple it sounds right now."

"Fine," he said, nodding as he rubbed his hands up and down his pants legs. "That's fine. We'll talk about it some more tomorrow."

When he had gone, Julie sat staring at the wall across from her desk and the tan metal filing cabinets lined up along it. There had been a time when she would have been thrilled to work with Bull, to be given the chance to huddle with him, discussing ideas and mechanics and the theories of what made interaction work between characters, and therefore what made movies work. The prospect still had appeal. Nevertheless, she could not get away from the feeling that she would be surrendering control of her movie if she agreed to what Bull and Allen wanted. It would no longer be hers.

It wasn't just the remaining scenes that would be different if Bull was involved. He would also have a hand in the editing process. It was in the editing, with the splicing of the miles of film, the rearranging of cuts and scenes, that the final story would take form. It was here that the whole content and feel of it could, and probably would, be changed. And it was not that Bull would set out deliberately to alter what she had done, what she was trying to say; it would come about because of his difference in attitude and vision, and most of all because of the weight of his past triumphs, past success.

She was not sure she could stand it.

This was her story. She had so much work and thought, so many months of her time invested in it, had such a need to see it playing on a screen the way she saw it in her head. To have it taken over, changed into something quite other than she had intended, would be a kind of sacrilege.

On the other hand, *Swamp Kingdom* was just a film; there would be others. Bull was her father. He had helped and encouraged her, given her her chance. Now he needed her help. How could she deny him?

She felt as if everything was disintegrating around her, both inside and out. The accidents on the set that should not have happened. Her unexpected and seemingly uncontrollable attraction to a man the opposite of all she held valuable, a man with a murky past. Allen's betrayal by trying to bring in another director. Her break with this same man who had been the center of her life for nearly ten years. The pressure to give up her movie. The realization that a number of the people around her hid resentment toward her behind their smiles. The discovery of the snake and the suspicion that for some the ill feeling went past mere resentment. The discovery of Rey's connivance with Bull for the encroachment on her film. The plea for help from her father, whom she had always thought of as being rock steady in his position of fame and achievement. Everything had changed and changed again. Nothing was as she had thought it to be, not even her own heart and mind.

"Hey, Bull giving you a hard time in here, or was it the other way around?"

It was Ofelia, standing in the doorway that Bull had left open behind him on his way out. The assistant director slouched against the frame with one of her long slim cigarettes burning in her right hand

and her left propped on her hip. Julie summoned a smile as she answered. "Both."

"Figures. The man knows his stuff, but he's as full of himself as they come, and I don't care if he is your old man."

"You may be right."

"Sure I am." She pushed away from the door and came forward, stubbing out her cigarette with a couple of quick jabs in the ashtray on the corner of Julie's desk. "Meantime, I was wondering about tomorrow's schedule?"

They discussed it for a few minutes, along with the props and permissions needed to begin shooting in downtown Lutcher the following week. Ofelia, taking the schedule and making a rapid check of the people who would need to be called in for the following morning, said without looking up, "Allen will be on hand."

"Really? I thought he might have gone back to L.A. since he wasn't around this evening."

Ofelia looked up. "Lord, Julie, I can't believe you don't know where he is and what he's doing. The two of you have never been like this before. What's going on?"

"I don't know," Julie said with a sigh. "One thing just led to another."

"Well, it ain't too smart, if you ask me. Allen's still the producer around here, you still have to work with him. Before too long we'll be through here and heading back to the coast. What then?"

"I guess it depends."

"On what happens with Bull? Or on this thing you've got going with your Cajun?"

Julie gave the other woman a straight look. "On a lot of things."

Ofelia grunted. "You and Vance. What is it, a contest?"

"What's Vance got to do with it?"

"There he is, boffing the brains out of that silly reporter—not a hard thing to do, I expect—all to prove something to you. And you're carrying on with Rey to prove something to somebody else, Allen at a guess, or maybe your dad."

"That's not true!" Julie said, rising to her feet in indignation.

"No? Could have fooled me. I heard the secretary telling Rey where you were staying and offering to make reservations. The two of you were absent together and showed up again together. Tell me what that means."

"It means you've got a nosy disposition." Julie's words were tart.

"True," Ofelia agreed with a grin. "And a deep and intensely lascivious interest in other people's affairs. Why is it they always sound more interesting than my own raunchy one-night stands? I must be doing something wrong."

"Maybe, maybe not," Julie said, her frown easing into a reluctant grin. "Are you never bothered by why men go out with you, what they want from you?"

"Hell, Julie, I know what they want; there's nothing complicated about it."

"Never?"

"No, damn it all."

"You don't think there might be if you approached it differently?"

A flush rose to Ofelia's face and she looked uncomfortable. "I don't know, but what would be the point in a place like this? We'll all be gone in a few days, back to the darling fleshpots, back to where we belong. I'm speaking of you and me, honey. I'm a career woman, just like you. We don't need complications; there's no place for them in what we do. There's only a place for our own kind, somebody like Allen who understands what we're after and can help us get it."

"You think so, do you?"

"Makes sense, if you think about it. But I'd be careful. Allen is patient, but it's not too smart, keeping him waiting around. There are a lot of women who would like to have what he can give them."

"If you mean what I think," Julie said slowly, "I have to remind you that what I have didn't come from Allen alone."

"Knowing him didn't hurt," Ofelia said with a shrug and a toss of her head that flipped her thick ponytail of hair back over her shoulder.

It was so, and yet there had never been anything quite that crude about her association with Allen. She hadn't moved in with him to further her career. She wondered if he thought that she had, if that was why he had always maintained the mentor-protégée element in their relationship, the slight edge of superiority that kept them from achieving greater closeness. She wondered if he had kept that distance for fear she would take advantage of greater intimacy. It was an unsettling thought.

"I'll go get started on this," Ofelia said, waving the papers in her hand. "I'll probably be around for quite a while, if you need me. You get to looking for me and can't find me, try Vance's motor home; he's been letting me keep my beer in his fridge. Bull threw me out of yours, said he couldn't stand the smell of my damned cigarettes—his exact words. This from a man who has more or less systematically made his way through every smoke-filled dive and joint in St. James Parish since he got here."

"He didn't really ask you to leave?"

Ofelia laughed. "Not exactly; there was just a strong hint. It's easier to avoid him than to listen to him carry on. You never can tell who's going to go all health conscious and self-righteous about it, can you? Next thing you know, Bull'll be drinking nonalcoholic beer."

It was late when Julie left the office. She had no idea what had become of Rey; his Cherokee was nowhere in sight. She wouldn't wait for him. The keys to her rental car were in the motor home where she had left them when she went to L.A., in case Ofelia or some of the others needed to use the car.

The motor home was dark and still, the light of the mercury vapor lamps reflecting off its windows. It was a relief to reach for a light switch in the kitchen area and have brightness flood the place, banishing the shadows and dark corners. Regardless, she had a tendency to watch her feet as she moved about.

Her throat was dry; flying was dehydrating, and she had stopped for only a cup of coffee since she returned. She moved to the refrigerator for a bottle of Evian, also taking out a can of tomato juice while she was at it. Spotting a small Gouda and a plastic bag of seedless red grapes, she set those out on the nearby table also, then went rummaging through the cabinets for a package of crackers. It was well past dinnertime and there was no way of knowing whether Aunt Tine would have anything to eat when she got to the house. The prospect of a light dinner had a certain appeal anyway; it seemed she had done nothing but eat over the last few days.

She was digging behind assorted boxes of cereal and packages of microwave cake mix when she felt an odd package. She brought it out, a pint-size plastic bag tied with a twistee and half-filled with a crystalline white powder.

She knew what it was, yet her brain refused to process the information for long seconds. She untied the closure and took a cautious sniff, then whipped her head aside.

It wasn't powdered sugar. It also wasn't powdered milk, baking powder, or soda or cornstarch or any other ordinary kitchen substance.

Cocaine.

Pure, unadulterated, easily accessible, mind-blowing cocaine.

What was it doing here? How long had it been hidden? Most of all, who had put it there?

Who did it belong to?

Her movements quick, jerky, she retied the package, rolled it back up, and pushed it back where she had found it. Slamming the cabinet door, she backed away to the kitchen table and sat down on the side bench. She picked up her water and downed most of it, then stared at the clear liquid left in the bottle, watching the air bubbles rise and subside.

Was this why Bull needed her help? Was an addiction to cocaine the reason his creativity had drained away and no one would trust him with a project anymore? Had he exchanged the traditional, macho pastime of drinking for the faster high of snorting coke?

Was this why he had wanted Ofelia gone, so he could indulge in his love affair with instant gratification uninterrupted, unobserved? But why would he care? He had been a part of the Hollywood party crowd long enough to have discarded all trace of self-consciousness about his vices. Unless it was his daughter he wanted to fool?

These and other questions swirled in her mind like the bubbles in the water, but there were no answers.

There was, however, a conclusion to be made, one based on emotion rather than logic. It was obvious, inevitable.

If the cocaine did belong to Bull, if it was the cause of his decline, then it would be an unnatural daughter who would refuse to help him in any way possible. She had no choice except to let him join her in the making of *Swamp Kingdom*. The only thing left was finding a time and place to tell him so. And the courage.

The doorknob of the motor home, not six feet from where Julie sat, rattled. It twisted from side to side. She watched it in frozen silence, knowing she had locked the door behind her, and glad of it.

There came a staccato knock. "Julie? It's me. Let me in."

Vance. Julie drew a quick breath, then shook her head. She was far too tense; maybe she needed to get more exercise. It wouldn't help with everything that troubled her, but it couldn't hurt.

"What are you doing still here?" she asked as she unlatched the screen then reached through its sliding-door panel and unlocked the outside door.

Vance's upturned face looked bloated in the light falling through the screen, and he was squinting against the brightness. He was wearing what appeared to be a short terry-cloth beach robe and a pair of thongs. His lopsided grin was a little loose as he reached and pulled the screen open, then stepped up inside.

"I took a shower and lay down for a nap in my bus—I was bushed from working in the hot sun all afternoon; it really takes it out of you. When I woke up, everybody was gone except you. I saw you through the window, thought I'd come and find out if L.A. is still out there."

"It's there and wet," she answered, then offered him a drink. He waved her back to her seat while he moved to the refrigerator and searched out a canned soda. With it in hand, he came to sit across from her at the table while they talked about the festival and also the virtues of the Bel Air versus the Beverly Hills Hotel.

"Tabary was there with you, wasn't he?" he said finally.

"It's no secret, apparently," she said, though her tone was cool.

"There's no such thing around here; you know that. What I want to know is, if you wanted company, why him? Why not me?"

"I thought you were busy with your girl reporter."

"I'd have got rid of her, for you."

Julie drank the rest of her water, then reached for the can of tomato juice, peeling off the foil seal. "That's very flattering, Vance, but the truth is—"

"I don't want to hear it! I hate sentences that start like that; they're always a slap in the face."

There was a grating edge to his voice that made her look at him more closely. His pupils were small in the blue of his eyes, his face was pale, and there was a tremor in his hands. He kept lapping the edges of his beach robe in his lap, as if its short length bothered him, or else he had something to hide. She had seen the signs too often in the past few years, and before that among her surfing friends, to mistake them.

"The truth is," she continued with scarcely a break, "that I didn't invite anybody to go with me. Rey flew out on his own. You know what else? We flew back today, and I've just realized that I'm exhausted. I think it's time I called it a night."

She rose to her feet, moving to the door. Vance drained his soda as he got up also. The can toppled over on the table as he set it down.

"You could sleep here tonight," he said. "I'd be glad to—tuck you in, and so on."

"Thanks for the offer," she said lightly, "but Aunt Tine will be wondering if I'm going to make it home."

"Not to mention lover boy. Or is he mending his fences with the foxy widow? I saw him talking to her after Summer left for the day."

"I wouldn't know, and it doesn't matter. It's been a long day, and I think jet lag is catching up with me." Julie looked around for her shoulder bag.

He moved to block her way, reaching to brace his arm on the door frame above her head so she was caught between him and the end of the bench at the table. Lifting his free hand, he ran it up her arm to her shoulder, then let his fingertips trail downward to the curve of her breast under her shirt. "What's your hurry?" he said thickly. "We got time for a quickie."

"Forget it, Vance," she said, keeping her voice even with an effort. "I have all the complications I can stand at the moment."

"Nothing complicated about this," he said. "I want you, you want me. We satisfy the urge. Easy."

"Except for one thing. What makes you think I want you?"

"A man can tell."

He was too close. The smell of his breath, the heat of him, was suffocating. She had to clench her hands to keep herself from shoving him away. It would be a mistake, she thought. For now he was open to reason; he might not remain that way if she used physical force.

"A man can make a mistake, too. I'm tired, Vance, and so are you; you said so yourself. Come on, it's time you got yourself back to your motel. Or would you like me to find somebody to drive you?"

"I'll take you, tired or not," he said in a hoarse whisper. "You don't have to do a thing, just lie back and enjoy."

He pushed his hand behind her neck, sliding it under her hair to drag her toward him. His mouth came down on hers, open, wet, engulfing in its rubbery softness.

Revulsion swept through Julie. She brought her hands up, the fingers closed into tight fists. The edges of her forearms smacked against his inner elbows, breaking his hold. Immediately, she slammed her wrists and hands into his chest so he staggered back.

He cursed her as he caught himself with one hand on the table. Then he recoiled, lunging at her again. Julie whirled and pushed the screen door open, clattering down the steps. He hit the door frame and careened off it, hurling himself at her. He caught the back of her shirt in one hand as he fell.

They crashed to the ground together. Julie lay for a stunned second. Then as pain flared through her she erupted in a kicking, scratching, punching fury, her mind so red blind with rage that she hardly knew what she was doing, what pain she was giving or receiving, and did not care. Somewhere she heard a shout, felt Vance start, but had no time to look, no time to think.

Abruptly she was free. Vance was jerked from her, lifted bodily into the air, and flung to sprawl in the rough white gravel of the parking lot. Julie glimpsed broad shoulders bunched with muscle, a dark, well-shaped head, and contorted, furious face, then Rey was leaping after Vance, dragging him to his feet again. She saw him draw back his fist.

"Not in the face!" she yelled out as she scrambled up. "Don't hit him in the face!" She hardly spared a glance for Ofelia, who came running up beside her, helping her to stand.

Rey threw her a look over his shoulder there in the dim light that seemed to reflect angry amazement, but the punch he swung sank into the actor's midriff to the wrist, doubling him over and taking his feet from the ground. Vance grunted as he staggered back to fall full length. He rolled over, cursing, crying, retching into the gravel with an arm clamped to his belly.

"God," Ofelia breathed. She sent Rey a look of wide-eyed respect before she turned back to Julie, asking with concern in her voice, "You all right, honey? Want somebody to drive you home, or maybe yell for the police?"

"No," Julie said, rubbing the palms of her hands together where the gravel had scraped them as she fell. She shook back her hair, lifting her chin as she repeated, "No. I'm fine, really. No harm done."

"Yeah, well, I suppose it wouldn't help the movie. God, what a business. Well, I bet you can come up with some way to make the joker sorry, anyway."

Julie managed some sort of smile, but there was no humor in it. She was the sorry one. She had made another enemy, she thought, and that was not what she needed.

Ofelia released Julie's arm, moving to stand over the actor. "Come on, Vance, you stupid idiot. What in the name of living hell did you think you were doing? Get up and get your dumb backside out of here before you get yourself massacred."

Julie turned toward Rey with slow reluctance. He stood watching her. There was a frown between his eyes and his still hands were still knotted into fists. His gaze raked over her, as if making sure there was no damage. Before she could speak, he gave an abrupt nod and swung on his heel, striding away.

Julie opened her mouth to call after him, then closed it again. He had no need for her thanks, apparently, and seemed disgusted by her caution over Vance. Well, let him go. There was nothing to be done, then. No doubt it was better this way.

No doubt.

Chapter 17

"Vance won't be a problem for you anymore," Allen said as he and Julie stood waiting for the preparations for filming a street scene to be completed. "Ofelia told me about his behavior last evening. I spoke to him about it a few minutes ago. I believe we came to an understanding."

Not far away, Vance was standing with his reporter friend, looking morose and tired in the jeans and T-shirt of his character, Jean-Pierre. In a few moments, he was going to have to walk down the street with Summer, exchanging greetings and handshakes with a few townspeople rounded up to represent friends and neighbors. It was a good thing that the script didn't call for a great deal of animation from him, Julie thought, because she wasn't sure he was up to it. It was difficult to say, of course; there were a great many actors who appeared half-dead until the cameras began to roll, then were suddenly on, alert and glowing with life.

"It's nice of you to be concerned," Julie said to the man beside her, "but I could have handled it."

"Possibly, though I believe my clout made a greater impression than your appeal to reason or Tabary's fists. At any rate, it seemed best that I speak to him so as to redirect Vance's natural resentment."

"*Natural* resentment?" she asked, looking at Allen with a frown. His bearing was stiff, his appearance as careful as always in a tan silk shirt with an ascot at the neck, and well-creased rust slacks. He made Julie in her cream cotton pants and muscle shirt feel rumpled and underdressed.

"At being reprimanded." The answer was brusque as he fidgeted under her gaze, reaching to adjust his ascot. "I was not suggesting that it was natural for him to resent you for rejecting his advances."

"Weren't you?"

"No. Though some men have that tendency, particularly if the rejection is public."

Julie searched his face, hearing the underlying accusation, but uncertain it was intentional. "They should learn," she said slowly, "not to make public advances."

"That would no doubt be wise. Shall we say I have now learned sufficient wisdom? Will you stop showing me that I don't own you and come stay with me in New Orleans?"

"It isn't that simple, Allen," she answered.

"I was afraid it wouldn't be. What is it? Are you going to sink into the arms of this swamp man because of a heroic gesture or two? Do you really think that you are going to give up all this for domestic bliss?" He waved toward the swarm of activity around them, the clutter of cameras and sound equipment and generators, of snaking electric cables and light banks and scattered reflectors, and at all the yelling, cursing technicians it took to make order of the chaos.

Her voice cool, Julie said, "Nobody has asked me to give up anything."

"Good, because you won't do it; you can't. It's in your blood, an obsession, something you eat, drink, and sleep."

"It's my job, that's all," she said.

"It's what you've worked at since you were a teenager, something you've put hours of sweat and mind-bending effort into; it's what you are. You can no more walk away from it than that building over there can walk away from its foundation."

"You hope."

He stared at her. "What?"

"You hope I can't leave it because you think that will mean that I will return to L.A. and to you. You don't want to ask me flat out to come back with you because that would mean more commitment than you are willing to make. Do you realize, Allen, that it's been nearly two years since we even talked about getting married?"

"I didn't think you wanted it."

She ran her fingers through her hair in a weary gesture. "Maybe I didn't. We had a comfortable, even a convenient, arrangement, but you'll have to admit that's all it was. There's no point in trying to make it anything more."

"I never knew you felt this way," he said, his face pale and his eyes wide with dismay.

"I didn't either, until lately. Don't you think that's sad?"

"But I love you, Julie," he whispered.

She met his gaze, her own somber. "Possibly, but it never kept you from going out with the starlets."

"You don't understand," he said, the words louder. "I love you. We were perfect together, you and I. We complemented each other: talent and money, contacts and organizational skills, old Hollywood and the new, old blood and new energy. We worked so well together. You made me feel young and powerful, and I helped you make it to the top. It can be that way again."

"I never stayed with you for what you could do for me, Allen. Why should I do it now?"

"Why did you stay?"

"I've been thinking about that." She stopped, uncertain how to go on. Finally, she said, "Years ago, I was impressed by the Harvard ties and quotes from Ibsen and Arthur Miller; I thought that was class. I was thrilled that you thought I had potential, delighted to be Galatea to your Pygmalion. Gratitude became liking, and affection became a habit. I can't explain it any better than that."

"Oh, Julie, couldn't you like me again? Couldn't you try? It will be different, I promise. It's only been the way it was before because I was afraid that if you knew how I felt about you, it would give you the upper hand, would make me the dependent one."

"You preferred that I have that role."

"It was fear that caused it. I've been afraid of something like this, afraid you would leave me if you ever realized what you could do and began to get credit for it like this Crystal Award, if you ever really became a success. It's a chance I'm willing to take, now."

"I don't know—" she began.

"Just think about it, that's all I ask. I've missed you so much in these last few weeks. I kept thinking of ways to get you off this picture, bring you back to L.A., especially after the accident with the stunt. It was almost a relief when Bull came to me suggesting he join you. I thought he might be able to take over, let you come back where you belong."

"That isn't going to happen; I can tell you that much right now."

"I can accept that."

"Good. Can you also tell me if Bull taking over was supposed to be retroactive? Was I not supposed to have credit for this film? Did you intend to be sure that I gained no more recognition?"

"God, Julie, don't say such things to me; it drives me insane. I was afraid for you and wanted you back in L.A. That's all there was to it."

She was the one who was being driven crazy. For just an instant, the suspicion that Allen had instigated the accidents that had killed Paul Lislet and nearly killed Summer in order to have an excuse to pull her off the picture had been so clear in her mind that she felt sick. She was still haunted by the idea that he would have replaced her the moment he arrived if she had not been involved with Rey. Her affair with another man gave her a degree of protection, since Allen could not be sure she would not abandon him and throw in her lot with Rey if she were pushed too far.

Crazy.

She was seeing threats and plots everywhere. It had to stop. She had all she could handle just finishing the movie. Once that was done, most of the other problems would take care of themselves as everyone went their separate ways. Most of them.

"Look, Julie," Allen said, his voice deep and low near her ear, "I'm not going to beg, but I'm not going to give up, either. I want you to think about what I've said. Think hard. And then, sometime soon, we'll find a time and place to get serious about it. A lot depends on it. More than you'll ever know."

It was pretentious and tantalizing, with echoes of an old song title, that parting remark. It was touching because of it; Allen was trying hard. Julie, watching him walk away, gave a slow shake of her head, then deliberately immersed herself in the business of making a movie.

The purpose of the scene was to show Summer off in a brand-new set of jeans and T-shirt with jogging shoes, as well as illustrating the place of Jean-Pierre in the community. Later, when the morning light was gone, and when the cold front with its rain that was supposed to be coming arrived, they would film the shopping spree where Summer and Vance buy the new clothes that become a part of Summer's metamorphosis from city girl to back-country tomboy.

Summer was with her mother over near where the motor homes had been drawn up in a grocery-store parking lot. Annette was fussing with Summer's hair, which had been braided down her back, using a fog of hairspray to subdue every stray wisp while the girl squirmed and coughed.

Julie turned from talking to the cinematographer to wave at the script girl. "Go tell Annette to leave Summer's hair alone. It's supposed to look like her father did it for her, not like some salon creation."

The girl moved off to do Julie's bidding. From the corner of her eye, Julie watched her approach Annette, saw Summer's mother throw hairspray and comb up in the air so that Summer had to duck to keep them from hitting her. Annette reached for Summer's head, tearing at the braiding. Summer ducked again, slapping at her mother's hands, then turned and ran. Annette started after her daughter, then stopped, weaving where she stood. She shouted something at the script girl, then whipped around and stalked to the motor home. As the door slammed behind her the script girl rolled her eyes and walked away.

"Drunk," Andy Russell said with a shake of his head. "Hard on Summer, putting up with it. If we get doodly-squat out of her this morning, we'll be lucky."

Julie agreed, though thinking of Vance and his condition the night before, she wasn't sure liquor was the sole cause of Annette's problem. A frown lingered between her eyes as she reverted to the topic she and the cinematographer had been discussing before the incident began.

Summer was not cooperative when the cameras finally began to roll. Her walk was self-conscious: she held herself too stiff and straight and barely touched Vance's hand. She had to be told again and again to look up at him instead of keeping her eyes on the ground. Her smiles were strained and had a tendency to fade too fast. Correction and suggestions brought tears instead of improvement.

As take followed take Vance grew irritable and snappish with the girl instead of trying to help. It affected his own manner, so he appeared to be stalking down the street half dragging Summer, and gritting his teeth in the close-ups.

At last, Julie called a break. Taking two canned Cokes from catering, she walked over to where Summer was seated on a pile of cable with her chin in her hands. She held out one of the Cokes to the girl, then sat down on the ground beside her. The two of them popped the tab tops of their drinks. They drank and watched the traffic being diverted around the street that was blocked off for the movie shoot.

Finally, Julie said, "Okay, honey, what's the problem?"

Summer rubbed her thumb over the condensation on the side of her can. "Everybody is staring at me."

"Sure they are. You're one of the stars."

"I mean the crew. They're feeling sorry for me. And Vance hates having to work with me; he says kids always steal the scenes."

"Part of being a professional actress," Julie said, "is learning not to care what other people are thinking. How would you like to have to play a love scene with Vance knowing he didn't particularly like you. Actresses do it all the time."

"This is different," the girl muttered, with color rising in her face.

"Not really. You do what you have to do, and let the others take care of their parts themselves. In a way, that goes for your mother. You aren't responsible for how she acts, only for what you do about it. If you don't want other people feeling sorry for you, then don't feel sorry for yourself."

"But you don't know what it's like! I can't act upbeat and happy or go prancing down that street with a million, trillion people watching when I don't feel happy."

"Yes, you can. You just have to remember a time when you were happy. Remember how you felt and what you did to show it, how you acted—how you moved and looked at people. Remember— remember how you felt when you were dancing with Rey at the wedding? You were having a good time then, weren't you?"

"Yes, sort of." A faint smile came and went on the girl's face.

"Yes, you were. So pretend that Vance is Rey. Pretend that Rey has bought you some new clothes and the two of you are on your way to go—boat riding, maybe, or fishing. Can you do that?"

The girl's eyebrows went up and down. She pursed her lips and twisted them from side to side. She lifted her canned drink and took a long swallow as if she were suddenly thirsty, then gave a quick gurgle of laughter. She said, "I can try."

"Good," Julie said, relief making her laugh in her turn. "Run tell the makeup girl to check you again, and we'll give it another shot."

As Julie stood watching the girl cross toward makeup there came the scrap of a footstep behind her. She knew it was Rey even before he spoke, recognized the sound, and also the spicy male scent of him. She was already turning when he spoke.

"You're good with her," he said.

"It doesn't take much; she's fine when she concentrates."

"But you're patient with her, which is something else again."

The compliment gave her more pleasure than she would have dreamed possible. She looked away to conceal the flush she could feel rising in her face. At the same time, a pulse began to throb in her throat as it occurred to her that he had not come to see about Summer as she had first thought, but had sought her out. She swallowed, then quickly, while the impulse was still with her, said, "Look, I want to tell you—"

"About last night—" he began.

They both stopped.

"Ladies first," he said quietly.

She met his gaze, her own troubled. "I'm not sure I know what you thought was happening there with Vance, but he—he wasn't himself."

"You mean he was doped to the eyeballs."

"Exactly. All I wanted to say was, I'm glad you were there."

He watched her long moments while the lines of tension about his eyes slowly faded. He took a breath and let it out on a sigh. "I lost it there for a second when I saw the way he had you on the ground— and the way you protected him. It didn't sink in until later what you were doing. I'm not used to considering things in terms of what's best for a movie."

She said, "It's a habit, one I carry too far sometimes."

He only smiled a little in acknowledgment. "I had seen your light, was coming to talk to you about the sunset scene. I thought you might give me a few pointers about how to act toward a woman who's too mad at you to speak to you, strictly as a director, of course."

"Of course," she repeated. "I'd probably have told you to try pretending that she isn't."

He tilted his head to one side as he looked down at her. "Meaning?"

"Bull told me why you talked to him about filming the scene for the credits. You might have tried explaining it yourself, instead of leaving without a word."

"Retreat seemed better just then. I wasn't too sure who was in the most hot water, me or Bull, and I didn't want to make things worse for either of us by saying the wrong thing."

"You'll have to tell me, sometime, what was wrong with the truth," she said lightly. "It's something I value highly."

He did not answer, and his face changed as she watched, becoming darker, less readable. Doubt crept in upon her, and with it depression, as she was forced to ask herself if Bull had given her the true facts after all.

They had to hurry. They were losing their light, the sun coming and going behind a slow gathering of clouds. The air had become heavy, oppressive in its heat. The breeze that had been with them all morning was picking up, swirling dust, gum wrappers, and also dried sycamore leaves like scuttling sea creatures, in gusts down the street. The cameramen were trying to protect their lenses. Ofelia had taken her Tokyo Rose chopsticks from her purse and was securing her ponytail out of her way. Annette was standing at the door of her motor home, watching the sky as if it was necessary for her to see the first drop of rain fall.

"Let's go, folks!" Julie called. "One final, perfect take."

People ran to take their places. Quiet was called. The clapper fell. The hum and whine of cameras began.

It was wonderful.

The sun found a clear spot in the gathering clouds, so the light became constant. The wind died. Summer pranced. She swung from Vance's hand. She admired her clothes in the reflective glass of the store windows they passed and chattered as if she had never heard of stage fright. She made Vance smile and seemed to add extra brightness to the scene. She was every child who has ever been delivered from a tight party dress and slippery Mary Jane shoes. She was every loving daughter and small femme fatale ever born. She was the personification of happiness and delight. She was great.

When the end of the street was reached, everybody cheered and clapped, while a few breathed sighs of relief. And then the rain began to fall.

It wasn't a sprinkle, nor did the drops come in scattered, warning cadence. One moment the warm wind was blowing and the sun was drifting behind a cloud, the next there was the deluge. The drops were warm and wet and saucer-sized. They splattered the pavement, plopping into the dust, merging and flowing together while steam rose and the musty smell of the sudden wetness filled the air.

Summer, riding the natural euphoria of her own performance, ran shrieking into the street where she spun like a top, holding her arms out and her face upturned to the rain. Julie could not help grinning at the girl's pleasure as she herself dashed to take shelter under the overhang of a storefront. It was contagious; for two cents she'd go out and join Summer.

The scream, shrill, animalistic, came hard on that thought. "No! No, no, no, stupid child! No!"

It was Annette, running from the motor home with her hands flapping and her bare feet splashing through the muddy water already sheeting the pavement. Her eyes were wild, her mouth wide open as she yelled. Her hair was quickly plastered to her skull while her flimsy cotton pants suit grew so wet it hung on her thin frame like fresh wash on a line.

Summer, her smile vanishing, began to back away. Annette bore down on her. The woman grabbed the girl, jerking her toward her, smacking her hand across her daughter's face. "Stupid! Idiot child! I'll teach you to make a spectacle of yourself! You can't get sick, you hear! You can't! You get sick, who will make us a living?"

Annette shook the girl like a scarecrow in a high wind, slapping at her while she raved, spewing out demands and threats. Summer cried out, begging her mother to stop while she dodged her blows with the skill of experience, dancing around at the end of Annette's hold, trying to break free.

Julie, appalled by the ferocity of the attack, startled by the sound of madness in the noise Annette was making, stood still while seconds ticked away. Then she was plunging out into the rain, jumping the curb, and running into the blocked street. She grabbed Annette's arm, shaking her, calling to her to stop it. At the same time, she was aware of Rey coming from the other end of the closed-off area, leaping cords and chairs and toolboxes, ducking his head into the rain.

Abruptly, he was there. Annette was wrenched from Julie's grasp and her arms pinned behind her. Summer fell, landing on her back in the rain-wet street. She stared at her mother while her face, fiery red but pale around the mouth, twisted with repressed tears. Then she surged to her feet and took off, running as if she could outdistance the storm and her mother's fury.

Julie took one look at Rey's face, masklike in his revulsion for the woman he held, but with his heated gaze following Summer. Whirling, Julie ran after the young girl.

She caught her beyond the end of the last motor home and generator truck, at the edge of the detour street, where traffic swished past going both ways, splashing water into the gutters. She caught her and, without a word, pulled her close, holding her wrapped tightly in her arms. There was resistance in the taut body of the girl for long seconds, then a small cry broke from her. She hugged Julie tight, burying her face in her chest while her whole body heaved with sobs. Julie stroked her hair, murmuring soothing noises that meant little, protecting her with her upper body while the rain beat down around them. She held her until a Cherokee pulled up beside them and Rey leaned to swing the door open, urging them inside.

"You know what they're saying, don't you?" Madelyn asked. She was filing her nails, making minute adjustments to her French manicure, while a fresh glass of champagne sat fizzing like a dose of stomach medicine at her elbow. Her voice was fairly loud, to be heard over the roar of the rain on the boat club's metal roof and the clatter of voices from the crew sitting all around them as if at some university student center, playing cards, reading books, or just shooting the bull. They had been working, filming a few views of the swamp in the rain to be used with the scene where Madelyn is supposed to wallow in swamp mud in her search for Jean-Pierre's fishing camp.

"Yes, I know," Julie said.

"They're saying this production is jinxed," the actress went on as if she hadn't spoken. "First the dead stuntman, then Summer's near miss, and now Annette in the hospital for 'observation,' though we all know she went nuts, nearly OD'd on cocaine and alcohol. Anyway, Annette was the last straw. Everybody's saying something has to happen to change the luck, or this movie is going to be a total disaster."

Julie said dryly, "Does *everybody* have any ideas?"

"Bull." The answer was blunt. "They think maybe he could turn things around."

"Their vote of confidence makes me feel all warm inside."

Madelyn pulled at the black sweater she wore around her shoulders that kept slipping off her black silk blouse. "I know, but that's show business for you, loyalty to the end, or until things go wrong, whichever comes first. But seriously, isn't it in the cards? I mean, why else is he here?"

"Visiting."

"Oh, sure, and I suppose you have some Louisiana gold-mining stock you'd like to sell?"

"I was—thinking of asking his opinion on a few things."

"I knew it! You can't fool me; I've been around the block too many times, not to mention the bed and the boardroom table. I know the brass gets itself in a toilet paper–using tizzy when things start to go wrong. First thing they want to do is replace either the star or the director. Frankly, my dear, I'd rather it was you who had to go."

Julie smiled to herself at the actress's calm assumption that she was the star of this vehicle. Madelyn would not have liked the idea that it was only her years in the business that gave her any claim to the place.

"How's Summer doing?" Madelyn went on.

"Fine. She and Aunt Tine are getting along great; they've been baking gingerbread. I expect the bruises on Summer's face will have faded enough by morning to be covered by makeup."

"It was nice of the old lady to let her stay while Annette is in detox."

"It was Rey's idea."

"She didn't have to agree, though," Madelyn said. After a brief pause, she went on in lower tones. "I probably shouldn't say anything, but it wouldn't surprise me to learn that Vance gave Annette the stuff that set her off. He's been looking a little blurred around the edges himself lately, and the two of them had an early-morning thing going there for a day or two, before the reporter showed up. Annette's older than he is by a few years, but what the hay, right? She was pretty hard hit when he started looking elsewhere."

Julie nodded her understanding. She had suspected what Madelyn was saying herself. Now she said, "You don't think the overdose might have been deliberate?"

"It's hard to say, isn't it? Could have been that Annette kept on with it, more and more, because she hurt. You know? But think of spending that much money on a painkiller. It's enough to make you sick, the billions of dollars going up in smoke, getting shot up, all for a bang and oblivion. When I think of the clothes and jewelry, the cars and beach houses I could buy with it instead! It's no wonder people sell dope when there's that much money to be made that easy."

"Stop the demand and you stop the supply, and the suppliers," Julie said, almost to herself.

"What was that?"

"Nothing. Something somebody said."

Madelyn stared at her a second longer, then gave a quick shrug as she put away her nail file. "You know, I've been thinking about dear old Bull. Maybe I should go have a talk with him, reminisce about our fun times. It might be good for another scene or two in the film. What do you think?"

"I really doubt it," Julie told her frankly.

"Ah, well, nothing ventured, et cetera."

Madelyn slid out of her chair and headed for the door, her bracelets jangling as she patted her hair and pulled at her sweater, heels clicking on the hard floor while the silk of her black divided riding skirt fluttered about her knees. Julie, watching her go, felt a little sorry for the other woman. She wondered if Madelyn recognized her own craving after clothes and jewelry and other fine things as an addiction of sorts. She thought of being considered washed up at forty, or feeling the need to step warily around people in authority like herself, of needing to cajole men like Bull for the sake of more scenes or lines. She wouldn't make a good actress; she didn't have the fortitude for it.

"I thought she'd never leave."

It was Stan, limping over to drop down on the seat Madelyn had vacated. He was nursing a Styrofoam cup of coffee the size of a flower vase and had the inevitable cigarette between his yellowed first and second fingers.

"Madelyn's all right," Julie said with a smile.

"Sure, but I didn't want to talk while she was around. Or anybody else, for that matter."

"Would you like to step out front? It's getting a bit like a smoke-house in here anyway."

They walked across to the end doors and out under the metal entrance canopy. The air that struck their faces was fresh and damp. The rain falling beyond the protective canopy was like thick layers of gray draperies wavering in the wind. The noise as it clattered overhead was loud, but without the roar caused by a confined space inside. Julie moved to lean against the building, waiting.

"Did I hear right? Is Bull really coming aboard?" Stan asked, the words jerked from him in a rush.

"I suppose, though I haven't got around to telling him yet, or anybody else for that matter."

"Then don't."

"What?"

"You heard me. Don't do it. That happens, I'm out of here."

"Why?"

"You know why. I don't like Bull, never have, and I won't work with him."

There was dreary earnestness in Stan's face. He meant what he said. Julie, facing that fact, felt a rush of tiredness so great that she had to lock her knees to keep them steady. She said quietly, "You've come so far with this movie, Stan, and there's such a little way left to go. Why can't you tough it out?"

"Can't do it. My hide's not worth much, but I value it."

His cryptic refusal even to consider what she was saying after giving her such an ultimatum brought a stir of anger. It was just too much on top of everything else, one final thing too much.

She said, "What are you talking about? Am I supposed to know? Because if so, you ought to understand that I don't."

"It's something between Bull and me, something from a long time ago. You want to know, you ask him. After he's gone from here."

"I don't want to ask Bull. I want you to tell me, flat out and without beating around the bush. What are you talking about?"

He was silent, eating at the inside of his lips as he stared out at the rain. His eyes were red-rimmed, moving in the sockets as if searching for some escape.

"Well?" Julie demanded.

He said nothing, only looking at her and then away again while his hands slowly curled into fists at his sides.

"All right," Julie said, "you don't have to explain. But you can't expect me to tell Bull to get lost just because you said so."

He puffed out his lips in a sigh, then moistened them with his tongue. Still, it was only as Julie pushed away from the wall, turning to go into back into the boat club, that he spoke. "It's about your mother."

She didn't know what she had expected, but it wasn't that. She turned back as if moved by rusty gears. "What could my mother possibly have to do with it?"

"She had an affair. With me."

Julie said nothing, could say nothing. She tried to picture her mother—ladylike, softhearted, with her love of flowers and antiques and old houses and her quick humor—embroiled in some clandestine series of meetings with Stan, tried to picture them together in a sweaty embrace. It couldn't be done.

"Don't look so shocked. I was different years ago. We were all different."

Her lips stiff, Julie said, "What happened?"

"Not much. Bull had been running around, as usual, with the star of his picture, a flashy blonde. I had been top stuntman on the same film. He sent me to take your mother to some party while he shacked up with blondie. Your mother was a beautiful woman; you look a lot like her. I fell for her the minute I saw her, started coming around after that on my own. Your mother found out about the blonde and, well, decided to pay Bull back the way it would hurt the most. I was handy. That's all it was, really, though she knew how I felt. I considered myself lucky, anyway."

"Well, all right, you had an affair, but I don't see why—"

"That ain't all. Your mother wasn't too good at keeping secrets. Fact is, I'm not too sure she wanted to keep this one. Bull found out. A few days later, he left to go on location on a western. I went, too. Bull put me on a stunt with a runaway freight wagon supposedly carrying a load of dynamite for a gold mine. The wagon was supposed to go over a cliff, explode on impact. I told him it was too dangerous, but he kept talking about how great it would look on film. The dynamite went off early. I jumped, got this gimpy leg, but I was lucky to be alive."

Julie watched him without moving. "You—you're saying Bull knew about you and my mother and put you in harm's way because of it?"

"That's about the size of it."

"I can't believe it."

"Believe it, because he did it. He wasn't really himself at the time, though, I'll admit that much. See, your mother wouldn't tell him whether the baby she was carrying was mine or his."

"Did she—tell you?" Even to her own ears, the question sounded faint. It was a good thing the wall behind her was sturdy, for there was no strength in her legs to hold her.

"She said you were Bull's. I used to wonder, anyway."

"Why was that?"

"Your mother was a special kind of woman, and I don't think she wanted me to feel obligated. She left Bull after the accident with the stagecoach, left him because of it, and came back here to Louisiana. Said she couldn't live with a man who was as good as a murderer."

Chapter 18

Julie sent her car skimming through the night along the dark double ribbon of Interstate 10 with the speedometer needle lying over a notch or two above the speed limit. Even so, most of the traffic flowing between New Orleans and the state capital at Baton Rouge, car after car with headlights stabbing through the pouring rain and taillights blurring into red glares, passed her as if she were standing still.

She let them go. She was in no real hurry to get where she was going, and had long ago outgrown suicidal impulses. The steady whip and clack of the wipers could scarcely keep the windshield clear. Half-hypnotized by the sound, she gazed ahead, trying to stay alert yet unable to stop the steady beat of her thoughts.

Julie had never considered Bull much of a father. It was one reason she had always called him by his first name; she had felt he didn't deserve a childhood title like Dad or Pop, hadn't been around when it counted to earn one. She had resented his absence, resented the lack of contact at birthdays and Christmas beyond the usual gift or card with money tucked inside. She had hated him, at times, for the way he had deserted her and her mother, never questioning her reasons. Reading in the tabloids and magazines about his glamorous life-style in Hollywood and New York and in Europe where he made movies, she often flung what she was reading away in scorn and adolescent rage. While her mother was alive, it had been the two of them against the world and, to a certain extent, against men, especially men like her father.

Later, after her mother had died, the invitation from Bull to come to live with him in L.A. had been a surprise. At the same time, it had

seemed no more than she deserved after the long years of neglect. She
had taken it for granted that he should feed and clothe her, give her
money for school and a car, finance her first efforts at making a film.
At the same time, she had refused to concede that he had any authority
over what she did or with whom. It wasn't amazing that their brief
few years together had been uneasy, or that they had finally parted
company.

The story Stan had told her changed everything. If Bull had not
been certain she was his daughter, then it was a wonder that he had
ever remembered her birthday or thought of her at other holiday times.
Asking her to live with him was a matter for astonishment. That he
had never, not even in moments of his greatest anger, suggested that
she was not his flesh and blood was a miracle. It required the rethinking
of her entire relationship with him.

It almost made it imperative that she tell him at once that he could
work with her. She could do no less.

Yet how could she?

Bull might have been wronged, but he was not an innocent party.
He had tried to kill Stan or, at the very least, had sent him into danger
in the hope that like the husband of Bathsheba sent into battle by
David, he would not survive.

Or had he? She only had Stan's word for that, and Stan was not
an uninterested party. He had been in love with her mother, but had
been used then rejected. It would not be surprising if he was bitter,
nor would it be unusual for the anger of his old pain to be directed
toward the wronged husband, Bull.

She was going to have to talk to Bull about this new development.
There was no way around it; the things he had done for her required
that she give him a chance to explain.

Oh, but what was she going to do if he admitted the charge? How
was she going to choose between Stan and Bull, the two men who had
loved her mother, who might either one of them actually be her father?

The green and white exit sign for Gonzales loomed ahead and she
flipped on her turn indicator. It had been a short drive, shorter than
she remembered. Within only a few minutes, she was making the turn
into the motel driveway and swinging around the redbrick building

with its foundation planting of rain-wet junipers to reach the parking lot. She sat for the time it took to draw a few steadying breaths, then turned off the car motor, shut off the headlights, and got out.

She had to make a run for the lighted line of doorways since she had not thought to bring an umbrella. Shaking raindrops from her hair and arms, wiping the splatters from her face with the heel of her hand, she double-checked the number on the door in front of her. She lifted her hand and knocked.

Bull answered the door with a newspaper in one hand and a pair of half spectacles in gold wire frames sliding down his nose. Seeing Julie, he whipped off the glasses and threw the paper aside before swinging the door wide.

"Come on in here before you drown, girl! What in the name of all that's holy are you doing out on a night like this anyway? Have you had dinner? Let me order us some pizza or something. No, don't argue with me, dammit. Why do you always argue?"

He moved to the telephone, dropping down on the king-size bed while he dialed. Over his shoulder, he said, "Have a beer, you want it. It's just lite Coors. I had some dark German brew in the motor home, but Ofelia swiped it when she moved over to Vance's bus. She didn't have to do that; I'd have shared it with her—the motor home, too."

His order completed, he turned back in time to see Julie pouring a small Jack Daniel's for herself. As he put down the receiver he said, "I didn't know you drank that stuff."

"I don't, usually."

"Good. It takes whole bites out of your liver, you know. So why now?"

It was as good an opening as she was likely to get. Julie told him.

"God," Bull said when she was through. He looked at her from where he was still sitting on the bed. Abruptly, he surged to his feet. Stepping to the setup tray, he poured himself a large Jack Daniel's. Only when he had tossed back a big portion of it did he speak again. "God," he said.

"Yes, well, that was about my reaction, too," Julie said.

"I can't believe Stan told you all that. Not after years of keeping quiet. I can't believe he would say those things about your mother at all, the way he worshiped her."

"He had a reason. He was afraid you might be working on the picture, working over him again."

Bull grunted, then gave a hollow laugh. "Asshole. He should have known years ago that if I'd wanted him dead I'd have taken a gun and shot his fool head off. Why would I mess around with stunts waiting for an accident? That wouldn't have been near sure enough."

"You mean you didn't try to kill him?"

"Hell, no. Not that the thought didn't cross my mind. But by the time your mother got through telling me what she had done and why, I knew exactly who was to blame."

"Her?"

Bull shook his head and took another swallow of his drink. "Me."

"But according to Stan, my mother left you because of your attempt to kill him."

"There was some discussion about it, but I told her I didn't do it, just like I told you. Maybe she didn't believe me, I don't know. I always thought the reason she left was she was tired of me and the way I was doing, tired of L.A., tired of the whole business. She was always out of her element out there, always pining for Louisiana and the family and country life, where she knew everybody and everybody knew her."

"I suppose it's possible," Julie said, since he was watching her as if he expected her to say something.

"What strikes me as wrong about all that is why she didn't marry Stan. That's if she was so sure she was the cause of him being hurt. It would've been like to her to decide he deserved that reward."

"Stan said something about her not wanting him to feel obligated to support her, and me, as if she may have thought he was proposing out of pity. But I remember asking her myself when I was little why she had never remarried. Her only answer was that once was enough."

"Sounds like her."

Julie, watching Bull swirl the liquor in his glass, thought how difficult it was to know other people, even the ones who were closest to you, particularly the ones closest to you. She would never have guessed that Bull and her mother had been part of a dangerous lovers' triangle. They didn't seem the type. There was little about them of the thwarted dreams, suppressed passions, and tragic intensity usually associated with such situations.

However, if Bull was to be believed, it wasn't like that at all. It was just an all-too-common and rather sad bit of domestic betrayal.

Their pizza arrived. It was thick and heavy with toppings and cheese and reasonably hot. Biting into it, Julie realized how hungry she was, how empty and cold she had been inside since she had talked to Stan. It was also then that she recognized she believed Bull. She wasn't sure whether it was because of his logic or her own need, but she was more than willing to consider that the whole long-ago episode had been a terrible misunderstanding.

"I've been thinking," she said as she finished her second slice of pizza and reached for another, "that I might wind up the shooting on the picture a week early, maybe more. Several of the scenes I intended to include were designed to add background and atmosphere or depth of character. They aren't really necessary for the thrust of the story."

Bull swallowed and took a hasty sip of the beer he had opened to go with his pizza. "Why the change?"

"I told you," she said without looking at him. "They will just use up money without adding anything material to the story line."

"Material, hell. You start cutting scenes and you'll ruin your movie. It won't be the thing you see in your mind. Besides that, you're gonna catch double hell from your actors. Madelyn has already been over here offering God-knows-what-all if I'll beef up her lines and add a few more feet of film showing her strutting her stuff. She'll scream so loud it can be heard clear to the Texas–New Mexico line if you actually cut something instead; I mean it, she can be vicious."

"It can't be helped."

"Wrong. All you have to do is stick by your guns. You thought these scenes were necessary once, so why cut them now? Unless you've lost your nerve?"

"My nerve? What are you talking about?"

"Two things. Either you've lost confidence in your own vision— or else you're just plain scared."

"All right, then I'm scared. Satisfied?"

He sat back in his chair. "Scared of what? You know?"

"Yes, I know!" she cried. "I'm scared somebody else will be killed on my set. I'm scared more people will be hurt or maimed or go nuts while I watch. I'm scared somebody is going to take this film away from me. I'm scared I'm going to go so far over budget that nobody will ever trust me to direct so much as a commercial again. I'm scared that somebody is after me, trying to make me fail—"

"What?" he asked, the power of his voice cutting across her trailing tones.

She put down her pizza and rested her head on her hand with her elbow propped on the table. "You heard me."

"I heard you, but I don't believe it."

"Well, neither do I half the time," she said, sitting up and glaring at him, "but common sense ought to tell you that something is badly wrong on this location. If that's not what it is, if somebody doesn't have a personal vendetta against me, then I don't know what else it can be."

"Have you told Allen about this?"

"I haven't told anybody."

"Ahuh."

"I don't want to sound ridiculous," she muttered, looking away from him.

He reached out and caught her hand. "But you don't mind looking ridiculous in front of me?"

She looked at him and started to smile. "You're Bull, you—"

Then she remembered. Her smile vanished. She lowered her gaze to his big hand on hers, studying the long fingers, the wiry hairs that grew on his knuckles, the shape of his fingernails.

"What's the matter now?"

"Stan said—he said that my mother told him I was your daughter."

"Well, of course you are. Who else's?" His tone was warm, faintly indulgent.

"Not his."

"Oh, that. Well, I tell you, Julie. You're mother wasn't a saint, but she was never worth shucks as a liar. She wouldn't tell me whose child she was carrying, but she wouldn't say it wasn't mine. I figured the odds; you know, a couple of one-night stands against whole days and nights of loving. I never had any serious doubts."

She laughed. She couldn't help it; it was so like Bull, immensely practical, more than a little egotistical. It was also, she realized, intentionally kind. Tears rose to shimmer in her eyes. As they spilled over her lashes she wiped at them with the edges of her hands.

"Here now, none of that," he said uneasily.

"No," she answered, "but you know what? I think I appreciated you more when I thought you had paid for my education and taught me your trade while thinking I might be another man's child."

"I'll be damned," he said, sitting back in his chair.

"Probably," she told him, and smiled with traces of tears in her eyes. "But you know I had to wonder. Stan used to come to see me. You never did."

He looked down at the beer in his hand. "I used to think about it a lot, but I knew your mother didn't want me around, didn't want me upsetting the both of you. Besides, it seemed like it hurt less not to go than it would to see you then have to leave. One thing, though, I always sent the alimony, and the child support."

The last was, she saw, a point of pride with him, and possibly a consolation. She said softly, "That you did."

She thought of telling him then, at that moment, that she would work with him on the movie. What kept her quiet was the memory of the cocaine she had found in the motor home. She had to talk to him about that, had to find out what it meant. Yet it didn't seem possible to do it at this moment. She could not bring herself to say anything that would spoil the warm rapport that lay between them, anything that would take away the sense of loving. It would wait another day. Surely, it would wait that long.

They had finished their pizza and were picking up the last crumbs of mushroom and sausage and onion with their fingers when Bull cleared his throat. He said, "So what are you going to do about Stan?"

"I don't know," she said, putting a bit of pepperoni in her mouth and chewing reflectively. "Try to talk to him, I guess, tell him what you said."

"Let me talk to him. I think maybe it's time."

She turned her wide gaze on him. "If that's what you want."

"It can't hurt. If I make no headway, then you can always give it a shot."

"When will you see him?"

"Tomorrow, maybe. It's getting a little late to start in on anything tonight. Besides, I'm going to have to do some hard thinking about what to say and how to go about it."

Julie left the motel a short time later. She was halfway out the door when she turned back and put her arms around Bull, giving him a quick, hard hug. He returned it, holding her tight, letting her go slowly and with a reluctance. She gave him a quick kiss on the cheek, her smile soft, before turning and running out into the rain.

"Be careful," he called after her. He didn't shut the door until she was safely in the car and rolling out of the parking lot.

On the following day, they returned to filming in town, shooting the scenes inside the clothing and shoe stores in the early morning, then using the rest of the day for the wedding scene. The next day, they would work on the scene with Madelyn and Vance hovering over Summer in a hospital bed, supposedly after the accident that had so nearly been real. They might also get to the scene where Summer, as Alicia, leaves her hospital bed and runs away, hiding in the swamp in the attempt to force her father and mother to stop fighting over her and cooperate with each other to find her.

Julie wasn't sure she wanted to get to it. She had been having second thoughts about that bit, and about the happy ending she had mapped out, derived from Alicia's plotting. Watching the interaction of the actors playing the characters and seeing the dangers of the swamp, that outcome seemed increasingly unrealistic.

She had never belonged to the school that considered happy endings as automatically less meaningful and artistic than downbeat ones.

She liked the idea of having Alicia take control of her fate, having her do something to force the issue and achieve the goal she desires. Yet it seemed out of character for Jean-Pierre and Dorothea to suddenly find the willingness and love to overcome their differences.

Perhaps she could come up with something different. But if she was going to do that, it would have to be soon.

Julie went back to the location after the shooting was over. She huddled for a couple of hours with Ofelia and Stan over the next day's schedule, then, when they had gone, sat on alone, scribbling on a yellow pad. She jotted down ideas of all kinds, from tried and true clichés to far-out solutions, free-associating in an effort to come up with something, anything new for an ending. She didn't have much luck.

She heard the parking lot emptying car by car, heard most of the company trucks pulling out. She knew when the catering van left, but still she worked on. This was Aunt Tine's bingo night, and Rey had said something about a business meeting in New Orleans before he had left the house after breakfast. No one would be expecting her.

Rey had been having a lot of business meetings in the last few days; she had, in fact, seen little of him. The rain had kept them from shooting any of the few remaining action scenes, of course, so he had not been needed on the set. She supposed she was still having a little trouble recognizing the extent of his other life in New Orleans. He had been so quintessentially the Swamp Rat to her in the beginning that she was still adjusting.

It was perhaps two hours later that a possibility for the ending came to her. She scribbled it down as fast as she could, added a few embellishments, then sat grinning at it in somber pleasure. It was good, very good.

No, it wasn't.

Dorothea, as played by Madelyn, was not the kind to let sentiment rule her heart for long. For her to find her daughter in the swamp after she runs away, then stand back out of sight and let Jean-Pierre make the rescue was all wrong.

Ripping the pages from her notebook, Julie balled them into a wad and tossed them toward the trash can.

She was tired. Her eyes burned, the back of her neck hurt, and she felt too stiff to walk. It was time to call it a night. Maybe something would come to her if she slept on it.

She rose from her chair and picked up her shoulder bag, hunting for her keys as she moved toward the door. She locked her office and crossed to the outside door, then locked this behind her also. She moved slowly down the trailer steps, looking up at the night sky. It was clear for the first time in days, but it was also cooler. The stars seemed close, and the harvest moon sinking down the sky had an orange tint like a pumpkin.

Her rental Buick was parked near a mercury vapor light at the edge of the parking lot farthest from the road entrance. She started toward it, glancing around at the emptiness, growing steadily more aware of the stillness the farther she went from the office trailer. She was glad to see the location guard on duty inside his metal building with its wide windows. He was kicked back in his chair, reading a paperback book.

She was almost to her car when she heard it. She stopped, tilting her head back once more, scanning the night sky, listening to the steady hum of an approaching plane. She had heard that sound before, on her first night in the swamp country. It was not a passenger plane, not a jet, not just any plane. It was a private aircraft, possibly a seaplane.

Possibly drug runners.

Possibly drug runners who had something to do with her movie crew.

The idea had been forming in the back of her mind for some time, even before she had found the bag of cocaine. It was too much of a coincidence that so much evidence of use had shown up on this location, or that drops of some sort were being made so close. A movie on location was an anthill of activity, with delivery trucks and vans of all sizes coming and going at all hours, plus there were vast sums of money flowing from it in every direction. It presented a unique opportunity, not only for channeling the drugs but for laundering the proceeds.

She had no proof that she was right, of course.

The plane was a black shadow against the moonlit heavens with lights that winked red and green. It was banking far out over the treetops some miles away, coming in low and slow. As she watched, its landing lights were switched on, shining out with startling brightness in spite of its distance from where she stood. Julie was aware of a host of feelings flooding over her in a tide, doubt and curiosity, anger and fear. But foremost among them was anger.

Suddenly she was running back toward the trailer, fumbling with her keys. She stamped up the steps, unlocked the door, and ran toward Ofelia's office. It was unlocked, since Ofelia never bothered with such things. On a board inside the door hung the keys to the company boats and trucks. Julie scanned them, considering and rejecting the key to one of the cabin cruisers—too big, too loud, though she noticed that only one set was in place. Possibly Stan was using the other one—the blue-tagged key to the company truck he usually drove was on its hook as if he was still around somewhere. For her needs, the skiff was much better. She jerked its key from the board and ran from the trailer, pausing only to lock the outer door once more.

There was only one cabin cruiser at the dock, all right. Julie barely glanced at it, however, as she pushed the skiff that lay on the bank out into the water and jumped into it. Starting the engine, she put it in reverse until it was free of the dock area, then sent it nosing quietly down the river. The location guard, she noticed, never looked out of his building. She shook her head, then craned her neck to stare up at the night sky.

The plane had disappeared, had probably landed. She had a fair idea, however, of where it might have come down. In her mind was a memory of a canal seen from the air, and of a cabin cruiser running into a boat house to one side of that long stretch of water. All she had to do was get there without being discovered.

The splash was loud, a hard slap on the surface of the water that sent spray flying for twenty feet. Julie's head snapped around. Her heart jumped and began to pound.

Then she saw it. A bull alligator. He had dived from the bank and was gliding along not six feet away, as if racing her boat. She took a deep, shuddering breath, gripped the wheel harder, and looked away back down the river.

———

Rey sat perfectly still while a cloud of gnats too small to see in the darkness danced around his head and made a feast off his face and the back of his neck. He should have known better than to leave the house without insect repellent, or to take up a post under a low-hanging tree limb. Unfortunately, it was the only cover available. He would be lucky if he didn't get a brown wolf spider down the back of his shirt. Still, if he could last a few more minutes, the plane out in the canal would be unloaded and he could go home.

The rain had interfered with the operation, causing a slowdown in delivery and a triple load that had meant a landing instead of just a drop. These things happened to the best of them. The planning was good, however; the business was proceeding at a snappy pace. There was no unnecessary talking and no banging and bumping the goods around.

The sound of a boat motor brought his head around. It was familiar. He swore under his breath, then as the motor was abruptly cut, swore with even greater virulence. Uninvited guests were bad enough; guests armed with some slight chance of knowledge and sneaky impulses could be a disaster, a deadly one.

Rey kicked off his running shoes and tied the laces together. With the shoes draped around his neck, he slid over the side of his borrowed skiff. He paddled and waded to the bank, climbing out. Slipping his shoes back on, he faded back among the cypress stumps and palmetto. When he was sure he could be neither seen nor heard, he set off at a steady jog toward where he had last heard the boat motor.

The light boat was nearer than he expected, actually turning into the canal instead of still in the river. The reason was the electric trolling motor on the front. Still, the greatest surprise was who was operating it. He stood staring for a long moment with his hands propped on his hips, then threw back his head, gazing heavenward as he whispered a fervent supplication of "Jeez, Mike, and Mary!"

There was no answer, nor did he expect one. No doubt he deserved this. Regardless, there was only one thing to be done. He eased once more into the water.

He came up on the side of the skiff, surfacing without a sound. He reached swiftly to place both his hands on the gunwale, but only allowed it to take his weight by degrees. When he had purchase, he heaved himself up and over the side in a single vault before the unstable craft could rock to the top of its arc and overturn. Coming to his feet as Julie swung around, he snatched her backward into his arms. The breath was driven from his lungs as they catapulted into the bottom of the boat. He gave a wheezing grunt. He felt the biggest scabbed place on his shoulder break open, then its burning sting; still, he managed to get a leg over Julie's thighs and a hand clamped across her mouth.

"Don't make a sound," he said against her ear, the words rough with fury and exasperation, "or you may get us both killed."

She went still. He could feel the quick rise and fall of her chest against him and the heavy thumping of her heart. Her body was soft and pliant and the smell of her hair was sweet. It crossed his mind, in the most fleeting and haziest of ways, how nice it would be to make love to her there in the floating boat, under the stars. But the boat was turning in circles caused by an untended trolling motor, and now was definitely not the time.

He shifted, heaving himself up onto one elbow beside her. His shoulder felt wet and sore. It didn't help his temper. "I'm going to let you go, and we are going to get ourselves back the way you came as fast as this thing will go without making any noise. Signify agreement by nodding your head, otherwise—"

She had the nerve to raise her brows in a question there, flat on her back in a runaway boat. He almost laughed aloud at the undaunted sassiness of it. To cover the impulse he said crudely, "Otherwise I'll see how much of your shirt it takes to gag you."

Her nod was slight, but still felt like a victory. In quiet relief, he said, "Good."

Letting her go, he eased forward and caught the handle of the trolling motor. Since it had been running all along, using it could hardly matter. He swung the boat, heading back toward the river. From the corners of his eyes, he watched as Julie sat up, then retreated as far from him as possible, to the rear seat of the boat.

He felt a hard jab of regret, but pushed it away. He would deal with it later, if there was a later.

He had to give her credit; she waited until they were nearly back to the location before she tried to talk to him, then she kept her voice low to keep it from carrying over the water. "I thought," she said, "that you were supposed to be in New Orleans?"

"It isn't far. How do you know that I haven't been and returned?" He tried the effects of a quietly firm tone, but could not tell that it made any impression.

"What are you doing in the swamp this late?"

"Fishing," he answered.

"Sure you were."

"It's what swamp rats do."

"Spare me," she said, and turned her head in disgust.

He did.

Neither spoke again until they had nearly reached the dock, until they could see in the glow of the mercury vapor lights that shone out over the water. The peculiar pinkish light reflected in the river's surface, edged the moss swaying in the trees, and slid over the white paint and chrome trim of the cabin cruiser that floated beside the wooden walkway.

It shone, too, on the body that hung facedown with arms dangling at the rear of the boat, and on the trail of red wetness streaking the white side, tracking down into the water.

Chapter 19

It was Stan.

Julie knelt beside him, where she and Rey had laid him on the rear deck of the cabin cruiser, and felt for a pulse. Rey had already told her that it was no use, but she had to see, to know for herself. Even then, even when she had felt the stillness as she held the flaccid hand and looked into the waxen, lifeless face, it did not seem possible.

Gone. Just like that. Only a short time before he had been walking, talking, worrying, hoping, feeling. Now, nothing. This man who for a short time she had thought might be her father was just gone.

A hard knot formed in her throat. She swallowed against it; still, the tears pooled in her eyes and trickled down beside her nose. She tried to ignore them, to concentrate on other things.

Stan had apparently been stabbed, though there was no sign of the weapon. How long ago it might have been was a matter for the coroner; still, Julie could not help wondering if Stan had been there, bleeding to death, when she had left in the skiff, wondering if she might have saved him if she had seen him.

"Come on," Rey said, laying a hand on her shoulder, gripping briefly. "We may as well call the sheriff's office and get it over with."

"You go," she said in low tones. "I'll stay with him."

"No."

She looked up at Rey there in the dim light, blinking away the obscuring tears, startled by the uncompromising hardness of his voice. "All right then, I'll go and you stay."

"We'll both go. In case whoever did this is still around."

She opened her mouth to argue, then closed it again. There was a flashlight flickering, swinging, over in the direction of the motor homes. It was the location guard, making his rounds. She had been afraid to ask where he was, afraid he might also be dead. He at least had a gun for protection. She said, "I think the problem is solved."

Rey called the sheriff's office. Since it was obviously a homicide, he told her, the sheriff would, in all probability, alert the state police; she could look for the investigation this time to be considerably more intense and prolonged than it had been for Paul's death.

His words were a reminder of her position, and her duty. As soon as he got off the phone Julie called Allen in New Orleans. Then she called Bull.

He answered on the fifth ring, sounding groggy and half-asleep. He woke quickly enough, however.

"God, how did it happen?"

Julie told him. Even as he said he was on his way and hung up the phone Julie stood there replaying his voice in her mind, trying to decide if his reaction was natural, if his voice was too calm and matter-of-fact, his response afterward too ready. She hated doing it, hated the slow creep of desolate suspicion inside her, but she couldn't help it.

She didn't know what to believe anymore.

Rey had appeared on the canal as if from nowhere. She could not imagine how he had gotten there in her boat, but could imagine all too well what he had been doing on the river. His roughness, his threats all pointed to knowledge of the plane that had landed. It also indicated that her guess as to its purpose had been correct.

The question was, how much of what she guessed was she going to tell the police? How much could she afford to tell them?

Stan was dead, and there was nothing she could do to bring him back. If she told the authorities that he had had a quarrel of long standing with her father, then Bull might be arrested. If she told them that his death might stem from some kind of involvement of the movie company with drug smuggling and the landing of a plane in the swamp, then production would most likely be brought to a halt for weeks on end, weeks that could spell disaster for the movie and for her future.

There would be a considerable delay in the production anyway; it was inevitable. She could expect another visit from Davies, the accountant with the bonding company, and more threats to take the movie from her. The thought made her want to scream. Or howl like a hurt child.

Oh, but it was ridiculous to think that Stan's death was directed at her. No one could be so vindictive, so without mercy as to kill a human being just to get at her. Could they?

Maybe she was wrong. Maybe none of what had happened had anything to do with her personally. It could be that it was all tied in some way to this drug business, from Paul Lislet's death to the murder of Stan.

There were so many possibilities and no way to know which was the right one. Until she knew, how could she decide what to say? How could she tell whether to protect her father and try to save her movie by keeping her suspicions to herself, accepting whatever risk there might be, or just to give the sheriff's men every single detail she knew or guessed, and hope for the best. She had maybe ten minutes to make up her mind.

Rey had moved to the window of the trailer office where they had gone to use the phone, looking out across the parking lot toward the boat pier. Julie glanced at him, troubled by his grim silence and the strain that hung between them. His hair was still damp and his shirt and jeans wet and clinging. There was a spreading patch of red on his shoulder.

"You're bleeding," she said, her voice sharp.

He swung to face her so she could not see, shrugging a little at the same time. "It's nothing, just the burn."

"Come in to the other office and let me look at it. Ofelia has the first-aid kit, I think." She led the way out of her office and into the other one, saying, "Somehow everything winds up in here."

He watched her take out foil packs of alcohol-saturated pads, a couple of large gauze squares, and a roll of nylon tape. "You were working tonight, I suppose."

She nodded in answer before she stepped toward him, tearing open a foil pack. He turned his back obediently, sitting on the edge of

Ofelia's desk so that she could reach his shoulder with greater ease. He winced as she touched the pad to the raw areas in the middle of the old scab.

"Sorry," she murmured.

He didn't move again, scarcely seemed to notice what she was doing as he went on. "You didn't notice anything unusual, see anybody around who didn't belong?"

"No, but then there are always so many people coming and going. Besides, I don't see much of anything or anybody when I'm at my desk."

"So far as you know, everybody left at near the normal time?"

"Except Stan," she said, wiping at the trail of blood down his back, remembering the blood on the side of the boat with an abrupt, convulsive shudder. She threw the alcohol pad in the trash can, picked up another one. "I saw his key still on the board—when I took the boat key."

"Nobody else's key had been left there?"

"I don't think so, but then it's not easy to tell. Some of the trucks are always here overnight. It depends on what's happening next day, who may be working late, who needs a ride."

"But you didn't recognize anyone's keys in particular?"

She answered in the negative. With the wound clean again, she picked up a gauze square and spread it over the place where the scab had been torn away, then began to use the nylon strips to hold it in place. She paused once with her fingers spread over the width of his shoulder as she pressed a strip of tape to it with her thumbs. Beneath her hands she could feel the tense ropes of his muscles and the warm resilience of his sun-browned skin. She swallowed before she went on, "What is it? What are you trying to get me to say?"

"I wanted to know if you have anything of importance to tell the sheriff and his men. If not, there's no real point in you getting involved beyond the normal questioning. I can just tell them I was out fishing, that I started back in and discovered the body."

"What you mean is that I won't be given the opportunity to mention what took place out on the canal, isn't it? I won't tell anybody about the plane? What you were doing out there? Why you wanted me elsewhere?"

"It has no bearing."

"How do I know it has no bearing? How do you know?"

"There may or may not be some connection with the plane and why it was out there, I can't say. I do know this much: The fact that I was out there had nothing to do with Stan being killed, any more than you being there contributed to it."

"And that's all you're going to say?"

He turned to watch her for long moments, his dark eyes unreadable. Finally, he said, "Trust me, Julie, this way is best."

There was in the quiet timbre of his voice a reminder of shared joy, a rapport of body and mind that had been fleeting, yet special. It was only in her mind, that reminder. She did not think that he was trading on past intimacy to persuade her.

Trust, he had said.

Had he saved her from running into trouble, or saved himself? She didn't know, wasn't sure she wanted to know.

She could not quite give him trust, but might be able to accept a pact of mutual cooperation. That was, in essence, what he was offering. Wasn't it?

"In case you've forgotten," she said, her tone irritable with her uncertainty, "you are still soaking wet. How do you intend to explain that?"

A deep breath swelled his chest while elation burned for an instant in his eyes and was gone. He said, "I could go and busy myself diving around the boat, looking for the murder weapon in case it went overboard when Stan fell against the side. Who knows, I might actually find something."

"You would start your shoulder bleeding again, or get it infected, if you haven't already." She hesitated. "There's another possibility. We could take the key to the wardrobe trailer and see what kind of dry clothes we can find."

He smiled a little without moving.

"Don't look like that," she said sharply. "You're not the only one with ideas."

"I see that," he answered, the words deep.

"All right, then. What about the guard?"

"He came on after ten-thirty for the midnight shift, claims nobody unusual has been in or out on his watch. Anyway, he's a friend of mine and Paul's. I think I may be able to make him see things my way."

Julie gave a slow nod. "That's good, then. Now tell me exactly what it is you think we should say."

It was not complicated. Basically, they would just leave out mention of Julie's being out on the water. She was to say, instead, that she heard Rey's boat motor and went to meet him. They had then found Stan together, just as had actually happened.

Julie, searching quickly through the wardrobe trailer for one of Jean-Pierre's outfits while Rey stood guard at the door, did her best to ignore the doubts that assailed her. It helped that the sheriff and his deputies arrived as she and Rey were walking back toward the office trailer, with the state police appearing shortly afterward. Once Rey had told his truncated story, once she had added her part by way of corroboration, there was no turning back.

It was a long night. Bull arrived, grim and unshaven and with his short graying hair standing like rows of harvested wheat where he had run his fingers through it. He had called Ofelia before he left the motel, and she came in a little behind him. Shortly afterward, there was coffee brewing for everybody in the reception area of the trailer office, which soon became the main gathering place.

The coroner came and went and a forensic team put in an appearance, did their job, and left again. By four-thirty in the morning, some three hours after Julie and Rey had found the body, it was established that death had occurred no earlier than eleven the evening before, and no later than one, a half hour before discovery. The autopsy, along with a close investigation of Stan's movements during the evening hours leading up to midnight, could possibly narrow the time, but that was as close as they could come for the moment. They would proceed on that assumption, if Ofelia would begin calling in the crew members who had been at the location at that time.

Julie had hoped for a more certain time of death. With the time frame given so far, there was no way to tell whether Stan had been dead when she left the location in her boat or if he had been killed in her absence. It troubled her, that uncertainty.

As the night turned into a pale dawn it became more and more disagreeable that she had to hide her reasons for wanting information, and also that she had to watch every word she spoke so that her time spent out on the river was taken into account. By the time Allen arrived, the sun was up and she was exhausted.

Allen took one look at her and demanded that she be allowed to go home and rest. There was no objection. Bull and Rey had been urging her to leave for hours and she had been refusing. She went then because she was tired of arguing, and because it seemed that Allen should be able to take over as representative for Excel Films, relieving her of responsibility. At least he, out of the three men present, had some right to do it.

Aunt Tine still had Summer with her, though Donna was on hand to see after the girl, as she had been every day since Annette was hospitalized. The two women had heard about the killing over Aunt Tine's police scanner. They sent Summer to play with Donna's two boys while they asked about it. Their curiosity was natural enough, neither overly pressing nor macabre; Julie didn't mind answering their questions, telling them who was at the location and what the police were doing. Aunt Tine cooked breakfast for Julie while she talked, but Julie could eat only a little of it. The older woman finally took away the plate, leaning to give Julie's shoulders a brief hug.

"Here, now, off to bed with you. You look tired clear into next year, and I should think shame on myself for keeping you up answering questions. Rest you need, and rest I'll see you get, or know the reason why, yes!"

Julie showered and put on a nightgown, closed and locked her door, and pulled the curtains at the windows. She got into bed and stretched out with a sigh. It did no good; her mind did not stop turning.

Trust me, Rey had said. She had not agreed in so many words; still, it came to the same thing. She had had her own reasons for going along with what he asked, of course, and yet she couldn't believe she hadn't demanded to know what he had been doing there on the river, or what it was about the plane that he had gone to such trouble to keep her from seeing.

She could hear the children playing in the yard behind the house, yelling and laughing. Now and then, Donna or Aunt Tine called out to them, but there was no alarm in their warnings and strictures, only indulgent concern. It was oddly soothing, that sound of women and children, like a dream of childhood.

Julie jumped as a knock came from the direction of the gallery. She struggled to sit up, then slipped from the bed as she slid into her robe and went to unlock the door. It was Donna who stood waiting, her expression serious as she faced Julie.

Julie invited her inside, tying her robe at the waist as she stepped back out of the way. Sitting down on the bed, she gestured at the same time toward a chair.

Donna seated herself and clasped her hands together in her lap, looking down at them self-consciously. "I'm sorry to disturb you, but there was something I wanted to talk to you about, and it seems there's never the right time on the set. There's always people around or you're so busy."

"You should have just flagged me down. Is it about Summer?"

"No. It's—about Rey."

"Yes?" Julie realized the comment wasn't helpful, but it was the most she could think of to say. She could feel her stomach muscles tighten as she remembered that Donna and Rey were supposed to have been teenage sweethearts, and perhaps something more than that just before Paul was killed.

"I'm concerned about him. He may have told you that his wife died?"

"There was some mention of it."

"What he probably didn't tell you was that she was angry with him, upset over his job taking him away from home so much. Actually, she was leaving him. She started down the steep back steps of the old house they were living in. It was pouring rain and they were slick, plus she overbalanced somehow because of her pregnancy and the heavy suitcase she was carrying. She fell, lay in the rain, and miscarried. She and the baby died. Rey's always blamed himself because he left her to go off on a special job that day, because he wasn't there."

"He didn't give me the details, but I really don't see how it concerns me."

"I'm getting to that," Donna said doggedly. "His wife was young and headstrong, beautiful in a Raphael Madonna fashion, though not very mature. I thought he was never going to get over her death, the double death really. The women he has taken out since then have all been—I don't know how to say this exactly, but—needy in some way. They were attractive enough, but had been deserted by family or husbands, had backgrounds of illness, mental or physical abuse, things like that. It was as if he was drawn to women who needed him, as if helping them was the basis of the relationship. Do you see what I'm saying?"

"I'm not sure, unless you're suggesting that's the way he sees me?"

"I'm just trying to make you understand that a sort of compassionate affection was about the most he could muster for the women in his life until you came along."

Julie wondered if Donna realized that she herself could be the latest in Rey's long line of needy women. If that was his preference, then he could hardly resist a beautiful young widow, mother of two children, and in need of the means to make a living.

Julie stood up, moving toward the door and putting her hand on the knob. "I'm sorry, but I don't see much point in this. If you don't mind, I really am tired."

"It isn't my concern, I know that, and I'm sure Rey wouldn't like it if he knew I was talking to you. My only excuse is that I've known him a long time, and I don't want to see him tear himself to pieces again the way he did over that silly little girl he married."

"Running away from a bad marriage doesn't make a woman silly," Julie said.

"Maybe not, but his wife knew what kind of job he had when she married him, and should have known he wouldn't always be there."

Julie's need to know more about Rey, to verify her fears, suddenly became greater than her need for privacy. She released the doorknob, turning to lean her shoulders against the wall. "What kind of job did he have exactly?"

"He was a special undercover agent for the DEA for years, until he became a supervisor."

Undercover.

"Oh, yes, I remember. I believe he resigned?"

"That's right, a couple of years ago."

"There was some problem, I think?"

"What?" The look on Donna's face was blank.

"Something about drugs missing after an operation. He told me so himself."

"Oh, that. He made a detour with a truckload taken off some boat, took it by one of the New Orleans inner-city schools where he was scheduled to give a talk on drug prevention. There was about a fifteen-minute flap over it, but every kilo was accounted for."

Julie stood absolutely still. "But—why would he let me think the worst?"

"Who knows? To see what you would say, maybe. It's not always possible to tell with Rey."

"I also don't understand why he went to work with the agency in the first place if he had such a wealthy background."

"That background wasn't always there for him. His New Orleans grandparents were difficult over their daughter's marriage to a Cajun. They didn't see or speak to their daughter until after Rey was born, and then they visited only once or twice a year. Rey grew up Cajun, following the swamp ways of his father, and his father before him, and his father before him back seven, eight generations. Back to the 1730s and a wedding in St. Louis Cathedral, because the Cajuns who came in the 1760s long ago intermarried with the Germans who came during John Law's Mississippi Bubble in the earliest days of French colonial Louisiana. We're all one big family on the river, you see, no need for this business of birth and riches."

Julie did see. She had been given only bits and pieces before, but now she could put them together. Somewhere in the back of her mind, there was another puzzle putting itself together, but she couldn't quite see the pattern.

She said, "Things began to change, I suppose, after his mother and father died?"

"Oh, yes. Then he became the heir, and went more often to stay with his grandparents in the house in New Orleans. But he never quite forgave them, and would take nothing from them except payment for his education. He had his pride. It was only after his grandfather died and his grandmother became ill that he resigned from the DEA and took over the management of the business interests and investments. For a long time, he would take nothing for his services, but recently the expansion and development of those interests has been so great, he has changed the operation to such an extent, that his stiff-necked attitude became ridiculous."

"Development in what direction?"

"Foreign investments mostly, I think, though he doesn't talk about it much."

"And with his tendency toward business matters—was it Rey who suggested that it might be reasonable to sue the movie company over your husband's accident?"

"Sue? I don't know what you're talking about."

Julie was not, somehow, surprised. She made a dismissive gesture. "Something else Rey said. I suppose I misunderstood."

She hadn't misunderstood, though, and she knew it. Rey had deliberately raised the specter of a suit in order to give himself an excuse for being in Julie's office, going through her files, that day.

"Anyway," Donna went on, "I would never do that, and Rey knows it. My husband went into the stuntman thing with his eyes open. It was Paul's job, and I understood that."

There was something sad yet proud in the way Donna spoke that sounded off key, as if the two of them were talking at cross purposes. Julie said in some confusion, "He didn't have to take it."

"No, but he wasn't the kind to turn it down, not when he knew it had to be done. That's the kind of man, the kind of policeman, he was."

"Policeman," Julie repeated blankly.

"Narc, if you'd rather. There's nothing wrong with saying it; it's what he called himself. He was proud of his work. Oh, he kept saying every year that he was going to quit and go shrimping for a living, but the money was good and he felt he was being useful, so he never did."

Narc. Undercover narcotics agent.

Julie felt cold. She wrapped her arms about her body, pulling the robe close. "Rey knew, I suppose?"

"I think Paul went into it, in a way, because it was what Rey did at the DEA," Donna said with a slow nod.

"Would many other people have known?"

"Close family, his co-workers, not that many. Are you trying to suggest that he might have been killed because he was on a job at the movie location? I've always known it was possible that it wasn't an accident."

"And you came to work there, anyway."

Donna looked away. "It wasn't easy, but I needed the money."

Julie stared at the other woman's averted face. "You're an unusual person. I'm sorry the movie is so near completion. It might have been nice to get to know you better."

"So you'll be going back to L.A.?" Donna said.

"Yes, of course."

"Yes," the other girl echoed. "I don't suppose you would listen if I asked you to leave Rey alone between now and then?"

"Leave him alone? I wasn't aware I was bothering him."

"You know what I mean. If you aren't serious about Rey, then tell him so and go back to your California lover. Rey is strong and good-looking and may be just foreign enough to you to be exciting, but he needs more than some brief affair. You're different—needy maybe, but not in quite the same way as the others. You're the kind of woman he could love if you would let him. That means you can also hurt him. He doesn't deserve that."

"Not even if it also means that you can hang around and pick up the pieces?"

"I'm a widow," Donna said with her chin high and her face composed. "I loved my husband very much. I love Rey, too, but not in the way you mean. He's always been there for me, and I think always will be, but that's all."

"For now, maybe."

Donna got to her feet, moving toward Julie and the door beside her. "I should have known better than to try to talk to you. I'm sorry I wasted your time."

Remorse rose inside Julie. She took a deep breath and released it on a soft sigh. "No," she said quietly, "I'm sorry. I expect you're the kind of woman Rey needs. Don't worry. I don't think I'm cut out for babies and diapers and waving a man off to a dangerous job every day. I'll be gone before long and that will be the end of it."

Donna paused with the door half-open and a frown creasing her forehead. "You're sure?"

Julie shrugged with a halfhearted attempt at a smile. But she didn't answer. There was, inexplicably, a knotted muscle in her throat that prevented it.

Chapter 20

Julie was back at the location by the middle of the afternoon. She felt better for the few hours of rest, though she hadn't slept. Her mind was too unsettled; she kept going over and over the same problems, or else wondering what was happening with the investigation and what everyone was doing.

She couldn't stop thinking about Stan. There were arrangements to be made for him; she thought there was a sister somewhere in Iowa or Illinois who should be notified and asked about preferences for the burial, whether in a family cemetery in the Midwest, in L.A., or even in Louisiana. A decision would have to be made about attending the funeral, wherever it was held. Or whenever. It would not be possible to make final plans until after the coroner's office had completed the autopsy.

In the meantime, she needed to begin to get some idea of how long the hiatus in filming would be, and maybe see if something couldn't be done about continuing on a small scale with the scenes to be done in town. If that proved impossible, then there would be a thousand logistical problems to be worked out, supplies and services to be delayed or canceled, permits to be extended, and so forth. There were people whose job it was to take care of those things, but with the upheaval caused by Stan's death, she wasn't sure it would get done.

Excuses, all of it. She simply couldn't stand being away from the location when so much was going on there.

Bull was sitting in Julie's office eating takeout chicken. He looked up as she came in. "I knew you'd be back," he said, picking up the red-and-white-striped chicken box and waving it in her direction. "Want a wing?"

She took the piece of chicken mainly to be companionable. Perching on the corner of the desk, she said, "Anything new come up?"

"They found a couple of different guys who saw Stan around twelve or so, which narrows the time of death down a bit. That's about it."

She ate her chicken wing in a few bites, then tossed the bone in the trash can and reached for a napkin. "I've been thinking, this thing with Stan almost makes the cuts I was telling you about a necessity."

"Not that again," he said, his expression pained as he chewed a mouthful of chicken.

"Listen, I don't like it any better than you do, but an ending of some kind on this film is better than nothing."

"I know the delays are driving you nuts, Julie, but they'll be over eventually. You still have time to do this thing the way you want it."

"I don't think so. It seems to me that the faster we can get done here, the better it will be. There are things going on here that you don't understand."

"You mean the drug business," he said flatly.

"How—" she began.

"I've got eyes, girl, and ears. Besides, Rey filled me in while you were gone."

"All right, maybe you do understand, but you can see that it isn't going to do the movie company any good to stick around and be used."

"That has nothing to do with you or with what you're doing. Your story, your art—if I can be so mystical about it—transcends that sort of thing. You ought to know that."

"Since I've never been encouraged to see what I do as an art," Julie answered with some tartness, "no, I can't say that I do know it. If I stay, and somebody else gets killed, then that transcends art, as far as I'm concerned. I'll be responsible, and frankly I've been responsible for enough."

Bull pushed aside the last of his chicken in distaste, picking up a napkin to wipe the grease from his fingers. "I've said it before, but I'll say it again: You'll be butchering your movie. You're not one of these directors who shoot miles more film than they need. I've watched you work, and I know that every scene you schedule has a purpose, makes an important point about the characters, the story, or both. Cut out a scene, and you'll be doing damage. That's just the way it is."

"There isn't a director alive who doesn't leave piles of film on the floor after a fine cut."

"That's different, and you know it. We're talking here about not filming scenes in the first place."

As they talked, there had come the sound of the outside door opening and closing and the low timbre of Rey's voice along with the throaty contralto of Madelyn de Wells. A moment later, the actress sauntered into the room. "Cutting out scenes?" she said in mock horror. "Those are fighting words, you know, my dear Bull. Which scenes, exactly, are we cutting?"

"Yours, Madelyn, all yours," he said, a sharp edge to his voice that showed his displeasure at the interruption.

Madelyn gave him a tight smile. "I don't doubt it. I'll tell you this much right now, though: Anybody who clips so much as a syllable from my hospital scene should prepare to die!" Delayed recognition crossed her face and she grimaced. "Oh, dear. That didn't come out right under the circumstances, but you know what I mean."

"The hospital scene is necessary," Julie said. "Of course it will stay in."

"I'm relieved. And the scene where I grovel in the mud and rain, totally undone by this hellish swamp? Promise me it won't, in that classic phrase, wind up on the cutting-room floor."

"I don't see it happening."

"Good. Those two I have to have. I really will commit mayhem if I lose either one, even if it's only on my agent for not getting me script control."

There was a short silence. Madelyn was not a large enough name these days to swing script control, if she had ever been in that league. It was embarrassing to Julie to see the actress play the star game when everyone knew it was false. She was about to make another noncommittal answer when Rey spoke from the doorway.

"Seems to me, Julie, that it will be a shame if everything you've outlined in the past few weeks doesn't make it to the screen." He gave her a slow smile as she turned to look at him in surprise. "Sorry. Just couldn't resist putting in my two cents' worth. I actually came to give you fair warning. I believe the guy I saw prizing himself out of the rental car out front is the accountant from your bonding company."

"Mr. Personality himself," Madelyn said, moving toward the door. "Last time, I signed autographs for his grandmother, his wife, his nephew, and his three nieces—everybody except his dog. Too bad there isn't a back door out of this place. I know you will all excuse me?"

The actress didn't wait for an answer. As Bull got up, too, Julie said, "Don't go. I may need moral support."

"Didn't intend to go," he answered as he reached to sweep his chicken box and other trash up in his big hands, "but you can have your desk back. You don't mind if Rey stays, do you? He might find it interesting."

Julie sent Bull a sharp glance, but he was busy dusting bread crumbs from her desk surface. "I suppose not," she said, then added, "Who called the bonding company, anyway?"

"Ofelia, maybe, on Allen's orders. It's a royal pain, but I guess they had to know. No point in putting off talking to their accountant."

"You haven't met this guy," Julie said in dry tones.

Moments later, the bonding-company representative was shown into her office. He hadn't changed. He still brought with him a smell of stale sweat and a look of snide superiority. Julie shook hands and performed the necessary introductions with as much cordiality as she could manage.

"Well, well," Davies said as he took her father's hand, "the great Bull himself. I was told you were here and wondered if I would have the pleasure. I'm a great admirer of yours, particularly your war pictures. Great battle scenes, just great! That one in *Death Among the Dunes* where you blew all those guys up? That's my favorite."

Julie exchanged a look of irony with Rey before moving around to lower herself into the chair behind her desk. She indicated that the bonding-company man should take the chair directly across from her. Bull pulled his own chair to an angle near the right end of the desk, while Rey had elected to stand, leaning with his back against the wall near the door on her left.

"Well, Miss Bullard, in trouble again, I see," the company man said, smiling tightly as he set his large, expandable briefcase on her desk and hitched up his chair by reaching for it between his large legs.

"Unfortunately, yes," Julie answered. "The stunt coordinator who was killed was a friend as well as a fellow worker."

"My condolences, of course. But we can't let that blind us to the facts. I understand this is not a matter of an accidental death. Is that correct?"

"You are well informed."

His lips moved in a brief expression of self-congratulation. "I try to be. You must be aware, Miss Bullard, that if that's the case, the publicity is going to be horrendous, simply horrendous."

"You're probably right."

"The curiosity seekers will swarm, the newspeople will descend like locusts—in fact, I'm surprised they aren't here already."

"They've been, and gone," Bull interjected.

"There, you see? It seems likely that work here will be disrupted, if not brought to a standstill, for some time to come. That being the case, I've been authorized to suspend all production."

"Suspend production!" Julie repeated in disbelief.

Rey stood up straight. "You mean, close down the location, send everybody home?"

"Exactly," the bonding-company man said with satisfaction. "To have everything and everybody sit here waiting until this mess has been cleared up is a useless drain on the budget."

"Wouldn't it be more expensive to close down, then bring all the equipment and technicians back again later?"

The bonding-company man barely glanced at Rey as he answered him. "There's no question of that. The footage shot already will have to suffice."

"But that's impossible!" Julie said. "There are still one or two important scenes that must be done here to preserve continuity."

The man across from her shook his head. "I'm sure the studio artists can mock up something so the average moviegoer will never know the difference."

"I can't agree. Anyway, what would be the point when it would be so easy to do them here if we only wait a few days."

"The point is saving money. Toward that end, I also have the authority to take the production out of your hands, Miss Bullard, and find someone who can do the job cheaper."

Julie felt the blood drain from her face, then return in a rush. "Now? When it's so nearly complete?"

"Now is when things have gotten so out of hand on this location that people are getting killed."

"I can't help that!"

"Maybe somebody else can."

There was a silence as Julie tried to decide if the decision was final, tried also to collect her thoughts, to marshal her arguments against it.

Bull, who had been listening in frowning silence, sat forward and cleared his throat. He said, "I can. I can get the job done for you."

Davies's face suffused with violent red color. "You? You mean you would be willing to take over?"

"I'm your man," Bull said expansively.

Julie felt as if she had been kicked in the stomach. She leaned back in her chair slowly, carefully, so as not to increase the pain. She was aware of a quick, abortive move Rey made toward her before he stopped himself, but she could not look away from her father's blandly smiling face.

Bull was taking her place. She couldn't believe it.

And yet, wasn't it better to have Bull finish her story instead of some nobody hired by the accountants, a yes-man who would chop it to pieces and do the final scene in a swamp made with a water hose and a forest of silk ficus trees?

The company man said, "Well, now, I'd have to check with the front office, but this puts a new light on the subject."

"I'd want to finish up the filming here," Bull said. "I think I can promise that any delay will be minimal, and quality will remain high. Since I only arrived at the location a short time ago, I'm not as directly involved as, say, my daughter; I don't believe there will be any objection to me going back to work with a skeleton crew while the investigation is under way. That should help control expenses for you."

"A very cooperative attitude, I must say, but the cost of your salary could cause problems."

"I'm not a greedy man. I expect we can come to an agreement if your front office okays the deal."

The company man smiled. "I'm sure you would like to bring in your own assistant and so on, plus a new stunt coordinator. But I don't think the budget will allow for a staff any bigger than the one already in place."

"No problem. I expect my daughter will be my assistant. As for a new stunt coordinator, Tabary here has already agreed to take on the job."

"Let me make a note of all this," the company man said, unzipping his briefcase and taking out a pad and pen. "We get everything on paper, we may be able to settle this today."

Julie opened her lips, then closed them again. What she had to say to Bull about his suggestion—and his gall in speaking to Rey about directing stunts without consulting her—would be better said in private. She would give Davies nothing more to gloat over. It was a pleasure to see, however, that the man was uncomfortable with the idea that she would still be involved with the movie.

She glanced at Rey. He was watching her with an odd combination of what appeared to be sympathy and apprehension in his eyes. *Compassionate affection* was the term Donna had used. It was, possibly, a good one. She looked away, picking up a pencil from her desk, turning it over and over in her hands. Abruptly, she flung it down and surged to her feet.

"You'll have to excuse me," she said. "I have an appointment."

Bull looked up from where he was dictating clauses to the company man. "Julie, don't go. I have to talk to you."

"Later," she said without looking at him.

Skirting her desk, she walked out of the room. She didn't stop in the reception area, but continued outside and down the steps, moving blindly, with no real idea of where she was going. She saw the open area between the end of the office trailer and the motor home beyond and moved toward it. The swamp was on the other side. The swamp with its tall trees and dim shadows, its dark green, shielding palmetto palms. She moved toward it and did not stop until she was out of sight of the trailers and motor homes, beyond the trucks and cars and boats, until there was nothing around her except the deep natural quiet.

She had lost *Swamp Kingdom.* It wasn't hers anymore. The one person she would never have expected to hurt her had taken it from her. If Bull hadn't spoken, she might have hammered out a compromise, made concessions that would have allowed her to finish her story the way she envisioned it. Now the chance was gone.

Her movie was gone and Stan was dead and Rey—what of Rey?

She leaned her back against the rough and enduring trunk of a giant cypress and tilted her head, staring up at the sky. The pure, serene blue was clear until slowly it was obscured by a shimmering haze of warm tears. The pain inside her grew, shuddering over her, rising in her throat, contorting her face so that she lifted her hands to cover it.

She had lost everything. Her father had betrayed her. Her chance to become a major director was gone; no studio would ever give her another chance at a feature film. Her life with Allen was shown for the empty, sterile pretense at love that it was. And Rey had never had anything to give her except a careful passion. Yes, and compassion; she must not forget that. Sympathy, concern, pity, but never love. Never love.

"Julie?"

She swung around, startled, backing away from Rey where he stood with one arm braced on the cypress beside where she had been standing. He had moved so quietly that she had no idea he was there so near, until he spoke.

"Go away," she said, wiping at the tears gathered in the hollows under her eyes with both hands. "Go away and leave me alone!"

"Let me explain. What went on in there isn't what you think." He pushed away from the tree, moving toward her with slow, smooth strides.

She took a step backward every time he took one forward. "You don't have to tell me anything. Bull needed a job and he thought he might as well have mine since they were going to take it anyway. That's fine. I'm glad for him. You needed to stay on the location to do your undercover work, so you talked him into vouching for you as stunt coordinator. He was probably supposed to make the suggestion to me before the bonding-company man came along, but what's the difference? It worked out anyway, so everything's just fine."

He stopped, his stillness absolute. "What are you talking about?"

"Oh, excuse me; I shouldn't have mentioned your work, so very hush-hush. Don't worry, I haven't told anybody, any more than I told them about what you were doing last night. But you might drop a hint to Donna not to tell anybody else that Paul was a narc. It might give them ideas if they also learn you worked undercover for the DEA. It took me a while, but I finally figured most of it out. I'm not sure whether you're in this on your own or officially, but I think it started with Paul. He was on a case; that's why he took the stunt job. You weren't interested in working for me until he was killed, then it became some kind of personal crusade to finish what he was doing. Only you went a step further, didn't you? You decided that as the person calling the shots around here, I was the one most likely to be behind the drug deal. You decided I would bear a close watch. Only you went too far, Rey, you really went too far."

"I'll admit that I thought you might be mixed up in it at first, but that's all I'll admit. What was between us, Julie, had nothing to do with the rest of it."

He sounded so sincere, but he was good at that, as she had reason to know.

"Oh, but it was so convenient, wasn't it? Such a marvelous excuse for being around at all hours, doing all sorts of things. For instance, being in my office where you could go through my files for possible leads. I caught you that time, but you lied your way out of that one. You wanted the name of the boat company, poor Donna might sue. But Donna never heard of a suit. If you're going to use her as an accomplice, you really should keep her better informed."

"You can leave Donna out of this."

"Willingly. Next time, you can take her to the Bahamas or sweep her off her feet in L.A. But you should make sure they are pleasure trips, not some trumped-up flight designed to check her knowledge of drug distribution or catch her out in negotiations for it—or pump her for information about the people around her. You used me, but you won't do it again."

His voice was low and soft as he said, "The trip to L.A. had nothing whatever to do with this business; you must know that. I don't see how you can think otherwise."

"You don't mention Nassau. That was wise. Oh, but L.A., yes. I think that by then you had made up your mind I was all right, but not exactly safe. You felt guilty because what you were doing had put me in some slight jeopardy, so you came to guard me. At very close quarters. I would be touched if I didn't think that you had been amply repaid."

"Now, there," he said with a deliberate and steady gaze, "I have to agree with you."

"That's something, anyway," she said with sarcasm.

He said, "It was the snake. I found it."

She stared at him. "The snake? How could you?"

"You have no idea how close the watch is I've kept on you. You killed it in the motor home and disposed of it out here along with a perfectly good towel. It's been puzzling me ever since."

She lifted a shoulder. "I thought it was either an accident or some kind of sick practical joke. If it was the first, there was no point in alarming everybody, and if the second, I intended to spoil the fun of whoever put it there."

"And if it was meant to hurt you?"

"I preferred not to think about that."

"What were you going to do, think about it tomorrow? This isn't a movie, Julie!"

"And I'm no Scarlett O'Hara! I just had a job to do and no time to waste on stupid tricks."

"No, you're no Scarlett. She would have screamed for Rhett and had ladylike hysterics."

"Oh, yes, but if there was no Rhett around, she'd have killed the damned thing herself and thrown it in the bushes."

"So you don't need protecting."

"No, and I don't need anybody feeling sorry for me; I'm perfectly capable of doing that for myself, too! I especially don't need the pity of a man so crippled by grief over the death of his wife that he can only care for women who are crippled in some way, too. Well, there's nothing wrong with me. I'm fine. So Donna can stop worrying and be happy. Everybody can be happy. There's no problem. Now, just go away!"

"I'll be glad to do that," he said tightly, "but first I have to ask what you intend to do about what you've figured out?"

"Why should I do anything? I have other things to worry about, such as a movie. You and Bull may think you've taken control, but I have news for you: I won't let you. *This is my movie!*" She thumped herself on the chest, hardly pausing to take a breath. "And I'll tell you something else. It makes me mad as hell to have somebody using *my* movie as a vehicle to bring drugs into this country and killing people on *my* set, at *my* location. If I find out who's doing it—and I well may—there will be hell to pay! So go away and leave me alone before I change my mind again and decide that the most likely drug trafficker of all might well be a former DEA agent working independently, one with a private plane who knows the swamp. At this moment, I can't think of anybody else I would rather have it prove to be!"

His face slowly hardened as he heard her out. He said then, "All right, I'll go. But I'd think twice about getting too mixed up in this drug business. Next time, it may not be the snake that winds up dead."

She swung from him with her arms crossed over her chest. She heard the sound of his retreating footsteps for three, perhaps four treads, then nothing. He was gone.

She had told him exactly what she thought. She should have felt better. Instead, she was chilled and depressed and tired beyond imagining. The thought of going back and facing everyone, of trying to finish *Swamp Kingdom* the way she wanted while having to contend with Bull and his ideas, filled her with revulsion. She couldn't think why she had ever wanted to make movies, didn't feel that she would ever want to make another one. It took too much out of her, too much strength, heart, and soul. It was no wonder that directors like Bull and John Huston became hard-drinking, loveless men with a streak of sadism.

The sunlight filtered down into the dimness of the swamp. The quiet drew in. She could hear the distant hum and throb of generators and car engines and the carrying shout of a voice, but the swamp sounds around her were more immediate: the call of a blue jay in alarm, the whine of a mosquito, the delicate rustle of a lizard flicking among the deep mulch of leaves around her feet with his tail trailing over the toe of her shoe. There was a nebulous peace in the stillness, but none inside her. Drawing a deep breath and letting it out in a silent sigh, Julie squared her shoulders and turned back toward the location.

It was then she heard the rattle of the palmetto. Someone was moving through it, coming not from the location but from the opposite direction, as if they had been deep in the swamps—or else had circled around to come from there. It was plain, however, that if they had ever heard Rey's lecture on how to travel through palmetto with stealth, they had forgotten it.

The blue jay's cry rose to shrieks, harsh and carrying. The dry clatter of the palmetto was like a drummer's brush moving in slow double time on a snare drum. Julie's heart jarred against her ribs, then began to pound. She loosened her arms, turning her head to listen. At the same time, she took a quick step toward the location, and then another. The clattering came closer. She broke into a run.

The shot exploded in the compressed quiet of the swamp. It sent the blue jay flapping into flight and made rolling thunder of its echo as the bullet whined among the tall cypresses.

Julie felt the sting at her temple, saw her vision cloud with red, then she was falling into darkness. She settled gently, nestling her cheek into a pillow of leaves.

Chapter 21

"Julie?"

It was Allen's voice. He spoke in a hushed tone, close to her ear. She opened her eyes by careful degrees.

There was a dull pain in her head. It hovered, barely suppressed. That suppression was, she knew instinctively, a temporary state. It could return at any moment, become a piercing pressure slicing inward toward her brain.

The room was dim. The first thing she saw with any clarity was the enormous bouquet of yellow roses, at least six dozen of them arranged in a vase with fern and myosotis. There were also bouquets of freesias and lilies, and pots of greenery. The granite ledge of the large window was so full that it looked like a bower. The walls of the room were papered in a subdued pattern of tiny blue stripes on a cream background. However, it still looked like a hospital room, for high on the wall was a television set on a heavy bracket, and the bed in which she lay had protective rails and white sheets.

Allen stood beside the bed with one of her hands clasped in both of his. He appeared tired, though that might have been the effect of the gray turtleneck he wore. Seated in a chair behind him was an older woman in a white uniform with a starched white cap on her graying hair and a white sweater around her shoulders. She smiled as she saw Julie looking at her. Getting to her feet, she moved around the bed to the opposite side from Allen. She picked up Julie's wrist, holding it while she looked at the large watch on her own.

"What is it?" Julie whispered with alarm feathering the words. "What happened?"

"You have a hairline skull fracture with mild concussion," Allen answered in soothing tones. "Don't worry; you're going to be all right."

"But—how?"

"Don't you remember?"

Julie made minute movement of her head from side to side, then paled as pain shifted inside her skull.

"Now, now," the nurse said, "you'd best keep still just a little longer, my dear. But don't upset yourself; people often don't remember things just before and after something like this."

"Something like—what?"

"You were shot," Allen said. "Apparently you were running, so you didn't make a terribly good target. The bullet plowed a shallow furrow across your scalp, clipping enough blood vessels to make it look as if half your frontal lobe—well, never mind. Anyway, what you have is a shaved spot on your temple, six or eight stitches, and bandaging like Boris Karloff in *The Mummy.*"

"Not really?" she said, freeing her hand to lift it toward her head.

He caught her fingers again. "No, no, I'm only trying to be funny; there isn't much to it. But actually, you missed the really comical part. You should have seen Bull come unglued when Tabary came running out of the woods covered in your gore and with you dripping blood from your hair—Tabary heard the shot, it seems, and knew just where to look for you. I had only that moment gotten back to the location from lunch when the farce began. I thought Tabary and Bull were going to have a fistfight over who was going to take you to the hospital, then both of them started yelling for the police at the same time, trying to send one squad to look for whoever fired the shot and demand that the rest jump in their cars and act as escort to get you here to the hospital as fast as possible. Between them, they had the poor sheriff and his men so confused it was like the Keystone Cops. It would had made a great movie scene; it's a shame you couldn't enjoy it."

"I'm glad you did," she said with a hint of dryness.

"I didn't mean to sound callous, but watching was about all I could do. Neither Tabary nor Bull would let me near you, much less have a hand in seeing after you. I wasn't too pleased about that at the time;

I would have liked to be the one to make the heroic rescue."

She smiled a little. "At least you're here now."

"On sufferance. Bull and Tabary both stood vigil through the night and part of the morning. I think the doctor finally sent Bull home because he was driving the nurses insane. Tabary took off as soon as he heard that your fracture was minor and you were coming and going in consciousness but expected to wake up at any moment."

She glanced around at the room and the flowers, at the nurse who had put her wrist back under the sheet with a pat and was now shaking down a thermometer. "If my fracture is so minor, why all this?"

He grinned. "I didn't know it wasn't serious, and I had to do something. Anyway, it can't hurt for as long as you're in here."

"How long will that be?" she asked.

"Don't be so anxious; everything can go along without you for a few days, especially now."

"I have a movie to finish, Allen."

"Bull is taking over, surely you recall that? All in all, this little episode will have its uses. It makes a perfectly plausible excuse for having him step in just now."

She stared at him. "I'm glad you've found some benefit, but I still want out of here."

"So all right," he said, throwing up his hands. "They are only keeping you forty-eight hours for observation. You can break out tomorrow, barring some problem they don't expect."

"Good," she said, closing her eyes. "Good."

"I don't know how good it is; the police want to talk to you. Again."

A frown creased the skin between her eyes. Her lips parted, but she only said, "About—what?"

"About who shot you, of course. What happened out there, and why."

She opened her eyes again, and there was a glaze of surprise on their surface. She said, "I don't—remember."

"What do you mean, you don't remember?"

"I mean there's nothing there," she answered in growing concern. "It's blank."

"Calm down, now. Tell me what you do remember."

"Nothing. Just—nothing."

"How can that be?" he said, an insistent note in his voice. "You know who you are, who I am?"

Her lashes fluttered, and her expression smoothed a little. Her voice quieter, she said, "Yes, I know that. And I—I remember talking to Bull and Rey with the man from the bonding company, then leaving the office. I have this mental picture of walking into the swamp a short way. Trees, leaves, birds. But after that—it's gone."

"You didn't see who fired the shot?"

She made a small negative movement with her head.

"Never mind," the nurse said comfortably. "It's nothing unusual with head injuries. Just a little temporary amnesia. Don't try to force it."

"Temporary," Julie said, her voice wavering.

"I expect so. We'll let the doctor know, and he'll talk to you about it. But I expect everything will come back to you in a bit without anybody's help, maybe this afternoon, maybe tomorrow or the next day."

"You think it will?" Julie asked.

The nurse patted her hand. "With the good Lord's help. And if it doesn't well, it's such a little piece of time missing when all's said and done. What can it matter?"

That was right, what could it matter?

But it does.

Julie wasn't sure whether she spoke the words aloud or if they were only in her mind. She drifted, thinking of bowers of yellow roses that turned slowly into floating, dipping water lilies. After a while, she felt Allen release her hand.

Less than thirty-two hours later, Julie was ensconced in the swing on the shady end of the back gallery of Aunt Tine's house. She had been released from the hospital just before lunch. After a light meal, she had rested in her room, regaining her strength. Her headache came and went, but required only aspirin to keep it bearable. Bull had always said she was hardheaded. Apparently he was right.

Toward the middle of the afternoon, Julie had enough of being an invalid and staying shut up alone. She had made her way out to the swing. Summer and Aunt Tine had brought extra pillows, some paperback books, a portable radio, and a tray holding tea cakes and a pitcher of lemonade.

Before Julie could get too comfortable, however, she had been paid a visit by the sheriff along with an officer from the state police. It was entirely cordial; Julie had seen so much of them of late that it was more like a social call than an interrogation. Having Aunt Tine join them, asking about the men's families, added to that impression.

Julie had grown to appreciate the professionalism and innate courtesy of the local and state police in dealing with the movie crew— many of whom had little respect for authority of any kind and less inclination to be helpful. More than that, she rather enjoyed being called ma'am. Nevertheless, she was not much help to them since she could still remember so little. At least they all enjoyed the lemonade and visiting.

When they had gone, Summer stuck her head out the back door, then shuffled out and threw herself down on the foot of the swing. Pushing out her lips, she said, "I'm bored."

"Where is Donna today?"

"One of her kids had to go to the dentist. She said I could go with them, but I don't like dentist offices."

Julie, looking at the girl's dejected face, couldn't help smiling. "I don't blame you. But everybody will be free to start shooting again soon, according to the sheriff. Then you'll have plenty to do."

"Tomorrow, Bull said. I asked him if I can have a bandage around my head like yours for my hospital scene. He said he'd see about it."

Julie said, "He did, did he?"

Summer, folding her legs up into a yoga position then leaning to prop her elbows on her knees and her chin in her hands, sent Julie a very adult look from the corners of her eyes. "Don't get excited. I think he meant he'd see what you wanted."

"What makes you think that?"

"I asked when would he see, and he said when you were up to it."

Something between hope and doubt shifted inside Julie at the girl's words. She did her best to subdue it, however.

To Summer, she said, "You're supposed to be burned in the scene coming up, not have a concussion."

"Yes, but there was an explosion, so I don't see why I can't have one like you, too. 'Course, if you wrapped my head all up, it would be like all my hair got burned off. That would be neat."

"You have a point there."

"And maybe I could have a broke leg? And a broke arm?"

"What, and lots of ropes and pulleys for traction? You don't think that the scene would play better with you just lying pale and small and pitiful under the sheet?"

"But with a head bandage?"

"That, yes," Julie said gravely.

The girl frowned with a terrible contortion of her eyebrows before moving them up and down as if to be sure they were still in working order. "I guess. So long as I don't have to have one of those green tubes up my nose. That's gross."

"No green tube," Julie agreed.

Summer unwound herself from her wet-spaghetti position and went to pour herself a glass of lemonade. Bringing it back, she sat back down with her feet splayed out in front of her. She drank half her lemonade and licked away the sticky mustache before she spoke again. "You know what? I wish Rey was my dad."

"Your mother might have something to say about that," Julie pointed out.

"Yeah. She checked herself out of detox."

"Did she?"

"Two days ago; said the food was terrible. She's been staying at the motel, but didn't bother to call and tell me until this morning. Now she wants me to run right over."

"That's good."

"Why? I don't want to go. It'll just happen again. She'll pop too many pills and drink too much booze and blame me for not being as famous as she was or making as much money. And someday she'll fall down dead instead of just going crazy."

There was too much knowledge, too much indifference as a mask for pain, to be in the voice of a girl so young. Julie reached out to touch her shoulder. "Maybe not this time."

"Nothing to keep her from it," Summer said, knocking the toes of her shoes together, watching the movement as if it had nothing to do with her.

"What about your real father? Could you stay with him?"

"Forget it. He has a second wife who needs a flea collar and three kids who all go to the bathroom standing up."

"Right," Julie said.

Summer turned red and scowled. "Okay, okay, I shouldn't say that, but it's true. He remarried and has three totally precious sons. He doesn't want me, just like he didn't want my mother after he found out she wasn't going to be this big star. They got divorced a long time ago."

"I'm sorry. I know how you feel; I used to think my dad didn't want me, either."

"Bull?"

"Turned out he just thought I'd be better off with my mother. At least, that was mostly it."

"I don't think that's it for me," Summer said in morose tones. "But if Rey was my dad, it would be different. He's great, like Jean-Pierre— he's a lot more like Jean-Pierre than Vance can ever pretend to be. And Rey really likes me, the way Jean-Pierre likes his daughter. We could do all kinds of things together. And I wouldn't be any trouble to him. I could stay here with Aunt Tine forever. The sleeping loft upstairs could be my apartment all to myself. I could make gingerbread boys and tea cakes and go to weddings and eat jambalaya and go fishing and—"

"And never make another movie?"

The girl closed her mouth, twitching one corner in a grimace of irritation and confusion. She muttered, "I don't know."

"It would be nice for you to be part of a family," Julie said.

"Yeah," Summer said under her breath.

The screen door into the dining room creaked as Aunt Tine opened it. "Summer, you bring me the lemonade glasses, *chère,* before the flies carry Julie away with them. And then I need you to chop me some onion for my *roux*. I'm making us a gumbo."

The girl scrambled up, running to do Aunt Tine's bidding. Aunt Tine held the door for Summer as she carried the glasses inside, balanced carefully on the tray with the empty pitcher. The older woman paused long enough to smile at Julie with a faint shake of her head, before she followed the girl back into the house.

Julie could hear their voices, a low murmur coming from the kitchen. Aunt Tine was a kind woman and a wise one; the tasks she had set Summer were no doubt helpful, but they also served to distract the girl from her problems. It was about the most that could be done for her so long as her mother was reasonably competent. It was doubtful that Annette would willingly give up her daughter, doubtful that she should even be asked to do it. The episode on the set had not been pretty, but things might not be as bad as Summer implied. Children sometimes said things in anger they didn't mean, and Annette had always given every indication of loving her child.

It was possible, too, that Summer was identifying with the character she was playing, the child of the warm and strong Cajun father, Jean-Pierre, a child learning the way of the swamps and the intense sense of family and community that ties of blood can bring. It wouldn't be unusual. Older and more levelheaded actors than Summer often found the line between make-believe and reality a bit blurred.

Thinking of it, of Summer and Rey, and of Jean-Pierre and Alicia, Julie realized in a kind of slow-moving surprise that she had been thinking about her movie all wrong. The story, as she had seen it, was about a young girl coming of age, learning to stand on her own feet, think for herself. Nearly killed by her mother and father's different kinds of loving, different ways of life, she was, in the end, supposed to force the two of them to reevaluate their lives.

That was all right in its way. But the story she had really been telling, Julie saw, was not about coming of age. It was about the relationships between fathers and daughters. It was about love that teaches self-reliance instead of dependency. It was about love that encourages individual growth instead of insisting on a reproduction in its own image.

The ending she had envisioned was all wrong, then. Alicia in her hospital bed would not be able to run away; Julie had found that out for herself the hard way. That meant that a decision would have to be made, and it wasn't Alicia's to make.

The decision must be made by Jean-Pierre. His was the greatest love, so the sacrifice must be his. There was no alternative.

That meant that the scene in the hospital was crucial. It must not be maudlin or sentimental, did not even have to be long. It should, instead, be gallant and loving beneath the roughness, with maybe even a touch of humor. It should, in fact, tear the viewers' hearts out.

She had to tell Bull. The ideas were coming fast; she needed a pad and pencil to get them down on paper before she forgot, and then she needed to get to her laptop computer and start writing and rewriting. There was a lot of both to be done if they were to start filming again with the hospital scene tomorrow.

Then she remembered.

She was not in charge; Bull was. And he might not see this scene the way she did.

Oh, but he would, he had to; he was her dad.

And sitting there, watching the shadows of the trees weaving patterns on the summer-tired grass, Julie saw something else.

This movie, her movie, was not about just any daughter and her father. It was about her and Bull.

There was nothing of her life in it, of course, but there was a great deal about her dreams as a child, her hopes and her fears even now. When she was small, especially when she was mad at her mother, she had entertained and consoled herself with a fantasy about a father who loved her so much that he would come and rescue her, steal her away, braving all dangers in order to have her with him. In this fantasy, it was always her mother who stood in the way, who kept him from coming. But Bull had betrayed her dream, or so she thought, showing plainly that he didn't love his daughter, or at least didn't love her enough. He had never come at all.

Somehow, that betrayal was tied in her mind to his betrayal of her and her mother with other women. She had never forgiven him for either of those things, not really, not even after she had gone to live with him. Somewhere deep inside she had always been angry with him. More than that, she had never trusted him. She had been afraid of another betrayal.

The more she thought about it, the more it seemed that her fears were a part of the reason she was so upset about the possibility of him working with her on *Swamp Kingdom.* She hadn't believed him when he said he wanted only to work with her, not supplant her. And she had been right. He had stepped in and taken over at the first opportunity. It was another betrayal, one which proved yet again how little he cared about her, how little he loved her.

Or was it?

She hadn't given him a chance to explain.

"Ah, *chère,* why you sitting here with a face as long as the bayou? You have the headache?"

It was Aunt Tine, coming out to check on her again, dropping into a nearby rocking chair for a moment of rest. Julie smiled at her, grateful for her concern. She answered the older woman's question with a shake of her head, then told her what she had been thinking, about Bull and the movie and the way he had taken it away from her, and whether he would give it back.

When she had finished, Aunt Tine sat rocking a few moments in the chair she had pulled up beside the swing. Her fine old face with its crepe-textured skin wore a look of shrewd concentration. "So you think your papa took your job for himself? It could be, these things happen. The papa alligator will smile as he eats his own newborn young, if he's hungry and they are not quick to run from the nest to the water. But men are, for the most part, human enough and more caring. It seems to me you must at least ask."

Julie nodded. "I had just about come to that conclusion, too. I guess, really, I have no one to blame except myself for getting myself shot after running off like that."

"No, *chère!* How could you guess someone would want to kill you? Don't be absurd."

"No, but there was Stan's death," Julie said ruefully.

"This is too bad," the older woman replied, her tone querulous. "All these deaths and murders and people in the swamp who don't belong. All this running of drugs. The worst of it is the young people they entice with their tainted money that makes big dreams; they die so easily, these young ones."

Julie said, "You think the problems on the location are connected with drug trafficking?"

"It isn't hard to guess, *chère;* what else is there in the swamp worth killing over? A few alligator hides taken out of season? No, no."

"And I thought it was a secret, kept quiet about it because I was so afraid that the news would affect my movie. I've made a terrible mess of things."

"The police always knew there was the possibility; they fight this thing every day with their drug task forces. Whatever you might have told them, it's doubtful it would have made a difference."

"Maybe. But it really seems that everything I touch turns out wrong."

"You only feel that way because you are not well. It will be different tomorrow."

"I don't think so," Julie said with a shake of her head.

"Well, then, that is something only you can change," the old woman said with simplicity. "Like making a gumbo, you get from this pot of living what you put into it. You can season it with love or hate, hope or fear, it's your choice. If something floats to the top you don't like, dip it out and throw it away; it's folly to leave it in and complain of the taste. Most of all, take pleasure in the eating. That is the purpose."

"I think," Julie said, "that I've scorched this particular pot. Do you suppose I could start over?"

"Always," Aunt Tine said. "It's what good cooks do until they get it right. Which reminds me that I should go and look at mine. Summer is watching it, but she won't know when it's done."

Julie sat quite still for a long time after Aunt Tine had gone inside. She watched the peacock spreading his tail in the sunlight slanting across the backyard, breathed the smells of richly browned flour and onion with celery and garlic, bell pepper and smoked meat and chicken stock that wafted from the house, and she thought about what Rey's aunt had said. She also thought of what Aunt Tine had left unspoken, her subtle intimation that people's lives were more important than a movie.

Bull, Rey, Allan, Ofelia—none of them seemed a killer. Why was it so difficult to imagine the people she knew as being guilty? She didn't consider herself naive, and yet it was almost impossible to picture any of them rigging an accident, wielding a knife, firing a gun. Regardless, someone had killed two people and tried to kill two others.

They had tried to kill Summer. Perhaps that was the key. Everything else could be looked at with some degree of reason, but the threat to Summer was senseless. What could anyone possibly hope to gain by harming a young girl?

The chance was that Summer knew something, had seen or heard something she didn't understand herself but that the killer was afraid she might mention to someone else. Summer was just the kind of precocious, inquisitive child who could be expected to notice whatever was going on, especially if it was something she had no business seeing.

Summer. If she really did know something, then she could still be in danger. Julie thought about that in grim concentration as she stared out into the gathering dusk. She would have to talk to the girl.

There were several others she needed to ask a few things, too. Somewhere in all the morass of her thinking there was something that bothered her, something someone had said that she needed to hear again, possibly something she had said herself to someone, something she had forgotten. It nagged at her, that small detail. She would not be able to rest until she had it.

She still could not remember the few minutes just before she was shot. Perhaps it had been something said then. Rey had been there, that much she did know. She would have to ask him what they talked about. Maybe he could help her bring it to mind.

One way or another, she was going to find out who it was that had dared use her and her movie for their own ends. One way or another, she was going to see to it that they didn't get away with it. She wasn't sure exactly how she was going to go about it but she thought she just might start by stirring this particular pot of gumbo that had to do with the making of *Swamp Kingdom.*

She would stir it hard—and see what came to the top.

Chapter 22

Bull came for dinner, driving up with Rey about the time that Julie was beginning to think about going into the house. He looked harried, and there were dark hollows under his eyes. His khaki clothes were rumpled, as if he were living out of a suitcase and had no time to bother with motel laundry and pressing services.

Rey, in jeans and a navy shirt worn with navy deck shoes, was unwrinkled and even sophisticated in a casual fashion. He appeared fit, vibrantly alert in a manner that, to Julie, was tiring even to contemplate.

In answer to Rey's question of how she was doing, she answered, "Fine." When she asked him how his shoulder was healing, she received the same answer in return. Both of them, she thought, were lying. He knew it, too, from the way his eyes narrowed as he watched her.

Julie turned to Bull. "I've been thinking about the final scenes for the movie and I have some ideas I'd like to talk to you about."

"Do you now?" he answered, with color rising into his face. "Happens I have a few myself. But do you think they can wait until after dinner? I'm hungry enough to gnaw on an elephant's hind leg, if he'll stand still long enough. Think I'll go wash my hands and give Aunt Tine a hand dishing up."

Julie frowned after her father as he went into the house. She recognized his usual evasive technique against something he didn't care to face. At the same time, she thought he had been pleased that she had wanted to discuss the movie. She would get to the bottom of it, but later. Now she turned to face Rey.

"I'm told you found me in the swamp and brought me out, got me to the hospital. I really—"

"If you're going to thank me, don't," he said, his voice tense as he moved to sit on the gallery railing, half-turned away from her with one foot on the floor. "I should never have left you alone out there in the first place. If I hadn't, it wouldn't have happened."

"You *were* there! I knew it, but I can't remember exactly what we were talking about. I suppose it was something to do with Bull and the movie; I do remember that part with him and Davies before I went running out into the woods like some wild woman."

He turned to look at her, a speculative look on his features. "You really can't remember?"

"I get little flashes, feelings, but that's about all."

"Like what?" he said, brightness growing in his eyes.

She was wary of the undertone of amusement in his voice. "I don't know, just—something."

"So if I told you that you asked me to make mad, passionate love to you under the open sky, you wouldn't know whether it happened or not, if I answered yes or no?"

"This isn't funny!" she told him in indignation that did not prevent the small flutter of her pulse at his words.

"I think it is. I can't believe you could forget something so important."

She turned her head slightly without taking her eyes from him. "Like what?"

"I'm not sure I should tell you; it might be embarrassing."

"Not as embarrassing as having you sitting there laughing at me about something I can't even begin to imagine!"

"I know, but it's just so irresistible."

She was skeptical, yet it seemed like weeks since she had seen that look of fun in his face. She said, "So are you going to tell me, or are you just going to sit there laughing to yourself?"

"It isn't always possible to believe what women say in the height of passion, but you swore that you adored me to distraction and wanted to stay—"

He stopped, and the laughter died out of his eyes. He looked down at his hands clasped together as he rested his wrists across his thigh.

"If I said that," Julie said slowly, "then I think it was wise of you to run away and leave me."

He got up with an abrupt movement, stepping to the nearest square column, leaning against it with his back to her. "You didn't. It was a bad joke; I'm sorry. Actually, what you said was that you thought I murdered Paul for the sake of his wife, then killed Stan because he was the one person who might have guessed what I had done."

"I—didn't. I couldn't have." She had to push the words from her tight throat.

"Maybe not. Maybe you just implied it. The effect was the same."

"What—effect?"

"I let my asinine pride get in the way of my better judgment, and you nearly died."

"It sounds as if there was plenty of provocation. But it didn't happen. Let it go."

He turned to face her, resting on the column with his good shoulder, tucking his fingers into the pockets of his jeans. Glancing at her, unsmiling, he said, "I'd like to, but I can't, not until you remember everything that was said that day."

"Is it so important?" she said in low tones.

"I think so," he answered.

"What if I never remember?"

There were footsteps approaching the open dining-room door, probably Aunt Tine coming to tell them the food was ready. He spoke quickly, before they could be interrupted. "That might be the best thing that could happen."

After dinner, Rey helped his aunt with the dishes, teasing and laughing with Summer so the girl was also drawn into the cleanup crew. At the same time, Aunt Tine pushed Julie from the dining room toward the parlor. Seeing Bull hovering as if about to make an excuse to leave, Julie caught him by the arm, reminding him that they were supposed to talk.

The parlor was not a large room, nor was it often used; Aunt Tine much preferred entertaining her friends on the back gallery or in her kitchen. The room, as a result, had about as much character as a hermetically sealed museum setting. There was an old pump organ with worn velvet pedals and silver candlesticks on its wooden candlestick arms sitting upright against one wall. A huge rococo mirror hung above the fireplace, tilted outward at the top in what looked like a dangerous angle but was the only way the room could be reflected in it. On one wall was a sepia print of some ancient Roman scene, and on another a faded Madonna and Child with brittle, dried palm branches from the previous year's Easter service stuck behind the frame. The parlor set, consisting of four chairs and two footstools, all covered with champagne-colored brocatelle that might once have been white, sat before the fireplace. The one halfway modern piece was a console radio dating from the thirties and covered with photos from the same era side by side with pictures of Rey from school.

The room with its venerable furnishings was not unlike a movie set waiting for the actors. Julie, reaching out to touch a bell jar that covered a cluster of wax flowers in delicate colors, spoke her carefully rehearsed lines with more ease than she had expected.

"I wanted to talk to you about the ending of *Swamp Kingdom;* there are some changes I'd like to make."

At the same time, Bull, standing in the middle of the floor, said, "About the end of this movie—I don't think it jells."

They looked at each other and laughed, both a little self-consciously.

"You go first," he said.

"No, you. You're the director."

"Brownnosing? You? Come on!"

The vulgarity was predictable, the scoffing when she was trying so hard to be reasonable was not. "You know better than that!"

"Damn right," he said. "We are the directors, the two of us, and don't you forget it. So give with the ideas."

For an instant, Julie thought she might cry. She swallowed hard, then began to outline what she had in mind.

The ideas worked; they found that out on the hospital set the next day. Julie, with Bull and Rey's help, had stayed up all night rewriting. Ofelia, warned in advance, had been on the phone for hours getting clearance to use more of the hospital and the street outside for a few hours. Madelyn, Vance, and Summer had had to huddle for a quick rehearsal of the new lines while everything was being set up. Regardless, it was worth it.

Summer, wrapped in her bandages and lying in the hospital bed, managed to look both angelic but sound like a tough little nut no longer afraid of anything, one who was going to be able to give her mother trouble in the future. The scene, as Jean-Pierre explained that he had to leave because he was wanted by the police for kidnapping her, unfolded with emotion so real it could be felt in the air. There was aching love in the few lines exchanged as they said good-bye, in the understanding that shone in their eyes, understanding of the sacrifices each was making for the other by being brave and of the sustaining power of shared dangers, shared memories. The way the young girl watched him walk from the room, then climbed out of bed and strained at the window to see him drive off, held the crew still, spellbound. Then as they heard the magic words "Cut, and print it!" everyone exploded into applause and congratulations.

Julie went to give Summer a hug and add her own praise, putting her bandaged forehead against that of the young girl as she sat beside Summer on the bed. There was the flash of a camera, and Julie turned in time to see the female reporter who had become Vance's shadow turning away. The woman had the nerve to give her a wink and a little wave.

Julie stared after her with a frown, then giving Summer a last pat, she relinquished her to Donna and went in search of Vance.

"All right, folks," Ofelia was saying to the camera and sound crew as Julie left the room, "I hate to tell you, but you're in the wrong place. Now we set up in the hallway. Let's go!"

Julie rounded a corner on her way outside the building, then sidestepped hastily as a woman came running around it from the other direction. The woman gasped and shrank back, then gave a shaky laugh. "Oh, I didn't mean to run over you, Julie."

Julie reached out to steady Annette. "I think it was nearly the other way around. Are you all right?"

Annette nodded vigorously. "Is the scene over? They said Summer was working, and I wanted to be there."

"I'm afraid it's done. You can help unwrap her from the bandages—fake ones, of course."

"You did scare me for a minute. I've been so out of it, I almost forgot the story line."

Annette was pale, and her hair lay flat and lifeless against her head, showing the definition of her skull. Her face without makeup showed fine lines and blurring contours, and there were shadows of illness under her eyes. She looked, in fact, as if she should still be in the hospital, if not in the chemical-dependency unit.

"Summer is fine," Julie said, then went on, driven by an idea that had been forming in the back of her head since the evening before. "Tell me something, Annette, is the story Vance told true? Did you really do a strip act with a python?"

Annette moaned. "That story. I could have killed Vance, or myself for getting high and telling him about it."

"It wasn't that bad," Julie said.

"I nearly died, I was so humiliated. I never wanted people to know I had sunk so low. I just feel lucky the tabloids haven't got hold of it. Sure as they do, they'll have it printed up that Summer is part snake!"

Julie would have laughed at the idea, except she wasn't sure that Annette wasn't right. "It's true then?"

"Sort of. It was an act with a man I was seeing, not a striptease. I only did it once because I couldn't stand the way the thing felt around me, dry and slithery and so—huggy." She shuddered in revulsion that had every appearance of being real.

"I didn't mean to stir up bad memories," Julie said. "It just seemed curious."

"Yeah, sure, well, a person will do a lot of things to make a living when they've got a kid to feed and no career left. But you wouldn't know about that. The day may come when you'll find out, though. When it does, maybe you'll remember me and the python."

"I expect I will," Julie said quietly.

Annette gave her a stabbing glance, as if suspicious of the lack of heat in the reply. Then, pushing past Julie, she went on into the hospital.

Julie found Vance, finally, on his way to makeup for repairs. He would be doing the hallway scene they were setting up, along with Madelyn. It was a small scene but important. Jean-Pierre was supposed to tell his wife that he's giving up, that she's won—he won't try any longer to keep his daughter with him, won't ask her, his wife, to come back to him—while Madelyn as Dorothea begins to see how much she has lost.

"You were great in that scene with Summer, Vance," Julie said as she fell into step beside him.

"Thanks," he said, shifting his shoulders a little as if shrugging off her compliment as trivial. "The thing belonged to the kid, but I guess I held my own."

"I would say so, too," Julie agreed, though privately she was amazed at the emotion an actor like Vance could evoke without, apparently, feeling a twinge of it himself.

Vance, summoning the makeup man, sat down in a wood-and-canvas chair. Julie waited until the makeup man had flung a cover-up cape around Vance and begun to powder his face before she went on.

"You understand the next scene, don't you? You see the necessity of showing the unbridgeable differences between you and your wife, and also the futility of the viewer expecting either one of you to change to accommodate the other?"

"Got it," he said in bored tones as he closed his eyes while powder was combed out of his brows.

"That doesn't mean that you don't still love her, or even that she doesn't care about you."

Vance looked up at her, his blue eyes as cool as his voice. "Right, Julie, I did read the script, you know. As I told you, I've got it."

"Good," she said, and abandoned the need to influence the way the scene would be played. "There's one thing more. Tell your girlfriend to either put her camera away or get off the set."

Vance jerked the makeup cape off and flung it at the makeup man as he stood up. "I was trying to be nice, so I listened to your suggestions, Julie, but I'd like to remind you that you aren't running this show anymore. Get off my back."

Julie smiled at him and even reached out and touched his cheek.

"You're a fair actor, Vance, but not a particularly bright man, though I'll try to reach your level of understanding. It's like this: Do what I said, or guess what? I'll tell my daddy on you."

She could have been more diplomatic, but he had irritated her. More, it was no part of her plan to have him love her. She swung away before he could answer, walking a few steps before abruptly turning back.

"Oh, Vance, you've known Allen quite awhile, haven't you? Was it friendship that made you feel it was necessary to keep him informed, or just a bad case of—as Bull would put it—brownnosing?"

"What in hell gives you the idea you can talk to me like that?" he shouted as he stepped toward her with clenched fists. "I'll have you know I'm the star of this damned picture—the brat may be all right, but without me she'd be nothing! Brownnosing, my ass! I'm not that kind of snake-in-the-grass; I don't have to do that crap! Now, get the hell out of my face or next time it may be me taking a shot at you!"

"My, my," she said with a lifted brow and a slowly growing smile as she turned away once more. "Thanks, Vance."

She left him staring after her. As she walked the expression he had used kept pace in her mind with her footsteps. Snake-in-the-grass. Snake-in-the-grass. Suddenly she had it, the words someone had said that had been nagging at her. Because of them, she could guess at who was behind the destruction of her movie, who had initiated the drug traffic, Paul's death and Stan's, the attack on Summer and herself. The why of it made no sense, but the rest of it fit together in a twisted fashion. It fit so well that she knew she had to be right.

She had to be.

The question now was what she was going to do about it.

The filming continued. Watching Vance and Madelyn play out the scene in the hall, one that would come before the farewell scene in the hospital room with Summer in the movie's sequence, Julie was forced to wonder if there wasn't something to the method of directors who stung their actors to rage with insults. The set was silent as everyone watched, even Summer, still in her hospital gown over a flesh-colored body suit.

Vance was superb as he faced the truth about his own nature and that of the woman he had married. He spoke with suppressed pain and bitter sorrow, yet with outward weary kindness and a need to make the parting as easy as possible for the woman who had been his wife and was still the mother of his child. There was conviction in his voice as he said that sometimes people were unable to change, even when it was in their best interests, that old customs and ambitions alike were often too ingrained to be altered, the security of old habits and learned ways too comforting to be abandoned.

"What of love?" Madelyn whispered as the cameras rolled, her eyes in their heavy makeup huge and liquid.

"Love or passion?" Vance said, his face shadowed for an instant with longing so intense it was like anguish. "Tell me the difference and I'll give you the answer." He waited, and when Madelyn could find nothing to say, paused another beat, then gave her his famous crooked smile and a Gallic shrug of resignation. "Whatever it was between us, it wasn't enough—it was never enough."

"What will you do?" Madelyn asked.

"Leave," Vance said, "because between us we are tearing Alicia apart, and it can't go on. Leave while I can, if I can. And I won't be back, because Alicia knows now what love is. And so do I. And it is, finally, enough."

Vance walked away then, entering the hospital room of his daughter as if to say good-bye, while both Bull and Julie signaled for the camera to move in on Madelyn's ravaged face.

Then from the back of the hall, behind the crew where the spectators were standing, there came a gasping sob. Summer plunged forward with her hospital gown flapping around her and her bandage coming loose about her head. She grabbed hold of Julie, wrenching at her arm. There were tears running down her cheeks and desolation in her thin face as she cried, "I didn't know he was never coming back, not ever! Make him come back, I know you can. Make him come back!"

Julie caught the girl in her arms, holding the small body close as she felt the press of tears in her own throat. "Oh, Summer," she murmured helplessly, "I'm sorry, so sorry."

Then Donna was there, and also Annette. Vance came out of the hospital room he had entered to stand awkwardly to one side. The rest of the crew gathered around while muttered whispers and low comments ran around the room.

"Poor confused kid."

"High-strung, just like her mother."

"God, I didn't know she even liked old Vance."

"It's not Vance she's talking about, dummy."

Then the crowd dissolved, moving back, as Rey strode through. He went to one knee beside Summer, touching her arm. Summer turned her head slightly. As she saw him she released Julie to fling herself against Rey's chest with a wrenching sob.

"I want to stay with you," she cried into his neck. "Don't go away. Don't leave me."

"I won't go," he said softly. "I'll always be here."

"If you leave, I'll have to go back with my mother. I'll have to!"

"Only if it's right," he said, his dark gaze unseeing, shielded by his lashes, "and if it's what you want to do. This I promise."

"You—you mean it?" The catch in the girl's voice almost, but not quite, covered the sound of reprieve.

"I give you my word."

Summer sighed and clutched him tighter, sniffing as her fingertips turned waxen with the choking closeness of her hold. If Rey felt its constriction, he gave no sign, but soothed the child with a gentle hand upon her back.

Annette, her face mottled with red, pushed her way through to the two of them. She tugged at her daughter's arm. "Summer, baby, it's Mama, I'm here," she said. "Don't cry, it's just a story. That's all it is, a story."

"No!" Summer cried, jerking away from her without looking at her.

Annette drew back as if she had been struck. She turned on Rey. "See what you've done! I knew it was wrong, you paying her so much attention, taking her off with you in your boat. See what happens when you tamper with a little girl's feelings!"

Rey stared up at Annette with stark anger in his face. "If you paid more attention to her, if you loved her for herself instead of as your own reflection, she wouldn't need me."

"It's not you she wants, it's somebody else, somebody not real. You filled her head with nonsense, letting her think you were like the Cajun in the movie. You're not. You never were."

Summer was still. Her crying had hiccuped into silence. Her eyes were wide, staring.

"Don't worry, Annette," Rey said quietly. "Summer knows too well that *Swamp Kingdom* is just a story. And she knows better than most that stories end. You at least taught her that."

Annette stared at him long seconds. Then her face twisted. "She's my child!" she wailed. "I'm nothing without her, nothing. She's all I have. I need her! Oh, God, I need her!"

As the echoes of that desperate cry died in the hallway Summer stirred. She lifted her head by slow degrees, loosening her hold on Rey. The girl looked from him to her mother, then back again. Her lips flattened together for an instant, then her small features congealed with a resolve that seemed to melt away the childish lines, sinking to the bones, so that her expression grew adult in its anguished recognition of reality.

Rey, his firm hands holding those of the young girl, spoke with gentle emphasis. "Summer knows you need her. She knows, too, that you love her in your own way, as surely as Jean-Pierre loved Alicia. More than that, she understands, I think, that though I'm not Jean-Pierre, she will always have a place here in the heart of the swamp, and in mine."

Summer, her voice small, said, "I do understand—I think I do."

"And you will remember?"

"Always," she said on a fervent breath that caught in the back of her throat. "We—we had fun, didn't we?"

"That we did." Rey's reply was low.

"I won't forget how to dance the Cajun waltz."

"No, don't."

"And I'll come back someday, I really will. We'll go fishing again. And ride on the river, ride all the way to where the swamp ends and the lakes begin."

"I'll be waiting. Until then, I'll see you in the movies, up on the big screen."

"Yeah," Summer said, "that's where I'll be." Then she repeated, the words almost inaudible, "Yes, I will."

In the silence that followed, Bull cleared his throat with a loud rasp, then lifted his bass voice in command. "That's it for the day, people. Strike the set, pack it up, and let's go. Everybody out!"

As the equipment was wheeled away and the hall began to clear Julie looked up to see Vance's reporter friend standing, focusing her camera on Summer and Rey. She stepped quickly to block the shot the young woman was about to take of the girl and the man with Annette standing over them. Then, her face set in grim lines, Julie advanced on the young woman with the camera.

"Wait a minute," the girl said, backing away. "I have permission to be here. Vance said—"

"I don't care what Vance said, you don't have permission any longer," Julie told her.

"What's happening here is news, the accidents, the killings, that touching business with the kid. You can't keep the public from knowing about it."

"Can't I?" Julie said, and reached out to wrench the camera from the girl's hand. Whirling around as the reporter jumped at her, snatching and clawing for her property, Julie sprang the latch on the camera case and dumped the film out into her hand, stripping the exposed portion from its roller. Turning back, she thrust the empty camera back at the woman. "Take it and get out. Set foot on my set again, and I'll have you arrested for trespassing."

The girl went. Julie, looking back toward where Rey and Summer had been, saw the two of them walking away down the hall with Annette at her daughter's side. They were heading toward an empty waiting room. She could hear Rey's low voice, see the way Summer looked up at him, with trust and hope and, yes, love. The girl's footsteps dragged, but she was holding both her mother's hand as well as Rey's, and she was no longer crying.

Julie was. The tears were inside. She was drowning in them, and in the deep, welling tide of passionate tenderness that had brought them. She loved the man who was walking away, a man who could understand a child's need and did not spare himself in answering it. She loved him for all the things he was, for his strength and kindness and humor. She loved him for the things he did for others, and the way he made her feel. She loved him, even if it made no difference.

Julie leaned against the wall and closed her eyes. She was shaking, she discovered. A part of it was weakness; it was possible she was trying to do too much too soon. A part of it was the shock of self-knowledge. But the rest was caused by sheer fury, a consuming protective outrage.

Summer was so vulnerable, so in need of loving security, yet had such courage. Anyone who could strike at her would stop at nothing.

Recognizing that, she saw something else as well. It was the last small piece of the puzzle she was fitting together in her mind. It was the reason behind it all.

And seeing it, feeling it, she knew what she must do.

Chapter 23

If she was going to be a target anyway, she might as well act like one. At least, that was Julie's rationale. It might not be too wise, but she was tired of wondering, tired of waiting to see what would happen next without having any way to change the outcome. More compelling than that was the deep anger that underlay all her mental effort, the anger that anyone would think they could attack what was hers, use what was hers for their own ends, and get away with it. There was also pity, but she preferred not to dwell on it.

She placed her call to the motel in Gonzales shortly after she had returned to Aunt Tine's house. Afterward, she sat for a long time, trying to compose a note that would tell someone what she was doing without setting off such an alarm that her quarry was frightened away. She thought hard about who to address it to, but there really was no question. There was only one person she could be sure would do what needed to be done. She put the note in the envelope, sealed it, and wrote Aunt Tine's name quickly across the front.

The khaki skirt and blouse she was wearing would not do. She stripped them off and threw them on the bed, and kicked out of her taupe flats. Digging a pair of jeans and a blue-and-white-striped T-shirt out of the armoire, she skimmed into them, then pulled on socks and running shoes. At the last minute, she tied a white cotton-knit cardigan around her waist by the sleeves; there was a damp stillness to the air this evening that she had come to recognize as a warning of rain.

Summer had come back to the house with Donna, since Annette, in the discussion after the scene at the hospital, had volunteered to check herself back into the drug-dependency program. She wanted, she said, to get her life back in order for the sake of her daughter, and that seemed the best place to begin. Later, Donna had gone home to see about her own children. Julie could hear the television playing now in Aunt Tine's bedroom, and thought Summer must be watching it. Aunt Tine was, as usual, in the kitchen. Rey had not returned after the day's shooting, nor had he told anyone where he was going.

Julie did not want any premature activity as a consequence of her note. She passed through the dining room into the parlor, and through it in the bedroom. Summer was there, lying on the bed wearing pajamas and a faded print housecoat that looked suspiciously like Aunt Tine's, watching a game show. Her nose was still red and her eyes swollen from her bout of crying earlier, but she seemed composed enough.

Julie stood watching her for a few seconds, thinking of the way things had turned out, and how little could be done to change them. Finally, she moved into the room.

"Summer?"

The girl looked up and gave her a wan smile.

"Would you do something for me?" Julie asked.

"I guess so."

"Wait an hour or so, then give this to Aunt Tine. Can you do that?"

"Sure," the girl said, taking the envelope, looking at it with mild curiosity.

"Make sure she gets it. It's important."

"All right."

Julie hesitated, wondering if she should say more. It didn't seem possible without frightening the girl. She turned to leave the room, smiling over her shoulder. "Thanks, hon."

"Where are you going?" Summer called after her.

"Snake hunting," Julie said before she could stop herself, though an instant later, she said, "Cancel that, bad joke. I'm just going to work for a while."

She had reached the steps of the back gallery when she heard the thud of bare feet coming after her.

"Julie! Wait!"

Julie swung back at once. Keeping her voice low, she said, "What is it?"

"Are you going to the location?" The girl's eye were large in her small face.

"Something like that."

"But it's almost dark."

"I know; I won't be long."

"But you just got out of the hospital, I mean really, not playacting."

"I'm fine. Don't be a worrywart."

"Aren't you afraid?"

The look of concern on Summer's face was touching. Julie moved back up the steps and put her arm around the girl. She said frankly, "Yes, a little, but it will be all right. I'll be careful. Just don't forget to give the note to Aunt Tine."

The girl agreed, though there was still doubt in her eyes. She trailed back into the house with Aunt Tine's house robe dragging on the floor behind her. Julie watched her go. When the door had closed behind Summer, she strode quickly toward her car.

Julie waved at the guard as she passed through the gate into the location. As she parked near the motor home she turned off the key and pressed the switch to douse the headlights. She sat in the dark looking at the big, cumbersome vehicle in front of her. It appeared dark and empty, as did the other three that were parked once more in their staggered line after being driven from the hospital set today.

Everyone was gone. The boat club was closed up tight, lit only by the yellow bug-repellent light at the entrance. The office and wardrobe trailers were deserted. Out at the boat pier, the two cabin cruisers swayed at their mooring lines, while the skiff bumped gently against the piling where it was tied. Nothing else moved. The only other person on the place was the guard who had gone back to reading his paperback book as soon as Julie passed by.

Julie got out of the car, closing the door with a quiet thud. As she walked toward the motor home she shifted the keys she held until she had the one in her hand that unlocked it. Pushing the key in the keyhole, she turned the knob and pulled the door open, then reached for the screen also. She paused, looking inside, but there was only silent darkness. Stepping up on the iron step, she reached inside and flipped on a light.

Empty.

She sighed and stepped over the threshold, moving into the dining area to put her shoulder bag down on the table. She turned back then to pull the door shut and lock it from the inside. As usual, the heat from the day was trapped in the metal vehicle. She turned on the air-conditioning, then started to untie her sweater from around her waist.

As she bent her head her hair swung forward around her face. She pushed it back with her fingers. The motion tugged the fine strands at her temple with a stinging pain where it was stuck to the tape of the bandaging on her forehead. Leaving the sweater for the moment, she went into the small bathroom to find a rubber band to pull her hair back out of the way. Locating one, she formed a rough French plait and fastened it low on the nape of her neck. Smoothing in the few stray ends that were still loose, she moved back into the kitchen.

Wine, she thought, and a little cheese with crackers. She got these things from the refrigerator, setting them on the table with two glasses and a couple of napkins. Filling her glass from the chilled bottle, she sat back on the bench seat. She sipped her wine with slow patience, and she waited.

The wine in her glass was almost gone when car lights swept the parking lot and a door slammed. A moment later, a knock came on the door that made it rattle in its frame.

"Julie? You in there?"

Julie got to her feet and opened the door. "Come in. Have something to drink."

"Lord, I can't believe you're out here by yourself after what went down," Ofelia said as she stepped inside. "You must have a death wish or something."

"I thought it would be quiet," Julie said, returning to her seat.

Ofelia laughed without much humor. "You got that part right. So what's the big deal?"

"Sit down and stay awhile." Julie poured wine into the other glass.

"I thought we might figure out the shooting schedule for the next couple of days. There are a few changes that need to be made since Bull and I rearranged the ending."

"I can't stay long; I've got this big *bourée* game," Ofelia said, seating herself on the edge of the opposite bench seat. "Anyway, shouldn't you be talking about this with Bull? I mean, he's the head man now, and you're the first assistant. I don't have much to do with it except make sure whatever you guys say gets heard by whoever needs to hear it most."

Julie lifted a brow. "What's in a title? Bull still listens to my ideas. Actually, I wanted him to join us, but seems he's a little nervous of this place for some reason, said he heard noises in the walls or closets or air ducts, or something like that. Can you beat it? I don't know what he thought it could be except maybe rats."

"Men can be such babies," Ofelia said with a shrug. "But what was it you had in mind?"

"I thought you might have some input on the kidnapping scene with Summer, the explosion where she was nearly killed. We got that footage, remember; the cameras were rolling when Rey picked her up and hit the water with her. It's so stupendous, it would be a shame not to use it."

"I can see what you mean about that bit," Ofelia said, nodding, "but what's the rest?"

"I was thinking of reshooting the last part of the chase scene just before the explosion. We'd have Rey—taking Vance's place of course—jump from his skiff into the speedboat going full blast, struggle with the two goons who are escaping with Summer, and take them out, flipping them overboard like some back-country James Bond. At that point, we cut to the footage of Rey with Summer that's already in the can. Then with that out of the way—" Julie stopped. She lifted her chin, turning her head to one side. "Did you hear that?"

"What?" Ofelia asked, her glance flicking quickly around the trailer.

"I don't know, a sort of hissing sound."

"I didn't hear anything."

"No? I guess Bull has made me nervous. What was I saying? Oh, yes, about the scene with Summer. We can set up to film Vance coming up out of the water with Summer draped senseless in his arms. Add a little artistic makeup on them both for their injuries, and voilà!"

"I don't see why it wouldn't work," Ofelia said.

"The beauty of it is that the footage was made without running afoul of the child labor laws since it was an accident. I'm happy now that we have it, but no sane person would ever have put Summer in that boat that was going to be blown up."

Ofelia gave Julie a lightning glance. An instant later, she smiled, saying, "Now, that's the God's truth. As for the scene, I don't know what I can add. You seem to have it all worked out."

"I don't know about that. I wondered if you have any feelings about Vance's reaction after he has Summer back on dry ground, so to speak. We saw what she was like, nearly drowned. Should he be simply terrified that she's dead at first, then have a 'Thank God' sort of reaction when he sees she's not? Should we see him enraged? Vengeful? What?"

"I think," Ofelia said slowly, "that maybe the reaction Rey had might be best."

"What was that?" Julie shifted in her chair, stretching one leg out under the table.

"Concern, boundless concern, but with all the rest of it held in, more or less set aside until he finds out about Summer."

"That's good," Julie said, picking up her wineglass and leaning back as she stretched out her other leg, letting her foot slide toward where Ofelia was sitting. "I like it, I really like it a—"

She broke off, recoiling with a choked scream, dropping her wineglass as she came up off the bench.

Ofelia shot out of her seat. She threw herself across the kitchen, so she slammed into the sink. "Kill it," she shouted. "Kill it!"

Julie stopped, frozen in a half crouch. She looked at her friend and assistant director across the width of the motor home's small kitchen while the sound of shattering glass and splattering wine died away into silence, saw the fear and vindictive instinct to destroy mirrored on her round face.

Her voice soft, Julie said, "Kill what, Ofelia?"

The other woman wasn't stupid. Comprehension of what she had done wiped all expression from her face before Julie finished speaking. She blinked rapidly, then her lips quivered into an expression more grimace than smile. "God, Julie, you really had me going for a minute there. I thought a rat must have run up your leg at the very least."

"I don't think so, Ofelia," Julia said, straightening to her full height. "I think you expected a swamp rattler. I think you've been waiting for one to surface for days."

"No, really, I—"

"Oh, yes. Only the problem is, it's already been found. Days ago. By me."

Ofelia tried a laugh that came out strained and uneven. "My lord, Julie, you sound as if you think I put it in here."

"Did I say it was in here?" Julie asked softly.

"You must have, you implied—"

"No." The word came out with quiet finality. "Nobody else knew, nobody else had any reason to be afraid to come here, only the person who tried to kill me. Only the murderer on this location. Only you, Ofelia."

The other woman stared at Julie while the planes of her moon face grew flat and hard with the knowledge of how much she had revealed, and the pupils of her eyes narrowed to pinpoints of hatred. Her pale, stiff lips opened. "Bitch," she said in a rasping whisper, "lucky bitch."

"Lucky, yes, at least that," she agreed with simplicity.

"I wanted you dead, I really wanted you dead."

Julie sank back into her seat as her knees suddenly threatened to give way under her. "Why?" she asked, her brows drawing together in a frown while sincere puzzlement threaded her voice. "Oh, I'm beginning to see some of it, I think, the part about Allen. You're in love with him, aren't you, have been for years?"

"Love?" Ofelia said the word as if it was in a foreign language. She laughed a little, a coarse sound with an edge of hysteria. "I worship him. Dumb, huh? What would he ever seen in a woman like me? He likes them refined, beautiful, preferably with something to add to his image, such as a famous father. So all right, I played up to him, kept him informed because I hoped he would give me my break the way he did you. Doesn't make any difference. I can't help it; I worship him."

"So much that you were enraged that I might leave him. So much that you tried to talk me into staying to protect him from losing me?"

"Maybe, I don't know. But if you left, then I'd have nothing, no reason for staying around. As long as you stayed, and as long as I worked with you, I would at least have a reason for seeing him."

"But you jeopardized all that by getting involved with the drug trafficking. It doesn't make sense."

Ofelia's mouth twisted in a grimace. "I'll tell you what makes sense, and that's money! I can't believe you didn't see how much I needed it all the time I was working with you. God, Julie, I've wanted your job, your resources for longer than I've wanted Allen. I've been wild to have everything you had, but especially the chance to make movies."

"Why didn't you do it?"

"Because I don't have a famous father, that's why! On top of that, I'm a woman, in case you haven't noticed, and women directors don't get money handed to them in L.A.. They have to have backers, mentors, lovers to help them get it. Look at me! Who's going to think sleeping with me is worth five or six million bucks? I need money and lots of it to back my first two or three pictures, show the studios what I can do, or else make something that grosses so big I can stay independent."

"I started out small, so could you," Julie said.

"Penny ante stuff? No thanks."

"It's like everything else, Ofelia. You have to pay your dues, make a few learning films. I'd have done my best to help you if I'd known it meant that much to you."

"But you didn't. It really pissed me off that you couldn't see it. You thought you were the only female around here with the balls to make movies. You thought I was happy following orders and maybe filming a street scene now and then. You make me sick!"

There was so much hate and resentment in the other woman's voice that Julie was perplexed that she could have lived close to it so long without sensing it.

"I thought you were doing what you wanted," Julie said. "Working with the movie during the day and hitting the juke joints here with the guys at night. I suppose that's where you got into the drugs?"

"You're dying to know all about it, aren't you?" Ofelia jeered. "I bet it gives you a charge, hearing how low I sank. But you're only partly right. It was the back-street bars in L.A. where I got into it. Coming here and getting hooked up with the local traffic was just more of the same. It was a sweet deal, really, until Paul Lislet started snooping around."

"So you killed him, and Stan got suspicious—"

"Stan got greedy, if you're looking for why I had to get rid of him. He knew there was something fishy about the stunt accident, not that I meant to kill anybody. I didn't know Paul was a narc until later; I just thought he was too nosy and needed either scaring off or a trip to the hospital until after everything was over. But then Bull came aboard, and Stan decided he wanted no part of a deal with his old boss. He decided, in fact, that he was going to retire from the movie game and wanted a cut of whatever was going down, one big enough to let him live high in Mexico. Trouble was, he couldn't stomach the business with Summer. Besides, I think he saw I didn't love you like a sister, saw I hated you. You didn't know that, did you, but I have, since you made me look like a fat clown, wallowing in the ocean in your surfing picture. Stan got afraid for you, too. He threatened me—me!—and I had the knife. He was surprised at how strong I was, I don't know why."

She wanted applause for her cleverness, Julie thought. Instead, Julie could only see the calculation that discounted everything except what Ofelia wanted. She shook her head. "That's the worst of this whole thing to me. I don't see how you could do that to a child, the explosion, the fire. As you said, you're a woman!"

"You think I wanted to do it? But the kid saw me taking the snake out of my truck, came up behind me before I knew she was there. I made up some tale about it being a pet; I mean the kid's from L.A., what does she know from snakes except in a pet store? But I knew she would remember once she heard about you being bitten. But the snake disappeared. Nothing happened."

"I killed it."

Ofelia laughed. "Who would figure?"

"You should have, knowing firsthand what some women are capable of doing."

"But you kept quiet about it; I never would have guessed that."

Ofelia didn't like the idea that she wasn't the only one capable of devious tricks, Julie thought. She said, "Turns out it was just as well. I knew it was you behind it when I was reminded that you didn't come in here anymore. You said Bull threw you out, but that wasn't so because he complained about you taking his imported beer to Vance's motor home, and as good as told me you could have stayed and helped him drink it. It followed that if you knew about the snake, you were involved in the rest."

"Very bright, but it wasn't too bright of you to come here by yourself tonight."

There was a flat, opaque look to Ofelia's eyes. She was leaning against the sink with her feet in brown leather saddles crossed at the ankles. Her hands were palm down on the edge of the cabinet with her elbows in the air, as if she might launch herself forward at any minute.

"No," Julie said, "I suppose it wasn't. But I had this idea that I might be wrong. I really wanted to be wrong, Ofelia."

She had not come totally unprepared. The preparations she had made seemed to have gone astray. All she could do was hope they were only delayed.

"Did you?" Ofelia said in cool sarcasm. "And if you weren't, then what? Did you think you could tell me to come along to the police station and I would do it because you said so?"

"Something like that. Because the fact that I'm here alone doesn't mean I'm the only one who has figured this thing out. Rey has been on to it, too. Did you know that he was once an undercover agent for the DEA?"

Ofelia snorted. "Once is right. He's on the take, Julie, dear heart, and has been since before his friend Paul died. How else do you think he supports his life-style? He asked for Paul's stunt job so nobody else from the sheriff's office could take it. That's all."

The glee in the other woman's face was sickening. Julie refused to let it affect her. She said, "Oh, yes, I'm sure. That's why he tried so hard to keep Summer away from you after the explosion, isn't it? He made sure somebody was with her every minute. He even took her home with him when he figured out you had been working on Annette, giving her some of your free drug samples, like the one you left behind here in the motor home."

Both were guesses arrived at in the past few hours and brought out now in the need of the moment. Regardless, Julie was almost sure they were right. Almost.

"So he felt sorry for the kid. He also kept her from babbling what she knew, didn't he? And he could have come after me when you were shot, if he was in with some kind of investigation. He didn't do it."

"Out of concern for me, the need to get medical attention for me."

"Hell, Julie, you're too naive to live. And this has gone on long enough. Come on, on your feet. Let's go."

Ofelia took the pistol from the back of her jeans, holding it steady on Julie's breastbone. Julie looked at it, at the round bore of it like a small black throat. A single tremor ran over her then was gone. A pulse began to pound in her temple, throbbing with sickening strokes in the front of her head. For an instant, she felt dizzy, then her vision began to clear again.

She stood up as slowly as she dared. "Where are we going?"

"The river, where I should have taken you the first time. Did anybody tell you it's a dumping ground for the bad boys out of New Orleans? It's the 'gators. They may not attack people, but they'll eat anything once it's dead."

"So I've heard," Julie said dryly.

"I thought you might've. Go on, out the door. We're going to walk across the parking lot like two ladies going to the little girls' room, all companionable and coy, until the guard can't see us anymore. Then we take a nice, quiet boat ride."

Julie did as she was told. Halfway across the parking lot, she said, "You'll be the last person seen with me. How are you going to explain that?"

"No problem. When I come back, I'll circle around like I did before when I shot at you, make sure the guard doesn't see me, maybe even go back inside the motor home. After a while, I'll leave with a lot of noise and fond farewells, maybe tell the guard on my way out what a terrible workaholic you are. With any luck, nobody will know you're missing until the middle of the morning."

"And just what reason will you give for us taking a midnight boat ride?"

"To look at a place to film? To see the river at night? It's not as if you haven't done it before."

There was a terrible cunning to Ofelia's reasoning that Julie preferred not to contemplate. "I have a better idea. If you come with me to the police and expose the drug operation, they may be lenient with you."

"Nice try, but they have the death penalty in Louisiana for murder and I prefer not to run the risk. Besides, talking won't make me a penny richer."

The guard in his shelter looked up as they crossed the open space in the dim light of the mercury vapor lamps. Julie could feel the pistol in Ofelia's hand jabbing into her ribs. Ofelia waved with her free hand. The guard, recognizing them both, lifted a hand in return. He watched them a moment longer, then went back to his book.

"We'll take the skiff," Ofelia said as they neared the dock. "We don't want to attract too much attention along the way, now, do we?"

There was something so inconceivable about what they were doing, Julie thought, that it was unreal, as if it were taking place in front of the cameras where someone would yell "cut" when the final frame was run. She stopped, refusing to walk as Ofelia gave her a push forward. "This is crazy," she said.

"Yeah, you think I'm bonkers, don't you? I got news for you; I'm as sane as anybody. Killing is like turning tricks. The first time is awful, the second not quite so bad, after the third or fourth you say, ah, what the hell."

"You've turned tricks?"

"Actually, no, but you get what I'm saying. Killing you won't be hard. So get in the boat."

"It would be a shame to make you shoot me here, and ruin all your careful plans."

"But you'd be just as dead."

Some logic was inescapable. At Ofelia's prodding, Julie moved forward again.

The other woman motioned Julie into the seat at the back of the boat. She shoved the skiff off and stepped in to take the forward seat, facing Julie, where she could reach the trolling motor. She swung the lightweight craft around so Julie was riding backward. A moment later, they were easing away down the river.

The night sky was overcast, with only an occasional star blinking through the cloud cover. The water reflected the little light available, but it was still dark on the river. Regardless, Ofelia didn't turn on the running lights. She sent the boat gliding along close to the right bank.

The darkness sang with insects and the chorusing of frogs, while now and then a bat or an owl swooped, gliding along the channel cut through the trees by the water as if along a highway. Night creatures were moving shadows that either dropped into the water and disappeared or else froze into stillness at their approach and did not move until they were past. The dank mists rising off the water smelled of mud and decay and the musky oiliness of fish. There was also a whiff of corruption, like a reminder of death.

Julie wondered about the battery for the trolling motor; she and Rey had used it quite a bit on their nighttime forays along the river. It must have been recharged, however, for it cruised on without a miss or sputter. It sent them gliding past the openings into the canals and bayous, past fishing and trapping camps and the dark shape of the wooden shrine known as Our Lady of Blind River.

The shrine reminded Julie of Aunt Tine. Thinking of her, she remembered a story Rey's aunt had told. It drifted through her mind with the memory of another time on the river. Rey had been there then, flying through the swamp with the boiling spume of his passage following him like a silver tail. Dark and strong and faintly mysterious, he had still been ready to drag her out of the water and haul her home, and even to laugh about it. And there were other times when they had raced along the water passages with the wind in their hair and the sun in their faces. How dreamlike it all seemed. Had she created it out of her own needs and desires, imbuing the time they had spent together with warmth and meaning that had never existed?

No, she wouldn't think about that. It wouldn't help.

She must concentrate. Clear the fog and memories and haze of pain from her mind. Think.

Rey and Paul. Two boys in a pirogue on the river. Not Blind River, but the mighty Mississippi. There was something there, if she could grasp it. Yes.

The dampness on the river clung to her shirt and jeans, making them clammy. That was the reason for the tendency of her teeth to chatter together, or so she told herself. She was still wearing her sweater around her waist; somehow she had never gotten around to taking it off in the motor home. She fumbled at the knot.

"What are you doing?" Ofelia asked sharply from where she sat with the pistol in one hand and the other reaching back to grasp the trolling motor's tiller.

"I'm cold. I was going to put on my sweater."

The other woman gave a short laugh. "Suit yourself, makes no difference."

A sarcastic answer rose to Julie's lips, but she bit it back. It would be better to let Ofelia think she was cowed, afraid of her. Maybe she should be. Maybe she was.

She shook out the loosened sweater and draped it around her shoulders, but did not slide arms into the sleeves. She put one hand on the gunwale beside her as she leaned to look back the way they had come.

"What are you expecting to see? Nobody's coming, you know. I saw to that."

A prickling sensation ran over Julie's scalp, aching in her brain. She said sharply, "What are you talking about?"

"I stopped by Aunt Tine's on the way here—thought I might catch you there since I didn't much want to go to the motor home. You understand. It's the old lady's bingo night; bet you forgot that. Donna was there with her two brats, baby-sitting as usual, and Summer was asleep on the couch. There was this note on the floor. I'd know your handwriting anywhere. I took it."

There was a dry rattle of paper as Ofelia patted the breast pocket of her shirt. Julie breathed again. For a moment, she had been afraid that Aunt Tine and Summer might be—but no, they were all right. For now.

At least they were all right.

She wasn't.

She was chilled to the last pale red corpuscle in the marrow of her bones, shaking in rippling rigors of sudden horror. No one was coming, not the sheriff and his deputies, not Rey, not anybody. There was only she and Ofelia out here on the river. That's all there was going to be.

Chapter 24

A soft rain began to fall, sifting out of the autumn night sky as if the air had become so dense with moisture it could be contained no longer. It whispered on the surface of the river and among the leaves of the trees. Julie could feel it beading on her hair, dampening the shoulders of her sweater. The wetness in her face was cold, but welcome at the same time; it helped to clear the fuzziness from her head. She knew it was worse for Ofelia, who was facing the mist that swirled toward her with their steady progress.

The other woman had become a pale blur in the darkness. Julie knew she herself must be the same. She reached out with her free hand under the cover of her sweater to clutch the gunwale on her other side.

They were slowing. Julie looked behind her at the river ahead. It was still some distance to the open stretch of water where they had been filming; somehow she had expected they would go at least that far, if not beyond. There was, however, the opening of an inlet off to the right, one of the bayous, she thought. The boat began to turn in that direction.

"No point in going on," Ofelia said. "One section of river is as good as another. Besides, it might look funny, us staying out too long in the rain."

"*We* might get wet, too." Julie's comment was laconic.

"Right," Ofelia said, letting out a spurt of laughter.

In that instant, Julia flung herself hard to the left, using her weight and the strength of her right arm and hand where she grasped the gunwale to destabilize the boat as she plunged toward the water. She went over the side, letting go with her right, grabbing with both hands for the left side of the boat to drag it down as she plunged into the water.

A shot cracked out, hissing past a foot from Julie's head. At the same time, Ofelia screamed as the boat flipped up on its side. There was a heavy splash as Ofelia hit the river.

The wet gunwale was dragged from Julie's grasp. It struck her shoulder and she plunged down and down into darkness. Her breath burned in her chest, her heart pummeled her ribs, and her nose and throat ached. The running shoes on her feet were like lead sinkers. Her jeans clung, making it hard to move her legs. The weight of the water dragged at her, depthless fathoms as thick and cold as molasses in winter.

She kicked upward with desperate strength. She rose for aeons, then broke the surface with a sudden harsh gasp. She treaded water with her chest heaving and the sound of her struggle for air whistling in her ears. Her head throbbed, so that she felt sick and blind. Dear God, but she was weak. And it seemed that what little strength she had left was draining away, melting into the river's imperceptible flow.

The skiff floated, bottom side up, a barely discernible outline some twenty feet away. Ofelia, thrashing from side to side as she searched the water's surface, was between Julie and the boat.

The riverbank was a misty shadow at a distance of perhaps seventy-five feet. Ordinarily, that would be nothing, but now it seemed impossible to reach. The only thing to be done was what she had intended to do from the moment she remembered Rey and Paul as boys on the river, turning their pirogue over deliberately for the consternation of the tourists.

The rain dimpled the water around her with small tinkling splatters. Far off, there came a low buzzing like a giant insect in flight. Did she hear it, or was it only the rush of blood in her ears, the reedy vibrating of her own pulse? She could not tell.

Ofelia was swinging in her direction. She yelled in harsh triumph, then lunged toward Julie, splashing into a powerful crawl.

Julie dived. She reached deep with a single thought burning in the mind, depending on the will of her failing body if not its strength.

She came up not three feet from the skiff, breaking the top of the water as quietly as a feeding fish, snatching air then diving again. When she surfaced once more, there was suffocating darkness above and around her head, darkness with the smell of gas and old fish bait. The top of her head, as she treaded water and fought for breath, bumped something solid that gave out a soft, metallic chime. She had done it. She was under the boat, breathing in the trapped pocket of air.

Holding to the submerged gunwale with one hand, Julie rested for a moment. The rain was getting harder, pecking on the aluminum boat bottom over her head. Out of the weather, it was perceptively warmer, so she felt a fleeting sense of safe coziness. It was false. Sound carried well through water. She could hear the splashes as Ofelia swam up and down, thrashing this way and that as she searched, hear her muttered curses.

How long would the air in the pocket last? Julie didn't know. She did know that to stay hidden indefinitely was impossible. At any moment, Ofelia might decide to give up the search, hoping Julie had drowned. She might then try to right the boat for the return to the location.

The floating skiff was not heavy. Julie prized off her running shoes, first one then the other. Kicking out with slow purpose, she began to move the boat downriver, angling toward the bank.

At least, she hoped she was moving toward the bank. She was no longer sure of her bearings in the total darkness of the boat's underside.

She couldn't hear Ofelia anymore. She was moving away from her. The only sound was the pinging of the rain and her own rasping breaths.

Her strength was flagging; she could feel the cold creep of exhaustion. The bank had better be close. Kick. Pull with one arm. Don't turn loose. There was no great amount of oxygen in the close air. The slight rock of the boat from her efforts seemed to be making the pocket smaller. The boat was weighing on her, pushing her further and further under with every kick and pull. Only a few more breaths, a few more kicks, and she was going to have to dive again to get out from under it. If she dived too deep, she might not come back up.

Her foot struck something soft and giving. Struck it again. Mud. The riverbank! She wanted to laugh, to shout. She had made it.

She stopped moving, letting her feet settle downward until she was standing on the mud bottom. Holding to the gunwale with both hands, she bent her knees, ducking out from under the boat.

The shadow rose up from the back of the boat, looming, clambering toward her. Ofelia screamed invective as she hurled herself at Julie. Julie, half crouching, was struck to her hands and knees, thrust down into the waist-deep water. Darkness descended with her. She was choking, strangling as she was pinned under Ofelia's weight, pressed beneath the surface.

Then from somewhere deep in her brain a painful, red-tinged brightness of rage exploded, propelling her upward. She twisted, throwing off the other woman, scrambling to her feet. As Ofelia plunged toward her again she staggered backward, squelching in mud while the water became more shallow. Ofelia caught her knees, pulling her down. Julie sank her fingers like claws into the other woman's hair, jerking her head back, rolling to shove her face into the water. As Ofelia coughed and spluttered and let go Julie pushed herself upright, floundering once more toward the bank.

Ofelia came up dripping water and mud, her face twisted into a snarl. She waded toward Julie with her hands outstretched. She leaped to catch the back of her jeans. As Julie swung around Ofelia drove her fist at Julie's face.

Julie flung herself backward away from the blow; still, it struck her forehead, so she felt the warm rush of her own blood under the wet bandaging. There was a roaring in her ears. The pain was blinding, an eruption of white light that seemed to wash the sky and make Ofelia stand out as pale and terrible as some ancient goddess of death carved in marble.

Julie cried out, a guttural scream of pain and vengeance. She surged upward, curling her fingers into a hard knot. Lunging at Ofelia, she brought her fist up from her knees in a blow with venomous gall and endurance and the last ounce of her strength behind it.

It smashed into Ofelia's round face with the sound of a hammer hitting a ripe melon, splitting skin, grinding bone. Ofelia grunted with the impact, spinning backward, falling to her knees. She looked up with blood running from her nose and her eyes glazing with pain. She went still as she stared at Julie—and also at what lay beyond her.

Ofelia cried out, a hoarse scream of despair, and covered her face with her hands.

And the look on the woman's full face, the redness of the blood, the tangled wet mess of Ofelia's long hair, and the muddy water spreading around her were as clear as day, shining in the light.

Julie could see her. There was light enough to see her.

Slowly Julie swung around.

Behind her was the brilliant, stabbing spotlights of two air boats, one with a red light on the prow, slowing turning, the other older and more stripped down. Through the light, running from the second boat, splashing water as high as his head, was the tall, broad figure of a man.

Julie waited, breathing hard, dripping water, smiling, for Rey to reach her.

There had never been another wrap party quite like it. True, the boat club was decorated with the usual blown-up stills, and seating was limited to either cloth-bottomed directors' chairs or folding metal ones placed at Formica-topped tables, also no surprise, but there any resemblance ended.

The skiff used in *Swamp Kingdom* had been filled with crushed ice and set up on trestles in the middle of the floor to hold beer and wine coolers on one end and oysters on the half shell in the other. The rich seafood smell of jambalaya and gumbo hung in the air with the smoky aroma of broiling sausages and smoked turkey legs. A long table was crowded with platters and hot plates laid edge to edge and stacked high with boiled shrimp, fried frog legs, and hog's head cheese, crab rolls and hot crab-au-gratin dip, German potato salad, piles of French bread, and every kind of cake and cookie and pie.

On a makeshift stage, a band played rock and roll and zydeco, country and western and Cajun fais do-do, all with equal ease and panache. The lead singer had a good sound system and a better voice, and did his best to help the proceedings along with quips and jokes.

But the real difference was the people. The boat club members were out in force with their wives, their sons and daughters, and their children's playmates. They brought aunts and great-aunts, uncles and great-uncles, plus nieces and nephews, in-laws and cousins, and friends of friends. Every technician brought his family along, and every supplier had done the same. Most of them brought food of some kind; all of them brought appetites. The drink flowed and the laughter came long and loud, and the sound of shuffling feet on the dance floor made a rhythmic counterpoint to the beat of the band.

Warmth, that was the biggest difference. There was warmth there, and humanity, and the perfect enjoyment of simple pleasures made better by the camaraderie of friends.

And the movie crew dived into it all as into a champagne bath. They drank and ate and talked to people they didn't know. They told tales of funny things that had taken place on the set, howling with glee—and some of them were even true. They flirted and postured as sophisticates from L.A. and were put down with a sidelong glance from dark eyes and a curling smile. They tried to dance, and made fools of themselves on the floor, unable to keep up with the quickstepping Cajuns. Still, they tried.

The nostalgia, that inevitable by-product of the end of something, came later. It came creeping in upon them all while the speeches of appreciation for the welcome and cooperation they had received in the community were being made, and while Vance and Madelyn and Summer were saying how much they had enjoyed their stay and regretted leaving. Julie spoke her piece with a lump in her throat, saying with honesty and conviction that she would never forget the time she had spent there. Afterward, she gave the floor to Bull.

"I'm no good at this," Bull said, "though I feel like all the rest that this movie, this place, this time spent here has been special. It falls to me to add one last thing, in memory of the tragedies we have shared. It's a venerable toast, one I've always liked because it says enough and not, hopefully, too much. Ladies and gentlemen, friends, I ask you to raise your glasses and drink with me: To absent friends."

"To absent friends," Julie repeated, the words a whisper.

She drank, and thought of Paul as she had seen him last, smiling and happy, waving at his wife. She thought of Stan, talking stunts and risks, his face animated, his fair thinning hair shining in the sun. Gone, both of them, killed by her ambition. And also their own.

There had been a memorial service for Stan, then his body had been sent home to the Midwest, to his sister. There had been no fanfare, but also no accusations against him. Had he tried to cut himself in on Ofelia's game? It was impossible to say; Ofelia was not the most reliable witness. In any case, as Bull said, there was no point in burdening his kin with it. Let it rest, they had agreed. Let him rest.

She turned to smile at Bull. He had done well. She should not have been surprised; for all his roughness, he was a sensitive man. It wasn't something he wanted to let get out, he said, for the sake of his reputation.

He had come, like the father in her dream, to save her. Hearing through the movie grapevine of trouble on the location, he had looked into the situation. He hadn't liked what he found out. Contacting Allen, he had talked his way into a place on the movie, not a hard task at all compared with the task of talking her into letting him near her set. He had never needed her help, really; that part about his lack of prospects, lack of creativity, had been a lie designed to play on her sympathy. He had never thought it would work, though Rey had told him different.

Later, when the bonding-company man had tried to take over, Bull had stepped in. But he hadn't done it for himself, he had done it for her, to keep the accountants from taking her movie away from her and to keep her from ruining it in her anxiety over the people who were being hurt. There was nothing in the way the final scenes had been filmed that was not true to her ideas, her concepts, both original and reconsidered.

In the process of completing the filming, she had learned a new trust and a new understanding for Bull. It was sad to think that it had taken her so long. She couldn't really blame her mother for the way she had been taught to see him; her mother had had her reasons. Still, she did think that in the years they had spent together Bull might have overcome his male reticence enough to explain his position. He had not done it, she thought, because he hadn't wanted to tarnish her image,

or his own, of the woman who had been his wife. She respected him
for that. Regardless, it was hard to think that if she had not come to
Louisiana to make *Swamp Kingdom,* she might never had learned what
he was really like.

Allen was gone. He had left for the West Coast several days ago,
when he had decided that the movie would come in only a little above
budget, when he knew the movie was in good hands with Julie and
Bull as co-directors, and when he finally figured out that whether he
went or stayed had no bearing on whether or not Julie intended to
return to L.A.

Allen, unlike Bull, had been ready to take her movie from her for
reasons that had nothing to do with her safety or well-being. He had
been concerned with money and his reputation, and with his fear that
he would lose her to success. He said he loved her, and possibly it was
true, but his concern was for his wants, his needs and feelings, with
little left over for hers. She wished him well, but she no longer loved
him, if she ever had. He had been her rebellion against everything that
Bull was, everything he stood for, his exact opposite in so many things.
The trouble was, he was also his opposite in feeling.

Ofelia was absent tonight also, sitting in the parish jail awaiting
arraignment before a grand jury on murder charges. It was still difficult
for Julie to believe the things she had done. Ofelia had not always been
like that; the years of accumulated grievances, accumulated bitterness
and jealousy had sent her over the edge.

Rey had been absent for a while, but had come in late. He was
sitting with Donna and her two children at a table that also included
Summer and her mother. They were an animated group, with the boys
and Summer all in high spirits. There had, a few minutes ago, been
a minor food fight in progress between the three younger members
until Rey had firmly quashed it.

Julie had not seen a great deal of Rey in the two weeks since
Ofelia's arrest. The assistant director had collaborated with the authori-
ties in a three-parish area to expose the drug ring in operation there,
one with roots stretching from the swampland to New Orleans, Baton
Rouge, and Shreveport, and reaching out wider to Houston and
Atlanta, New York, and L.A. Ofelia had cited names and dates and

supply routes, pickup points and carrier methods. The result was a series of lightning raids and enough arrests to clog the courts for months. Rey had been in the thick of it as a special agent attached to the DEA.

He had resigned from his position with the agency some time ago, but had been called back on this assignment because of his specialized knowledge of the swampland and its people. He and Paul had been cooperating with each other, both as friends and as members of two different teams both interested in the same operation. It had been Paul's death that had triggered Rey's acceptance of Julie's offer of a job; that much of what Ofelia had said was true. The reason had been because he had suspected that Paul's death was no accident, that his friend had been killed because he was getting too close to something important.

Rey had been watching Ofelia since the day Julie was shot. The woman had been in the other office listening while he and Bull and Julie were talking. She had kept quiet, but he had heard a small noise, and made an excuse to watch for her, saw her leave. It was in part what she had overheard, that she was going to have to give up her position as assistant director to Julie, that had touched off the shooting. Since that time, Rey's dossier on her had grown, but the agency had held off on reeling her in, in the hope of catching larger fish.

Julie allowed herself to think of the night Ofelia had tried to kill her, of the way Rey had come splashing toward her through the light beams, of the solid, comforting warmth of his body as his arms closed around her there in the rain and the glare. She had been so wet and so staggeringly weary, and in such pain that she had flung herself upon him and clung as if she meant never to let go. It mortified her to remember it.

Rey had wrapped her in a raincoat and held her while they skimmed homeward in the air boat. At Aunt Tine's house, he had given her a Percodan that his aunt had insisted she wash down with a hot toddy of bourbon sweetened with honey. Julie had little recall of the older woman helping her change her clothes or of Rey driving her to the hospital to have her injuries attended to and dressed again, and none whatever of the return or being put to bed.

It was Aunt Tine who told her that Summer, waking after Ofelia had gone and not being able to find the note, had become hysterical. The girl had insisted that Donna call Aunt Tine and tell her Julie had gone out, where she had gone, and that the note was missing. Aunt Tine, knowing something of what Rey was doing, if not all of it, had called the sheriff and had him, literally, chased down. He had come home with a police escort. He made Summer go over every detail of Julie's departure, every word she had said. The minute he heard the phrase *snake hunting,* he was out the door and on his way. Finding the motor home deserted, he had questioned the guard, who had pointed them toward the river. The keys to the cabin cruisers had been locked up in the office, but both air boats had been at a river camp the DEA had been using during the investigation. The drive to reach them had been short, but even so, the delay had nearly been too long.

Rey had been busy, yes, but Julie thought that was not the only reason she had seen little of him. He had been distant, remaining near her no longer than necessary, since the afternoon she had been shot. Slowly, during the last few days, she had begun to see the probable cause. It seemed that now was the time to set it right. There was not likely to be another chance.

She rose to her feet, moving across the room toward the table where Rey sat. Her progress was slow as she was stopped for greetings and congratulations and expressions of sympathy; still, she did not let herself be distracted for more than a minute or two.

It almost seemed that he was watching her, waiting for her. His gaze strayed to her progress often as he lay back in his chair with his long legs stretched out before him and one arm lying along the table with a beer in his hand. His hair had been recently cut short, so the curl was tamed. The cream shirt he wore reflected a glow into his face, so he appeared fit and sun-bronzed and much more attractive than any nonactor had any business being. It made her feel at a disadvantage with the red line of a scar tracking through the clipped spot in her hair and her hand in a splint.

He came to his feet as she neared. Their greeting was polite and smiling, but hardly more than that. Julie spoke to Donna and Annette and the children. Then as Rey put his hand on a chair back as if to pull it out for her she looked at him with an appeal in her eyes.

"Could I speak to you for a moment?" she said. "I won't keep you long."

His expression was narrow, yet intent, as he agreed. He looked at Donna with a lifted brow. The widow, glancing quickly from him to Julie, gave a nod as a slow and generous smile curved her mouth.

"We're all fine, here," she said. "You two go on."

He returned her smile and winked in Summer's direction, then moved to follow Julie away from the table. Catching up with her, he gestured toward the open door. "Is outside all right?"

She nodded, and a moment later, they were strolling away from the noise and food smells, down toward the dimness of the boat pier and the huge old cypress that overhung it.

"I'm sorry to take you away from the party," she said when they paused near the water. She was glad of the few feet that separated them, afraid that otherwise he might hear the heavy thud of her heart in her chest. It seemed to shake her body, that beat, making it difficult to concentrate.

He glanced at her, then slid his hands into his pockets, looking away again. "It doesn't matter."

"I just wanted," she began, then had to stop to clear the huskiness from her throat. "I wanted to tell you—before I left—that I finally remembered what was said between us the day Ofelia shot at me—or rather what I said. And I wanted to tell you I didn't mean it, not about your work or Donna or your other women. I was boiling inside with rage, and you happened to be around when I exploded."

"No, you were right, at least in part. I know I've made a habit in the past of going out with women who needed me. I wouldn't call them cripples exactly, but I was substituting pity, or maybe compassion, for love. I felt less guilty that way, I guess, as if I was giving something in return, even if I didn't have love to give them."

"I still shouldn't have said it. It was none of my business."

"I don't see that it matters. Anyway, it certainly didn't apply to you. I've never seen a woman who had less need for pity, or compassion either."

She looked at him a moment, but could not decide if what he said had any meaning before the bare words. She went on with dogged determination. "I also said, or implied, that I thought you were mixed up with the drug business in the swamp."

"You were supposed to think it," he said with a shake of his head. "I had gone to a lot of trouble to have you and a lot of other people think it was possible, including Ofelia."

"It didn't work; I didn't believe it entirely because I saw you watching the seaplane so closely that first night. After I talked to Donna, I was sure you were working undercover, that you suspected me and you had gotten close to me to—that you were—"

"I did and I was. It was part of the job, not that anybody told me to take it that far. I just had to be sure, for Paul's sake, that you were clean. That was before L.A. and the Bel Air. L.A. was for no one's sake except mine."

"Not even because you were afraid for me? I had the distinct feeling of being guarded."

"If I was even remotely right in what I had started to suspect, it seemed a good chance that you might not be allowed to live to accept your award."

"So you had yours."

His head came up, but he didn't flinch. "You—might say so."

"Well, that's all right, because you didn't have it alone."

"No?"

"I won't pretend that I wasn't willing to give you whatever you wanted." Before he could speak, she went quickly on. "Tell me something, do you remember the night you took Percodan for your shoulder and Bull plied you with Jack Daniel's?"

He turned his head slightly, as if in wariness, as he looked at her. "Yes?"

"Do you remember what you did, what you said that night?"

It was a long moment before he answered. "I remember waking up in your bed."

"Before that," she said hastily.

"I wanted to talk to you, but your light was off and I thought you were asleep. I sat on the gallery railing for a while. I think I even walked on it."

"You did."

He looked up into the branches of the cypress overhead as he sighed. "What else?"

"You said you couldn't surf and you couldn't act."

"That much is right, as far as it goes."

"And you made me a proposal, not necessarily indecent. You did not propose, for instance, that you make mad, passionate love to me under an open sky."

"I take it," he said in low tones, "that my sins are coming back to haunt me."

"I think so, yes," she answered with a faint smile.

"There's no need to be kind, then, just let me have it."

"I intend to," she said, but could not go on for the taut hold of fear on her vocal cords.

"Julie?" He turned, tying to see her face, taking a tentative step toward her.

She wanted to retreat, but could not. She felt sick with the chance she was taking, desperately fearful of what he might say, or what he might not. There was no way to get out of this, nothing to be done except plunge on.

She moistened her lips, swallowing hard. "What you said, in fact, was that you wanted to take me away with you into the swamp like Jean-Pierre. But you were not him, and not bound by the old ways, by old pride, as he was. You said that, instead, we would be married and live half our time in New Orleans and half in L.A., or wherever I might be making a movie, at least until after the children come. You said that then we would live as need be, that you were a modern man who could cook and look after our children and run an empire all at the same time."

"I said all that?" he asked, his voice husky as he reached to put his hands on her shoulders.

"You did," she answered, and gathering her courage, looked up at him and did not allow her gaze to waver from his.

"And what did you answer?"

"I said, I'm glad you're not Jean-Pierre."

He bent his head, his lips hovering inches above hers. "Was that all?"

"I said I rather liked the plan," she replied with a catch in her voice, "so long as you promise to let the DEA find itself another swamp rat."

He whispered, "Anything else?"

"I said I love you. So much, so very much, though I tried not to let you know, tried to think I could live without it, without you. And found I was wrong."

"Did I answer that you are my life, the damnably independent mistress of my soul, and that I intend to love you and keep your feet warm for as long as I live—and someday soon make mad, passionate love to you under the open sky or be damned for all eternity for trying?"

"There was some mention of it," she said, the words barely audible before she sighed. "Rey? Do you remember me telling you weeks ago that I don't play games."

"I remember."

"I was wrong. I love to play with you."

"Thank God," Rey said, "also Jesus, St. Michael, and Mary."

"All of them?"

"Every one," he said, his voice firm, deep.

They tasted each other's mouths, savoring the warmth, the sweetness, the willing surrender. Finally, Rey lifted his head, but did not loosen his hold as he rubbed his forehead gently against hers.

"I think," he said, "that I should tell you I know exactly what happened on the gallery that night and afterward in your bed, especially every word that was said."

"Do you?" she murmured with her eyes closed. "And did I get it right?"

"Just right," he said as he sought her lips once more. "Exactly right."

About the Author

Jennifer Blake was born near Goldonna, Louisiana, in her grandparents' 120-year-old hand-built cottage. It was her grandmother, a local midwife, who delivered her. She grew up on an eighty-acre farm in the rolling hills of north Louisiana and got married at the age of fifteen. Five years and three children later, she had become a voracious reader, consuming seven or eight books a week. Disillusioned with the books she was reading, she set out to write one of her own. It was a Gothic—*Secret of Mirror House*—and Fawcett was the publisher. Since that time she has written thirty-four books, with more than nine million copies in print, and has become one of the bestselling romance authors of our time. Her recent Fawcett books are *Surrender in Moonlight, Midnight Waltz, Fierce Eden, Royal Passion, Prisoner of Desire, Southern Rapture, Louisiana Dawn, Perfume of Paradise, Love and Smoke,* and *Spanish Serenade.* Jennifer and her husband live in their house near Quitman, Louisiana, styled after old Southern Planters' cottages.